Verndale
Brotherhood Headquarters
Raidenya
I0694941

Shadow of an Unknown Past

JESSICA DUCKWORTH

CHAPTER ONE

OMENS

Mariea

Mariea didn't know where she was—everything was unfamiliar, and she couldn't remember how she had ended up there. All she knew was that it was too dark to see, and the air was heavy with moisture and a metallic scent she couldn't place. She shivered, hugging her arms to her body to fight away the cold that seemed much more than just the temperature. It seeped into her soul, chilling her deep inside. She desperately wanted to leave, but with no idea how or where to go, she found herself paralyzed by fear.

When she heard a noise behind her, she jumped, certain it would be some terrible evil coming to end her. But when she turned, she found a man she didn't recognize. He simply stared at her, and something about his gaze unnerved her. He looked at her but didn't **see** her, his eyes slightly glazed over. He was only visible to her because of the faint glow of his aura. There was something wrong with it—it didn't glow the way it was supposed to, looking sickly and weak. It cast erratic shadows as it flickered and shifted, partially obscuring her view of his face.

Deciding there was a chance the whole scenario wouldn't be so bad if she could see better, she brought her own aura to light, *surrounding herself in the familiar aqua blue glow. Its power briefly chased away the chill, and for a moment, she felt relieved. She gathered some in her hand and raised it, and it grew brighter, turning white as she muttered a simple word to turn it into a spell. The orb floated just above her head, illuminating her surroundings.*

As her eyes adjusted to the new lighting, she immediately regretted the decision, wishing desperately for the darkness to return. There were bodies everywhere, in a thousand different states of decay and dismemberment. Some were relatively fresh, and seeing them made it possible for her to finally identify the smell. It was blood. She began shaking violently, her breath rattling through her body as her hands slowly raised to cover her mouth. She glanced back at the man, wanting to see his reaction, and wondered if that was why his expression was so blank.

"Mariea, don't!" a voice yelled behind her.

She glanced back and saw Bracken approaching her through the sea of bodies. His face was ashen—clearly, he hadn't missed their surroundings—but he fought to reach her, anyway.

"But what about him?" she wondered, turning back to the man slowly.

"Don't, it's dangerous!" Bracken called. She noted he had used the pronoun it, not him, like it was some sort of animal or object. What could he possibly mean by that?

When she faced the stranger again, she realized he had moved several steps closer while she had been distracted. The harsh white glow of her spell pushed away the shadows that had previously hidden his face, yet none of the light reflected in his eyes. He was sickly pale, like he belonged with the corpses at their feet more than the living. When he reached out a hand towards Mariea, she took an uncertain step back, but something crunched under her foot. She flinched forward again; sure she had just stepped on a human bone.

"Mariea!" Bracken called. She looked back at him. He had made no progress towards reaching her. She desperately wished he was by her side. She glanced around, still unsure how to escape the macabre scene, but the stranger moving closer added a new level to her desperation. His hands were mysteriously dark. She absentmindedly wondered why as she searched for a way out. The floor was disappearing under a sea of blood rising to claim the victims' remains. It seeped towards her, darkening everything in its path.

Then her gaze snapped back to the man as she realized his hands were darkened for the same reason as the ground was now—they were covered in blood. He had killed all those people. And there was a high chance she was supposed to be his next victim.

Letting out a small squeal of fear, she turned to run, determined to find a way to Bracken and out of that horrid place, but a hand closed around her shoulder from behind, yanking her back. She screamed as she was engulfed in an unholy pain.

Mariea shot upwards, gasping for air as she tried to escape the pain. Luckily, it faded, and her bleary gaze made out her room. *Was...that a dream?* she wondered as her disoriented brain realized she was sitting in her bed, her blankets pushed off her and tangled around her feet. It *was* just a dream. She was cold because the blankets were gone, and her mind had crafted strange images to explain it. Strangely morbid images, to be specific.

She just wouldn't question why the pain lingered for a moment after she woke up.

Shuddering, she decided she couldn't stay in bed any longer. Her alarm wouldn't go off for another hour, but she knew she wouldn't be able to sleep. She glanced to her side at Bracken to make sure she hadn't woken him. Thankfully, he was still resting peacefully, blissfully unaware of the scene she had just witnessed. She quietly slipped into the restroom and began preparing for the day.

Once she was finished, she headed out into the main room of their home. The small three-bedroom house had a clean, modern design with a large, open kitchen and living room combined. The bedroom door opened into a small hallway that led to the restroom to her left and the front door to her right. Stepping through the archway, she entered the light-colored sitting area, which faced the large windows along the back wall. Cutting across the space, she made her way to the kitchen, which lined the opposite wall. It was well lit by the windows surrounding the breakfast nook adjacent to the sitting room. Beyond the kitchen was the dining room, though it was hardly used with only two people living in the home.

Glancing around the kitchen, she mentally took stock of what they had on hand and then glanced at her watch again. "I've got time," she muttered before she started pulling breakfast ingredients from the fridge.

By the time Bracken was up and dressed, she had cooked them each an omelet and bacon. She was pouring orange juice when he stepped into the room, running a hand through his short, dark brown hair in an attempt to flatten the slight curl. He shuffled to the fridge as Mariea called, "Good morning."

He glanced towards her to return the greeting and then noticed the table was set. "What's this?" he asked.

"Breakfast," she replied, smiling slightly at him for asking such an obvious question.

He immediately perked up, clearly excited. "I guess I mean, what's the occasion?" he wondered, moving towards the table.

Mariea shrugged. "Do I need an occasion to spoil my husband?" she asked, stepping towards him.

He smiled. "Oh, I'm definitely down for that idea."

She chuckled, and then he pulled her into a hug. When she closed her eyes, the images from her dream briefly returned, and she suddenly felt immensely relieved to feel his embrace. She tightened her grip slightly, lingering a bit longer than she figured he had expected.

As if sensing something wasn't right, he held her, gently tracing circles on her back with one hand. "You okay?" he muttered after a moment.

"Yeah, I just...had a weird dream last night. Made me grateful I have you," she told him as she finally stepped back.

He gave her a sympathetic smile. "I hate dreams like that. You want to talk about it?"

"No, I'd rather forget. And eat these eggs; they're going to get cold," she decided.

He nodded. "Don't have to tell me twice. Man, I miss breakfasts like this," he told her as his smile returned and he moved for the table.

She couldn't help but brighten at his enthusiasm. "I know. It seems we never have time to sit down and have a proper meal anymore."

"Well, there's no reason I can't get my lazy bones out of bed sooner and help. So I shouldn't complain," he told her with a shrug. Mariea smiled slightly, deciding not to dissuade him from his rest. Bracken was a terrible cook. His brain functioned too much like a spell—it needed exactness, and cooking was too much of an art for him to manage.

They ate their breakfast with companionable small talk, and soon Mariea found the nightmare fading into memory. They cleaned up together when they were finished eating, and then Mariea had to head to work. She gathered her things, kissed Bracken goodbye, and headed for the door.

Outside, the city of Verndale sprawled out below her, and in the distance, the ocean surrounded Raidenya like a protective barrier. She loved Raidenya in spring, and despite having lived on the island for fifteen years, she still couldn't get over how beautiful it was. It was only February, but the snow never lingered long, and the first signs of life returning to the island were beginning to show. She had grown up in New York, and though it had its charms, it just couldn't compare to where she was now.

She was sure part of the difference could be blamed on the magic the people of Raidenya used. The rest of the world knew nothing of the island, and the Auraes were careful to keep it that way so they could practice their gifts without trouble. Their power—which came from their auras—was often hated and feared by those who did not possess it. Raidenya was a haven, and its people treasured it.

It was only a ten-minute drive from her home to the academy where she taught. She made her way down the hillside, passing from the suburban streets of her neighborhood into the bustling downtown. Verndale wasn't a huge city, but it had grown considerably even in her years on the island.

About a block from the city center was the Aurae Academy, a sprawling campus with accommodation for education from six years old and up. She parked in the faculty parking lot behind the main building, which housed most of the advanced classes and the dormitories for those students who chose to live there. Most of the students who did were adults, but the academy also reserved some rooms for younger students who didn't have anywhere else to go. This included those few that had just discovered their magical gifts and had come to the island seeking safety from the outside world. Mariea had once stayed there when she had first learned of her own power.

The main building was called Rybolov Hall, after the Aurae family who had once owned Raidenya. They had chosen to open their island home to others in need of a safe place to practice their magic in peace. The hall was built to mimic Rybolov's old manor. Over the years, the building had undergone several renovations to update its facilities, though it maintained the classical architecture and theme as much as possible.

Mariea's classroom was on the second floor. It was a large, rectangular space with a wall of windows opposite the door and a whiteboard dominating the wall in between. Rows of tables allowed the students to work together efficiently. Mariea had a desk tucked in the corner against one window. She placed her purse and other belongings in one of the drawers before hanging her jacket on the back of her desk chair.

For the past five years, she had taught at the academy, helping to introduce the new generation of Auraes to their auras. Her focus was on the elemental magics, which manipulated the four base elements of water, earth, fire, and air. After only a little time learning to control her aura, she had found a preference for them and had devoted her time to mastering them. The magic she taught was usually introduced to students in their teens.

As another class gathered, she felt the last of her worries from that morning melt away, replaced by a slight excitement that never failed to amaze her. It didn't matter how many times she introduced the elemental magics to another group of students, it simply never got old. And since they had begun a new semester in February, they were just starting to handle the elements again.

Moving to the front of the room, Mariea leaned against the long cabinet there and waited for the class's attention. As they settled down, she smiled slightly. "Today is the day you've all been waiting for," she announced to start the class. "Over the past few weeks, I've introduced the concept of and prepared you for handling the first of the elemental magics, fire. Now, it's time to show you just what this magic can accomplish and allow you to handle it yourself."

Excitement rippled through the class, making her smile grow. Her aura came to view around her hands, its aqua glow adding an extra splash of color to the classroom. No two auras were the same—their color varied from person to person—though the way they manifested was similar. The light hovered just above her skin, not quite touching her, like a steady, thin outline of bright color. She used only a minimal amount of power from it, meaning it barely showed, instead of encasing her entirely as it did when she drew on its full strength.

"Fire is a dangerous element, but it can also be of great benefit when used correctly," she stated as she raised her palm before them. Fire sparked to life just above her hand as she continued. "When you use this magic, you are using the pure energy of your aura to light the fire, meaning the strength of your fire is directly connected to that of your aura. Because this is a magic, not a spell, all you have to do to summon the fire is simply imagine the flame, will it to be, and then supply the energy of your aura. It takes time, and at first, even a small flame will cost a great amount of energy, but as you familiarize yourself with the magic and your aura grows, it will come more naturally. To start with, it's easier to bring a flame to light with a natural fuel, hence the matches on the tables. You'll start with those today. Any questions before we get started?"

A few were voiced, and she explained further. When they stopped, she invited them to try it. "It's your turn. Remember the spells we learned earlier in the class to protect you if the flame should get out of hand. You'll want to use these every day before working with fire until you're confident in your control."

Auras blinked to life in various hues and shades around the room as the students reached for the matches and began the necessary spells. Then the room fell silent as the students turned their concentration to the magic at hand. She observed quietly, waiting for them to discover the power of their auras.

A girl gasped from one side of the room as a small flame flickered to life at the end of the match she held. It died as quickly as it appeared, to her disappointment. Mariea approached her with another match. "Good job," she congratulated quietly. "Try giving it a little more power this time."

As the class continued, fire blinked to life throughout the room in tiny flickers as more students managed to light their matches. Eventually, she called for them to finish. "This is only the beginning of fire. Throughout the rest of the semester, we'll explore its limits and see just what your auras are capable of," she informed them.

The class filed out as one hour ended and the next began. This time, the room filled with an older group working on learning water, the third elemental class she taught. She began explaining the prep exam they were required to take before handling a new element as the class started.

The rest of the day flew by, and eventually, Mariea found herself home again, ready for a good night's sleep. Her mind briefly strayed to the nightmare again, but she quickly pushed it away, knowing dwelling on it would only freak her out again and cause her to have another nightmare. She was determined to put it behind her.

— ℰ —

It was a week later when the next nightmare happened. This time, the same morbid stranger followed her through the streets of Verndale, never getting too close. He would appear in the corner of her eye and then disappear when she turned to him, like a shadow she couldn't quite shake. But every time she turned around to continue her desperate attempt to escape him, she'd find another person she loved dead at her feet, almost as if she had somehow murdered them.

That dream, and the one before, were the start of a new, terrifying pattern in her life she couldn't begin to understand. Every week throughout February, she would have a nightmare. And when she woke, something would always linger for a brief amount of time—a feeling of pain, temperature, or the textures around her. It was almost as if the dreams were bleeding over into her reality, something she had never experienced before. And with each passing one, she found it harder and harder to shake the overwhelming feeling something was coming, even when she was awake.

Bracken began to notice as well—she often woke him in her panic, as much as she tried not to. When she woke from the second nightmare in the first week of March, he sat up to comfort her, pulling her to him. "I'm really starting to hate seeing you this way. What's causing all these nightmares?" he muttered as her breathing slowed and her heart rate slowly returned to normal.

She shook her head, not sure how to answer. "I'm sorry I keep waking you. This is ridiculous," she muttered, feeling childish. She just couldn't understand why her mind seemed fixed on such dreadful scenes.

As if deciding neither of them would be sleeping soon, Bracken switched on the lamp next to the bed. "You're not bothering me. I'm worried about you. This just isn't natural. You must be exhausted after so many nights without sleep."

"It is becoming a nuisance," she reluctantly admitted. The consistent pattern and the lingering emotions were what upset her the most. The longer they went on, the clearer it became to her that these weren't regular nightmares. "I'm...beginning to think there's more to them."

"There has to be something triggering them," he agreed with a nod.

Mariea shrugged, realizing Bracken hadn't entirely caught her meaning, but she went with it. "I've been trying to figure that out, but there's literally nothing I'm dealing with to cause it. I'm not overly stressed or worried about anything in particular, nothing out of the ordinary. I don't know."

"Could it be that what stress you are dealing with is finally starting to take its toll?" Bracken asked. "There have been a lot of changes recently. It wouldn't be that surprising." She knew he was referring to her recent election to chancellor of the governing council of Raidenya, a position she hadn't expected to receive and felt unqualified for. Still, she didn't feel she was stressed enough for such a reaction. At first, balancing two jobs had been a bit much, but now she enjoyed the busier pace.

Beyond her new job, she had scoured her life for anything that could be triggering the dreams. She had been to a couple of medics, and neither had found anything physically wrong with her. She had even altered her diet, wondering if it was some sort of strange allergic reaction, but nothing seemed to help. She tried sleeping in different rooms, even staying at Bracken's parent's house for a night to see if it was something to do with her house. Nothing had changed the pattern.

"It can't be that simple," she muttered, her gaze on the wall across the room.

"Then what could it be? It's weird to continually have nightmares for no reason," Bracken mused, looking stumped.

"Yeah," she muttered. After a pause, she glanced up at him and cautiously ventured, "Is it too crazy to think they are a warning of some kind?"

He considered that for a moment, his head tilted slightly to one side as he thought. "Not necessarily crazy. There are many things about this world and magic we don't understand, so it could be possible. Is that what you think they are?"

"I'm starting to," she confirmed with a slight nod. She paused a moment to collect her thoughts, knowing it wouldn't be easy for her to get Bracken to see what she was seeing. "They're too consistent. And normal nightmares don't leave me this rattled. The things I feel tend to linger. I'm left grieving a death that hasn't happened, terrified of highly unlikely events, even sometimes dealing with phantom injuries after waking up. No matter how much I tell myself it's just a dream, it doesn't stick. They...." As she finally met Bracken's gaze, she felt the dark worry overwhelm her again even as she spoke of it. "Every time they fill me with dread. Of what, I don't know, but I can't shake it. As crazy as it sounds, I...I think something *is* coming, something I should be afraid of. I just don't know what it is."

Bracken held her gaze for a moment in silence, his expression troubled, and then let out a long, heavy sigh. "Which leaves us with little idea what to do about it."

Mariea nodded in agreement, feeling a little relieved he believed her. "That's the most frustrating part. They leave me with no clues as to what's happening. I just..." her hands tightened into fists in the blankets as the image of Bracken's death from that night's dream came to mind. "I can't allow what happens in those dreams to become reality."

Bracken wrapped an arm around her shoulders, making her realize how tense she had become and how uncomfortably close she was to tears. Quickly, she blinked them away as she fought to gain control of her emotions.

"We'll figure it out. I trust you," he told her with a bittersweet smile. She nodded, hoping he was right. After a pause, he added, "Maybe it would be good to start writing these dreams down. If we could compare them, we might find a pattern of some sort or something that could give us a hint about where they're coming from or why."

"I'll try it," she agreed, deciding any sort of plan, as weak as it was, was better than doing nothing.

He nodded. Then he stifled a yawn, clearly trying not to let on how tired he was. *Of course, he must be exhausted as well,* she thought, feeling guilty once again for disturbing him. "Let's go back to sleep," she muttered.

"If you want," he decided.

She glanced at the clock. "Yeah, it's only midnight."

He nodded and settled back against his pillow, gesturing for her to join him. She curled up close, grateful for his presence. She had to fight the urge to ask to leave the light on. All her life, she had never feared the dark, but now, at twenty-four, she couldn't list anything she was more afraid of.

Chapter Two
Raidenya's Council

Mariea

Fire blazed all around Mariea, the only light source in the dim world she found herself in. The streets of her home lay in ruins behind her, but she had long since accepted there was nothing she could do to stop the fire. It was unnatural, fueled by a power she could not combat.

But that didn't mean she couldn't use the fire against her enemies. Her aura flared brightly around her as she reached for the flames. It gave in to her will and bent from its path to gather in her outstretched palm. Her anger and despair poured strength into her aura, making the fire she controlled burn sharp white and scorching. With a wave of her hand, she sent it flinging towards the dark shadows surrounding her in a wide, blinding arch. Few perished, just as she had expected. She could feel their power and knew her enemy was strong enough to destroy her, but she fought on, her only thought of vengeance for those she had already lost.

Suddenly, she did not fight alone. Bracken appeared nearby, disoriented and struggling to survive against the same foe. Realizing he could never match their power, Mariea rushed to assist, just as she had hundreds of times before, despite knowing she would never reach him in *time. As she watched, helpless to intervene, his defenses failed him, and he perished.*

He was the last of those she loved to fall. With him went her desire to fight. She could survive the loss of her community, her friends, and neighbors, but not her husband. She had no one left to fight for, and her life seemed pointless. Her aura snuffed out, leaving her vulnerable to the shadows around her. She simply stared ahead without seeing as they engulfed her, a part of her welcoming the endless darkness they brought.

Shocked awake by the echoing whine of her alarm clock, Mariea sat up abruptly, expecting to find the dark world she had left behind to be her reality. When the confusion faded and she finally realized it had been another dream, she sighed heavily and reached to turn the alarm clock off.

With the blaring annoyance finally silenced, she glanced to her left, where Bracken was stirring. Despite how many times she had lost him in her dreams, she found she had to see him once she awoke, just to confirm it was a dream. They still felt so real, even after nearly a month of dealing with them.

Pushing herself from bed, she numbly began the day with a level of somberness she couldn't shake. Every time she lost her focus—which wasn't hard, considering how exhausted she was—her mind began rehashing the details of the latest nightmare in an endless loop, refusing to allow her to forget.

Part of her quietly despaired the dreams would never end. Bracken had once again consulted with a medic friend and offered her a few medicinal remedies, but none of them had kept the dreams at bay. He tried protection spells, even a spell designed to render a person unconscious, and still, the nightmares made their way to her. Recording them didn't reveal a pattern other than the fact she was often stalked by a mysterious murderer in her dreams. Sometimes there were more than one, like last night, but one thing was always clear—their goal was to take everyone she loved and destroy her home. This only reinforced her worries there was *something* out there, something real she needed to fear, but she still had no idea what it was.

After a quick shower, she dressed in a simple blue blouse and dress slacks and then made her way to the mirror to tame her thick, blonde hair into something presentable. It fell in loose waves just beyond her shoulders when she finished brushing through it, and she settled on that being good enough for the day. Taking in her appearance as a whole, she frowned slightly, noticing the dark circles under her eyes, and if she wasn't mistaken, she looked a little ashen. It seemed the lack of real sleep was starting to impact her health. Muttering a quiet thanks to the inventor of makeup, she did her best to hide the effects and make herself presentable.

Making her way to the kitchen, she perused the cabinets for something to eat. Nothing looked appetizing, like most mornings, but with the little energy she was running on at this point, she knew she needed to try to eat, anyway. Settling on a simple bowl of cereal, she prepared it quickly and headed for the table.

Bracken was already there, munching on a bagel while he read the newspaper. He looked up as she approached and smiled. "Good morning."

Managing a smile, she returned the greeting. His attention returned to the newspaper, leaving her alone with her thoughts. Immediately, her mind wandered back to the latest dream despite her desire to think of anything else. She began comparing the details to other dreams she had experienced with a forced detachment, trying to keep herself from reacting emotionally.

After a moment, Bracken glanced back up again and seemed to notice her somber mood. "Are you alright?" he asked, his gaze filled with concern.

Blinking, she shook herself from her stupor and nodded. "Yeah, I'm okay," she reassured him with a sigh. He didn't seem to believe her. After a moment of enduring his silent scrutiny, she gave in and admitted, "It's just, I had another nightmare last night."

His frown only deepened. "Again?"

Mariea gave a hesitant nod. "They're no big deal though, really," she dismissed, knowing he worried about them insistently. She was grateful this one hadn't woken him, at least.

"This is the fourth one this week," Bracken pointed out.

"Fifth, actually," Mariea corrected softly, her gaze falling to her cereal. She absentmindedly realized it would quickly become an unappetizing mush if she didn't eat it soon, but the tight knot of worry in her stomach made it seem an impossible task.

His brow furrowed in worry. "They're happening more frequently."

She nodded. "I would do anything for a good night's sleep at this point."

"I asked around the office for solutions for sleeplessness. I'll follow up today and see what they've learned," he decided.

She nodded, unable to admit she had long since given up on any hope he might come up with a solution. Mariea returned to her cereal, attempting to eat a bit more, and Bracken's gaze became unfocused as he got lost in thought, clearly dwelling on the problem. She felt horrible dumping all this on him, but she didn't know what else to do. At one point, she had even tried to convince him they were gone so he wouldn't worry about her, but she was a terrible liar, so he hadn't believed her for a second.

Suddenly her watch beeped, shattering the tense silence that had fallen over them. She barely prevented herself from jumping, but instead raised her wrist to discover the time. "Oh, I've got to go," she realized, standing in a rush. She hurried to the bedroom, gathered her keys and purse, and then returned and gave Bracken a quick kiss. "See you at the meeting tonight."

Catching her in a quick, one-armed hug, he teased, "Try not to be late this time." She rolled her eyes and smiled slightly as she slipped out the door.

Outside, the warmth of the early morning sun enveloped her, chasing away the lingering chill of spring and making her smile slightly. At least it seemed it would be a pretty day. *Maybe I should try sleeping outside. I always feel better out here,* she mused. It seemed ridiculous, but at this point, she was willing to try anything.

As she drove, she told herself she wouldn't let the nightmares ruin her day, as she did every morning they bothered her. It would be easier said than done, but teaching had a way of simplifying the world for her. If she could figure out how to explain the power of her aura and the wondrous things it could create in a way her students could understand, she could figure out anything.

When she reached her classroom, she was just dropping off her things at her desk when someone called her name from behind. She turned to see Francesca, an older woman who ran the early education program in the building across the campus. Mariea turned and smiled in greeting.

"Good morning, Mariea," Francesca stated, moving to stand with her. "You have your prep period first thing, correct?"

"Yes, for the first hour of the day," Mariea confirmed. "Why, did you need something?" She silently hoped Francesca would say no. Her prep period had slowly devolved into time for her to mentally recover enough to actually face the day, and she wasn't sure she'd manage without it.

"Oh, good. Molly's baby came early—luckily, she and the baby are doing fine, but obviously, we didn't have a substitute planned for another few weeks. Thankfully, the substitute said he'd be able to start next week, so now I'm desperately searching for someone to fill in for the rest of this week. I've been asking since Monday and have yet to find anyone available this morning. I know you usually only work with the older kids and college students, but is there any way I could get you to cover, just for one hour? I can take over after that."

Mariea glanced back to her desk, mentally considering all the work there that was slowly beginning to pile up. She wanted to say no, but she felt guilty about abandoning her fellow teacher. "Well...I don't know anything about teaching younger children. What would you need me to do?" Auraes were typically introduced to their auras and the power they controlled very early on, but their aura wasn't developed enough to start using magic until they were eight. That was pretty much all she knew when it came to educating anyone younger than about fourteen. Children as young as Molly's class would also be studying reading and writing and other standard subjects, things Mariea had never learned to teach.

"Oh, nothing too complicated," Francesca quickly reassured her. "The children usually start the day with reading practice, but if you would prefer to cover their magic studies instead, it won't hurt to mix things up. They are just reviewing their basic understanding of the difference between spells and magic, so they will be ready to take their first test in a week or so.

It's a group of eight-year-olds, so not small children, if that's concerning."

"No, not at all," Mariea quickly corrected. For some reason, she felt a little miffed Francesca was implying she might not like kids. Was it because she had none of her own yet?

"Oh, so you can do it?" Francesca asked, brightening slightly.

Realizing that Francesca had misinterpreted her response, she scrambled to correct her and then paused, feeling herself relent to the idea. "Yeah, I've got the time. Just for an hour, though; I have my first class at nine."

"Of course, I have my prep period then and can take over. Oh, thank you so much. You have no idea how stressed I've been about this. Let me show you to Molly's room."

Mariea managed a smile as she moved to her desk and locked up her purse. "Let me just get a few things," she told her, gathering a small handful of ungraded papers in the hopes she could get through them in between managing the class. Then she motioned for Francesca to show the way.

The pair made their way outside and crossed the sprawling lawn between the buildings to the smaller, more modern early-education building. They stopped at the first door on her left. Stepping inside, Francesca quickly gathered the children's attention and then introduced Mariea to them. Mariea stood near her, studying the group hesitantly. There were twenty kids in total, less than her regular classes, and for the most part, they seemed well behaved. Hopefully, it would be an easy hour.

"Well children, be good for Mrs. Rolondo, alright?" Francesca told them, and then promptly left her alone.

Once she was gone, Mariea couldn't help but feel a bit nervous, which was so rare for her as a teacher. But she smiled and decided to just jump straight in. Sure, she'd be making it up as she went, but they were eight-year-olds. How hard could it be?

"So today, your regular instructor is sick, but she asked me to quiz you all and see if you're ready to try some real magic soon. So, let's get started. First question: Who can tell me the difference between spells and magic?"

After only a moment, hands began to raise. She called on one boy, who replied, "Spells use words and magic don't."

Smiling slightly at his simplistic explanation, Mariea nodded. "Right. Spells are a form of magic that relies on the use of a certain language. Who can tell me what it's called?"

"Shidokian!" one girl called before hands could even be raised.

Mariea nodded. Shidokian was the second language of the Auraes, used primarily for their magic. Though the language was used for everyday conversation, every word held power, so most found it safer to stick to more traditional languages. It was also challenging to learn, and Mariea still had difficulty grasping it due to her late start.

"Good. So, can someone explain to me how a spell works?"

This time, Mariea was allowed to choose a student to answer. Fewer hands were raised now that the questions were more complicated. "Spells are built of sequences, kind of like math equations," the girl explained. "But they're all written in Shidokian."

Mariea nodded, amazed they understood the concept so well at such a young age. It had seemed like such a foreign idea to her when it was first introduced, and she had been nearly twice their age. "Correct. And these sequences, they teach the spell its purpose, right?" The class nodded obediently. "So, why do we have both spells and magic?"

The class seemed to struggle for an answer, so after a moment, Mariea decided to supply it for them. "Remember, spells were created to allow us to do more complicated things with our auras, such as healing someone who is sick or building something. Regular magic is more based on emotion and imagination—it's something you do quickly and without much thought. For example..."

Her aura came to view around her hands, and a small fire sprung to life above her open palm, eliciting excited gasps from the classroom as they stared in wonder.

"This is magic. I didn't have to build a spell to create it. I just imagined the fire in my hand, and it appeared. You still have to learn this type of magic, but it doesn't require any knowledge of Shidokian."

The fire disappeared, and her aura grew brighter as she muttered a short Shidokian phrase. After only a few seconds, she was encased in lightweight, aqua-tinted plate armor. Then her aura faded. "This, I created with a spell. Even when my aura isn't active, it'll stay until I want it to disappear."

The armor disappeared after a moment, and she continued to ask more questions. She found she could settle into a nice routine with the kids, and despite her earlier worries, she enjoyed herself. Before long, Francesca returned, and she was allowed to return to her regular schedule.

At the end of the day, she spent a little time catching up on grading assignments before leaving the academy behind to fulfill her other regular duty. It was still odd, knowing all the Auraes around her looked to her for leadership. Her election as chancellor had come as a complete shock. She hadn't wanted it, hadn't even been seeking it, but that was how the Auraes governed themselves—they felt everyone was equal, even current elected officials, and everyone had a part to play in keeping the city safe and running. They were required by law to fulfill the assignment handed to them when called upon.

Though Mariea didn't consider herself a great leader, she had warmed to the position quickly. Being able to help others and play her part in a society she had once felt she would never find her place in brought her a surprising amount of satisfaction—almost as much as teaching at the academy.

At least, it had until the dreams had begun. Now she found herself exhausted and wishing for a way out of the weekly evening meetings and other duties required. It was why she had been so late to the last one—she had fallen asleep at her desk at the academy and nearly slept through the meeting.

The Academy and Capitol Building were close enough that she often walked, but today she was too tired, so she drove the short distance and parked outside the grand marble building. Climbing the stairs, she passed the statue of the original colonists and its accompanying sign, which declared the name of the island and city, and the date the community was established. It stood as a constant reminder of how long the Auraes had managed to stay hidden—and safe—from the rest of the world. The colonists stood guarding the capitol building, declaring their joy over their newfound home.

Passing through the double doors at the top of the stairs, Mariea glanced around the crowd of busy men and women. A row of the city's peacekeepers, known as sentinels, stood just beyond the doors. They silently stood guard in their crisp, light-colored uniforms. Mariea passed through them and started across the lobby to the marble staircase that dominated the room's back wall.

The second floor was mostly office space, and she passed by quickly. Tucked in the far-left corner of the floor was a more modest stairwell that led to the smaller third floor. At the top, a short, mostly empty hallway led Mariea to a pair of great oak doors. The room beyond was lit by the afternoon sunlight pouring through the windows along the back wall and the chandelier hanging from the domed ceiling far above. Covering one wall was a wide mural of the island from a distance under the light of a setting sun, adding a splash of color to the room.

Present in the room were several familiar individuals. Their conversations briefly paused as Mariea joined them, taking her place in the center of the U-shaped table that dominated the room. Ila Layne sat to her right and glanced up to give Mariea a brief greeting. To Mariea's left, Gavin Conover, Shawn Williamson, and Bracken were deep in conversation. Misha Eisen sat at the far end of the table next to Bracken, her head bowed over a stack of papers. Not long after Mariea entered, Jocelyn Pharr joined them as well, adjusting the sleeves of her uniform as she made her way to her seat next to Ila.

Across from Bracken and Misha were two empty chairs. Mariea sighed when she noticed them. It was past time for their occupants to be present, yet the chairs were still vacant. Glancing at Ila, she asked, "Samar isn't here, again?"

Ila nodded, causing a strand of her thick, dark curls to slip loose from her bun and hang along her face. "He left a note informing us he wouldn't be coming, still with no explanation." Though she did her best to keep the comment neutral, her annoyance leaked into her words, nonetheless.

With a shrug, Mariea muttered, "I guess he can't complain when we make decisions without him that affect the Brotherhood."

"Oh, you know he will," Ila promised.

Mariea nodded wearily, knowing all too well how difficult the Brotherhood's Council representative could be. Sometimes he acted as if he led the entire island, not just the Brotherhood. To the rest of the group, she called, "Alright, let's get started."

One by one, the Council members reported on events under their jurisdiction. They started with Gavin, who served as Mariea's councilor and oversaw public relations between the Council and the general populace. He was a somber man with a thinner build, black hair, warm-toned skin, and dark eyes. He often had plenty to worry about, but he was good at what he did. He kept the Council carefully informed of the wishes of the general populace, so they could serve the people to the best of their abilities.

His report was brief, so they moved on to Ila. Ila was also considered Mariea's councilor, and her duties lay simply in the general operation of the city, helping Mariea manage the burden. Mariea had known Ila since she had come to the island; when she first came to Raidenya, the Layne family had allowed her to stay with them for a few weeks before moving to the academy housing. Ila came from a rich heritage; her mother was originally from Africa, and her stepfather could trace his line back to the island's founders. Her report was a positive one, and Mariea was happy to hear the affairs of the city continued forward well.

Bracken was in charge of a group known as the spells masters. They were tasked with maintaining the spells that protected the island from the outside world and designing new spells when needed. Despite having been married to Bracken for a few years now, Mariea was still amazed by how easily he navigated the world of spells. They came so naturally to him, it was astounding. After giving a brief positive report on the state of the spells over the island, he turned the time over to Shawn.

Shawn Williamson oversaw the educational department and was the headmaster of the Aurae Academy. He was in his early fifties but dressed as though he was from an older age and was always meticulously well-groomed. He greeted everyone with a friendly smile and gave good-natured but sometimes unwanted advice.

As he placed his glasses on the brim of his nose and glanced down at his notes, he shared information about upcoming enrollment plans for summer classes. Then he added a bit about a new pilot class they were trialing to introduce students to medical magic earlier in their studies in hopes of sparking more interest in that field.

As he finished, he glanced at Misha and gave her permission to continue the meeting. Misha served as Head medic and was the oldest member of the Council in her late sixties. However, Mariea often forgot just how much older she was than the rest of the Council; though her dark hair was almost entirely gray now, and her hands were weathered with age, she refused to slow down and faced every day with more enthusiasm than the rest of the group combined.

But, surprisingly, she lacked her usual pep this morning. Instead of giving her report, she stated, "I think Jocelyn should give her report first, as everything I have to say would make more sense when taken in context with the information she has."

Jocelyn met the old medic's gaze and nodded. The sentinel department dated back to the first Aurae communities, guarding the Aurae world and keeping order among them. Considering this, Mariea couldn't help but be a bit worried Misha felt Jocelyn's report was so important.

"I hate to be the bearer of bad news, especially since, for the most part, things are going well," Jocelyn sighed, her gaze on the table before her and her arms crossed against her chest. "There have been several mysterious attacks on the city, some resulting in the deaths of a quickly growing number of Auraes. They started a few weeks ago, and since they're increasing and I have yet to find a cause, I figured it was time to mention it to all of you. Among the lives lost have been sentinels, meaning whatever this threat is, it's strong."

Mariea's heart skipped a beat, briefly wondering if she had nodded off and this was now a dream. Though the events themselves were nothing like her dreams, they left her feeling the same way, and she didn't like noticing that connection. Forcing herself to focus, and for her voice to remain steady, she carefully asked, "Any theories as to what it could be?"

"Not yet. Unfortunately, I don't have much to go off of. One thing is consistent—these attackers seem to have some sort of power over auras. They can disable or destroy them, somehow. The victims who survived reacted quickly enough to kill their attacker before they managed to disable their aura. When this happens, the attacker's body frustratingly disappears, which leaves me with no information regarding a motive or who they are. When the victim dies, there are usually signs of a struggle near where the body is found, but there are no clues about who or what attacked. I know of no magic that can do this to auras. Have any of you heard of such a power?"

Mariea shook her head, stumped, and the group reflected her answer almost as quickly. Such a power seemed impossible. To take an Aurae's aura would mean certain death, so why would they bother to invent a magic that could do it?

Jocelyn nodded. "That's what I thought." Her gaze turned to Misha. "Have you learned anything from the autopsies?"

"It's definitely not caused by disease or poison, that much I can tell," Misha said with a small sigh. She seemed weary just speaking of it, which surprised Mariea. The old medic saw the worst the world could dish out in her career, so for something to upset her, it must be serious.

"The victims are rarely injured, at least not seriously enough to cause death, leading me to believe their attacker surprised them with this weird ability of theirs," Misha continued. "This does seem to line up with what Jocelyn found. But there's never any clue as to what exactly made their aura disappear."

"Is this the work of some sort of...serial killer?" Ila ventured cautiously, clearly not liking that she had to suggest it.

"It's possible, but so far there hasn't been anything to even connect the victims back to the same killer. Considering some of them have died, and the attacks continue, I'm assuming it's some sort of group," Jocelyn responded. "I've ruled out almost anyone on the island with a criminal record. It's not a long list to begin with, considering how strict we are about who is allowed to live here." She paused briefly, hesitating to mention something more, and then admitted, "At this point, I'm contemplating a possible outside source, something new to the city."

This caused the group to pause, and for good reason. There wasn't much on Raidenya outside of Verndale, so something not already in the city most likely meant from off the island.

But it seemed not everyone came to the same conclusion. "It's not Tarapor related, is it?" Gavin asked. He often mentioned the pests the Auraes dealt with in the surrounding forested areas of the island. Mariea couldn't blame him—they had been the cause of many deaths in the past, and if they weren't careful, she didn't doubt it could happen again—but she frequently doubted if they were capable of some of the things he attributed to them.

Jocelyn shook her head. "Most of the survivors said their attackers look human, which the Tarapor don't," she responded.

"Though I'm not entirely willing to rule it out as a possibility, considering most of the survivors didn't get a good look at their attacker before they killed them," Misha interjected. "Maybe it's a new strain of Tarapor that live off auras instead of blood?"

"Could a new strain just develop like that?" Mariea asked. She knew very little about the disease causing the Tarapor's existence.

With a slight nod, Misha explained, "It is possible, I assume. Maybe the virus sustaining them has mutated. The only reason I doubt is that it has never happened before, but that doesn't rule it out as impossible."

"I wonder if the Brotherhood knows anything about this," Bracken mused, glancing towards the empty seats.

"Wouldn't it be nice if we could ask them," Ila grumbled sarcastically.

"If these attacks are happening more frequently, and in correlation with their repeated absences, could it be the Tarapor are getting out of hand?" Gavin ventured carefully.

"If that is the case, we need to step in," Ila immediately stated. Mariea knew her old friend had a lot against the Brotherhood, fueled by past disagreements. Often, she found herself wishing Ila would just let it go.

"There's nothing we can do to fight the Tarapor," Mariea reminded her. "They would kill anyone we sent. We have to trust the Brotherhood to handle it."

"That is their role, after all," Shawn agreed with a nod. "Besides, if things were out of hand, they would inform us."

"I hate to disagree with you, but I'm pretty positive they would keep it to themselves as long as they could," Jocelyn stated.

Bracken nodded. "It wouldn't be the first time they've failed to report on important matters. They do tend to insist on their secrecy a bit more than necessary."

Mariea had to admit he had a point. "I guess it wouldn't hurt to send someone to their headquarters just to make sure there isn't more of a reason for their lack of communication and frequent absences," she admitted.

"I could go," Gavin offered. "I've been meaning to head that way, anyway."

Mariea knew it was because his sister was a member of the Brotherhood, and he rarely had a chance to see her. She nodded in agreement. "Remember, you're only there to make sure the Brotherhood is still functioning. We can't get involved with the Tarapor."

"Will do," Gavin agreed with an acknowledging nod to Mariea's command.

Chapter Three

Headquarters

Mefune

"So, Mefune, why does the Brotherhood use swords? I mean, I know the rest of the world has better weapons. Why stick to something so old-fashioned?" the boy asked.

Mefune glanced at him. Aron couldn't have been more than twelve, but Mefune had noticed he learned quickly and was good at thinking outside of the box, putting him ahead of most of the other recruits his age. Unfortunately, his intelligence made him arrogant. His tone was almost flippant as he spoke with Mefune, and he often questioned his orders, despite him being at least fourteen years the boy's senior and one of the most accomplished members of the Brotherhood. Mefune knew his cocky attitude would have led him to trouble with others, but he was more patient than most. Still, Aron had the amazing ability to annoy even Mefune.

I asked for this, though, he reminded himself, reflecting on his request at the announcement of the match for a younger member to assist him in preparing. He didn't necessarily need the help, but he liked to keep tabs on the newest recruits, to see what the future generation of the Brotherhood was shaping out to be.

Menial tasks such as what he had recruited Aron for were an easy way to get a chance to speak with them without their interaction going to their heads.

Turning back to preparing the sword in his hands, Mefune answered, "Because modern weapons are as useless against the Tarapor as an Aurae's magic."

"Why?" the boy pressed.

"Their auras, though destroyed by the disease that made them what they are, naturally repel almost anything. The metal in these weapons had to be specially crafted. It's a tedious and dangerous process—they're deadly to anyone with an aura but can only be made by an Aurae—so we stick to weapons that can be used multiple times. Besides, even modern weapons such as a gun made of this metal aren't very effective. A sword or knife is the quickest way to kill a Tarapor."

Aron seemed to consider this for a moment, granting Mefune a few minutes of silence. He continued his work, running a cloth down the length of his sword to polish it. The blade was long and thin, with a gentle, almost imperceptible curve. The edge was deadly sharp, and he meticulously maintained it as such. With little decoration, the weapon was practical, lightweight, and efficient, just like Mefune preferred.

Setting it down, he picked up a second blade, which was a perfect reflection of the first, the other half of a symmetrical object. With the help of embedded magic, the swords actually became one when pressed together, becoming a slightly heavier weapon for when needed.

"Didn't the Auraes teach you these things back in Verndale?" Mefune wondered, bringing the boy from his thoughts.

Aron shook his head. "Not really. They focus mostly on those with auras, and since I don't have one..." He shrugged and fell silent.

"Hmm," Mefune muttered. It wasn't the first time he had heard of such prejudices. It created a bit of animosity between the Auraes and Brotherhood at times, since the Brotherhood were mainly auraless. But he didn't think it was extreme enough that they entirely neglected the education of the auraless children, as Aaron was implying.

Straightening, Mefune commanded, "Go keep tabs on things, let me know when Altaira's ready."

"I thought I was supposed to help you," Aron countered. He had already spent plenty of time completing small tasks, but apparently didn't appreciate being dismissed.

"This is how I want you to help. Go," Mefune insisted, his tone leaving no room for argument.

Aron sighed, but finally did as he was told.

Satisfied with his swords, Mefune pressed them together to make one blade and then placed it in its sheath before resting it on the table before him. As he pulled on a pair of fingerless gloves, a member of the Brotherhood Council walked in. Garrett was close to Mefune in age, with light brown hair and steel-gray eyes. Though he didn't often spend time with him, Mefune considered him something of a friend.

"Hey, good luck out there," Garrett commented as he approached. He moved to lean against the table, crossing his arms against his chest. "Think you'll win?"

Without hesitating, Mefune replied, "I know I'll win."

Garrett looked a bit surprised and then smirked slightly. "Somebody's confident. You sure?" Mefune nodded simply. "I don't know. I've seen Altaira fight. She's pretty good. What makes you so sure?"

"I've seen her as well. She is good, but not unstoppable. I'll win," Mefune reassured him. He wasn't trying to seem cocky or boastful, he just knew he was good at what he did. There weren't many who could match his natural talent, and combined with the amount he practiced, it put him well ahead of almost all the members of the Brotherhood. Most saw him as quite the prodigy; despite being young and being born outside of the Brotherhood's ranks, guaranteeing a late start, his career was already shaping up to be quite successful. He had been leading his own patrol for a few years now, something usually reserved for the more senior members, and helped train new recruits on occasion.

"You want to win?" Garrett wondered, considering Mefune with his head tilted to one side slightly. He knew of Mefune's original reluctance to involve himself in the politics.

Mefune considered how best to answer before shrugging slightly. "I accepted the duel, did I not? If I hadn't wanted it, I could have just given the position to her. I have no objections to being part of the Council."

"So, you are a bit ambitious, after all," Garrett teased. When Mefune didn't respond, Garrett rolled his eyes, annoyed he hadn't gotten a reaction.

"Mefune?" a voice asked from behind. He turned to see Aron had returned. "Altaira's ready. The fight can begin once you enter the ring."

Mefune nodded and reached for his sword. Garrett pushed away from the table. "Well, I guess I'll see you on the other side. I'd wish you luck again, but it seems you won't need it," he teased.

This time, Mefune allowed the faintest hint of a smirk. "I'll take it anyway," he muttered before following Aron out of the small preparation room.

He stepped out into a large arena. The ground was sandy, leftover from the cove that had once occupied the space. He glanced up at the surrounding stands. They were overflowing with the Brotherhood, who waited silently for the fight to begin, the tension almost audible in the air. It was rare they witnessed such a duel, and anticipation ran high.

Across the circle, a woman about Mefune's age stood confidently, one hand resting lightly on the hilt of a sword strapped to her waist. Her dark brown hair was pulled back into a tight braid, and she wore flexible, dark clothing, perfect for fighting in. Her gaze followed him as he moved to stand opposite her, his stance relaxed.

He was more than ready for this fight—he had known intuitively their almost subconscious contest wouldn't be able to remain as such, so he had familiarized himself with her fighting style to prepare himself for when the moment came.

They were about to battle for a place on the Brotherhood Council, and not only any spot, but the chair for Raidenya itself, giving whoever held it authority over the Brotherhood's headquarters. Recently, the former chair holder, Creta, had passed away from a long struggle with illness, leaving the spot up for grabs.

Tradition had it that the Council members could choose their successor, but anyone who thought they were good enough could challenge for the position. Creta had appointed Mefune. Altaira hadn't hesitated to challenge him, as he had guessed she would. She wouldn't pass up the chance to take power, but Mefune wasn't about to hand it to her. Even if he tried to pretend otherwise, he did enjoy the idea of being part of the Council.

Samar, the senior member of the Brotherhood Council and the Council leader, stepped into the circle, appraising the two silently as they approached. "You both know the rules. Fight fair, no acting on murderous intentions." He smiled slightly, a bit of dry humor seeping into his words.

Mefune had to resist the urge to roll his eyes. Altaira muttered her agreement, and Mefune nodded in consent.

"Good luck to the both of you," Samar continued. Taking a few steps back, he called, "Draw swords!"

Mefune drew his sword and slipped into a fighting stance as Altaira reached for her own weapon. Once Samar stepped out of the circle, the fight began. Altaira rushed at Mefune and swung her blade at him. Obviously eager to win, she attacked fast and hard, pushing Mefune to maintain his defenses. He found himself delighted by how much her skills forced him to try; rarely amongst the Brotherhood did he find someone who could keep up with him.

Once, she nearly cornered him against the wall of the bleachers, but he quickly slipped out of her grasp. She didn't give him a single moment to rest, immediately following his escape with another onslaught. *She's good*, Mefune had to admit. *I can see why Garrett questioned me.*

He allowed the fight to continue a moment more before deciding it was time to turn the battle in his favor. After deflecting a couple more of her blows, he pushed the first hole in her defenses that he saw, and she was forced to retreat a step, pausing in her onslaught. He pressed his attack, and suddenly she was on the defensive. Altaira frowned slightly, but continued to match his attacks with her own.

It wasn't long before he started to see some of the weaknesses in her form he had noticed before when he had seen her fight. The most prominent one by far was how her grip weakened after parrying a blow aimed at her left side. If he could get her to deflect a quick strike at that angle, there was a chance he could disarm her. He circled around, focusing on her weaker side, attacking hard and fast when he saw an opening, but giving her little time to add any real offense of her own.

Then, his opportunity came; when she absorbed a blow directly with the blade of the sword, the combined force of his attack and her vulnerability loosened her grip. Before she could retreat and correct it, he spun his sword around her blade and pushed it away with a hard shove, sending it tumbling from her grasp.

To her credit, she reacted well; darting away, she moved out of his reach, her confusion from losing her weapon only lasting a split second. Her gaze trailed briefly to her sword, which rested on the ground to his right, glinting in the sunlight. He waited, knowing she wouldn't be willing to give up yet, but the real question was whether she went for the sword or simply attacked unarmed.

He saw the shift in her stance, the subtle hint she intended to lunge for the fallen weapon before she moved, and reacted first. Just after her hand wrapped around the hilt of her sword, Mefune was in front of her, his sword point pressed against her neck. If it had been a real fight, he would have just landed a fatal blow. Triumph filled Mefune, and he smirked slightly as Samar called the match.

Altaira let go of her sword again, standing slowly, and Mefune backed off. After sheathing his own weapon, he retrieved her sword and returned it to her. Altaira practically ripped the sword from his grasp, clearly infuriated. Mefune expected nothing less, so he quickly dismissed it. They were swept up in celebrations almost immediately, and he forgot about her, focusing instead on his victory.

— ❧ —

Altaira

Leaving the arena, Altaira and Mefune were escorted by the crowd to the dining hall, Mefune surrounded by well-wishers, and Altaira left to sulk in her defeat. The grand room echoed with the buzzing excitement of the group as they entered. Altaira didn't follow, too angry to even consider going to the party. She left the group behind, heading instead to the stairs up to the living quarters.

The stone halls were dimly lit and almost entirely empty. She reached her apartment without interruption, to her relief. Locking the door behind her, she removed her sheathed sword from her belt and tossed it on the couch across from the entrance. She ran her hands through her hair, pulling half of it free from the braid. When it snarled around her fingers, she yanked the band out and allowed her hair to fall the rest of the way free, chucking the band into some dark corner of the room. She didn't bother with a light, just quickly turned to pacing as she tried to wrap her mind around just what in the world had happened.

Through her anger, she felt a spark of grief as her father came to mind. She had never met him that she could remember, but he was the reason she had challenged Mefune for his spot on the Council. After hearing his story from her mother, she had sworn to avenge his wrongful death, which had been caused by corrupt former leaders of the Brotherhood.

Considering the Brotherhood's governing Council was manned almost entirely based on fighting prowess, she had thought that she could quickly climb the ranks with the talent she had inherited from both of her parents and her determination to back it. With her newfound place of power, she could change the Brotherhood so nobody had to suffer the same injustices her father had. However, she quickly discovered two obstacles. Though the positions were never meant to be for life, Council members never stepped down from their positions, and there weren't any laws forcing them to do so. So she had to wait for one of them to pass away.

And the other obstacle was Mefune, which had come as a shock. He had joined not long after she had. After meeting him, she hadn't worried much about him; despite him being a few years older, he had been a scrawny, nervous kid, and a stark contrast to Altaira's confidence. She had almost pitied him, wondering if he would make it anywhere in the competitive and dangerous world that was the Brotherhood. Soon she started to impress her trainer and even some high-ranking Brotherhood members, and her success began to take shape.

But to her surprise, she found she wasn't alone in her success; Mefune had kept up with her, even surpassed her, in everything she did. As she grew in strength and skills, he did as well, to the point that Altaira found herself falling behind. It wasn't long before her superiors shifted their focus from her to him, almost forgetting Altaira. Suddenly, he wasn't just the scrawny blond boy but a very skilled, well-known fighter amongst the Brotherhood, and she his shadow, nothing more than second best. Despite his habits of sticking to himself and his almost cruel reputation, she knew his skills would get him considered for succession before her.

And, just as she had predicted, Creta had chosen him. Even though she had known there was a good chance she wouldn't win, she had challenged Mefune, almost out of spite. Despite this, the outcome was still infuriating.

After a few moments of oppressive silence, a knock came at her door. "What?" she snapped, whirling towards the sound.

"It's Daya. Can I come in?" a voice asked softly from the other side.

Sighing, Altaira moved to the door and allowed her friend in. Once she moved across the threshold, Altaira shut the door again with more force than intended, and it rattled in the frame with an echoing bang.

Flipping around to face Daya, Altaira threw her hands in the air and exclaimed, "I lost!" as if it wasn't already obvious.

"I'm sorry," Daya attempted, trying to soothe her. She moved to the wall next to the door and flipped a light on as she added, "We'll figure something else out."

"Like what? Creta was the oldest member of the Council. The rest are healthy and young, and unless something goes wrong, they won't be giving up their spots any time soon. Now I have no chance of joining the Council!"

"Hey, we managed with me," Daya pointed out.

"That was just a stroke of luck," Altaira sighed.

"A stroke of luck? My uncle died," Daya pointed out.

Wincing slightly at her own rudeness, Altaira quickly told her, "I know. I mean—" she sighed, feeling anything she might say would only dig her into a deeper hole. She was too worked up to form a complete sentence.

Daya waved her hand in a gesture of dismissal. "I know what you mean," she muttered. "He made things easy for me." His passing had resulted in Daya's surprising appointment to the Council, something neither of them had expected but hadn't protested.

But the little influence with the Council that had given them hadn't been enough for Altaira to reach her goals, leading her to try to join her friend despite how difficult it would be. But once again, her plans had failed, thanks to Mefune.

Her anger renewed, Altaira exclaimed her disgust again in a series of curses aimed at Mefune.

Daya sighed, her shoulders slumping. "Maybe I'll give you time to cool down. We can talk later." She moved towards the door but paused and glanced back, a concerned look in her brown eyes. "Just don't do anything stupid, okay?"

Altaira sighed, melting onto the couch next to her forgotten sword. "I won't," she grumbled as she leaned forward and rested her head in her hands. Unsatisfied, Daya hesitated before giving in and leaving Altaira alone to sulk.

— ℘ —

Altaira didn't wake the following day until well into the afternoon, and when she did, she found she had little motivation to get up. The Council would be holding a ceremony to make Mefune's new position official, and she had no intention of attending. Since she didn't have a patrol that day, she decided to allow herself a day to sulk.

Around seven, she heard a knock on her door. At first, she ignored it, but when the knock came again, and more persistently, she sighed and dragged herself out of bed. Caring little for what she was wearing, she shuffled to the door.

Opening it a crack, she discovered Daya on the other side. Letting out a sigh, she told her, "No, I'm not dead, just sulking."

"I figured," Daya told her with a small, sympathetic smile. "But I'm not about to let you stay here and waste away. Despite what you think, all is not lost."

"If you say so," Altaira muttered, leaning her head against the doorframe. When it didn't seem Daya had any intention of leaving, she glanced up and told her, "So what's your scheme for resurrecting me from my dreary mood this time?"

"Ice cream and a movie," Daya told her with a smile.

Altaira raised an eyebrow in surprise. "That means going to Verndale." There was a movie theater downtown, the only one on the island, and it hadn't been around for very long. The Auraes were slow to accept technology. Getting a ticket could be tricky.

"Yup, and I paid good money for nice seats, so you're not getting out of this one," Daya told her with a smirk.

Altaira sighed, shaking her head, but she couldn't resist a smile. "Fine, fine. Let me get dressed."

After she let her in, Daya took a seat on her couch while Altaira headed back to her room. Deciding she cared little for dressing up, she threw on a simple t-shirt and jeans and ran a brush through her hair. Then, remembering it was still early enough in spring to be pretty cold at night, she grabbed a jacket, pulled on her sneakers, and rejoined Daya in the main room.

"You know I seriously hate you sometimes, right?" Altaira grumbled as she started for the door.

Daya followed her out. "I know, I know. I'm the worst friend ever, trying to cheer you up. What was I thinking?" she lamented with a shake of her head and a smirk.

Altaira shook her head, but she couldn't resist a small smile as she locked her door and started down the hall. "What horrible movie are you subjecting me to this time?"

"I think it was some romance. I don't know, it was the last one with seats," Daya informed her as she fell into step with her.

By the time the two reached Verndale, it was getting dark. Daya glanced at her watch. "The show doesn't start for another half hour. Let's grab ice cream first," she decided.

Altaira agreed, so they made their way to a small shop across the road from the park. It sat between a barbershop and a small bakery. The three buildings were some of the first built on the island after the town was founded, and the older design had been meticulously maintained. The bakery and ice cream parlor shared the patio outside, and they had just put the tables out for the season. It was lit by strings of soft white lights. The whole scene was surprisingly charming and one of Altaira's favorite places in Verndale. She smiled slightly, knowing Daya was well aware of that fact and had brought her there on purpose.

The two bought their ice cream—Nutella for Altaira and traditional chocolate for Daya—and headed outside. Claiming a table, Daya plopped down and said, "See, now we can leave that duel and everything about it behind us."

Altaira smiled slightly. "Yeah. So how did the officiation go?"

Daya gave her a pointed look. "Did you not hear what I just said? We're trying to forget all that, remember?"

"Well, yeah, but I'm just curious," Altaira defended.

Daya shook her head slightly, but relented as she told her, "It went well, I guess. I'll at least give Mefune this: he did look great in that dress uniform."

Altaira scoffed, surprised her friend thought as much.

Daya quickly defended, "Hey, even you have to admit he's attractive."

"I mean, if 'I could kill the world with my bare hands without even blinking' is your thing, then sure, he's pretty good looking," Altaira deadpanned.

Daya shook her head in exasperation. "You know, I really don't believe the rumors about him."

"The only one I think could be true is the one about Brandon," Altaira admitted.

"You seriously think he killed him?" Daya asked, sounding surprised.

"I don't know; you know he really bugged Mefune when we were younger. He wouldn't give him a break. I think Mefune had enough and ended it permanently. He was the last person seen with Brandon at headquarters."

"Yeah, but that was days before people realized he went missing. He went to Verndale to visit his parents—they reported him missing. And the sentinels did a full investigation. They didn't find anything that linked Mefune to his disappearance. They never even found a body, meaning he might still be alive. He wouldn't be the first recruit that ran away. Some people just don't know what they're getting themselves into when they join."

Altaira shrugged. "Guess we'll never know. Still don't think I can trust Mefune."

Daya shrugged. "But enough about him, seriously. We're supposed to be enjoying ourselves."

Altaira nodded. She didn't want to dwell on the topic either, despite how she kept finding herself going back to it. The conversation switched to something lighter. After only a little while, Daya had her laughing, and she completely forgot about her troubles back home.

Just as they were about to leave, the door to the barber opened, and out walked Gavin, Altaira's brother. When she saw him, her smile immediately disappeared, and her gaze dropped to the table as she hunched her shoulders in an attempt to hide. Noticing the change, Daya glanced over her shoulder and then shot Altaira a knowing look.

"Just pretend he's not there, maybe he won't notice me," Altaira hissed.

But her luck was never that good.

"Altaira?" Gavin called.

She let out a quiet groan, and Daya's lips pressed into a thin line, clearly annoyed her attempts to cheer Altaira up had been so completely thwarted.

"I'm surprised to see you here," Gavin stated as he approached the table.

Clearly, she wasn't going to be able to avoid him, so Altaira forced a smile as she looked up at him and said, "Hey Gavin. Long time no see."

"Yeah, I tried to visit yesterday, but the Council wouldn't let me in," he told her.

"They were busy," Altaira replied.

"With what?" Gavin immediately pressed, all too eager to delve into Altaira's business as usual.

When Altaira didn't answer, Daya smiled and told him, "Nothing important. We were just replacing a member of the Council who passed away."

Realization dawned on Gavin's face, and Altaira shifted slightly, hoping he wouldn't ask about the duel. She had only told him she was challenging Mefune to show him she was actually getting somewhere in terms of rank at the Brotherhood. Now she'd have to admit she had lost.

"Oh, that's right, I remember now!" Gavin nodded. "You were competing for the spot, weren't you?" Altaira only managed a sharp nod, knowing what question would come next and seeing no way to avoid it. "How did it go?"

Altaira found it impossible to answer without snapping at him. Clearly catching on to how she was feeling, Daya quickly responded, "You know, it didn't go as planned, but I'm sure it won't be her last opportunity." Her tone was forcefully light as she tried to zip past the issue.

Gavin frowned. "You lost?" he asked Altaira. When she didn't bother to answer, he shook his head slightly. "I was really hoping this would work out for you. I'm sorry it didn't. Maybe you'll reconsider my offer to move back here now?"

"Why would I do that? My entire life is at the Brotherhood," Altaira responded, barely managing to keep her tone civil.

Gavin frowned slightly. "We've talked about this, Altaira. You have a life here too; you've just forgotten it in your obsession with avenging Alec," he told her, his tone borderline condescending. He didn't even have the decency to call him Father, and hadn't in a long while now, blaming him for their family's troubles.

"Oh, well," Daya started with a weak chuckle, "I wouldn't say she's obsessed—"

"You know what? I think we need to get going, Daya. Don't want to be late," Altaira stated as she stood abruptly. She didn't feel like sitting through her friend's latest attempt to smooth over the situation, nor did she want to continue arguing with Gavin. She knew she wouldn't get anywhere. Without waiting to see if Daya would follow or Gavin would protest, Altaira started toward the theater, leaving Daya to scramble to catch up.

"Wait, Altaira!" Gavin called after them almost immediately. She let out a sigh, but reluctantly turned back to him. He quickly caught up. "I did have something important I wanted to ask the Council about."

"Yeah, well, I'm not on the Council, so I guess you'll have to ask someone else," Altaira griped, folding her arms against her chest.

"Yeah, but Daya is," Gavin added, turning to the woman in question.

Daya glanced between the two, looking as though she were debating whether helping Gavin would somehow betray Altaira. When she didn't leave, Daya finally turned to Gavin and stated, "I don't know what help I can be, but what did you need?"

"Have any members of the Brotherhood ran into a new strain of Tarapor lately? Anything that might indicate the disease is now targeting auras?" he asked.

Daya's brow furrowed in confusion, and she shook her head. "No, not that I can think of. We haven't received any reports like these. Why?"

Gavin gave her a small smile. "Nothing. Just something the Auraes were wondering about," he told them, clearly dismissing the question.

Altaira rolled her eyes, annoyed Gavin felt he could demand any information he wanted from the Brotherhood, but couldn't afford them the same courtesy. It was typical of the Auraes—they looked down on their auraless counterparts. It was part of the reason for the tension between her and her brother. Grabbing Daya by the arm, she stated, "Let's go." Daya didn't protest, and neither did Gavin, so Altaira was thankfully set free.

"I'm sorry we ran into him," Daya told her once they were out of earshot.

"It's not your fault. Seems just like my luck these days," Altaira muttered. Then, after a moment, she admitted, "I've been avoiding him ever since..."

"Since he pestered you about coming back again?" Daya finished.

Altaira nodded. She had no intention of abandoning her goals, but Gavin was convinced one day she would wake up and come crawling back to him like a child that needed comforting. He was only six years older than her, but he had spent so much of his time caring for her and their mother when she was sick that he sometimes forgot he was her brother and not her father. And it infuriated Altaira to no end. He thought she was crazy for wanting to try to fix the corruption that had led to their father's death and for joining the Brotherhood. He just wanted a quiet life and to overlook their family history. She could never settle for that.

By the time they reached the movie theater, she had calmed down a bit and somehow managed to enjoy the movie. But as she left and her and Daya's conversation over the film died out, she found herself reflecting on her conversation with her brother. If anything, it made her even more motivated to try harder, if only to prove him wrong. She wasn't done fighting for her goals yet.

Mefune

The morning after Mefune was officially appointed to the Council, he woke early to prepare for his first formal meeting with them. Yesterday had been spent in celebration, but he knew he now had a lot to catch up on. The base had been without a leader for nearly two weeks now, dealing with Creta's death and Altaira's challenge, so he was a bit behind.

As he pulled his uniform from his closet once again, he let out a small sigh, part of him reluctantly coming to realize he would be spending a lot of time in it moving forward. The uniform wasn't exactly comfortable. But it was the only negative factor of his new job so far.

Once ready, he made his way up to the Council room at the end of the top floor. The double-oak doors were open when he arrived, and he could hear quiet chatter from inside, signaling at least part of the Council was already there.

The room beyond the doors was surprisingly grand. Despite being one of the closest sections of the base to the surface, it was still built deep enough to be allowed a high, vaulted ceiling. Skylights above allowed in shafts of sunlight along the aisles between the rows of spectator seats, making the center of the room bright but leaving the edges in shadow.

The Council met on a raised, curved table that was far too big for the seven members that were usually present, but it was designed to fit the entire Council. Technically, the Brotherhood's governing body was made up of twenty-two people, but because of the Auraes' strict policies concerning traveling to Raidenya, it was rare they all gathered. The seven that usually attended were sometimes referred to as the High Council, and comprised Raidenya's seat, the Council leader, and five regional leaders who oversaw sections of the Brotherhood internationally. The other fifteen members were responsible for specific international areas and reported to one of the five regional members, keeping the High Council apprised of the Brotherhood's situation as a whole.

Mefune made his way down one of the aisles and, as he drew near to the table, noted who was already present. It seemed he had arrived before all but Samar, Garrett, and a woman named Desiree. Samar was by far the oldest member of the Council now that Creta was gone. His black hair was mostly gray now, and his tan skin was worn by the sun, but his dark gaze was still sharp, and Mefune knew he was still one of the best fighters among the Brotherhood. He had won his position on the Council years ago in a duel not unlike the one Mefune had just participated in.

Desiree was probably in her late thirties with curly red hair she usually kept in a braid or bun. Mefune didn't know much about her, and, judging by the fact that she sat quietly at her end of the table reading instead of talking with her colleagues, he guessed she liked to keep to herself. He could respect that.

Samar glanced up from his conversation when he noticed Mefune enter the room and gave him a small smile. "Welcome! The rest of the Council is late, as usual, so we'll have to wait for them, and then we'll introduce everyone."

Mefune nodded and claimed a seat at the table next to Garrett. He and Samar returned to their conversation as they waited. One by one, the rest of the Council trailed in.

Darius, a shorter man with wavy brown hair and gray eyes, arrived first. Mefune didn't know much about him either, but he had seen him hovering around Samar frequently enough to realize he seemed to be trying to gain the Council leader's favor. Daya, the newest member of the Council after Mefune, arrived next. Considering her connection to Altaira, he could only hope she wouldn't hold the duel against him as her friend did, or working with her could get interesting. But when she greeted him with a pleasant smile, his worries subsided. Daya was a thinner, tall woman with chin-length black hair and brown eyes. Soon after she sat down, the last member of the Council, Ezequiel, joined them. He was also one of the more senior members of the Council but wasn't quite as old as Samar—Mefune guessed he was in his late fifties. He had a sturdy frame and graying blond hair that still had some curl, even cut short.

"Alright everyone, let's get started," Samar announced, urging Ezequiel to hurry up the short step to the table so he could join them. Gesturing to Mefune, Samar continued, "I think you've all met our newest member. Welcome again, Mefune. For the most part, these meetings are pretty quick. I just like to discuss the reports the regional members are receiving from the rest of the Council regularly and bring up anything we want to change." Mefune nodded, so Samar turned to Garrett and said, "Let's start with you."

One by one, the Council leaders reported on their regions. It surprised Mefune how many of them mentioned number shortages. It wasn't because there weren't enough members to cover the bases they already had—the problem seemed to lie instead in the fact that there weren't bases positioned to reach new areas the Tarapor had spread to. The more vigorously the Brotherhood hunted them, the farther they went in search of safe hunting territory. That worried Mefune, considering how much pushback they received from the Auraes when they tried to expand their current operations. If they weren't able to keep up with the Tarapor, their numbers would grow as they attacked more people and, eventually, those not from Raidenya would notice.

After the meeting ended, Samar showed Mefune to his new office just down the hall from the Council room among the others that belonged to the High Council. They were a more recent addition to the base and were furnished nicer than most rooms on that floor.

They spent the next hour reviewing the specifics of Mefune's new responsibilities. His new tasks included reviewing patrol reports and maintaining their schedule, approving mentor and trainee pairings, vetting new recruits as they applied and at the end of their training, and keeping track of the base's finances. As he listened to Samar's explanations, he quickly realized he would be kept busy over the next few days.

And busy he did remain. Between learning his new duties, contributing to the governing of the Brotherhood as a whole, and the regular patrols he still participated in, the next few days passed in a whirlwind of activity that left him surprisingly worn out but not unhappy. It wasn't his first busy job—being a patrol leader hadn't been easy to adjust to, either—and, just as he had suspected he would, he found he enjoyed the faster pace.

However, there was one thing that quickly became annoying. He discovered early on that Samar tended to meddle in his business quite a lot. As head of the Council, he technically wasn't supposed to have much to do with how headquarters was ran—his focus was on the Brotherhood as a whole—but Samar seemed to think he could waltz in and change things whenever he liked, without even consulting Mefune first. Because he didn't spend much time with the patrols, he often made changes that left Mefune scrambling to reorganize or put out fires in his wake. But since he was so new, he wasn't certain if he had misinterpreted the situation or if he should say something. One thing was sure, he didn't want to start making enemies so soon, so he kept his frustrations to himself and learned to adapt.

On a slower night, Mefune took a much-needed moment to enjoy dinner alone in the dining hall of the Brotherhood. The hall was a large, low-roofed room filled with rows of tables. A large hearth sat near the center of the room, consistently lit. One side of the room was dominated by serving stations, where food was prepared and dished out. The space was always pleasantly lit and equally warm, and no matter what time it was, there were always people present, filling it with the quiet sound of conversation.

Mefune chose a table away from the crowds, enjoying his meal in peace. He was about finished when Garrett appeared across from him, claiming one of the empty seats at the table, a drink in hand.

"Well, how's the new job suiting you?" Garrett asked.

"I'm enjoying myself," Mefune answered honestly. "It's a little hectic, but it's good."

Garrett nodded. "I figured you would be fine with it." He paused for a minute, his gaze on the room around them, before eyeing Mefune. "What do you think of the other Council members?"

Mefune didn't answer for a moment, wondering what it was he was probing for. Something about his words made Mefune wonder if there wasn't more to his comment, but he could only guess. He still didn't know much about the other members, and he wasn't sure that would change. He wasn't interested in their personal lives, and they didn't seem too interested in him. Eventually, he simply replied, "Not sure yet."

Garrett took a sip of his drink and then shrugged. "Some of them are alright. But I would be careful of Samar and Darius. I don't trust them."

"Why?"

Garrett glanced around again, leading Mefune to believe he was a bit paranoid that people were listening in on their conversation. Then he turned to Mefune and met his gaze. "They're planning something. I don't know the details, but most of the Council from off island is in on it, possibly some of the High Council. They won't like you. You won't let them push you around. People like you, they don't last long."

"What do you mean?" Mefune asked warily, his gaze narrowing slightly.

Looking a bit remorseful, Garrett told him, "I don't think it was a disease that killed Creta. He was poisoned."

He stated it so confidently, Mefune didn't think he was just repeating gossip. He knew what he said was true. At first, Mefune wasn't sure he wanted to believe him, but it honestly made more sense than Creta dying of disease—since the older man had spent a good portion of his life serving the Auraes as a medic, illnesses were simple for him to treat. But if he hadn't known he was poisoned and couldn't trace it back to the source, he might have failed to find an answer before it was too late.

If what Garrett was saying was true, Creta had been murdered. That changed things. And Garrett was implying Samar and Darius had something to do with it. He had Mefune's full attention now.

"And he wasn't the only one," Garrett continued, the weight to his words leading Mefune to believe he intended this comment to be a warning. Garrett knew if Mefune wasn't careful, Creta wouldn't be the last death the Council caused.

"I see," Mefune muttered. "I'll keep an eye on them." He paused, considering the information Garrett had given him, and then asked, "Why are you telling me this?"

With a small, wry smile, Garrett told him, "Mostly so you know I'm not involved." With that, he quickly finished his drink and stood. "Nice talking with you. See you around."

Before he could get far, a man approached and informed them Samar was waiting for the Council to gather. Garrett seemed surprised. "A meeting wasn't planned for tonight. Has something come up?"

"Sorry, I wasn't given any details," the informant replied with a shrug. "He just told me to find all of you and tell you he wants you there quickly." Garrett glanced at Mefune, and the two shared a knowing look; a spontaneous meeting at such a late hour wouldn't be called for any small matter.

"Well, guess we better get going then," Mefune decided as he stood, abandoning the remains of his dinner.

When they arrived, they took their seats as the rest of the Council joined them. Glancing at the others with him, Mefune quickly noticed Darius was scowling at the ground, and Samar seemed a bit upset too, though he made more effort to hide it. It also surprised him to realize more members were present than usual; four international members had joined them, all people Mefune didn't recognize. If there were international members of the Council present on Raidenya, it must be for some critical need, or the Auraes never would have given permission for them to travel to the island.

Samar began the meeting with a huff, bringing Mefune from his thoughts. "I have news from Verndale. The Auraes are unhappy."

"Why?" Daya asked, sounding confused. Mefune couldn't help but agree; with Creta's death and the subsequent events, Samar had been forced to miss meetings in Verndale, leaving them with little news of what was happening amongst the Auraes.

"They think we aren't keeping the Tarapor under control," Samar grumbled. "There have been recent deaths amongst them, and they're blaming us."

Mefune's brow furrowed in confusion, wondering where this had come from. The Auraes relied on the Brotherhood to control the diseased monsters and were always grateful for what the Brotherhood did. He couldn't help but doubt they would risk jeopardizing their relationship with the Brotherhood by angering the Council. In the past, they had been understanding of any surges in Tarapor attacks, knowing their task wasn't an easy one. When Garrett muttered something along the same lines as Mefune's thoughts, he realized he wasn't alone in his wondering. Others seemed confused as well.

Samar nodded, obviously agreeing. "Usually, that would be the case, but ten people have died. They're so frenzied, they're quick to blame us." He scowled. "I've never liked working with them. They take advantage of us, with little more than words of gratitude in return."

"I can't understand how Tarapor are the cause of these deaths," Ezequiel exclaimed with an exasperated gesture. "We cleared them out near the city, and there's always a patrol nearby. The only Tarapor left on the island are so deep in the forest we don't even bother with them unless they come closer."

"I don't think these attacks are Tarapor either, but the Aurae was insistent," Samar stated.

Mefune wished he could have been present for that conversation. Something about Samar's retelling seemed off, but he couldn't decide if he was just being paranoid; Garrett's earlier warning still echoed in his mind.

"So, what do we do about this?" Darius ventured.

Samar sighed, sounding reluctant. "We'll just have to do what we can to reassure them we're still doing our job and hope they don't retaliate in anger." He paused for a minute, contemplating their options. Glancing at Mefune, he instructed, "Let's send out two extra patrols daily until things calm down. Send them near the city. That'll guarantee there aren't any Tarapor near Verndale, and allow the Auraes to see us working. Have them make a point to enter the city."

Mefune nodded, his lips pressing into a thin line as he considered the extra burden this would put on an already barely staffed schedule. *People will have to serve on two patrols every rotation,* he thought, knowing that wouldn't sit well with most. He'd just have to somehow try to balance it so that those on shorter patrol routes took the extra shifts every week.

As the changes took effect, Mefune quickly felt the growing annoyance amongst the Brotherhood. He didn't care if they didn't like his orders, but it was quickly obvious they didn't blame him—they blamed the Auraes for their troubles. It didn't make sense for them to even know the Auraes were connected to the change—he hadn't told them *why* they were adding more patrols. But after only a little digging, he quickly discovered Samar and Darius, as well as some of the visiting Council members, had allowed it to leak. It almost seemed purposeful, as if they *wanted* them to feel angry towards the Auraes. Considering Garrett's claim that they were conspiring, it worried Mefune that it appeared the Auraes were somehow involved. He could overlook conniving amongst themselves as long as it didn't hurt the Brotherhood, but this seemed more significant than small-time corruption. It had already led to one death. He didn't want to find out if it could lead to more.

Deciding he needed to figure out what was going on, Mefune resolved to approach Samar. Despite Garrett's warning, he wasn't afraid of the Council leader. Creta's greatest weakness had been his blind ability to trust people long after they had proven they shouldn't be; he never would have suspected his comrades would do him harm. In contrast, Mefune had never been so naïve. Now that he knew Samar was possibly dangerous, he would be cautious, but wasn't overly concerned.

It took a few days to find an opportunity, but one night, Mefune found Samar alone in his office long after everyone else had left. Seeing his chance, he stepped in and closed the door behind him. Samar glanced up from his work, one eyebrow raised in surprise.

"We need to talk," Mefune stated softly.

"It would seem so," Samar mused.

"Word is, you're planning something."

"And who told you this?" Samar wondered. He seemed more amused than concerned Mefune was asking about what he had assumed would be a sensitive matter.

"I'm not blind," Mefune admonished with a small shake of his head. "I see how you're trying to turn the Brotherhood against the Auraes. I want to know what this is about."

Samar considered him in silence for a long moment. "I don't take threats lightly," he stated, his voice as soft as Mefune's, his cold gaze meeting his without wavering.

"The only threat there was one that you implied," Mefune corrected.

"Hmm," Samar muttered with a small, mirthless smile. "I've heard things about you, Mefune. People say you'll stop at nothing to get what you want. You'd even kill, if necessary. Are these rumors true?"

This wasn't the first time Mefune had heard of those particular rumors. He was somewhat amazed they were still circling, though he admittedly hadn't done anything to squash them. Though he wasn't entirely sure what had started them, he had to admit, the reputation they gave him came in handy. It kept people out of his business and out of his way. And now, that reputation would definitely be helpful. "Perhaps," he stated evenly.

"I'm inclined to believe them," Samar admitted. He stood and made his way around the desk. "Why do you want to know of my plans so badly?"

"I want to help."

Samar nodded slightly, looking a bit surprised. "And why should I trust you?" he mused as he leaned against his desk.

"If I had wanted to expose you, do you think I would bother to pester you about the details? I already know enough to incriminate you," Mefune warned. Allowing the smallest hint of a smile, he added, "And I would hate to make the rumors about myself true by dealing with this matter in any other way."

"As would I," Samar agreed, his smile a bit more strained. But after a pause, he brightened a bit. "Luckily, it's something I've been meaning to bring up with you, anyway. I need the Council to back me if my plans are going to work, and I could have use for someone like you." He fell silent for a moment, collecting his thoughts. "The Auraes have been pushy lately. It's caused a bit of tension between us and them, as you've probably noticed. I see it as an opportunity."

Mefune raised an eyebrow in surprise. "An opportunity? What do you mean?" He couldn't see how angry Auraes would benefit them.

"We've protected and served them for decades now, but they give us little say in the governing of the island and place huge restrictions on our operations. Many Council members abroad want to expand our efforts to fight the Tarapor, but the Auraes are so stubborn they refuse to allow it. They claim we'll jeopardize their safety in the process. But they don't understand what it's like to fight these things, to watch as they take advantage of our lack of numbers and slaughter innocents. The Brotherhood would do anything to put an end to this struggle, but they would prefer to wipe the deaths away with magic and pretend it's not happening. As long as the Auraes are in full power, things won't change."

He paused for just a moment, whether for effect or to gather his courage to drive home his point and face Mefune's reaction, Mefune wasn't sure.

"I intend to take the power we need," Samar finally announced.

"Why not just move forward without their approval?"

"We tried. The failed base in Moscow wasn't because of a lack of supplies like we told the public. The Auraes shut us down."

It took Mefune a minute to recall the incident Samar was referring to. "That was…six months ago," he mused.

Samar nodded. "The Council kept it quiet because we didn't want to cause conflict. But now the Auraes are starting to throw the deaths they suffer at our feet, with no proof the Tarapor are even involved." Though his voice remained even, Mefune noticed the first signs of anger as his hands tightened into fists, and he slowly frowned. "So, I'm going to show them what it would really be like if we stopped fighting the Tarapor."

"You're going to stop protecting the city?" Mefune asked, unable to completely keep the surprise from his voice.

"Not exactly," Samar clarified with a slight shake of his head. "Just abandoning our guard would make us look negligent, not powerful. I intend to capture Tarapor and let them loose in the city. We'll make it clear we allowed it on purpose, but we're willing to stop it if the Auraes agree to a new arrangement."

"Hmm...." Mefune mused, debating this for a moment. "What makes you think the Auraes won't just retaliate?"

"They wouldn't dare, not after they realize how easily we can turn our enemy upon them," Samar dismissed.

Mefune couldn't help but think he was forgetting the might of the Auraes. He was definitely overlooking the plight of the people that would be caught in the middle of such a fight. It seemed, despite the original cover of good intentions, Samar's plan was entirely focused on the power he could gain.

Power which Mefune wasn't about to hand over to him. But he realized there were still many details he didn't know, like how far Samar's reach went or how he could stop him. In a split-second decision, he concluded the easiest solution would be to get Samar to trust him with those details instead of hunting them down himself.

"Well," he mused, smiling slightly. "What can I do to help?"

Samar seemed a bit surprised, but then his expression turned to one of triumph as he slowly smirked. "I need you to capture some Tarapor for me."

Mefune nodded. "That shouldn't be too hard. How many?"

"As many as you can," Samar requested. "The timing of everything is still up in the air, but I'd like to be prepared."

Mefune nodded. "I better get started then," he decided. With that, he turned towards the door. "Oh, keep me informed of the details, will you? I'm interested to see how this will play out."

"Of course," Samar readily agreed.

As Mefune stepped out, to his surprise, Garrett appeared not long after they were out of earshot of Samar's office. "What was that about?" he asked as he fell into step next to Mefune.

"I just mildly threatened details out of Samar and then led him to believe I'm willing to help him with his plan," Mefune admitted with a shrug.

Garrett blinked in surprise and glanced over his shoulder at Samar's closed door. "Wow. That was easy."

"It helps that it seems he's already trying to recruit the Council to his cause. He wanted me to help. But there's still a lot he wouldn't tell me; he clearly doesn't completely trust me," Mefune mused.

"I'm sure your charming personality had nothing to do with it," Garrett joked.

Mefune didn't respond, letting the comment slide despite the slight hint of annoyance it brought up. He would have thought at least his friends would realize he wasn't the man the rumors had made him out to be.

After a minute, Garrett asked, "So what is he trying to do?"

"Not here," Mefune decided. Stepping into his office several doors down from Samar's, Mefune closed the door behind them and then explained what he had learned.

As he finished, Garrett let out a dejected sigh. "All over a little disagreement in Moscow," he grumbled.

"Is this really what this is about?"

Garrett shrugged. "I doubt it. But that's just when Samar first became bold enough to state his dislike of the Auraes. It's also when opinions began to turn against Creta. He spoke in favor of the Auraes' decision. The base in Moscow was ill-planned and ill-timed. We had no business being up there, but most of the Council hated being told they were wrong. Especially Samar."

"Hmm," Mefune muttered, considering this and what little information Samar had bothered to tell the Brotherhood as a whole. Like he had with the visiting Aurae, it seemed he was using the situation to sour the Brotherhood towards the Auraes. "We need to stop him. A lot of people will die on both sides of this argument if he gets his way. I'll do what I can to find out details of his plan. In the meantime, we need to think of a counterplan."

"How many members support him?" Garrett wondered.

"He alluded to several from the International Council, and I get the feeling he at least has Darius and Ezequiel's support here on the island. He admitted he's trying to recruit the whole Council."

"And the general populace is already souring towards the Auraes because of the strain their extra demands are placing on us, so it won't be long before he has their backing," Garrett added, looking worried. "He might actually have the support to pull this off."

Mefune frowned, realizing just how quickly the situation could get out of hand. If the Auraes were as angry and desperate as Samar claimed, and they did blame the Brotherhood for their troubles, he wouldn't be surprised if a full-scale war broke out over this. "We need to remove his support. See what we can do to sway public opinion against him."

Garrett shifted uncomfortably. "Speaking out against him isn't the best plan."

"Why?" Mefune was confident that once the public heard what Samar was trying to do, they'd turn against him.

"He poisoned a man to protect his plans," Garrett reminded him with a pointed look. "He's good at lying, clearly, and with your reputation, nobody will believe you over him. And if we tried to say something to the rest of the Council, nobody would back us. They're either loyal to him, or he's scared them into submission."

"Then we take it to the Auraes."

"With people like Ila on the Aurae Council? That'll just fuel the flames. Have you seen her? She's almost as ridiculous as Samar," Garrett pointed out.

"Mariea's in charge," Mefune reminded him.

"Only superficially," Garrett countered with a dismissive wave of his hand. "The minute we tell Ila the Brotherhood Council is acting against the Auraes, she won't stop yelling for justice until Mariea caves. From what you just told me, if the Auraes moved against us now, Samar would be all too willing to act in kind, and we'd still have a war on our hands."

Mefune didn't answer for a long moment. He did have to admit Mariea deferred to her councilors more often than he thought wise. There was a chance Garret was right. But it still left him frustrated and without answers to their current problem. "We have to do something," he protested, trying not to grow frustrated.

Garrett gave a dejected shrug. "I'm just trying not to start a war. Or end up in an early grave."

The two fell silent, clearly stuck on the issue. After a moment, Mefune cautiously suggested, "What if we didn't address the overthrow he's clearly trying to pull but instead focused on some of the smaller crimes the Council has committed?"

"Like what?"

"You and I both know there's plenty of corruption among the men and women on that Council. All we need is proof. Like proof of Creta's death, for instance," Mefune suggested.

"Sadly, I have none," Garrett admitted with a small shake of his head. "At least, none that would hold up in court. But there's a chance we could dig up information about other members of the Council. Though, if we do this, won't it lead to the same result? Angry Ila, angry Samar, etcetera?" he wondered.

Mefune shook his head slightly. "If we play it right, I don't think so. We use Ila's hatred of the Council to our advantage by feeding her one lead at a time. Without a big enough threat, she'll never be able to convince Mariea to do anything irrational. But she'll be more than happy to remove even one member, and Mariea won't argue if we have evidence. And instead of being able to use the Auraes' accusations as fuel for their martyr complex, Samar and his ilk will be scrambling to hide their corruption from the members, which we'll make sure gets out. This will break up their support among the general populace."

Garrett considered this for a moment and then shrugged slightly. "It's something of a plan, at least." Then he glanced at

Mefune warily. "I'll do what I can to help, but I don't want to end up taking the fall for this."

"I guess I'll do the digging then," Mefune reluctantly agreed. "One more thing; if we manage to remove his supporters on the Council, we'll have to make sure they're replaced by people who aren't loyal to him."

"Which would be who?"

"Good question," Mefune grumbled. "Any ideas?"

"I'm not sure of anyone off the top of my head, but I can do some listening," Garrett offered.

Mefune nodded. Then Garrett shook his head, smiling softly in disbelief. "When I warned you to be careful of Samar, this wasn't exactly what I had in mind."

"Well, when I realized this may be bigger than petty power play amongst ourselves, I knew I had to look into it," Mefune admitted. "I'm not about to stand by and let Samar destroy the Brotherhood. Not if I can help it."

Garrett didn't answer for a moment. Then he stood and turned towards the door. "I hope you know what you're doing," he muttered before leaving Mefune alone.

"Me too," Mefune agreed, leaning against his desk with a sigh.

Chapter Five
Messages

Mariea

Mariea floated in a white expanse of nothingness, a passive numbness settling over her mind and body. Somewhere in the back of her mind, she vaguely remembered falling asleep, but reality and all its problems seemed a million miles away. Willing to allow them to remain that way, she let out a contented sigh—which, oddly enough, made no noise. It was amazing just how quiet it was; like a forest caught in the grasp of heavy, slow snowfall, the lack of sound was obvious but not unwanted. Mariea allowed her gaze to slide closed as she settled on the idea of just relaxing.

But before she could completely slip away, a gentle blue light pulsed to life at her left, drawing her attention. Blinking, she turned to it, her curiosity piqued by its sudden appearance. It looked much like a messenger spell—a simple orb of auric power—but it seemed unusually large, like the message it carried was bulky. As she thought of moving towards it, she began floating in that direction, her body moving without effort.

When she stood before the light, she slowly reached out a hand for it before hesitating. She was content to stay in the problem-free void she had found herself in, and part of her worried the light would be the way out. But the longer she stared at it, the more curious she became.

Eventually, she gave in, reaching out to touch its surprisingly smooth surface.

Warmth spread from her hand and into her body as her fingers passed through its surface, making her realize how cold she was. Streams of color suddenly burst from the ball of light, slowly filling the void with life. Mariea watched as a picture gradually formed before her; she could make out a blurry silhouette surrounded by a cream and gold landscape. Eventually, the image of a woman appeared before her, but her backdrop remained blurry.

The woman seemed to finally take solid form, and then she turned her gaze to Mariea. She was taller than Mariea and had an ageless quality to her, as if time seemed to have no effect on her. There was a definite sadness to the deep blue of her eyes and the bittersweet tilt of her half-smile. Her warm brown hair stood out in contrast to the white of her long dress.

"Mariea," she stated with the fondness of someone who knew her well. "The past has been forgotten, but it needs to be remembered."

"What?" Mariea wondered, confused by the statement. It didn't help that she spoke in Shidokian, which Mariea knew but wasn't entirely fluent in. It took twice as long for her to understand what she had said.

Suddenly, the woman disappeared, replaced by flashes from Mariea's nightmares that made her flinch. If this was what the woman was bringing to her, she wanted no part in it. But after a moment of watching, she realized it was no longer herself fighting for her life, but the woman before her.

"You must come to my home," the woman stated as she reappeared, and the dark images retreated, taunting Mariea at the corners of her vision. "You must learn of what happened. Follow the dreams. They will guide you. Trust in what you see." The woman disappeared again, replaced by glimpses of familiar streets.

Realizing the images were of New York, realization dawned. "You want me to come to New York?"

The woman seemed to miss what Mariea had asked. "Please hurry. Time is short, and everything depends on you knowing," she warned.

The void slowly faded to black, but not before Mariea was once again surrounded by the haunting images of her nightmares, the scenes all too real and encompassing.

Jolting up in bed, Mariea quickly scanned her surroundings searching for the woman, but as she took in her room, she realized the dream was over. Sighing, she rubbed a hand over her face, laying back down. Instead of returning to sleep, she mulled the nightmare over repeatedly. Despite it not being nearly as terrifying as the usual nightmares, it still left her with the same feeling of dread.

Before she could fall asleep again, the blaring of her alarm clock informed her it was morning. Sighing, she turned it off, silently grumbling about how much she hated its noise.

As usual, it took a long while for her to shake off the weight of the dreams and move on. She wanted to discuss it with Bracken, but he had left early that morning to give him some time to work on projects before a few meetings he had that day.

The message haunted her throughout the day, permeating every quiet moment even more than any of the nightmares had. She knew it wouldn't let up until she discussed it with someone, so during her lunch break, she decided to track down Bracken. The spells master's main lab was actually on the academy campus, allowing them to meet up during her lunch break frequently. Luckily, when she messaged him, he said he was available and would meet her in the professor's lounge.

Mariea reached the lounge before he did. It was a decent-sized room with tables and a few comfy lounge chairs around the edge of the room. There was a fridge, sink, a couple of microwaves, and all the utensils, silverware, and dishes a person could need. She prepped her lunch quickly and claimed a table.

It wasn't long before Bracken joined her. "So you had another dream?" He asked warily.

She hadn't mentioned anything about it in her message, but she wasn't entirely surprised he had guessed the topic of their conversation. "Yes, but this one was different," she told him before she began to explain the message from the mysterious woman.

When she finished, he sat in silence, contemplating the added information. Eventually, he asked, "You think this was connected to the nightmares?"

"I'm sure of it," Mariea confirmed. "Maybe this woman was sending them to me somehow, trying to warn me. What she said definitely felt like a warning."

"Did she mention what she was trying to warn you about, exactly?" Bracken asked warily.

"No," Mariea sighed. He looked disappointed. "But there is a way I could find out," she added carefully, knowing what she was about to suggest wouldn't sit well with him.

His gaze met hers, a knowing glint in their dark depths. "You aren't suggesting—"

"Going to New York? That's exactly what I'm suggesting," she finished for him.

One eyebrow raised, Bracken mused, "That's a long, possibly dangerous journey just for a dream and a gut feeling."

"But I have to know if this is real," Mariea pressed, forcing the annoyance from her voice. After everything he had done to try to help her, she didn't want to take out her frustration on him. "These have to be more than just dreams. Either that or I'm going insane. I can't keep living like this."

Bracken sighed, clearly conflicted. "If we were certain, then I would jump at the idea of going. But there's so much to consider with such a trip. The world out there is dangerous for Auraes."

"We don't even know if the auraless would attack us," Mariea griped as she folded her arms against her chest.

"Every time we've interacted with the *Shikani* in the past, they've immediately reacted in violence," Bracken countered, using the Shidokian word for those without auras. "It's like it's ingrained in their DNA to hate and attack us. You know the history as well as I do."

Mariea let out a small, annoyed sigh. She hated it when he brought history to their debates about the world beyond Raidenya, because he practically always won when he did. Reluctantly, she had to admit he had a point—she had seen a glimpse of their almost immediate hostility when her aura had first appeared while still living in New York. If it weren't for the Brotherhood stepping in, she wasn't entirely sure what that hostility would have led them to do.

"I guess I'll just let it go until I learn more," she reluctantly muttered.

He nodded, looking relieved but still slightly wary. Mariea could only imagine what he was thinking. *He's probably wondering what's possessed his wife*, she thought. It wasn't like her to do things on a whim, especially not something as crazy as leaving Raidenya. But often the Auraes forgot their leader hadn't been born on the island. The world beyond Raidenya wasn't nearly as intimidating to her. *I would be fine. If this keeps up, I'm going*, she decided. She wasn't about to allow some unknown danger to destroy her home and kin if she could avoid it.

After a moment, Bracken changed the subject. "Jordan was wondering if we wanted to come to his place for dinner on Sunday."

It took Mariea a moment to pull herself from her thoughts enough to form a response. "That should be fine."

"Are you sure you're okay to go? You know Jordan's kids can be a handful. If you're not feeling up to it, we don't have to," Bracken stated.

Forcing a smile, she shook her head. "No, I want to go. You know I like your brother's family. As long as it's just Jordan and not both of your brothers, it doesn't get too crazy. Besides, I don't want to stop living just because of a couple of dreams."

Bracken nodded, despite seeming a little uncertain. "Alright, I'll tell him we'll be there."

Eventually, their lunch hour ended, and she and Bracken parted ways. After her last class, Mariea stopped by her office at the capitol building to finish some quick paperwork and check in on a few projects she was managing around the city. Just as the sun began to set, she started packing up her things, ready to head home, when she heard a knock on her door.

"Come in," she called, and Gavin opened the door.

"If you have a moment, I wanted to tell you what happened when I went to speak with the Brotherhood the other day," he informed her.

"Sure," she agreed, gesturing to the seats across her desk.

Gavin claimed one and then began. "The Brotherhood Council wouldn't see me. There was a lot going on, so that might be why, but it still seems a bit suspicious. Even when I explained to Darius that I was just looking into something for the Council, he wouldn't take the matter to the rest of the Council or answer my questions."

"Hmm," Mariea muttered, frowning slightly. "I guess we'll just have to ask them what they know during our next meeting, assuming they'll actually show."

"I did learn a bit," Gavin admitted. "I ran into Daya in town, and she told me she hasn't heard anything about a new type of Tarapor."

"Interesting." It was odd to Mariea that the Brotherhood wouldn't encounter them, considering how heavily involved with the Tarapor they were. Maybe the problems weren't related. "Well, thanks for telling me. I guess we'll just have to look for answers elsewhere, won't we?"

"I guess," Gavin muttered, but he didn't sound convinced. Like many of the Auraes, it seemed he had a hard time trusting the Brotherhood. As he left, Mariea let out a little sigh. *Will this conflict ever go away?* The incident in Moscow had been one of the first things she had dealt with after being elected. It had happened three months before her election, yet the tension was still palpable when she had taken her place on the Council. For the most part, she had managed to convince everyone to move past the issue, but the deep-seated resentment between some leaders refused to fully fade, making trust difficult.

Adding it to the list of things she had to worry about, Mariea numbly gathered her things and headed home, wondering if Bracken was right—maybe the stress was getting to be too much after all.

— ∅ —

The mysterious woman delivered the same message to Mariea again for the next three nights. Eventually, it no longer disturbed her sleep, and it was a welcome relief to the nightmares. But she couldn't ignore it. It taunted her, but she had no idea what it meant. And she still wasn't sure she was willing to leave her home to follow it. Not when there was so much going on.

Sunday came, and Mariea found herself grateful for the time to spend with her family. Jordan lived with his wife and two daughters in a house on the edge of town, about a ten-minute walk from Mariea and Bracken's place. Because the weather was nice and Mariea felt good, they decided to walk.

She and Bracken arrived at Jordan's house just before dinner. His wife, Nora, met them at the door, along with her two daughters. They hid behind her, glancing out the door curiously, but their fear disappeared the minute they recognized Mariea and Bracken.

"Yay, Aunt is here!" one of the girls squealed as she rushed towards Mariea.

She grinned and bent to catch her, barely managing to keep her balance as the girl slammed into her with a giggle. "Hey, Emilie, it's good to see you," Mariea greeted.

It wasn't more than a minute before the younger girl, Rylee, joined her sister, though she didn't come with nearly as much force.

Nora smiled at her girls, resting a hand on her hip. "They've been waiting for you two all day."

Bracken shook his head. "Seems they were only excited to see Mariea," he teased.

Mariea scooped up the two and took a step towards her husband. "Of course. I spoil them rotten. It's no wonder I'm their favorite." Bracken shook his head with a small smile, not about to argue. He knew it was true.

"Come on," Nora told her, motioning them inside. Bracken followed, and Mariea carried the girls inside.

At the sound of the closing door, Jordan poked his head out from the kitchen. "Hey family! Dinner's just about done!" he called.

"Sounds good!" Bracken stated with a smile. He headed for the kitchen to see what he could do to help, so Mariea carried the girls into the living room to play with them.

Dinner passed uneventfully, and then the girls went to play upstairs. After cleaning up, Nora and Jordan invited Bracken and Mariea into the living room.

Nora sunk onto the couch with a sigh and pulled off the scarf she wore around her hair, letting it fall free. "So, how has work been treating the two of you?" she asked, glancing between Bracken and Mariea.

"Busy as always," Mariea replied with a weak smile. She didn't want to talk about work, not with everything going on. She doubted Nora was all that interested in her teaching career.

"Come now, I know how crazy things are getting. Jordan has told me. So, how is it really?" she insisted.

Mariea sighed, knowing she wouldn't be able to convince Nora to drop the issue. Her sister-in-law hated knowing her family was ill or unhappy for whatever reason. But Mariea also didn't want to admit she was struggling to maintain the peace. "It's been...messy lately," she finally admitted. "But we're getting to the bottom of the issue."

"That's good to hear," Jordan said with a sigh.

Glancing at him, Mariea was surprised to see just how stressed he seemed. Jordan was very much like Bracken in appearance, so much so Mariea joked they should have been twins. But Jordan was nothing like him in personality. Where Bracken was soft spoken and gentle, Jordan was stubborn and sometimes disagreeable. But it came with the job—he had one of the hardest on the entire island. Being a sentinel wasn't easy, especially now. She couldn't imagine what he was going through.

And now, she had accidentally given him false hope. But it wasn't like she could take back what she had said. It left her feeling stuck for a moment, and she shifted slightly to avoid Jordan's gaze.

Luckily, Bracken took advantage of the silence to ask his brother a question. "Have you seen these things? Whatever it is that's attacking the city?"

Jordan shook his head. "Luckily, no. But I've been on mandatory leave this whole week."

"Why?" Bracken demanded. "Did you get hurt again?"

Jordan managed a sheepish smile. "No, no. I just hadn't had a day off in what...a month? I guess I forgot to request my day." He shrugged slightly.

Nora glared at him. "That's not true. They were short men on his shift, so he volunteered for the extra hours. Left me all alone with the babies for days."

"Yeah, when Jocelyn found out, she literally told me, 'Are you trying to wreck your marriage? Go home and don't come back until Nora's not mad at you,'" Jordan told them.

The four shared a laugh. "I can see Jocelyn saying that," Bracken mused.

"Yeah, so when she calls to bring him back in, I'm going to tell her I'm still mad so I can keep him home longer," Nora said with a mischievous grin.

Mariea laughed. "Man, I wish I could use that with Bracken."

"Unfortunately, my boss isn't very conscious of my time or that I have a family," Bracken lamented, clearly attempting to smother a smirk.

"You *are* your boss," Nora reminded him.

He couldn't resist the smile any longer. "My point exactly."

Nora chuckled and shook her head before asking Mariea, "What are we going to do with them?"

"Love them," Mariea sighed with an exasperated shake of her head, though she smiled at Bracken. She knew he meant well. He just had an impressive ability to lose track of time.

They all laughed again. Then the conversation changed gears and, thankfully, stayed on safer topics for the rest of the evening. Eventually, it grew dark, and Nora wanted to put the girls to bed.

"I guess we better head home," Mariea decided, glancing at Bracken.

"Yeah. Don't want to be out too late," Bracken muttered, glancing out the window. Mariea frowned slightly, realizing why he was nervous. Most of the attacks had happened after dark.

"Let me send you home with some food," Nora stated as she stood.

"Oh, no, that's fine, Nora, you don't have to," Bracken protested.

The two kept bickering playfully for a moment more, but then Jordan abruptly called for them to stop, standing and turning towards the door. They all turned to him in surprise, wondering what had caused his sharp tone.

When he didn't say anything more, Nora cautiously asked, "Is something wrong?"

"Did you hear the scream?" he asked, turning towards them to glance between the three. Mariea glanced at Bracken and Nora, who both shook their heads. She shrugged, shaking her head as well.

Jordan didn't respond, his gaze unfocused, wisps of his dark amber aura appearing around him. "Jordan?" Nora called, her brow furrowing in concern as she stepped towards him, resting a hand on his elbow.

He blinked, looking up at Bracken and Mariea. "You need to go now if you want to make it home. Something's happening, but I can't get a good read on what. Come on, I'll escort you home."

"I knew we should have driven," Bracken muttered as he pulled on his coat.

"I'm sorry, that was my idea," Mariea stated as she hurried to gather her things.

"Oh, please be safe," Nora called, following after them. She met Jordan's gaze and ordered him, "You come home quick."

He nodded and stole a quick kiss. "Make sure the girls stay inside. Lock the door after we're gone. I've got my key." Nora nodded, so Jordan stepped outside, Mariea and Bracken following.

They started down the street, which was mostly empty save a few others heading home. Bracken took Mariea's hand and pulled her close, his gaze scanning their surroundings. Mariea kept watching Jordan, hoping to pick up on some cue from him to help her figure out what was happening, but it was impossible to read him.

As they came to an intersection, a noise farther down the street made Mariea jump, and Jordan raised a hand to pause them. Mariea edged closer to Bracken, her heart rate accelerating slightly. It wasn't like she was incapable of protecting herself, but she knew whatever was attacking the city had killed sentinels. She was well aware she wasn't a fighter, not like Jordan and the rest of the sentinels. And neither was Bracken, really. Spells weren't good in a fight. She just had to hope Jordan would be strong enough to defend all three of them if it came to it.

Jordan remained silent, his eyes closed and his aura flowing around him freely. "There's a fight up the street. Let's take a different route."

"Should we help?" Bracken asked.

Jordan shook his head. "I'm not about to risk you and Mariea. I'll get you home first, then come back and help."

He motioned them forward, turning down a less familiar street, hurrying past darkened rows of houses, his aura still surrounding him. Mariea kept glancing over her shoulder, wondering if whatever it was would finish that fight and find them next. Without a face for the attacker, her imagination quickly created plenty of gruesome images of what it could be to fill the gap—much of which came from the images the nightmares had supplied her with. The longer it went on, the more scared she became, to the point that her hands were shaking, and she felt the urge to run the rest of the way home.

When their house finally came into view, Mariea audibly sighed in relief despite her attempts to remain composed. She fumbled in her pocket for the keys and unlocked the door while Bracken and Jordan stood watch at the bottom of the stairs.

Stepping inside, she motioned for the other two to follow. Bracken did, but Jordan hesitated.

"I'll start back. I think whatever it was is gone. I can't sense it anymore," he told them.

"You could sense it? What was it like?" Bracken asked.

Jordan didn't answer for a moment, his gaze on the streets below them. Then he sighed. "Dark. I don't know. It didn't feel like anything I'd sensed before. Like an aura, but...different. Corrupted."

For a moment, it seemed neither knew what to say, but then Bracken stated, "Well, let me know when you get home, alright?"

Jordan nodded. "Be careful," he told them both before he glanced at Mariea and added, "If I were you, I'd consider enforcing a curfew."

Mariea nodded. "I'll bring it up on Thursday."

Jordan nodded again and then hurried down the stairs. Bracken watched him go for a minute, clearly worried for his brother, before Mariea reached out and pulled him inside. She shut the door behind him, locked it, and then leaned against it with a sigh. Her heart refused to settle.

It seemed the pair were frozen in the narrow entryway, neither wanting to break the tense silence their fear had created. "When did our home become this?" Bracken wondered softly.

"I don't know," Mariea agreed with a shake of her head. "But I don't like it." Her shoulders slumped slightly, and she met Bracken's gaze. "I'm failing everyone. Someone might have died tonight." She folded her arms against her chest, frowning as her anxiety and fear only grew.

"You're not failing," Bracken quickly replied. He took a step closer to pull her towards him, comfortingly running his hands along her arms. "You can't expect to have all the answers."

"I guess," she muttered. She had hoped her tenure as chancellor would be short and uneventful. It seemed that wouldn't be the case.

"Come on. There's nothing we can do about it tonight," Bracken told her before he gently began pulling her away from the door.

They spent a little time waiting for Jordan's message. When they knew he was home safe, Mariea headed for bed, surprisingly exhausted. But she struggled to fall asleep, her mind playing over the events of the evening relentlessly. She couldn't help but wonder once again what she was supposed to do.

It was no surprise when the mysterious woman's warning came to her again. It was the only thing close to a possible solution she had ever received, and she dwelt on it almost as frequently as she had the nightmares.

But this night, there was one different part. Just before the image ended, and she woke again, the woman told her, "I know you are struggling. I want to help. Please come."

Mariea

Once again, Mariea gathered with the Aurae Council. She was running late, so she figured the rest of the Council would already be present. As she entered the room and glanced around, she was delighted to see Samar was present for the first time in a long while.

When Ila joined her, she leaned close as she sat down and muttered, "We're grateful you have graced us with your presence, Samar." Her words dripped with sarcasm, an only half-hidden smirk playing at the corner of her lips.

Mariea couldn't help but chuckle, feeling only slightly less annoyed with Samar. Glancing at Samar, Mariea noted she hadn't met the man sitting next to him. Samar often brought the Council member who ran Raidenya's base with him to the meetings, but lately, he'd been coming alone or with another Council member due to Raidenya's chairholder's poor health.

Noticing her attention, Samar glanced her way and dipped his head in greeting. "Mariea."

"It's good to have you back," she said with a smile.

His smile turned a bit strained, but his voice remained civil. "I apologize for the unintended long absence. Creta's passing necessitated it." Then, glancing at his comrade, he added, "This is Mefune, the newest member of the Brotherhood Council. He replaced Creta."

"Ah. Nice to meet you, Mefune," Mariea greeted. "I'm Mariea."

"Likewise," Mefune agreed politely with a dip of his head. "I look forward to working with all of you." His words carried the faintest hint of an accent, making Mariea wonder where he was from.

"Though we'll miss Creta, I'm always open to getting a fresh perspective on things," she mused with a smile. Then her attention was pulled away by Ila tapping her arm.

"Mariea, do you think the weather will stay nice this weekend?" Ila asked, but she seemed unfocused. Her gaze trailed towards Mefune, narrowed slightly in suspicion.

Mariea looked at her in confusion, wondering why in the world she was talking about the weather. It wasn't really like Ila to dwell on mundane topics. She glanced back at Mefune, wondering what Ila's fascination with him was.

When Mefune turned away and began conversing with Samar, Ila whispered, "I don't like the new guy."

"Why?" Mariea questioned.

"There's something off about him," Ila replied.

Mariea raised an eyebrow and turned back to him, trying to see what Ila was getting at without staring. He was tall, with a pale complexion, lean build, and pale-blond hair pulled back into a short ponytail. He had the look of a fighter, as did most of the Brotherhood, and seemed a bit older than Mariea. He was dressed in the formal attire of the Brotherhood; a crisp black uniform jacket, dark pants, and boots. Though he didn't seem overly friendly as he contemplated the Council around him, there was nothing Mariea noticed that would make her agree with Ila.

"I don't know, I don't see it," she told her friend.

"It's not something I see, it's something I sense."

"Like an aura?" Mariea wondered.

"No, definitely not an aura. I don't know, it's hard to explain," she muttered with a helpless shrug.

Brow furrowing, Mariea focused on what her aura could tell her about him. It was like a sixth sense, an understanding of the world around them on a different plane. Mariea was so used to picking up on the smallest of things she didn't bother to contemplate it.

This time, she did notice something different about Mefune, something that, if it weren't for the fact that she was searching for it, she would have entirely overlooked. She couldn't pinpoint exactly what it was, but it felt dangerous, as if she just subconsciously knew she needed to be cautious around him. Like Ila had said, it wasn't like the feeling of an aura—it was clearly too subtle to be one. Even inactive auras left a mark of power on a person who had one. Plus, Mariea guessed it was safe to assume he didn't have an aura, since very few among the Brotherhood did; it was too dangerous, considering the weapons they carried could kill them if they interacted with their auras. So, what was it she and Ila had picked up on?

Without realizing it, as she had contemplated these things, her gaze had trailed back to him, and her aura appeared in the smallest amount around her hands, reacting to her emotions. As if he could sense her watching him, he turned to her, a hint of suspicion in his gaze. She blinked, caught off guard, and then quickly looked away.

"See what I mean?" Ila muttered, clearly reading her reaction and realizing she was thinking the same thing.

"Yeah," Mariea muttered.

"Hey, we should start," Gavin stated from her right, drawing the two women's attention.

"Right," Mariea agreed, trying to compose herself. She called the meeting together, forcing herself to ignore Mefune. As the meeting continued, she pushed it from her mind, focusing on the reports presented by her colleagues.

"These attacks are getting worse. More people are dying," Jocelyn told them when it was her turn to speak. "We need to find a solution, but I'm running out of ideas to keep everyone safe."

Mariea sighed, disappointed to hear such news. "It was suggested to me that we consider a curfew, since most of these attacks have happened at night. Do you think that would help?"

"I've considered it, but the attacks haven't been exclusively at night. I think that would just encourage them to be more active during the day. And they've broken into homes on more than one occasion. Keeping everyone indoors probably won't make a difference," Jocelyn responded.

"It would serve to make them afraid, though," Gavin added. "Everyone is already nervous, as much as I'm trying to keep things under wraps and reassure him." Mariea nodded. Of course, it wouldn't be as simple as hiding in their homes all night while the danger passed by.

Jocelyn turned her attention to Misha across the room. "Have you learned anything new since we last spoke?"

Misha shook her head. "I have yet to hear of anyone who has survived the attacks, and the autopsies continue to leave me with few answers." Jocelyn nodded, clearly disappointed but not surprised.

Glancing at the two Brotherhood representatives, Mariea asked, "Has anyone on your patrols encountered anything like Jocelyn described?"

"If your suspicions are accurate, and a new strain of Tarapor has developed that targets auras, I doubt we would see any cases. Considering ninety percent of the Brotherhood is auraless, these new Tarapor wouldn't focus on us," Mefune guessed.

"Besides, I do not appreciate the implication that we are not doing our job," Samar inserted, sounding frustrated. Mefune glanced his way, one eyebrow raised slightly in surprise.

Mariea's brow furrowed in confusion. "Nobody accused you, Samar."

"No reason to be defensive if you haven't done anything," Ila added coldly.

"Your accusations may not be vocalized while I am present, but I know you feel we are responsible. That was clear when you sent Gavin to chastise us."

"Hey, I didn't do any chastising," Gavin said, his hands raised before him defensively. "You wouldn't even speak to me! I had to get all my information from Daya when I randomly ran into her here in town."

"So you were investigating us, then?" Samar snapped, his gaze locking on to Gavin.

"You weren't present at the meetings, so we figured the worst had happened. If you attended regularly, we would have no reason to suspect you," Ila retorted in response, defending Gavin. Samar returned his attention to Ila, obviously seeing her as the cause of his problems as the tension between the two quickly intensified.

Before an all-out argument could start between the two, Mefune laid a hand on Samar's shoulder. "It's not worth it," he muttered.

Samar's gaze snapped to Mefune, and the two seemed to have a silent debate for a brief moment. Then Samar let out a small huff, obviously annoyed Mefune had involved himself, but he gave in to his comrade. He leaned back in his chair and crossed his arms against his chest, his gaze shooting daggers at the blank wall behind Misha.

Mariea sighed, relieved. After a brief pause, she addressed the group. "Obviously, nobody wants these attacks to continue, and arguing about who is to blame won't fix it. We need a solution. Any ideas how we can address it, find out more information, and better protect the people while we work on it?"

The discussion began, but Samar and Ila were still tightly strung. Their comments were always backed by plenty of spite, and the weary Auraes around Mariea quickly became annoyed by them as well. Pinching the bridge of her nose and leaning against the table, Mariea tuned them out, her thoughts trailing elsewhere in search of solutions.

The dream of the woman started to play in her mind as if called up by some force that refused to let her push it aside. *She had wanted to help us*, Mariea remembered, recalling the change from Sunday night. It had become consistent since. *Maybe this is what she wanted to help with?* The more she thought about it, the more she warmed to the idea. It wasn't like they had answers anywhere else, and she didn't find it a coincidence this mysterious possible warning had cropped up almost simultaneously with the mysterious threat.

I have to go to New York, she decided. *If this is possibly an answer, I can't ignore it.* As crazy as everyone would think she was for acting on the dream, she was quickly beginning to believe it was their only chance for answers.

"I think the answer to these attacks may lie elsewhere," she interrupted. The conversation stuttered to a halt as the Council turned to her. "As much as we would like to believe these attacks are Tarapor related, I wonder if there isn't something else, something we previously haven't dealt with, causing them." She glanced at Samar. "And I trust your people are doing their job. There must be another explanation."

"What did you have in mind?" Shawn asked.

"I...I received a message of sorts. It was vague, but it pointed me to where I could look for more answers. It will take me off the island. I'll be gone for at least a week, but it could be much longer...I'm not sure. But I think this is what I need to do."

"That may not be the wisest idea. It's too dangerous beyond the island. We can't do anything to allow those beyond our shores to see our auras, or it could lead them back to Raidenya and start their witch hunt all over again," Jocelyn warned.

To Mariea's surprise, Bracken spoke up in her defense. "Mariea actually mentioned this warning of sorts to me a couple of days ago, and we discussed the dangers at length. I originally agreed with you, Jocelyn, but I think we need to act on this. We're clearly not finding answers here."

Mariea shot her husband a grateful smile before turning back to Jocelyn. "Besides, I know the risks. I once lived in that world. I wouldn't be doing this if I didn't think it was best for everyone."

"If this is really what you feel is best, then...we can't stop you," Jocelyn relented.

"I'm coming with you, though," Bracken added, giving her a small smile.

Mariea returned it. "I wouldn't have it any other way."

"I can keep things in order while you're gone," Ila offered, her way of pledging her support.

"And I'll get a substitute to cover your classes," Shawn offered.

"Thank you," Mariea told them, grateful for their impressive support of her harebrained plan.

"You should bring a medic with you, just in case," Misha suggested. "Who knows what you'll find once you're out there?"

Mariea nodded in agreement. "Do you have anyone in mind?"

After considering it for a moment, Misha stated, "Mae Anderson. She just finished her training with a focus on emergency medical situations and could use some real experience. It would be good for her. Plus, she was born off the island, and though she was young when she came here, she may still remember something of it, which could prove useful. She's an incredibly talented medic. I would trust her to handle anything."

"If you could ask if she'd be willing to come along, I'd appreciate it," Mariea requested. Misha nodded.

Glancing at Samar, Mariea said, "I know the Brotherhood has a way of handling our...lack of existence according to the rest of the world, in terms of official documents and such. Think you could help supply the three of us with what we'll need?"

Samar nodded. "It'll take our records department at least a day to put it all together."

"Good. Keep me posted," Mariea requested. She paused, considering her plan, and then nodded, satisfied she had addressed all the issues. Then she frowned slightly as something of a sadder note came to mind. Addressing Ila and Gavin, she requested, "See to it that the families of those that have died in these attacks are taken care of. It's the least we can do since we failed to protect their loved ones." Gavin and Ila nodded, sharing in her sudden solemnity.

"When will you leave?" Misha asked after a moment, breaking the mournful silence that had fallen over them.

"As soon as Samar has what I need and Mae is ready to leave," she stated, suddenly filled with a sense of urgency as she remembered how desperate the woman had sounded to share the information she had. "The sooner, the better."

— ℰ —

Mariea stood just inside the front entrance to Dublin airport in Ireland, staring at the throngs of people, one hand gripping the strap of her backpack tightly. People hurried past them, talking in a hundred different languages and fussing with technology Mariea simply couldn't grasp as possible. When she had last stepped beyond Raidenya, the world had been much slower. Staring at it all now, it was suddenly overwhelming.

Bracken stood at her side, wide-eyed and slightly pale as he studied the crowds. He had never left their island home, and after all they had experienced so far, it seemed Dublin airport was the last straw. He looked even more overwhelmed than she felt.

Mae stood nearby, her green gaze attempting to take it all in as she ran a hand through her short, dark red hair. She was younger than Mariea had thought when Misha suggested she come; barely nineteen, she was the youngest medic ever to complete her training. Mariea had to admit that it was impressive, but part of her worried her inexperience would lead to trouble. Luckily, she seemed more excited than overwhelmed by their journey so far.

After a long boat ride from Raidenya to the nearest lightly populated area in Ireland, and two train rides to Dublin, they found themselves at the airport, trying to figure out the next step on their trip to New York. The whole adventure had been a series of Mariea stumbling around, somewhat knowing what to do, with the others following her like lost children. The confidence she had boasted before leaving Raidenya had left her soon after discovering just how much the world had changed in thirteen years.

"So," Bracken stated lamely, reminding her they were waiting for her to tell them what to do next.

She bit her lip, staring up at the signs and watching the traffic, hoping to get a hint from their movements. Memories slowly returned to her from her last trip on a plane, and she started to piece together their next step. "We need to check in." Locating the needed line, she approached the desk but then hesitated, feeling she was forgetting something important.

"Something wrong?" Bracken asked as he came to stand next to her.

Suddenly, it dawned on her. "We need IDs," she informed them.

"Eyed ees?" Mae wondered, sounding confused.

Mariea laughed. "Identification cards. Like a driver's license or something. It's what all these people use to identify themselves, like we use our auras. They should be in with the stuff the Brotherhood gave us." She propped up her suitcase next to her and pulled her backpack off one shoulder to rest against her stomach. She rummaged through its contents and then produced a folder. From it, she pulled out three cards and passport books and then passed them to her companions.

After briefly explaining what they should expect, Mariea replaced her backpack on her back and returned her attention to the check-in desk. The process went well enough, other than a slight hiccup with the fee for the bags; she had no idea how Euros worked and gave the woman the wrong amount twice before she decided to help her.

Once all three were checked in and had their boarding passes, Mariea started towards their next obstacle—security. "The fun has just begun," she sighed to Bracken and Mae before explaining the ridiculously long demands security would require them to adhere to before passing through.

Mae and Bracken looked shocked. "Why so strict?" Bracken wondered.

Mariea shrugged. "They're paranoid, I guess," she muttered, though she knew there was more to it than that. She didn't think a history lesson on how bad things had gone before the security was so strict would come as much comfort to the two, so she kept it to herself.

Joining the painfully slow line, Mariea began removing anything metal she had on her person, as did Mae and Bracken. Watching the metal detectors at the end of the line, she was surprised by how complicated they were compared to those she remembered from her childhood flights. As she continued towards them, the attendants began asking her about a myriad of items she could have in her bag, half of which she didn't even know what they were. *Eyepad? What could that possibly be, and why would it set off a metal detector?*

Finally, she reached the metal detector and passed through without incident. As she collected her things, she glanced over at Bracken as he passed through. She could see the monitor displaying the x-ray image and was surprised to see his aura seemed to surround him in the image on the device. *That's interesting*, she mused, taking note of it. For a minute, she watched others passing through, wanting to see if the silhouette showed up on more people than just him.

Mae eventually joined them, drawing Mariea's attention away from the x-ray. They regathered their belongings and then made their way to the gate, where their plane was just beginning to board. Once they found their seats on the plane—Mariea and Bracken next to each other and Mae across the aisle from them— Bracken let out a heavy sigh.

"Will it be this crazy in New York?" he asked.

"Probably worse," Mariea admitted, knowing New York was a much larger city than Dublin. "Though the security process should be relatively similar."

Bracken nodded. As the plane took off, he turned to the window, his eyes widening in fascination as the world shrunk below them. At least this part of the journey was enjoyable for him.

Several grueling hours later, the plane finally lowered itself to the ground again. Mariea was jolted awake when the wheels hit the runway and sat disoriented for a moment before she remembered where she was. After stretching as best as she could in the cramped space, she glanced out the window as the plane taxied to the airport. The glowing New York skyline was visible in the distance. When she saw it, a wave of nostalgia washed over her, and she smiled slightly, allowing herself to enjoy the fact that she was returning to her old home.

"Welcome to New York," the attendant announced. "The current time is eleven PM."

Slowly, the plane began to disembark. The passengers were let inside through a long tunnel, and then once again, they found themselves facing a security checkpoint—this time through customs and regulations. As she watched the process unfold for passengers ahead of her, she realized she had entirely forgotten to explain to her companions that the officers were most likely going to ask them questions about why they were visiting the United States and where they had come from. She had meant to spend some time coming up with a story beforehand—they couldn't very well tell the officers they were following a magical message to save their nonexistent home from some unknown threat—but the stress of the day had made it slip her mind.

Realizing it would be suspicious if they didn't say anything, she quickly told her companions, "They're going to ask us a ton of questions about why we're here. Just follow my lead." She nearly forgot not to use English—it still wasn't easy to rely on Shidokian, even after years of practice, and in moments of stress, it became more challenging.

Bracken and Mae shared a nervous glance, and then Bracken asked, "Think we could get away with pretending we don't speak English?"

Mariea considered it for a moment and then shook her head. "I think they'll expect us to since your passports say you're from Ireland, and I'm a US citizen still," she admitted.

Bracken nodded and then let out a nervous sigh. "Here's to hoping this goes well. I think I'm starting to figure out why we don't leave Raidenya, and it has nothing to do with magic. This is just ridiculous."

Mariea didn't answer, though she somewhat shared in his sentiment. However, she understood the people outside of Raidenya couldn't rely on magic and secrecy to protect them as she and her people did. She supposed such tight security was the next best thing.

Finally, they reached the front of the line, and Mariea dutifully handed over her documents to the officer at the counter. Her gaze passed over her passport, and then she scanned her ID at her computer. "It's been a while since you've been here, it seems. What's brought you back?" the woman asked.

"I wanted to show my husband where I grew up," she decided quickly, gesturing to Bracken.

The officer glanced up at him. "And you're from Ireland?"

"Correct," Bracken confirmed with a nod. The officer returned Mariea's papers to her and gestured him forward, so he handed over his papers.

"Do you plan to stay in New York while you're here?" The officer asked next.

"Probably," Bracken confirmed, glancing nervously at Mariea.

"We haven't entirely decided how long we're staying. There's some family I'm trying to track down, and it might take a while," Mariea added.

"Why not just call them?"

"I was adopted," she told them. It was close enough to the truth she figured she could get away with the lie and still manage to keep her story straight if asked for more details. "I'm trying to see if I can contact my birth family. It's a...bit of a long shot, but family is important."

The woman nodded, showing a surprising lack of emotional reaction to Mariea's story, making her worry she hadn't been believable. She glanced up at Bracken and then at Mae. "You're traveling with them too?" she asked.

Mae nodded, presenting her documents. The officer scanned her ID and then shuffled through the rest of her papers for a moment, her questions oddly absent. Considering she hadn't returned Bracken's papers before taking Mae's, Mariea grew nervous.

"Give me one moment," the officer said and then stood and carried Mae and Bracken's documents with her.

"Not good," Bracken whispered.

Mae turned to Mariea and Bracken, muttering a quick, "What do I do?"

"Don't panic," Mariea reassured, trying her best to sound calm, but in reality, she wasn't having much luck remaining calm herself. She glanced nervously after the officer, hoping whatever had caused her to leave wouldn't be a major issue.

After a painfully long moment, she returned with another man wearing a jacket with a CBP logo on the pocket. He glanced over the three with suspicion in his gaze and then turned to the screen.

"See?" the woman officer stated, gesturing to her computer screen. "I've never seen it do that before."

"Hmm," the man muttered, running a nervous hand over his goatee. "And it happens with both of their IDs?"

The first officer nodded, pulling Bracken's ID from the pile of papers and scanning it again in demonstration. The man nodded and looked up at Mae. "I'll need you to come with me." His gaze turned to Mariea and Bracken and added, "You two as well."

"Did we do something wrong?" Mariea asked impulsively and then cringed inwardly, hoping such a question wouldn't incriminate her.

"Your IDs aren't reading correctly in our systems. We will have to verify they're legitimate and ask you a few questions before allowing you into the country," the man explained. He then turned and gestured for them to follow.

Mariea glanced warily at her two companions, knowing this was way beyond her ability to safely guide them. Bracken shrugged wearily and started after the officer, so Mariea and Mae followed.

They were escorted to a security area in a secluded corner of the airport. There, they were placed in a small, bare room with three chairs and a table. A half-empty coffee pot and a few granola bars sat on a smaller side table.

"We'll return once your belongings have been moved to a secure location for processing. Please wait here," the officer stated, and then he left the three alone.

Mariea sighed and plopped into a chair. "Just to be safe, let's use Shidokian. They could be watching us somehow," she muttered. Mae paced on one side of the room, clearly too nervous to stay in one spot.

Bracken nodded as he leaned against the wall, his arms crossed against his chest. Following her advice, he asked her in Shidokian, "So how do we get out of this? I mean, we all know our IDs were fake. We could probably break out of here somehow, but I doubt they'd just let us go, and we still have things to do here in the city, so we can't just leave. But I'm sure if we cooperate, things won't go well. The rest of our documents are forged, and we know nothing about this world."

"Wait, couldn't you use some of the spells you use to hide Raidenya?" Mae asked, looking at Bracken. When he didn't seem to follow, she added, "You know, the spells that made people forget my family when we came to the island. The ones the Brotherhood got from the spells masters. Didn't you invent them?"

Bracken shook his head. "No, I had nothing to do with those spells. They're old and hard to use. I never learned them." Mariea was surprised by this. He glanced at her, noticing her expression, and gave a helpless shrug. "I never intended to leave the island, so I never bothered to learn them. Memory spells are too hard to get right and too easy to do permanent damage with."

"I guess that makes sense," Mariea muttered.

They fell silent for a moment more before Bracken asked, "How does the legal system here work, anyway? Is there any way we could get some sort of...pardon?"

Mariea shook her head slightly. "I don't know about that, but we might be able to prove our innocence if I can contact the Brotherhood. I think they have a base here in New York." After a pause, she frowned slightly and added, "Though, I have no idea how to do that here. I should have asked for their contact information before we left." Briefly, she debated sending a message to someone back home to get in contact with the base in New York. She glanced around the room, searching for any indication that they were being watched, but considering her unfamiliarity with technology, she worried she wouldn't know what to look for. Deciding using magic was too risky right now, she settled on waiting to see what happened next.

The door opened again a moment later, and the same man stepped into the room, followed by two others. "Mariea, Bracken, come with me," he stated. "Mae, Officer Tristan will interview you here."

Mae nodded, glancing nervously at the officer that entered the room. Mariea and Bracken were led out. As Officer Tristan closed the door behind them, Mariea watched Mae hesitantly take a seat at his instruction, her hands wrapped into a knot under the table. Mariea shook her head, swallowing around her growing fear. There was no way Mae would be able to answer the questions to their satisfaction. Mariea needed to get out of there so she could get help.

"My ID worked, didn't it?" Mariea asked the officer as he led her and Bracken to another room. The officer glanced at her, clearly wondering why she was asking, and she worried she had made things worse by wording her question the way she had—she could see him wondering if she had expected it to *not* work.

Hoping she wasn't digging herself into a deeper hole, she added, "It's just, since I'm a citizen, and my documents cleared in your system, are you even allowed to hold me?" She was grasping at straws with the comment—she didn't know enough about immigration laws to know if it was true—but she could only hope she'd manage to convince the officer to let her go.

Begrudgingly, the officer admitted, "If we find no fault with your documents, I can't legally detain you, but we still have to complete our investigation. But traveling with two individuals with potentially bogus IDs doesn't look good."

"Oh," Mariea muttered. Bracken glanced at her, his worry only increasing at the idea that she might be released while he was detained. She took his hand, giving it a quick, reassuring squeeze—the best she could do in the situation—and then turned her attention back to the officer. "Well, we'll cooperate. I'm sorry this whole ordeal is wasting so much of your time. I really don't know what happened with the IDs."

"No need to apologize, ma'am. We're just doing our job," he reassured blandly. Then, he gestured inside a room and stated, "I'll interview you in here. Officer Jepson will take your husband."

Bracken shared one final nervous glance with Mariea, and then he followed the third officer farther down the hall. Mariea hesitated, staring after him for a moment, before the officer that waited with her impatiently stated, "Come along, please."

For the next hour, he asked her dozens of questions that she somehow managed to keep answering, though she was sure none of her answers were convincing. Between her worry for Bracken and Mae and her growing, jet-lag-induced exhaustion, it was getting harder and harder for her to keep her story straight.

She slumped in her chair when he finally left her alone, running a tired hand through her hair. She could only imagine how Bracken and Mae were fairing with their limited understanding of the world they had stepped into. What was worse, since they hadn't discussed their story ahead of time, there was very little chance they would end up telling it the same way. That alone might be incriminating enough to get all three of them arrested.

She was left alone for what seemed like hours. She dozed once but then woke in a panic, immediately feeling oddly guilty for falling asleep. Finally, the door opened again, and the same officer stepped in. "It looks like your documents all check out. You're free to go."

Mariea stood in a rush. "What about Bracken and Mae?"

"They're still under investigation and will remain here until that is finished. If it turns out they're innocent, we'll allow them to contact you," the officer responded. Mariea was about to protest, unsure of how she would find her companions again, but one look at the officer's expression showed he would only find any further comments from her suspicious and unwelcome.

With a sigh, she asked, "Alright, where can I find my luggage?"

"Right this way, ma'am," he replied, gesturing for her to follow. He led her to an office, where her luggage and backpack were waiting. After thanking him, she claimed her belongings and quickly headed out of the airport, feeling incredibly alone and worried about Bracken and Mae.

Outside the airport, she found herself alone on the curb of a drop-off area that was still surprisingly busy, despite the late hour. She glanced around, realizing she had little idea of where to go next. She felt so disoriented after what had just happened that it took her a moment to remember what they had planned to do before being arrested. *I had hotel reservations,* she thought, reaching into her backpack to find the papers.

The address wasn't far from the airport. Mariea just had to figure out how to get there. Glancing around, she noticed a sign for rental cars and started towards it. Luckily, it didn't take long to rent a car.

By the time she made it to the hotel, it was after one in the morning, and Mariea was exhausted. Luckily, the hotel still had someone to check her in, and she was gratefully allowed to head upstairs. She glanced briefly around the two-bed hotel room and simply flopped down on one of the beds, kicking her shoes off as she did. Her brain was fried after spending all day trying to keep herself, Bracken, and Mae safe and where they needed to be. Despite her best efforts, they had still run into trouble.

"I'll contact the Brotherhood tomorrow morning, first thing. We'll get out of this mess," she muttered, needing to reassure herself before she could attempt to sleep. She changed her clothes in a half coherent state and fell asleep as soon as she managed to find her way into bed.

Mariea found herself looking over New York, her eyes wide as she realized she was far in the air with no parachute and no way to catch herself. She stared at the gleaming city, breathing hard while trying to remain as still as possible, hoping whatever kept her suspended wouldn't give out.

Suddenly, she turned away from the city, the surrounding landscape spreading out before her. Beyond the busy streets of New York, the rest of the state wasn't so crowded. Large chunks were open farmland, with miles of acres between houses. It all seemed to belong to a different day and age, which carried a certain charm.

In the northwestern part of the state, her attention focused on a small farmhouse. It seemed very old, and though it was well maintained, it was showing its age; the paint was peeling, giving it a distinct blue and gray speckled pattern. There was a fence around the front yard that was missing a few boards in places, and the mailbox looked like it had fallen off its pole and been reattached several times. For some reason, the door was painted a bright red. She lingered outside it for a long while, and she took the time to study it in detail, soaking it in. She had the distinct feeling she would need to remember everything she could about it.

Then, the house faded, and she found herself standing on a pier. It was late now. Something important was happening, but she didn't know what. She just knew she needed to find it.

Mefune

After returning from his first meeting with the Aurae Council in Verndale, Mefune found himself even more worried about Samar's scheming. Since confronting Samar, he had spent a good amount of his time trying to convince the older man that he was on his side, but Samar refused to give any more details about his plan. Part of him had begun to wonder if his secrecy wasn't caused by a lack of planning instead of a lack of trust—maybe there was nothing to share, and all of Samar's ranting was empty air. Mefune had almost been ready to dismiss the issue until they had gone to Verndale.

It was clear, within the first few minutes of the meeting, Samar hated the Auraes enough to pull off something as ridiculous as the plans he had shared with Mefune. And after witnessing Ila's open hostility towards the Brotherhood firsthand, he knew any chance of having the Auraes help resolve the issue without causing an all-out war was gone. Even if Mariea could have managed it, it was clear Ila wouldn't be able to in her absence.

And Samar's angry rant on the walk back to headquarters made it clear he had every intention and possibly the means to go through with his schemes. That left Mefune with a quickly growing issue that seemed way bigger than one man could handle. He needed allies, ones willing to do more than Garrett was. But who could he trust with such an issue? Who could he turn to that Samar hadn't already swayed to his side?

As he sat debating it at lunch one afternoon, he glanced over the crowd, considering what he knew about those around him. He had always been good at keeping tabs on the members he served closely with, knowing their strengths and weaknesses, but he knew little about them personally. Even his old patrol seemed distant now that he had left them to serve on the Council. It made him wish he hadn't insisted on keeping to himself so much.

Towards the back of the room, he noticed Altaira eating alone. He almost immediately passed over her, but his gaze trailed back as he reconsidered what he knew about her. Altaira was fiercely loyal to the Brotherhood, and she had an Aurae brother. She had never done anything to show she harbored ill will towards the Auraes. She had even spoken in their favor when nobody else would. That lead Mefune to believe she was most likely no friend of Samar's. On top of this, she had the skills and experience necessary to easily make it on the Council and wouldn't allow Samar to bully her into submission once she was there.

She...could work, he mused, frowning slightly at this realization. Because, despite how good a candidate she seemed upfront, he couldn't easily dismiss the tension between them. She hated him, that much was obvious. She was jealous of his success, as many others were, but he felt it was personal for her for some reason. Why, he could never guess. If they were to work together to stop Samar, he was certain they would have to address the issue, and he couldn't help but think it wouldn't go over well.

But what else am I going to do? he wondered for the umpteenth time. Altaira was at least trustworthy. Grumbling his frustration in a quiet, ineligible curse, he stood and approached her.

As he reached her table, he called her name. She glanced up and blinked in surprise when she realized it was him before quickly looking back at her food with a scowl. "What?" she snapped.

Mefune sighed. This was going to be more complicated than he had thought. "I need your help with something," he stated quickly. "But clearly, you're still angry over that duel."

"I'm not angry," she protested, to which he raised an eyebrow. She fell silent, her lips pressed into a thin line.

"This isn't a small matter, and I don't know who else to trust it with. I wouldn't bother you if it wasn't urgent. If you are willing to put our differences aside, come find me, and we'll talk." He paused, wondering if he should add more to try to convince her, but as he met her gaze, it was clear she was hardly even listening. Shaking his head in frustration, he turned and left. *I'm wasting my time.*

— ℰ —

Altaira

After finishing her lunch, Altaira immediately sought out Daya, needing to rant about the strange occurrence she had just experienced. She still couldn't comprehend why Mefune would approach her. And he had admitted he needed help with something. It wasn't like he couldn't work with others, but it was well known he liked to operate on his own when he had the choice. She couldn't guess why that would change now—and why he had asked her, of all people, for help.

Finally, she located her friend working on repairing a jammed emergency exit on the slope of the underground fortress. Dressed in an old pair of overalls and with her short black hair pulled into a ponytail, Daya was covered in grease from the hinges and bolts but didn't seem to care. She had always enjoyed working with her hands, and the dirtier, the happier she seemed to be.

As Altaira approached, she looked up from her work and waved. Noticing Altaira's sour mood, she frowned slightly and asked, "What's wrong?"

"I was at the dining hall earlier, and Mefune asked me to help him with something."

Daya raised an eyebrow, clearly surprised. "That's different. What did he want help with?"

Altaira shrugged. "Didn't say. Something about me being too angry." She rolled her eyes at that.

Daya scoffed. "Sounds like a very appealing proposal. Vague and unconvincing. Perfect," she deadpanned as she shook her head and started tampering with the door again.

Altaira couldn't help but smile, but that was all Daya was rewarded for her sarcasm. "He made it sound like it was important, though. And...he said he would tell me later if I asked about it," she muttered.

"Hmm." Daya eyed Altaira with a searching gaze, an idea forming, but she seemed reluctant to speak it.

"What?" Altaira pressed, too impatient to wait for her to make up her mind.

"Maybe you should ask him about it."

"No," Altaira immediately dismissed with a shake of her head. She would not willingly associate with him, much less work with him. "Whatever the problem is, he can take care of it himself."

Daya's former amusement now completely gone, she insisted, "Altaira, can't you see how good an opportunity this is? He has power, the one thing we lack, and maybe, in exchange for your help, he'll be willing to return the favor. He's way more influential than I will ever be; he'd be able to get things done I can't." When Altaira didn't respond, she continued, "At least hear him out. He wouldn't have come to you unless it was important."

"Or he's gloating," Altaira argued, despite knowing Mefune had stated it was important.

Daya shook her head, obviously thinking Altaira was being ridiculous. "And we both know Mefune's not that type of person," she stated, eying Altaira pointedly. Sighing, she folded her arms, spreading the grease stains further. "Look, I have to be honest with you. As much as you think he's standing in the way of your goal, he's actually not; it's your anger that's in the way at this point. You have a chance. As difficult as it might be to admit that, you should take advantage of it."

Altaira almost snapped back, but she couldn't find the heart to do so. She had to admit Daya had a point, which pulled the force out of her argument. With a defeated huff, she said, "Fine, I'll try talking to him."

Daya brightened, obviously surprised Altaira had agreed. "Good! Let me know how it goes. And please resist the urge to knife him or something. It won't go well."

Altaira rolled her eyes at Daya's teasing, but she couldn't resist a smirk. "Fine, fine. I'll tell you all about it if I survive."

After chatting with Daya for a bit longer, Altaira left her friend to her work and made her way back into the shelter of the Brotherhood headquarters. Once in the halls, she hovered for a second, trying to decide what to do next. Even though she had agreed to talk to Mefune, it didn't make approaching him any easier.

For a few days, she stalled, trying to build up the courage to act but never finding the strength to do so. Finally, she decided if she didn't just talk to him, the suspense would drive her insane, so she went looking.

She had a lot of ground to cover. Built deep into the towering cliffs that made up Raidenya's southwest shore, the base was a sprawling maze of stone corridors, lit by sconces along the walls that had only been converted to electrical lighting in the past ten years or so. Bringing in modern conveniences hadn't been easy, and since it wasn't a priority for the Brotherhood, they had been slow to bother.

The hallways were often cold and dim, but the warmly lit dining hall on the lowest floor and several gathering rooms scattered throughout the rest of the base made it more inviting. There was a library with skylights adjacent to the Council room on the top floor. The second and third floors were filled with housing. Accompanying the dining hall on the fourth floor were several large practice rooms, allowing the Brotherhood to keep their skills sharp even when the weather wasn't practical for training outside. Below that were maintenance rooms and storage space.

Starting near the bottom, she wound her way up, checking public areas and scanning the passageways in search of Mefune. Since the Council wasn't currently in session, she figured he was somewhere else in the base or on patrol. Usually, it would be easy to guess when he was out—since the Council served on the same patrol, he and Daya would be gone at the same time—but there was a chance he was on one of the extra patrols.

As she approached the Council room, she realized she was quickly running out of space to search. Her shoulders slumped slightly in defeat, but she decided to check anyway after a moment's hesitation. Entering the grand meeting hall, she passed by the long rows of seats.

To Altaira's surprise, Mefune sat alone near the front of the room. He had claimed a spot in one of the last rows before the Council seats, his gaze on the ground as his thoughts wandered. Altaira paused when she saw him, apprehensive once again, but gathered her courage and pushed forward.

As she approached, Mefune glanced her way. "Did you decide you wanted to talk?"

She sighed. "Yes. I have to admit you sparked my curiosity...and you're right, it's time I put the duel behind me." She almost couldn't get herself to say it, but knew she would never be able to move on if she didn't admit it. "So, what did you want my help with, exactly?"

"We probably shouldn't discuss it here," he stated before he stood and gestured for her to follow. He led her out to the hallway and then turned to his left towards the offices. He stepped into his own and then waited for her to join him. When she did, he closed the office door and then moved to lean against the desk. Glancing quickly around the space, she found it surprisingly bare, almost as if he had yet to move in properly.

"If I tell you, you have to swear not to repeat this information to anyone," he started, bringing her mind back to the conversation at hand. His voice took on a dangerous edge, the implied warning clear to Altaira.

"Of course," she readily agreed. There was something unnerving about his calculating gaze, and she already knew he could easily beat her in a fight. She didn't want to find out what would happen if she angered him.

He nodded. As he continued, his expression darkened slightly, a hint of frustration in his gaze. "I assume you had your goals for joining the Council, as did I, but I've discovered those goals are irrelevant now. I've stumbled across something that could be fatal to the Brotherhood and possibly the Auraes. I want to stop it, but can't do it alone. I was hoping we could put our differences aside and work together."

"Why me?" she couldn't help but wonder.

"You're capable," he said with a shrug, as if that explained everything. "There are few people I would trust to handle such an issue."

"Ah," she muttered. She wanted to mention the obvious rift between them and how it would complicate things, but decided against it. All it would succeed in doing was remind her of her anger. So far, the conversation was going well enough, and she didn't want to jeopardize its status now. "Well, if it means protecting the Brotherhood, I'm in. What exactly is this threat?" she asked instead.

"The Council."

Altaira paused, surprised by this. "I've known for some time the Council acts on its own agenda on occasion, but I have a hard time believing they would do anything to directly threaten the Brotherhood."

Mefune sighed. "At one point, I thought so too, but Samar sees a chance to grab power. He's slowly convincing the Council and the general population that the Auraes are abusing the Brotherhood. His support grows steadily, especially after the Auraes threatened us. He wants to reorganize our alliance somehow, so he's in charge."

"How does he expect to do that?" Altaira asked.

"He plans to use the Tarapor to his advantage. He thinks if he releases some into the city, the Auraes will be desperate to stop them, so they'll cave to his demands."

Altaira's brow furrowed in confusion. "Wouldn't that just upset the Auraes?"

"I pointed that out as well, but he thinks if he releases enough and makes it clear he did it on purpose to show the Auraes what would happen if we stopped doing our job, the threat of so many deaths would be enough to dissuade them from acting against us. I doubt that's how it would go, but I'm not willing to wait and find out either way. Too many people would die if he had his way."

Altaira stayed silent, staring at Mefune in amazement as she contemplated the deaths Samar's plan would cause. It sent a shiver down her spine. *I can't believe he's willing to go that far. And all for what?*

As if thinking the same thing, Mefune fumed, "It's disgusting. He's willing to murder hundreds just for a little power. Apparently, having the entire Brotherhood under his control isn't enough."

Altaira sighed. "People like him never stop," she muttered, her thoughts on the things her family had suffered at the hands of people just like Samar. Forcing herself to focus on the here and now, she asked, "Why don't we tell the Auraes about this? They have authority to remove members of the Council, even arrest them, if necessary."

"With tensions as they are, if we approached the Auraes and they confronted the Council about it, Samar would just play the role of martyr. He'd have the full backing of the Brotherhood at that point. He's not afraid to start a war over this, and with Ila left in charge in Mariea's absence, the Auraes would be all too willing to answer. Besides, all the evidence I have of this scheme is what Samar's told me. With nobody to back my claim, Samar could just say I lied and the Auraes wouldn't know who to trust."

"So...what do we do about it, then?" She doubted he had come to her without some sort of plan.

"I have an idea in the making," he admitted, confirming her thoughts. "If we can break down his support, starting with those on the Council, we could then move against him without risking an all-out war. I'm sure we could find some sort of dirt on at least a couple of the Council members to challenge them one at a time. This would expose the Council's corruption, swaying public opinion against it while giving us an opportunity to place those actually loyal to the Brotherhood on the Council. All we have to do is find the evidence we need."

Altaira nodded slowly. "That'll...take time."

Mefune gave a short nod. "Time we may not have, so we need to work quickly. In the meantime, I've convinced Samar I'm loyal to him so I can learn as much information as I can about his plan. If I find a more direct route to shut down his plans, we'll take it. But until then, undermining Samar's support seems our only option to prevent an all-out war."

Altaira sighed. "Alright. What do you need me to do to help?"

"Mainly two things. To replace Samar's allies on the Council with people actually loyal to the Brotherhood, I need people I can trust. I thought of you. Once we find something to challenge one of the members, if it proves substantial enough to have them removed, the seat will go to a vote, and you can challenge and easily win whoever is elected."

Once again, Altaira couldn't help but be amazed Mefune actually wanted her, of all people, to help him with such a delicate matter. She had resisted asking earlier, but after he had openly offered her a position of power, she found she had to address the concern. "How can you say you trust me? We've been at each other since we both joined the Brotherhood."

Mefune gave a small acknowledging nod, but stayed silent for a moment, clearly choosing his words carefully. "I never understood what caused that competition, to be honest. Maybe it's just the way the Brotherhood is structured. But I never intended it to get as big as it has." He allowed a small smile. "And I know you don't think highly of the Council. Because of this, I'm assuming your ambition to join them has nothing to do with loyalty to them. Plus, the fact that you have an Aurae brother leads me to believe you wouldn't want to see a war between our people."

She couldn't help but be surprised by how well he had analyzed her. He wasn't wrong, and even if he didn't know all the details, it didn't seem to matter. "So you're going to help me get a spot on the Council, basically." He nodded. She stood in stunned silence for a moment, realizing the irony of that fact; the man she had felt was standing in the way of her goal all this time was suddenly offering to hand her precisely what she wanted. And he was inadvertently helping her address the issue that had led her to the goal in the first place—dealing with corruption on the Council.

"I'm assuming you won't protest this?" he guessed, looking a bit amused.

"No, of course not," she quickly confirmed, unsure how to explain what she was thinking or if she even wanted to tell him. After a pause, she asked, "Where will you find the evidence we need against Samar's followers?"

"The Council keeps meticulous records. I have access to those records now. I'm hoping they've gone unchallenged long enough that their guard is down, and I might be able to find something," he told her.

Altaira shook her head slightly. "You won't find anything useful there," she informed him reluctantly. When he raised an eyebrow in question, she added, "I had Daya search those records weeks ago. She found nothing worthwhile."

"Maybe she just didn't know what to look for," Mefune mused, but it sounded like a speculation made in an attempt to maintain some semblance of hope.

"We were looking for something specific."

"And what was that?" Mefune wondered.

Altaira hesitated briefly, not sure she wanted to tell him why she had tried for the Council seat, but she realized it could be helpful, and he might even be willing to help her look into her father's murder further. "My father was once part of the Council. He was wrongly accused of something, and it led to his death. The Council covered the whole mess up. I've been trying to find evidence of it, but all I have so far is my mother's word."

"Hmm..." Mefune muttered, resting his chin in his hand. "This is good, though—you already have a lead. We might have to do some digging, but this is the perfect type of situation to challenge them over." He glanced up at her. "As long as you don't mind me making a big deal over this."

She shrugged. "It's why I was trying so hard to join the Council."

He seemed to contemplate this for a moment. "That makes sense now," he muttered. "Your father deserves justice. We'll find what we need."

Altaira blinked in surprise, amazed he so willingly agreed to help her—she didn't even have to ask. Feeling the slightest glimmer of hope she might actually be able to achieve her goals,

Altaira found her excitement growing. "Well, I have to admit, this is not how I expected this conversation to go," she mused.

He allowed a small smile. "Honestly, neither did I."

"But I also have to say I'm glad I decided to talk to you," she admitted.

He nodded. "Things are a lot easier with allies." It sounded almost as if he was coming to this realization for the first time.

"Which was the one thing I think we've both been lacking," Altaira agreed. Then, remembering Mefune said there were two things he needed her help on, she asked, "What else do you need me to do?"

"To keep Samar from being suspicious, I may actually have to help him a bit. He's asked me to help capture Tarapor—something I would rather not do on my own. Garrett reluctantly agreed to help me, but I have yet to get him to actually go. If you came as well, I think he might be more willing, considering the odds are more in our favor with a larger group.".

Altaira nodded. "I can handle that. Though it may be interesting to find time around all the patrols we're now assigned to."

"I can schedule us time off," Mefune stated.

Altaira nodded, remembering he was in charge of the patrol schedule. "Right. That's convenient."

Mefune allowed a small smile. "Hey, the position had to come with some perks, didn't it?"

She smiled slightly at the joke, though she could think of several other perks she had been looking forward to that he seemed to be overlooking. Realizing this would only make her annoyed again, she quickly pushed that thought away and told him, "If you don't mind, I'm going to include Daya in all of this. She's been doing what she could on her own to uncover the Council's corruption, but after Creta's death, she became reluctant to act alone."

Mefune nodded slightly, something akin to regret crossing over his features. "That would make sense, considering Creta's death wasn't by natural causes. He was poisoned by Samar."

Altaira let out a disbelieving sigh, shaking her head in disgust. "I was worried something had happened to him. Daya was suspicious. I was hoping she was wrong. Do you have any evidence?"

"Garrett's word, but he refuses to do anything about it," Mefune sighed.

"Coward," Altaira grumbled.

Mefune let out an amused huff, clearly agreeing. "But with what you've told me, we may not need him."

"Hopefully," Altaira agreed. She desperately wanted their plans to get somewhere.

"I'll start searching. I have some ideas of areas I could look," Mefune decided. "I'll let you know if I find anything."

Altaira nodded. "And let me know when we're going to go Tarapor hunting."

"Will do," Mefune agreed. Then he smiled slightly. "This just might work out."

Chapter Eight

New York

Mariea

When Mariea woke the next morning, she couldn't figure out why the room felt so quiet and empty until she remembered Bracken wasn't with her. She let out a shaky sigh as she sat up, feeling surprisingly alone. New York was a big place, and even though she had once lived in the city, that was a long time ago. She didn't remember nearly as much as she had hoped. As she sat there contemplating it, she realized just how much she had been subconsciously relying on the fact Bracken would be with her. She really wished he still was.

And she couldn't imagine how he and Mae felt, being in custody in a strange land they knew very little about. She just hoped they hadn't managed to get themselves into more trouble as they were questioned. It would be quickly evident how little they knew of the world beyond Raidenya. With that thought, she pushed herself to her feet, filled with a new sense of urgency to get them released.

Okay, so how do I contact the Brotherhood? If she were trying to reach an Aurae, it would be simple—a messenger spell could easily be sent to anyone with an aura. But things were a little more complicated for communicating with the mostly auraless

Brotherhood. She couldn't send a message to someone without an aura because it wouldn't know where to go.

Luckily, the Auraes had thought of a solution for this. At each base throughout the world, at least one person had essentially been given something of a magical caller ID through a complicated series of spells. However, because they didn't have an aura to sustain the magic, they could still only receive short-lived written messages instead of the longer call Mariea would have preferred in this situation. It would mean attempting to sum up her entire situation in the limited amount of text the written messages could carry.

And she quickly realized another issue; she didn't know the name of New York's contact, which was required to send the message. So, she thought of contacting the Brotherhood's headquarters on Raidenya. Surely, they would know who she could reach out to in New York. Glancing at her watch, she realized it was nearly noon. *Well, I don't have to worry about waking them up too early,* she mused as she brought her aura to light.

Thinking back to the last meeting with the Council, she remembered Samar's new companion's name—Mefune. Since he now held Raidenya's chair, he would be the contact for headquarters. Hoping it had been long enough since his election for him to already be capable of receiving messages, she quickly crafted the needed spell, addressing it to him. Creating a message spell was simple enough; she simply made the container to insert the message—which was nothing more than a small orb of light the same color as her aura—and then mimed writing the information she wanted it to include. The magic would pick up the words and translate them to Shidokian before inserting them into the container. Once delivered, they were reverse-translated if the receiver desired, and then displayed in the center of the container.

It took her a couple of tries to explain her situation in enough detail that it would make sense but simultaneously concise enough that it would fit in the spell. When she was finally satisfied, she sent it with a final Shidokian word, *annin,* which meant go. She let out a sigh when it disappeared, knowing it would have collapsed instead of sending if Mefune couldn't receive the message.

For a moment, she waited for a reply, not sure how quickly Mefune would be able to respond. If he had an aura of his own, it would be instantaneous, but since he didn't, she'd have to wait until he had a bottled messenger spell that he could use to reply. Suddenly, she understood why the Brotherhood hated that they refused to allow technology on the island a bit more. The process of messaging without an aura seemed tedious.

After a bit, she decided to see if she could find something to eat while she waited. It was risky, venturing downstairs where others could be around to see Mefune's reply appear next to her, but she hadn't eaten since yesterday morning, and she was famished. As long as she was quick, she figured she'd be okay.

Heading downstairs, she found where the hotel offered breakfast, hoping there would still be something available. The hot food and most other offerings had been put away, but there were still granola bars. She sighed and grabbed a couple, deciding it would have to do, and then quickly started back up to her room.

As she munched on her tiny breakfast, she sat at the small writing desk in her room and wondered what to do next. Her mind strayed to the dream from the night before. It was odd compared to her usual dreams, but she wondered if she would start to receive more guidance now that she was on the trail for answers.

"So if that's the case, I need to find that pier," she muttered to herself. But other than going towards the ocean, she had no idea where to even begin looking. New York had a lot of areas that could include an old pier, like the one she had seen in her dream.

But then her thoughts returned to the house. There had to be a reason she had seen it first. Maybe whoever lived there could help her find the pier.

Just then, a silver ball of light appeared to her right, and she felt a wave of relief and anticipation as she realized Mefune had replied to her message. Reaching for the orb, she tapped the surface to reveal:

Your contact for New York's base is a man named Cato. Here's the base's address as well, in case you need it. You're safe to message him whenever. I'm sorry about the mix-up with the IDs—I'll look into it and see if something on our end went wrong to cause it.

Mariea read the note, quickly scribbled down the included address on a piece of paper, and then waved the message away. After sending Mefune a quick thank you note, she turned to messaging Cato; again, she wrote out her situation, hoping he was nicer than some of the Council she had dealt with. It wasn't like she could order him to help—at this point, she felt she was far beyond the reach of the power her position gave her.

Luckily, it didn't take Cato long to answer. An orange orb appeared next to her with the simple reply, *I'd be happy to help. We should probably talk in person. Could you make your way to our base?* He then gave her the address, which she quickly checked against the one Mefune had supplied. Once she was sure she had the correct address, she sent a short reply to tell him she'd be there soon. After waiting a bit to make sure he didn't reply again, she headed downstairs with the address in hand. At the front desk, she found the hotel offered free city maps and grabbed one, figuring she'd need it to find her way to the Brotherhood's base.

Unfortunately, it took her longer than she had expected to locate the base. She wasn't good at reading maps, and the downtown area turned out to be way more confusing than she remembered. When she finally located the building, she quickly realized driving there was a bad idea. Finding parking was nearly impossible. What parking she did find was several blocks away, and she had to pay. She sighed as she left the car behind and started the walk back to the address, sure she'd get lost trying to make the trip on foot.

Luckily, she made it without incident. Standing outside the building, she stared up at it, feeling a bit uncertain that she was in the right place. The address was the one she had written on her paper, but nothing about the building indicated it had any connection to the Brotherhood. It looked just like the two next to it, if a bit shorter. She had passed beyond the huge skyscrapers New York was known for, but these buildings were still much taller than any on Raidenya. One of many brick buildings along a busy street, a steep staircase gave access to the front door. It was definitely not a place Mariea would associate with the Brotherhood.

However, as she glanced around the busy street, she realized she didn't have a clue what she was supposed to do if this wasn't it. It wasn't like she could message Cato again to confirm the address, not while standing on a busy street. *What could it hurt if this is the wrong place? I'll just ask for Cato, and if they don't know who I'm looking for, I'll go back to the car and find a place I can message him,* she decided. With a sigh, she climbed the short steps to the door and stepped inside.

The lobby beyond did nothing to reassure her. It was nice, blending well with the rest of New York with its up-to-date styling. A long reception desk occupied one side of the room, with a sitting area opposite, including a small TV that quietly played random shows. There wasn't much to indicate what the office was used for.

"Can I help you?" A voice stated to her left. Glancing at the desk, she noticed a woman there for the first time. She smiled at Mariea, but something in her gaze made Mariea feel she hadn't expected to see her there and didn't particularly like that she had appeared. It didn't make her feel all that welcome.

Swallowing her growing nerves, Mariea managed a smile and stated, "Um, yes. I'm looking for Cato. I was told he worked here."

The woman blinked in surprise. "And what is your name?"

"Mariea Rolondo."

The woman's confusion faded immediately, and her smile seemed more genuine. "Ah, he told me to expect you. I'm glad you found the base okay. Let me go find him," the woman told her as she stood. She gestured to the waiting area and then headed for a door next to the counter that was marked EMPLOYEES ONLY. As she left, Mariea couldn't help but note that was most likely the only time she had seen a member of the Brotherhood in a pencil skirt and heels.

She waited for a few moments before the woman returned with a man in his thirties. He was dressed in what Mariea had come to recognize as the Brotherhood's typical style—a simple t-shirt, cargo pants, and sturdy boots, with at least one weapon present on his belt. He had short dirty blond hair, and a kind face.

"Mariea, it's nice to meet you," he greeted as Mariea stood.

"Cato, thank you for seeing me," Mariea told him.

He smiled and nodded, and then gestured to the seats as he told her, "Of course. I'm sure we can get this mess cleaned up quickly. How long has it been since Bracken and Mae were detained?"

Glancing at her watch, Mariea replied, "A little over twelve hours."

"Alright, then they probably moved them to a holding facility by now. Why were you detained?" Cato wondered.

"Mae and Bracken's IDs didn't scan through their system properly. Luckily, mine was fine, but it's probably because it's a bit more legitimate since I'm technically still a US citizen," Mariea explained.

"Interesting. It's been a while since one of our IDs failed. I wonder if they changed something." He turned to the woman from the desk, who hovered nearby. "Charity, could you grab Mathew, have him look into this? We need to act quickly before this causes a big problem." Charity nodded and hurried off. Cato turned back to Mariea and told her, "We'll figure this out, don't worry."

"Thank you," Mariea breathed, relieved. "This won't compromise Raidenya's safety, will it?"

"No, we won't let it get to that point. That's why we've spent so much time working with the spells masters to make sure we have a magical solution to these problems. A few memory alteration spells, and this will all go away."

"That's good."

Cato nodded in agreement. "It's just important we catch it before it gets out of hand. It can be a pain to track down everyone who needs a memory wipe. And, as computers get more sophisticated, making *them* forget is proving to be the real challenge. Keeping track of Raidenya's safety and keeping magic under the radar seems to be what most of the larger cities' bases spend their time on."

Charity returned, drawing Mariea and Cato's attention again. "Mathew says the IDs were never properly activated, so the security systems at the airport wouldn't be able to search for them. He activated them, so if they're scanned now, they'll show up just fine."

"Good. Now, all we have to do is convince the officers that arrested them it was a glitch." Cato turned to Mariea. "You want to come with me, I'm assuming?"

"Yes, please," Mariea responded, standing up in her urgency. "We can take my rental."

"Works for me. Let me just grab a few things." Cato hurried from the room and returned dressed in a dark business suit a few minutes later. As he gestured for her to follow and started for the door, he told her, "So, I'm going to play the part of your attorney, who you contacted over the issue. This will make things seem more official."

Mariea nodded, hoping such a ruse would work. "They won't be able to find out you're not actually an attorney, would they?"

"For that, they'd have to rescind my law degree," Cato stated with a small smile. Mariea's gaze widened slightly, making Cato's smile grow. "What, did you think we were all just a bunch of sword-swinging dummies around here?"

"No, I just...a legit law degree?" Mariea repeated, surprised. "I didn't know anyone in the Brotherhood had an education from anywhere off Raidenya."

Cato shrugged. "I debated leaving for a while, so I got permission to attend school. But then we needed a new cover for the base when we moved to this building, and they asked me to use my knowledge to start a legitimate practice. It slowly evolved into something of a law firm, private investigator hybrid, since not all of us have time to get law degrees. We don't take many clients, just enough to keep up the ruse mixed with a good paper trail to fill in the blanks, and we suddenly look legitimate while the government looks the other way."

Mariea nodded. She had to admit the strategy was brilliant and convenient—dealing with straddling two worlds had to be made easier by in-depth knowledge of US law. She was at least grateful for Cato's knowledge.

After a bit, they reached the car and started into the busy city once again. It was much easier to reach their destination with Cato to guide her. Mariea glanced warily at the nondescript building as they parked outside the facility. "Are you sure they're here?"

"If not, they'll be able to tell me where they are," Cato replied. He glanced at her. "It's probably best you wait here. There's a chance they won't discuss anything with me if you're present, since you're not part of the alleged illegal border crossing."

Mariea nearly protested, wanting to see Bracken desperately, but she understood Cato's concerns. She nodded, so he hurried inside.

When Cato didn't return quickly, she decided to take that as a good sign—he must have located Mae and Bracken. She spent her time flipping through stations on the radio, trying to get a feel for what was going on in the city around her. Being up to date on the local news might prove helpful. But she found the details of what she was listening to impossible to absorb, her attention glued to the building before her.

After a while of fidgeting and glancing at her watch, she climbed out of the car and began pacing, her ability to wait patiently quickly evaporating. A few hours had passed already. She couldn't imagine what was taking so long. What would they be asking Cato that would require such a long wait? On Raidenya, if the sentinels received evidence that someone had been wrongfully arrested, the response would have been immediate. *I guess that's the benefit of a small, close-knit community*, she mused. *These people probably have so many legal hoops they have to jump through just to keep the city running.*

By eight-thirty, she was starving, exhausted, and nearly ready to storm in after Cato and break Bracken and Mae out herself. *Something must be wrong*, she guessed, wondering if Cato would be able to free them. If that happened, she figured Bracken and Mae would be deported. Thinking of them being dropped back in Dublin with no clue how to get home or back to her, her fear only grew. If something terrible happened to them throughout the whole process, she was sure she'd never forgive herself for dragging them to New York in the first place.

When Cato finally did reemerge, she first thought he was alone, but then she noticed Bracken and Mae following, luggage in tow. Bracken smiled when he saw her and waved. She allowed them to reach the car and then hurried to him and met him with a hug, letting out a relieved sigh.

"You have no idea how good it is to see you," she muttered as he returned the hug.

"Same goes for you," Bracken said with a chuckle. "I did not want to spend another minute in that prison. They've been asking all sorts of questions ever since you left. I had no idea how to answer most of them, and I'm sure I was digging my own grave."

"Told you pretending we didn't speak English would have been a good idea," Mae grumbled as she began loading their luggage into the car.

"Yes, but they already knew we could speak English by the time you suggested it. That would have looked even more suspicious," Bracken pointed out. "Either way, though, I was sure they were going to lock us up for a painfully long time. I was seriously debating breaking us out, but I think Cato here wouldn't have appreciated the mess that would have caused him."

Cato smiled slightly. "As it is, this is a bit of a mess, but much more manageable than it could be. So, thank you for waiting patiently. I'll take things from here if you need to be on your way."

"Won't you need a ride back?" Mariea wondered.

Cato shook his head. "I can get around town fine. You seem to have a lot on your mind, and considering how rarely Auraes leave Raidenya, I'm assuming it's pretty important."

Deciding to take him up on the offer, Mariea gave him a grateful smile and told him, "Thank you again, Cato."

"No problem. Oh, one more thing...." He reached into his pocket, pulled out a small notepad and pen, and wrote down a couple of phone numbers. "Here's my number and the main office's number here in New York. That way, if you run into trouble on your way home, you'll know how to get in touch without the use of magic."

Mariea smiled and nodded, mentally telling herself to make sure she stuck the numbers somewhere safe. She appreciated having a non-magical way to reach out to someone, just in case. With that, Cato started back towards the facility.

"Can we grab some food? Prison food is nasty," Mae asked as she climbed into the car.

"I second that," Bracken called as he and Mariea joined Mae.

Mariea smiled slightly. "I'm down—all I've eaten today were granola bars. First stop, food, then we can plan our next move. I've been busy while you guys have been in prison."

"Really?"

"Yeah. I think I know where we need to look next," she replied.

Chapter Nine

Searching

Mariea

Mariea woke early the next morning, her thoughts immediately turning to the house from her dream the night before. It was still dark, and Bracken and Mae were sound asleep. Mariea quietly prepared for the day, hoping they would wake up as she moved around, but she quickly realized that wasn't going to happen. She stood in the darkness for a moment, sighing softly to herself as she debated what to do next. Part of her wanted to wake them, but she knew they were both exhausted after everything that had happened the past couple of days.

I guess I could start looking for the house, she thought as she glanced at the map she had left on the desk the night before. Next to it was a pad of paper and a pen. Scribbling a note to let them know she'd be downstairs, she grabbed the map and slipped out of the room.

Downstairs, she headed for the lobby. She remembered seeing a public computer there when she had passed through earlier. Maybe, with some work, she could figure out how to search for the house.

Claiming the computer, she pressed the spacebar to wake the machine up. At first, everything on the screen was a bit unfamiliar to her—it had been a long time since she had used such a device—but she figured it out quickly enough.

She remembered what corner of the state the house was in, so she started by pulling up a map of New York. Zooming in on a mostly empty corner that looked somewhat familiar, she scrolled over aerial views of the houses. *This is going to take forever,* she thought, but with no idea how else to search for the house, she kept scrolling.

A couple hours passed, and she had to stop to give her eyes a break. They stung, and she rubbed at them, amazed people spent so much time staring at screens. She was already developing a headache, and her search wasn't over yet. She'd paused on several houses already, sure they were the one, but then as she'd zoomed in, they'd always looked different up close.

"There she is," a voice called behind her, and she looked up to see Bracken and Mae approaching.

"Hey guys," she greeted, feeling disappointed she hadn't found the house yet. She had hoped that she'd have an address by the time they were up, and they'd be ready to head out.

"Any luck?" Mae asked.

Mariea shook her head. "I feel like I'm getting close, but no luck yet."

"Well, let's take a break. Have you eaten breakfast yet?" Bracken wondered.

Mariea frowned slightly. "I'm not hungry. I'll eat before we leave. I don't want to lose the computer," she informed him.

Bracken shook his head slightly. "I'd admonish against skipping breakfast, but that would be highly hypocritical considering my track record. I'll save you something."

Mariea chuckled and turned back to the computer as she told him, "Thanks."

Breakfast came and went, as did lunch. Bracken and Mae returned to their hotel room to try to find something to pass the time with. Mariea quickly grew frustrated with her search. She knew it was somewhere in the northwestern part of the state. She remembered a clump of trees off to the left before she'd seen the house up close. Where could it possibly be?

Maybe it was just a dream, she thought, and then quickly pushed the thought away. She couldn't let herself begin doubting now. That would mean she had dragged Bracken and Mae all the way there for no reason. She wasn't ready to believe that was the case.

Finally, one house caught her eye that looked vaguely familiar. Zooming in, she discovered she could see pictures of the house up close and smiled when she recognized the little details from her dream—the paint color, red door, and mailbox were exactly as she remembered them. *Well, these dreams must be something if I'm seeing real places,* she decided, feeling vindicated. Jotting down the address, she jogged back up to the hotel room.

Bursting through the door, she held up the piece of paper in triumph and announced, "I've found it!"

"Finally," Mae sighed, flopping back on her bed. "I can only watch documentaries about random animals for so long."

"You want to go now?" Bracken asked.

Mariea glanced at her watch. It was nearly five. She didn't know how long it would take to get to the house, but it had looked like a bit of a drive on her search. Letting out a small sigh, she admitted, "We probably don't have time. I'd rather not be driving in unfamiliar territory through the middle of the night."

Bracken nodded while Mae wondered, "So we get to waste more time?"

Mariea shrugged slightly. "I mean, this is New York. I'm sure you could find something nearby to do," she pointed out. "I'm sorry. I'd much rather go tonight, but I just don't think it's safe."

Mae nodded. She glanced between Mariea and Bracken and asked, "Do we dare go look around? Last time we were out there, things didn't go well."

"Honestly, there are a few things I could be getting done right now, and I think I've had my fill of interacting with the *shikani*," Bracken admitted.

Feeling a bit disappointed they weren't more interested in the city, Mariea sighed and sat down on the edge of the bed. "I guess we'll just stay here, then."

Bracken turned to his work, even though using so much magic made Mariea nervous. She just hoped it was relatively safe in the hotel. She and Mae did their best to stay entertained, but Mariea couldn't help but feel antsy. Eventually, they went in search of food, and Mariea convinced them to stay out long enough to buy supplies they could take with them tomorrow so they wouldn't have to worry about finding places to eat while driving. Then she spent a bit of time on the computer again, figuring out just how long it would take them to get to their destination. When she finally figured it out, she realized it would be about a five-hour drive.

Mariea and her companions got ready early the next morning, all equally eager to start the trip. They ate breakfast downstairs and then headed back up to pack up their things. As Bracken gathered their food, he asked Mariea, "Ready?"

She debated it for a moment and then realized she was the only person who knew where they were going, but she knew neither of her companions felt comfortable driving in a city like New York—she hardly did either, but she at least recognized the street signs and sort of knew the traffic laws here. "Let me mark the house on the map. You'll have to direct me there," she told Bracken and then sat down at the desk to relocate the address and circle it.

"I'll do my best," Bracken agreed, reminding Mariea he had grown up on an island small enough that maps weren't entirely necessary.

"That'll be good enough," she decided.

Soon, they were back in the rental car and heading to their destination. To start, they had to cross from Long Island to Manhattan and then onto the mainland. That required a detour through downtown to reach the nearest bridge. They drove through the busy streets of New York as familiar and new areas flashed past, making a bittersweet smile spread on Mariea's face. Yesterday she had been too stressed to enjoy the city, but now, she felt more at home.

"These buildings are huge!" Bracken muttered as they approached downtown.

Mariea's smile turned into a smirk. "Yeah, makes Verndale look like a tiny village, doesn't it?" she joked.

"I had no idea they even built buildings this big," Mae muttered.

"I mean, I'd heard of them, even seen pictures, but it's way better in person," Bracken admitted. He was pressed up against the window with his head tilted back, clearly trying to see the tops of the buildings as they passed under them.

"See, the world beyond Raidenya isn't all bad," Mariea couldn't resist saying.

"I don't know. I'm not convinced; it includes crazy security guards and prisons with real bad food," Mae grumbled, to which Mariea and Bracken chuckled.

After reaching the mainland, they started seeing signs for Newark, and Bracken pointed Mariea in a northwestern direction. As the city fell away and the endless trees of New York surrounded the road, Mae and Bracken's fascination faded, and they turned to other means to entertain themselves as Mariea drove.

"So why do you think you saw this house in your dreams?" Mae asked after a while.

"To be honest, I don't know. I'm hoping that I'll be able to figure that out once I see it. There was also a pier, which I think is our end goal, but the dream didn't give me much information about it. So, I hope we can learn more about that pier if we find the house," Mariea explained.

"Alright then," Mae muttered. "Honestly, this is not what I imagined this trip looking like."

"What did you imagine?" Mariea wondered.

Mae shrugged, and Mariea caught a glimpse of it in the rearview mirror. "I don't know. Not house hunting, that's for sure."

Mariea let out a small sigh. "Yeah, I don't know what I was expecting to find. I just hope something at this place leads us to understand what's going on at home."

"You and me both," Bracken muttered.

They fell silent again as the day wore on. They stopped briefly for a break around noon. After roughly an hour and a half, Mariea pulled off onto a side road as they approached what looked like a long row of empty fields, a house perched in the middle. When the road met with the end of a short gravel driveway, she pulled over and glanced up at the house. Sure enough, it was the one from her dream.

"So, is this it?" Bracken wondered.

"Yup."

"Now what?" Mae wondered, looking at the house skeptically.

"I...have no idea," Mariea muttered. They fell silent, staring at the house, almost as if they expected *it* to tell them what to do.

"Do you think talking to the owners would help?" Bracken wondered after a bit.

Mariea shrugged. "It might. But what do we tell them?"

"We're doing some research?" Bracken suggested.

"About your family history, like you told the guards at the airport," Mae added. "A lot of families have ties to this area, if I remember US history correctly."

"That's true," Mariea agreed with a nod. "My family is from this area." This made her consider the odds of her returning to her old home for the first time. Of all the places the dreams could lead her, why there?

"Okay, so we tell them we're looking into your past, and you know this house is significant, but you don't know why. Sounds...vague, but possibly believable," Bracken mused as he considered it.

"I'll tell them I found pictures of the home in an old photo album, and I'm trying to figure out what connection it has to my family history," Mariea decided. Then she took a deep breath to steady herself. "Remember, no references to magic or anything like that, alright? I don't want another airport fiasco." Her companions nodded, so she climbed from the car and started down the driveway.

As they approached the house, Mariea rehearsed what she was going to say to this complete stranger, hoping they would be willing to hear her out. She heard a dog barking and couldn't help but hope it was friendly. To either side of the yard, fields of tall grass spread out for as far as she could see. She wondered what they were used for.

As they passed through the gate into the yard, the screen door creaked open, and an older woman poked her head out. "Can I help you?" she called.

"Hopefully," Mariea replied as she paused.

Before she could explain, the woman asked, "You're not selling something, are you?"

"No, ma'am. I just have a few questions about your house," Mariea responded.

"It's not for sale, if that's what you're wondering. Neither is the land."

"No, nothing like that. It's about the house's history."

"Hmm," she muttered. Then she stepped from the door and waved them closer. "Well, come on up here then."

Mariea approached, feeling a little more comfortable now that she knew who was behind the door. As she reached the stairs, she stated, "I'm Mariea. This is my husband, Bracken, and our family friend, Mae."

"I'm Iris. So you're curious about this old place, are you?"

"Yes. I've been trying to fill in my family history a bit—you know, just want to figure out where we came from and all that." Iris nodded, so Mariea hoped her story was somewhat believable. She continued. "I was looking through old family photos, and I came across one of this house. It took me a while to find where it was. There wasn't any information about why the picture was there, but it seemed important. I was hoping you might know who originally built it, or...or if anything significant ever happened here." She frowned slightly at the end, realizing she had no idea what to ask about.

"Well, you're out of luck. I don't know much about it. My husband bought the property a decade or two ago. He was determined to fix this old place up, but well." She shrugged. "It hasn't really happened. It's a nice place, though." She seemed to get lost in memories for a moment and then turned to her. "I'm sorry I couldn't be of more help."

Mariea tried to hide her disappointment with a smile. "That's alright. I'm sure we'll find information elsewhere."

The woman nodded, but she didn't seem ready to dismiss them. "Though I might know someone who would know. Hold on one second." She disappeared back into the house for a moment.

The door squeaked open again, and the woman stepped out, holding a piece of paper in her slightly shaky hands. "Here. This is the number of a man in town who's a bit of a history addict. I'm sure if anyone knows, he'd know."

Mariea accepted the paper and read the name. "Alvin Willards...alright. You say he's somewhere here in town?"

"Well, truth be told, I don't know where he lives. A few years back, he came knocking on my door asking if he could photograph the house for his 'archives', whatever that's supposed to mean. I'm honestly amazed I managed to hold on to his number, but it felt important, for some reason."

"We'll give him a call, then. Thank you so much, Iris. This gives us a direction to head in," Mariea told her with a pleasant smile.

Iris smiled. "Good luck, dear. I hope you find what you're looking for."

Mariea nodded, agreeing all too much with Iris. The three of them headed back to the car, the number in hand.

"So, now what?" Mae asked as they neared the car.

"Well, we have no way of calling the man Iris mentioned," Bracken pointed out.

Mariea considered it. "I guess we could ask Cato for help. He obviously has a phone since he gave us his number."

"Right," Bracken said with a nod. "We should probably wait and ask him tomorrow, though, considering we still have to drive home, and it'll probably be too late by the time we get back to call our newest contact."

Mariea glanced at her watch. The whole visit had been less than an hour, so it didn't seem that late to her, but she had to remember it would take another five hours to make it back to their hotel. "Yeah, I guess we wait until tomorrow. Let's head back," Mariea decided as she climbed into the car. Her companions joined her, and they started the journey back.

$-\ \mathscr{C}\ -$

Mefune

After talking to Altaira, Mefune went to work searching for what they would need to begin removing Samar's support. He spent a few good hours comparing notes with Daya to learn all the places she had searched. It didn't take long for them to mark off all the obvious locations, meaning he'd have to get a little more creative.

Still, he felt the need to double-check the places Daya had searched, simply because he wasn't sure where else to turn, but didn't like waiting while he came up with an answer. First, he stopped at the vaults, hoping maybe there were places Daya had failed to think of. He wouldn't put it past the Council to have an entire secret vault kept from even some of their own somewhere inside the structure.

The vault was located behind a sliding stone door at the back of the Council room, locked behind a password only the Council members knew. After pressing in the correct pattern, he passed into the dimly lit room beyond and glanced over the many dusty shelves. Some of them were occupied by random relics, but most were filled with boxes upon boxes of old meeting notes, member records, and other such documents. Since Daya had spent plenty of time searching through the paperwork and the artifacts for anything obvious, he decided to look for anything less obvious hidden around the room.

He walked the perimeter of the room, checking for seams in the rock where something might be stashed or other signs of a hidden compartment or door, but the walls were made of solid stone. He checked the air vents, but they were nothing more than thin slits close to the ceiling, too narrow for even his fingers to fit in. If they were hiding anything, whoever had stashed it there would be hard-pressed to retrieve it.

So, he returned to the files, knowing he was probably wasting his time but feeling he had to check, anyway. It took him a few days to read through them. He couldn't spend all day in there—he still had a job to do, and he didn't want anyone getting suspicious of his absence. What he found aligned well with Daya's notes—unless the Council had written in code, it seemed they were more meticulous than he had hoped in making sure any less than honest deeds were kept from the record books.

As he replaced the final file in its box in the vault, he let out a sigh and turned towards the exit, wondering where he was supposed to search next. Anything of worth was most likely kept away from prying eyes in the Council's homes or offices. Though he wasn't opposed to snooping in their belongings, considering how important a matter it was, he knew that would take a lot more stealth and planning to get away with. And he could only hope whatever evidence he did find wouldn't be quickly dismissed by the Auraes because of its mysterious origins.

A growing part of him worried he wouldn't find any evidence. He knew, simply from Creta's ranting and Altaira's story, that the Council wasn't as unscrupulous as it would like the members to believe, but that was all hearsay. He couldn't get people arrested over that, nor did it mean evidence of their crimes even existed.

Briefly, he debated planting something or creating some sort of scenario to frame one of the members. It would be difficult to pull it off, and it wasn't exactly the most honest solution, but in the end, it was for a good cause. What Samar was planning would be much worse. There were just so many loose ends that he found himself reluctant to go down that route.

So, he looked to the Council offices next as he decided they would be the next most likely place to contain what he was looking for. Finding a day where the Council was absent when he could search their offices without being discovered took some time. He spent four days simply watching their habits, trying to map out a time when nobody else would be around.

Eventually, he settled on returning to the offices after dark on a day the Council had met. He noticed the others tended to leave earlier after meetings as if they counted it as work enough and allowed themselves to have the rest of the day off.

Well after midnight, he started from his apartment, moving carefully in the darkened hallways. Only emergency lights along the base of the wall remained on overnight throughout the living quarters, but once he passed into the public areas, the halls were lit again. Once in the lighted sections, he continued more cautiously. Often, a patrol would leave or return at odd hours of the night, and though seeing him out and about wouldn't be too suspicious, he didn't want anyone to be able to place him anywhere but his apartment, just in case he did find something in the offices and Samar began asking where it had come from.

When he reached the offices, he lingered in the hallway for a few moments, making sure they were empty. When he was sure he was alone, he silently crossed the hallway to Samar's office. After pulling on gloves, he checked the door and found it locked, though this wasn't unexpected. Luckily, he knew how to pick a lock—a skill taught among the Brotherhood in case they needed to enter restricted areas while hunting Tarapor. Reaching into his jacket pocket, he pulled out a small tool and got to work opening the door.

The lock finally gave with a quiet click. Mefune cracked the door open slightly and peered in, once again checking for vacancy, despite how it seemed redundant at this point. Stepping inside, he closed the door behind him and pulled a flashlight from his jacket pocket.

The offices weren't large, and Samar's was no exception, though they were furnished better than other parts of the base. The stone walls were covered and painted, and there was carpet. Since it was so close to the surface, it was allowed a small window that looked out over the ocean. Samar's desk sat in the center of the room. There was a single filing cabinet with three drawers and a couple of extra chairs for guests.

First, he checked for any sort of surveillance, though he knew the Auraes would never allow such devices onto the island, and though Samar had an aura, it was too weak to manifest, much less use it for complicated security spells. When he was sure the office was clean, he turned his attention to finding the evidence he needed.

The filing cabinet was the obvious first choice, so he headed to it and carefully began thumbing through the files. Surprisingly, he found all but the top drawer empty, and nothing of interest was stored there. Glancing around, he wondered where else Samar might possibly stick items he didn't want people to find.

Noticing the picture on the wall, he wondered if it could possibly cover a hidden safe of sorts. He lifted the frame away from the wall and glanced behind it, but found the surface smooth, so he so he let it rest against the wall again and straightened it. Turning back towards the door with a small frown, he debated where else to search. The whole escapade couldn't have been for nothing.

That's when he noticed the weird way the carpeting under Samar's desk seemed uneven. Crouching, he pushed the chair out of the way and looked closer. Sure enough, there was a thin line in the shape of a square, where it seemed the carpet was parted, almost as if it had been ripped and then patched.

Feeling around the edges, he discovered a narrow groove that his fingers fit in as if there was a panel in the floor. He tried to lift it, but it didn't give. After fiddling with it for a few seconds, he found it pushed in and then slid back, revealing a small compartment in the floor. He allowed a small smile, sure he'd find something useful there.

There wasn't much present; a few maps, a lockbox that jangled quietly with the sound of money when Mefune bumped it, and a small stack of files that drew his interest the most. Carefully, he started through them.

As he skimmed over the files, it quickly became evident Samar had been gathering incriminating information about many members of the Brotherhood, possibly for bribery or blackmail purposes. *I wonder if this is how he's convinced so many Council members to look the other way*, he mused. He even found a few notes about himself, though none held any truth to them, so he dismissed them.

He spent a long time reading under the light of his flashlight, long enough that he grew nervous he'd run out of time. There were plenty of things in the files that had potential, but it took a while to find something he felt would be enough to start an investigation but wouldn't make the Auraes feel threatened by the Brotherhood. The last thing he wanted was to fuel Ila's apparent hatred towards them.

When he came across handwritten pages that seemed pulled from a notebook, he almost passed over them, but a sticky note attached to the first page caught his eye. Listed on it were two names: Ezequiel Rydinski and Alec Conover. The second name sparked his interest; Conover was Altaira's last name, and if he remembered correctly, she had said her father's name was Alec. The pages were kept in a sheet protector, along with a cassette tape not much bigger than a coin. Knowing what he did about the situation of Alec's death, he guessed there might just be something useful in the pages, so he pulled them from the sheet protector.

After only reading for a few moments, Mefune realized he wouldn't find anything about Alec's death—they were his journal pages. However, what he had recorded quickly caught Mefune's attention. Apparently, Ezequiel had paid Alec to choose him as his successor to save Alec from financial ruin. This meant Ezequiel's election, and therefore his presence on the Council, was entirely illegal.

This was precisely the dirt he was looking for, and considering the connection to Altaira's father, he felt motivated to pursue the issue. However, journal pages were easy to fabricate, and he would need pretty solid evidence to get Ezequiel removed. Glancing at the cassette tape, he wondered what it could possibly be. Reading over the pages, he searched for anything about it.

Sure enough, towards the end, he found this line: *I don't know if this will play out alright. That's why I made the tape. It's plenty enough evidence to take Ezequiel down. I'd most likely burn with him, but if I ever have to use it, I'm sure I'll already be in a bad enough situation it won't matter.*

Mefune smiled slightly, realizing he had what he needed. He set the sheet with the journal pages and tape aside and gathered the rest of the files, carefully placing them back in the corner where he had found them. After sliding the compartment door shut and replacing the chair, he slipped the sheet protector into the inside pocket of his jacket.

Leaving the office behind, he double-checked the door locked again behind him and then hurried back to his apartment. By the time he made it back, dawn was quickly approaching, and his lack of sleep was starting to catch up with him. Deciding he'd sleep for a few hours and then inform his allies of what he had found, he placed the papers in the safe in his closet and allowed himself to rest.

When he awoke again, he found it was mid-afternoon. Despite how hungry he was, he quickly went in search of Altaira, Garret, and Daya. He found Garrett and Daya first, close to the base entrance.

When Garrett saw him, he smiled and said, "Hey Mefune, we missed you on the morning patrol."

Mefune paused, and then his brow furrowed in confusion. "There was a patrol this morning?"

Daya nodded. "One of the extra ones, remember?"

Mefune shook his head as he put a hand to his forehead, grumbling his annoyance over forgetting under his breath. "I could have sworn that was tomorrow."

"It's alright. You weren't the only one who forgot. Darius overslept, so we left without him, and Desiree was almost late," Daya told him with a shrug. "Samar planned it late last night, so it's no surprise he didn't get everyone to show up. I swear he's trying to work us to death."

Relieved he wasn't the only one who had forgotten about the patrol, Mefune nodded and told them, "Well, I've had a busy night. Let's find Altaira, and I'll fill you in."

Daya supplied, "She should be home right about now. She'll be leaving for her patrol in half an hour, so we better hurry if we want to catch her."

She led them to Altaira's apartment and knocked. Altaira answered the door quickly, glancing between the three of them in surprise. Before Mefune could say anything, Daya eagerly announced, "He found something."

Altaira quickly brightened. "Let's talk inside," she offered as she opened the door wider and gestured them in.

They followed her inside and gathered in her small living room. Her apartment was much like Mefune's, but that was no surprise; most of them had a similar layout. The kitchen and living room shared an open floor plan, and a hallway in the back of the room led to the bedrooms and bathroom.

They gathered in the small seating area in her living room. Altaira sat on the edge of her seat, obviously eager, as she met Mefune's gaze. "Okay, tell me everything," she demanded.

He allowed a small, triumphant smile as he explained, "I found information that proves Ezequiel had a hand in what happened to your father." Pulling the journal pages from his pocket, he passed them to her as he added, "This is all the evidence we need to get him removed from the Council."

Taking it, she pulled the pages out and began thumbing through them, her gaze passing over them quickly. "What are these?"

"Journal pages, from your father's journal, actually."

Altaira looked up at him, surprised. After taking a moment to process that fact, she glanced back down at them and continued to skim over the pages. "How do these help?" She asked. With an almost flippant shrug, she added, "I mean, for some reason, I think it would be hard for him to write about his own death."

Daya chuckled, and Mefune couldn't resist a small smile at her sarcasm. "True, but they do have other evidence," he told her. "Apparently, Ezequiel was chosen as Alec's successor not long before Alec's death. It wasn't what your father wanted, but he ended up in a tough situation. He was almost financially destitute because of your mother's health and desperately in need of options. Ezequiel came from a rich family. He offered Alec an impressive sum of money if your father elected him as his successor."

"Bribing your way onto the Council is illegal," Garrett interjected.

"Exactly," Mefune agreed with a nod. "Alec accepted. These pages detail that transaction, and apparently, the tape still in the sheet protector has more information."

Altaira glanced back at the sheet protector, noticing the small tape for the first time. She pulled it out, frowning slightly. "It'll be interesting getting the recording off of this."

"Yeah, I'll have to track down something that'll play it, but it'll be worth the effort. The journal pages say Alec had planned to use the tape as insurance if things didn't go his way. It's enough information to start an investigation, which would force Samar to make Ezequiel resign."

"But it doesn't prove he or the rest of the Council had anything to do with my father's death," Altaira muttered, looking a bit disappointed.

"No, but I'm hoping they'll find out how Alec died and learn who killed him while they investigate this," Mefune added.

"Either way, we need to act on this opportunity," Garrett pressed. "This is exactly what we're looking for."

"If this is so important to you, why don't you speak out about Creta's death?" Daya challenged. "That would be an even better opportunity—we could go after Samar instead of beating around the bush."

Garrett's lips pressed into a thin line as he debated how to respond. "The only evidence I have of what happened is what I witnessed. It would be Samar's word against mine, and he would win. Then I would join Creta on his list of murders."

Mefune was quickly growing frustrated with that argument. He had to pause a moment to squash his first response in order to keep his words somewhat civil. "We don't need to push that issue if it isn't going to get us anywhere. Let's just use what we've learned about Ezequiel for now." Then he met Garrett's gaze. "But don't think I haven't dismissed Creta's death. If I find any more evidence of it, I will pursue it, whether you like it or not."

This seemed to upset Garrett a bit, but he didn't argue, just nodded, staring at the coffee table before him. If Mefune wasn't mistaken, he almost looked nervous. His gaze narrowed slightly. *There's something he's not telling us. He's way too desperate to keep that story quiet.* When he glanced Altaira's way, she was watching Garrett carefully too, and he guessed she was thinking the same thing.

"Alright, so...what do we do now?" Daya asked, breaking the surprising level of tension in the room.

Mefune turned to her, pushing aside his frustration towards Garrett. He'd deal with that later. "The three of us won't be able to bring the evidence forward, since we aren't allowed to challenge other Council members. Apparently, it's so we can't use false accusations to remove competition."

"I could bring it up," Altaira suggested.

Mefune shook his head slightly. "If we want you to replace Ezequiel, we can't have you challenging his position. It would look like a power grab. I doubt Samar would willingly let you take his place. The Auraes are the only ones with the authority to arrest Ezequiel, so we'll have to take it to them. That, though, you could do."

Altaira nodded. "Think the Auraes will allow me to remain anonymous? If the Council finds out I gave them the information, they may still question my motives."

Mefune considered it for a moment. "Knowing Ila, she'll probably just be grateful for a chance at the Council. She hates Samar. Challenging him should be enough of an opportunity for her to agree to your wishes." Altaira nodded.

"After that, how is the new Council member elected?" Daya wondered.

"It goes to a vote amongst the entire Council," Garrett supplied.

"Wait, it does?" Altaira asked, surprised. "I thought his replacement would be chosen as usual."

Garrett shook his head slightly. "The founders figured if a corrupt leader was allowed to be replaced like normal, there was a high chance his chosen successor would be just as bad, and if nobody could challenge him, the Brotherhood would be right in the same boat. So, they made it go to a vote in this situation." He shrugged slightly. "Though whoever is voted in can still be challenged, as usual, so if the vote doesn't go in our favor, Altaira can just challenge whoever is chosen. She'll win."

Altaira nodded. "I'll head to Verndale tomorrow then."

CHAPTER TEN
THE ARCHIVE

Mariea

After a quick message to Cato, Mariea made arrangements for her, Bracken, and Mae to stop by the Brotherhood's base in order to secure a phone. Once there, they found Charity at the desk again, though she didn't seem surprised to see them this time. "Hello again, Mariea," she greeted.

"Hey. How are things going with cleaning up the mess we caused?" Mariea asked.

"Actually, that's all taken care of now. Cato just had some paperwork to deal with. We didn't even have to use magic," Charity told her with a reassuring smile.

Mariea let out a small, relieved huff. "Good. Next time, we'll be more careful to make sure we're better prepared before leaving Raidenya."

"Don't stress about it. It's more on us at the end of the day; we were supposed to prepare you," Charity told her as she stood. "Cato let me know you'd be dropping by. Let me go grab him."

Mariea nodded, and she and her companions claimed seats in the lobby while Charity left to get Cato. Bracken glanced around as they waited, clearly just as curious about the setup as Mariea had been the first time she had visited.

"This is nice. I wonder what it poses as," he mused after a bit.

"Cato told me last they actually run a small law firm and private investigator business on the side," Mariea explained.

"Which would explain how he had such an easy time getting us out of jail," Bracken realized.

"It also helps fund the Brotherhood, which is a nice perk," Cato added as he joined them. Then he reached into his pocket and pulled out a simple flip phone, offering it to Mariea. "Here, it's all set up and ready to go. You can use it as long as you need to. When you're finished with it, just bring it back here, and we'll take care of it."

"Thank you. I owe you big time. This is twice now you've helped us out," Mariea told him with a smile.

"Hey, don't worry about it. We heard things are getting a little rocky for you guys on Raidenya. We're here to help," Cato told her with a sympathetic smile.

"Well, thank you again. I'll find a way to repay you somehow," Mariea promised.

With that, Cato headed back to his work. Mariea returned to the couch and reached into her pocket for the phone number Iris had given her. Instead, she found a pile of papers, and she pulled them out, feeling slightly surprised she had collected so many. It was quickly obvious that all of them had addresses or phone numbers from their trip. *I need to find somewhere safer to keep these,* she decided.

It took her a second to locate the correct note. Dialing the number, she waited impatiently while the phone rang. Eventually, an older man answered the phone with a simple, "Willard Archives, this is Alvin speaking."

"Alvin, hello. My name is Mariea. I was told you could help me learn more about an old house in the area."

His voice seemed to brighten at the suggestion. "Yes, yes! That's the point of the archives, of course. Come by the shop, and I'll tell you everything you could know about any old building."

Mariea smiled, surprised by his enthusiasm. "Alright, we'll do that, then. Could I get the address of your shop?"

"Sure, sure—wait, how do you know my name and number but not my address?"

Mariea blinked, surprised by the sudden level of suspicion in his voice. "An old contact of yours, Iris, gave us the information. She said you could be helpful, but she didn't remember where you lived."

"Huh..." Alvin muttered, clearly considering it deeply. Then, he dismissed it as quickly as he had first considered it as he said, "Well, most people find me from my sign in the yard, so I assumed you'd be the same. No worries then!" He quickly relayed the address, and Mariea scrambled to write it down, hoping she got everything correct. "I'll be seeing you soon, I suspect," he finished.

"Yes, soon," Mariea agreed, but then she realized the line was dead. She pulled the phone away from her ear and glanced at it, surprised.

"Everything okay?" Bracken asked. He and Mae were staring at her expectantly, clearly worried as they read her reaction.

"Yes, I got the address. That conversation was just... bizarre. I think we're in for an interesting experience."

Mae shrugged. "Hey, considering this trip so far, it can't get any worse. Still beats prison."

"I'll second that," Bracken decided, and then he stood. "Let's get going then. Do you know where the address is?"

"No, but I should be able to find it on the map once we get back to the car," Mariea decided as she stood as well and started for the door.

They walked back to the car, and Mariea immediately grabbed the map once they were all inside. It took her a minute, but she eventually located the address just northeast of New York. "Guess we're headed in the other direction this time."

Bracken let out a sigh as he took the map and glanced over it. "This will be a lot harder to direct you to," he muttered. Once they had left the city, the trip out to the farmhouse had been relatively straightforward, but this one would require a lot more time navigating busy suburban areas.

"Just do your best. It's okay if we get lost; I'll just pull over, and we'll figure things out. We've got the time," Mariea reassured him, despite how desperately she wanted to get to Alvin's and get answers quickly.

They started off, and Bracken did his best to keep them on track. They only had to turn around a couple of times, and they made it to their destination before noon, so Mariea wrote it off as a success. The neighborhood had a storybook feel that Mariea quite liked. The house was a small cottage-style two-story dwelling with a meticulously maintained lawn and garden. Near the sidewalk, an oversized homemade sign announced the home as the location of "the greatest archive of historical knowledge."

Bracken leaned around Mariea to read the sign. "Seems a bit bold of a claim, don't you think?"

Mariea shrugged. "Guess we'll have to wait and see."

They made their way to the door, and Mariea rang the doorbell. It took only a moment for Alvin to answer. He grinned when he saw them, his bright white teeth and equally white smock of curls a sharp contrast against the dark shade of his skin. He wore a surprisingly ugly plaid vest over a crisp white button-up shirt and slacks, and he wore a name tag near his collar that looked surprisingly official. It declared him the "headmaster of the archive", though Mariea had the feeling he was the only employee.

"Ah, come to peruse the knowledge these humble walls contain?" he stated as he straightened, clearly proud of his home.

"Um, yes," Mariea replied.

"Very good! Come in, come in! Am I safe to assume you are the woman I spoke to a half hour ago on the phone? Morgan, was it?"

"It's Mariea, but yes, that was me," Mariea corrected.

"Very good! Right this way, and we shall discover the answers you seek!" He spun on his heel and strode down the hall at a surprisingly brisk pace.

Mariea glanced at her companions. Bracken was clearly trying to suppress an amused smirk, and Mae had covered her mouth with a hand to douse the sounds of her quiet chuckling.

"Well. At least he's enthusiastic," Bracken whispered, earning a smile from Mariea as they started after Alvin.

Alvin led them to a neat library lined with bookshelves. He claimed a seat at a large oak desk in the center of the room. "Please, do sit," he urged, so Mariea and Bracken claimed the seats at the desk, and Mae hovered behind them. "Now," he muttered as he pulled a pair of glasses from his pocket and perched them on the edge of his nose. "I don't actually need these. I just feel they make me fit the part better. Alright, what is it—oh, where are my manners? Please, Morgana, introduce me to your companions."

Mariea briefly debated correcting him on her name again, but decided against it. Turning to the two with her, she quickly introduced them both, sure Alvin would forget their names within moments.

"Very good! It is a pleasure to make your acquaintance, all three of you. Now. Would you like any refreshments? I always offer my clients, though I can't say I'm much of a cook, so it's probably safest to say no."

Mariea couldn't resist a chuckle at this. "Alright then, I guess we'll pass. Thank you."

"Very good! Clearly, you're all business. Let's get to it, then. What is it you're looking for?"

"I'm searching for information about a house I think might have ties to my family history. I was told by the house's owner you might be able to help me track down information about it," Mariea explained.

"That I can, my dear Molly! I know more about this here state than anyone else! May I ask what you would like to know in particular?" he asked.

"I found a picture of it in an old photo album. We were able to track down the house, so I have the address. I don't know what connection it has to my family, but I want to learn as much as I can about it."

"Very good, my dear. May I see the address?" Alvin asked. Mariea nodded and pulled the paper from her pocket. He read over it—clearly looking around the glasses so he could actually see—and then nodded. "Ah, a nice dwelling, to be sure. Blue paint, red door. Quiet neighborhood, though a bit too sparse for me. If I remember correctly, it has quite the history."

"You got all that from reading the address?" Mae asked in amazement.

Alvin glanced up at her. "I have a photographic memory for places I've visited. I never forget a house's face, so to speak!" He chuckled at his own joke as he stood and made his way to the nearest bookshelf. "Give me a moment to locate the correct binder."

He began perusing, muttering random things under his breath as he did. That's when Mariea realized none of the shelves contained books, just neatly labeled and stacked binders in multiple colors.

Eventually, he pulled out a large black binder and carried it back to the desk. "It would seem saying this old thing has an interesting history was quite the understatement. This binder is all for just this address," he stated as he set it down. "I thought the address sounded familiar when I read it."

He flipped open the binder to reveal a neat, handwritten table of contents on thick, cream-colored cardstock paper. "My daughter keeps begging me to switch to typing, but then my skill for calligraphy would be waisted, now wouldn't it?" he mused with a small, modest smile. Then he flipped the binder around and slid it towards the three across the desk. "Feel free to peruse at your own pace. If you have any questions, do ask." He rested his hands on the desk and sat on the edge of his seat, clearly eager to answer any questions they might have.

Mariea pulled the binder closer, and Mae and Bracken leaned in to see. The table of contents contained an extensive list of dates and labels, each with a page number listed—some even included a paragraph number.

Bracken leaned forward, his brow furrowed slightly. "What's this?" he asked, pointing to a line that read 'Disappearance, 1785.'

"Ah, that is a fascinating point in that house's history indeed!" Alvin stated. Mariea began flipping to the page marked with the date, but it seemed she didn't need to. Alvin was already relaying what had happened.

"It was the summer of 1785. The house was owned by a good man and his wife. They were elderly. With them also lived their adult son and his wife and their young daughter. The house owner was a farmer, but the son, he was ambitious. Rupert Tamberlaine, that was his name, if I remember correctly." Mariea glanced down at the papers—it was actually Reuben, but she'd let it slide. He seemed to have a good memory for the details, but not the names.

He continued, oblivious to his blunder. "Rupert left the family farm behind to start a successful shipping company. He traveled to and from the motherland—England—dozens of times and owned a nice fleet of ships by the time he was forty. And then, that summer of 1785, he, along with his wife and daughter, and about 200 other souls, disappeared."

Mariea quickly glanced up from the binder to Alvin. With one eyebrow raised, she questioned, "Did they ever figure out what happened to them?"

Alvin shrugged. "There were rumors, but no definitive answers. He ran into a bit of trouble—something about witchcraft. There wasn't much about it that I could find, and trust me, I dug quite deep. They say he went crazy and sailed one of his passenger ships into a storm. The ship never returned and was never seen again."

"Interesting," Mariea muttered, feeling this was significant. Stories of Auraes fleeing for being accused of witchcraft riddled the peoples' history. She wouldn't be surprised if this Rupert—or Reuben, whichever name was correct—was an Aurae.

"Interesting indeed, my dear! Fascinating little story. After his son disappeared, the farmer—whose name I forget—eventually moved away, and the house passed hands for a while. Then, about 30 years later, a young man shows up in this very port, looking much like Rupert's young daughter, Elinore. He carried the last name Remar, so nobody could prove the connection, and he denied it himself. But everyone still believed this boy was Rupert's grandson. If their theories were correct, Rupert and the ship did not perish."

"Huh," Mariea muttered. This intrigued her even more—her maiden name was Remar. Could it be this house ironically actually had some connection to her family? She didn't know much about her family history—her parents hadn't been very open about their past. But if the stories were true, why would Rupert's grandson return to a world that was hostile to his kind?

Shaking her head, she forced herself to focus. In her dream, she had also seen a pier, and now she was beginning to realize the possible connection. "Alvin, this has been very helpful. Do you happen to know the location of the pier that the missing ship left from?"

"I do, my dear, I do! Turn to page fifty-two in that binder, and you'll find everything you need to know about the ship's departure."

Mariea did as instructed and scanned over the page. Pictures of a worn-out pier and an address dominated most of the page, accompanied by several notes in the margins.

As she studied the images, Alvin opened a drawer in his desk. "Here you are, a pen and paper," he said as he handed her the items.

"Thank you," Mariea muttered, grateful he had anticipated her need. She wrote down the address and added it to the growing collection in her jacket pocket. Then she stared at the picture for a moment, trying to commit it to memory, before she closed the binder and placed it back on the desk. "Thank you again, Alvin. Your insight is priceless. I feel like I'm starting to get somewhere now in filling in the blanks of my family history."

"Very good!" he stated with a grin. He stood and offered a hand for her to shake, which she did. "I am most grateful I could be of service to you!" Then, from the same desk drawer, he produced a small stack of business cards written in the same neat penmanship. "Here, please, take my number. If you ever require my services further, do call. I never charge. Knowledge is too priceless to put a tag on it! And give them to your friends and family. The more, the merrier!"

She smiled. "I will remember that, thank you," she stated as she accepted the business cards.

He showed them to the door, and they hurried to the car. As Mariea began driving away, Mae glanced back at the house and stated, "If that guy gets any more eccentric—or happy—he's going to become a cartoon character."

Bracken laughed. "He's definitely interesting."

"I enjoyed his company," Mariea decided.

"Oh, don't get me wrong, I did too," Bracken quickly corrected. "I was waiting to see just how many names he could come up for you. I just hope he kept his facts a little more in order."

"It seemed accurate from what little I read in the binder," Mariea stated.

"Yeah, but he made those. Who knows if those are accurate," Mae pointed out.

"I'm inclined to trust him. But you have to wonder," Bracken added when he noticed Mariea looked a little worried. "So, I'm assuming you want to find this pier next?"

"Yes. It has to be where we're supposed to go next," Mariea decided.

"You think those people were Auraes?" Bracken wondered.

"I'm sure of it. Why else would 200 people disappear after one of them was accused of witchcraft? If they're not dead, they were fleeing. And at the time, America was the place people went to get away from bad situations, not where they ran from them. So I'm assuming whatever they were mixed up in was pretty bad."

"Seems likely to me," Bracken agreed. Then he glanced sideways at her. "Did you catch that the possible grandson had the same last name as your parents?"

"I did. I don't think that's just a coincidence."

"I'd guess not," Bracken agreed with a nod. "Our family history cover story may have ironically led us to actually learn something about your family."

Mariea shook her head in disbelief. "Yeah, it just might. Let's just hope this pier gives us more answers."

They drove for roughly an hour until they found themselves standing on an abandoned pier, staring out at the ocean as it lapped lazily against the shore. Despite it being empty and long forgotten, Mariea could sense something else to her surroundings.

"Is...this where we're supposed to be?" Mae asked doubtfully. It seemed there was absolutely nothing of use around, and Mariea couldn't entirely blame her for feeling unsure.

But Mariea was sure it was right. "Yes...I just...don't know what we're supposed to do now that we're here," she replied. Taking a step forward, she laid a hand on one of the old poles to steady herself as she looked out at the bay.

Suddenly she found herself in eighteenth-century America, the busy pier around her bustling with people. It was late, too late to be starting a sea voyage, and yet several people clamored to get on the ship anchored at the end of the pier. Despite the number of people, they were nearly silent, which amazed Mariea. She caught glimpses of their tired and scared faces as they passed under the light of a few candle lanterns. It took her only a moment to figure out what was happening; they were Auraes, she could sense it, and they were fleeing, driven from their homes by the witch-hunts of the past.

A man appeared next to Mariea and looked at her. "Elinore, come along," he hissed, gesturing Mariea closer. Surprised, Mariea pointed at herself, wondering why he had called her Elinore. Suddenly the woman she had seen in her first dream materialized before her, moving to stand next to the man. She was younger now, about fifteen, and didn't seem to carry the same weight she had when Mariea had first seen her. So this must be Rupert and his daughter, Elinore, *she guessed.*

Following Elinore, the scene morphed, taking Mariea onto the ship. Then, time seemed to speed up, and days flashed by like a time-lapse video. Mariea watched their vessel, like a little toy in a bathtub, bob its way across the ocean to a small, unfamiliar, and wild island.

Slowly a society was born from the rugged wilderness, and Elinore grew with it, maturing in beauty as well as Auric strength.

The vision ended as quickly as it had begun, snapping her back to reality. "Mariea!" Mae yelled, placing a hand on her arm and shaking her slightly.

"What?" Mariea gasped as she raised a hand to her forehead in an attempt to steady herself. She felt incredibly disoriented, jumping from one reality to another so quickly.

Mae sighed in relief. "Man, you were gone. I feel like I've been yelling at you for a solid five minutes."

"What happened?" Bracken asked. "Are you okay?"

"I'm fine, I just...when I touched this pillar, I saw more of the message," she informed them, gesturing to the wood in question.

Bracken brightened, looking slightly relieved. "So we're getting somewhere then."

"It would seem so," she confirmed. Staring out at the horizon, she suddenly knew the direction the ship had taken, and that she needed to follow it. "And I know where to go next. We're going to need a boat."

Chapter Eleven
Intervention

Ila

Ila sighed as she slumped into her office chair and scanned over the list of names Jocelyn had given her over a half-hour ago. It was her third or fourth time through the list, yet she still found herself unable to process how long it was. She had known there had been attacks, several resulting in deaths, but this? This was too many. *Mariea needs to hurry*, she thought for the thousandth time since her friend had left.

A knock came at her open door, and she sighed inwardly, wishing she had shut it. Now was really not the time for company. "Ila?" her visitor called. She finally looked up to them, discovering her attendant, Braxton. "There's a member of the Brotherhood here wishing to speak with you."

Ila frowned, realizing this would do nothing for her mood, but saw no way to avoid it. "Send them in," she wearily invited. She could only hope it would be worth her time.

Braxton returned a moment more with a woman Ila didn't recognize but seemed vaguely familiar. "This is Altaira," he introduced.

"Altaira, nice to meet you," Ila stated as she stood and extended a hand for her to shake, managing a pleasant smile. Contemplating the name, she remembered why it was familiar—this was Gavin's sister. Now, it was easy for her to see the resemblance between the two; though Gavin's hair was darker, they had similar facial features and skin tones.

"Likewise," Altaira returned with an equally civil smile.

Ila dismissed Braxton and closed her office door. Gesturing to the two seats before her desk, she invited, "Please, have a seat."

Altaira nodded, sinking into one of them gracefully as Ila reclaimed her spot behind her desk. "So, tell me, what brings you to Verndale?"

"Before we begin, I would like to make it clear that I don't want word of my involvement in this conversation to reach the Brotherhood Council," she warned, her tone firm.

"As you wish," Ila agreed with a nod. It seemed an odd request, but she had nothing against keeping secrets from the Brotherhood Council. It seemed only fair, considering how many secrets they kept from her.

Altaira nodded. "I have information about illegal activity amongst the Council," she began. Ila nodded, unable to hide her surprise, but she made a good effort to hide her triumph. This was just the opportunity she had been looking for.

Unaware of Ila's inner joy, Altaira continued. "Ezequiel, a member of the Council, bribed his predecessor to get his seat, which is against our laws. But I don't have the authority to challenge him, and I have reasons to believe the Council would not believe me if I brought it to them. I know you have certain jurisdiction over the operations of the Brotherhood, since we aren't an entirely independent entity, so I figured you could help." Her dark gaze regarded Ila carefully as she explained, clearly gauging her reaction.

"Hmm," Ila muttered, sitting back in her chair as she made a show of considering the ramifications of such news. In reality, she wanted to agree to arrest this Ezequiel right away, but she was learning the benefits of playing diplomacy. "This is a pretty high accusation, and the Auraes prefer to stay out of the Brotherhood's affairs if we can. Do you have proof?"

Altaira nodded as she slipped a sheet protector onto Ila's desk, several pages covered in scrawling handwriting and a small cassette tape tucked inside it. Ila pulled the slip to her and began examining the pages. "These are from the journal of one of the men involved. The last page promises the tape has more details," Altaira told her before explaining in detail the account, pointing out the corresponding areas on the pages as she did.

As Altaira finished, Ila nodded slowly, taking in the information. "This is definitely enough to open a case. I would like to hear the contents of this disk first, though," she stated, studying it. She didn't exactly have anything lying around that could play it. "Wait here," she instructed Altaira before she went searching.

After asking around and recruiting Braxton to help search, Ila eventually tracked down a recorder that would play the tape back. After returning to her office, she and Altaira listened to the tape. To Ila's immediate delight, she realized it was a recording of the very conversation where Alec and Ezequiel had made their deal.

"We need to act on this quickly," she stated as the tape ended. "I hate to entangle myself in such an internal matter, but Alec and Ezequiel need to be dealt with."

"Alec's dead," Altaira stated quickly. "This is just about Ezequiel."

Ila nodded. "Just Ezequiel then. Either way, thank you for coming to me about it. I can't stand for such corruption."

Altaira nodded. "It was the right thing to do. The Brotherhood is full of good people. They don't deserve to be led by someone like this." Her expression darkened slightly with this, and something about her tone suggested to Ila she meant her words more than she let on.

"I couldn't agree more," Ila stated as she stood, though she couldn't care less what happened to the Brotherhood. "I can come with you to your headquarters today if that would be convenient for you."

Though she seemed a bit surprised, Altaira nodded. "That would be perfect."

"Very well. I'll bring a couple sentinels, we'll arrest Ezequiel, and he'll stand trial for this. We should be able to handle this matter quickly and efficiently. Wait here, please." Altaira nodded, so Ila stepped from her office again and went a few doors down to where Jocelyn worked. Knocking on the head sentinel's door, she waited a moment.

"Ila, is there something I could do for you?" Jocelyn greeted.

"I need to borrow a couple sentinels. There's an arrest that needs to take place at the Brotherhood's headquarters, and I would rather not deal with it alone. You know how they can be."

Jocelyn nodded, her aura already appearing around her. She switched to Shidokian for a moment to send out the needed messages. "There will be two sentinels here in a moment. Considering who is involved, would you like me to accompany you? Tension between the Brotherhood and Auraes is at an all-time high."

Feeling a bit miffed Jocelyn was implying she couldn't handle the situation, Ila had to bite her cheek to prevent her first reaction. Managing a strained smile, she told her, "I'll handle the matter, thank you. Tell them to meet me at my office."

Jocelyn nodded, her gaze flicking away, but not before Ila caught a glimpse of the doubt that passed over her expression. Ila didn't bother to linger long enough to allow her to say anything else. She hurried to her car and grabbed the spare clothes she kept there, knowing the path to the Brotherhood headquarters wasn't even paved. Making the trek in a business suit and heels wasn't entirely practical.

After changing into the more suitable outfit, she rejoined the sentinels and Altaira, and then the group headed for the forest. They drove as far as they could, but most of the journey would be on foot once they passed beyond the city limits. The road ended at a cul-de-sac with a narrow dirt trail between the last couple of houses. Here, the residences all had high stone fences around their yards, their surfaces kept smooth to make it hard for the Tarapor to climb over. Though they weren't entirely necessary anymore—the Brotherhood had at least managed to push the Tarapor away from the city enough so the people living there didn't have to live in fear constantly—Ila still felt it was essential to maintain the fences. She didn't trust the Brotherhood enough to believe the Tarapor couldn't return.

She pulled her car over to the side of the road, and the small group piled out. As they started into the forest, Altaira took the lead. She followed a path Ila couldn't see but she clearly knew well, moving almost silently, obviously comfortable with her surroundings.

On the other hand, Ila had to resist jumping at any unfamiliar noise as the trees closed in around her. The thick canopy made it darker than the bright city streets, and there was so much about the forest that unnerved her. She knew all too well there were monsters lurking in the shadows. The dried pine needles and leaves crunched underfoot despite how careful she was to be quiet. Compared to her companions, she felt like she was stomping and yelling to attract as many Tarapor as possible.

The pair of sentinels trailed behind the two women, almost as silent as Altaira. Ila was grateful for their presence, even if she knew Altaira was the only one of the four equipped to deal with Tarapor if they attacked. At least the sentinels would be helpful once they reached the Brotherhood's headquarters. Keeping her mind focused on her goal, Ila did her best to ignore her fear and pressed on.

They walked for a long time as the day wore on. Passing around the southern tip of a lake, they started upward as the forest floor climbed towards distant cliffs and the shoreline. Altaira glanced over her shoulder. "We're close," she informed Ila, who couldn't help but be grateful. She was starting to tire.

After another half hour of the mostly uphill climb, the forest fell away to give them a grand view of the ocean far below to their left. A final hill rose before them, which Altaira approached confidently. *We're in the middle of nowhere,* Ila protested silently. *Where is she taking me?*

As she stepped up behind Altaira, the surface of the hill seemed to flicker in and out of focus before a large stone door appeared in its side, large enough for a few men to pass through side by side. Ila's eyes widened in surprise despite herself. Clearly, powerful magic had hidden the door from view, but she hadn't even sensed it. It wasn't an easy feat to hide magic, especially as it ventured into more powerful types, so whoever had crafted the spells had been a talented Aurae.

Altaira stepped up to the door and pressed in a few select pieces of the surface, as if putting in a code. The door sunk inward and then up with the sound of stone grinding against stone, allowing the group passage.

Stepping through the shadowed doorway, Ila paused a moment to allow her eyes to adjust to the dimmer light inside. Beyond the entrance was a long stone hallway lit by periodical sconces. She was surprised to find they were electrical lights—the Brotherhood seemed so old-fashioned that she had expected fire. Altaira pressed into the crowds, who eyed the Auraes following her suspiciously. Ila met their gazes evenly, despite the twinge of nervousness their presence caused. The Brotherhood had always made her uneasy, and she couldn't push from her mind the fact that she was clearly stepping into their territory.

They wound through stone corridors for a few minutes, traveling steadily downward. Ila quickly felt lost. *It's much bigger than I thought*, she marveled silently.

Eventually, Altaira stopped before a pair of large wooden doors, their grandeur surprising after the lower ceilings of the passageways behind them. "I'm going to pretend you came on your own. Meet me at the front gate when you're done, and I'll get you back to Verndale," she instructed.

"We can make it back on our own," Ila stated.

Altaira raised one eyebrow and fixed her with a pointed look. "There are Tarapor out there, and by the time you start back, it'll be dark, meaning they'll be far more active. They corner you, you'll be slaughtered," she stated bluntly.

Ila sighed, annoyed that despite all the power her aura lent her, Altaira was right; she was helpless against the Tarapor. "I'll meet you at the entrance, then." She didn't miss Altaira's faint smirk as she nodded. Glancing at the two sentinels, Ila added, "Wait here until I call you. No reason to upset the Council immediately before I have a chance to explain." The pair nodded.

Altaira pushed the doors open, allowing her and Ila in. The Council was already in the middle of a meeting, but their conversations halted as they turned to Altaira.

"Altaira, I'm assuming you knew the Council was in session," Samar stated, his annoyance only barely contained.

"Yes, sorry. I found Ila by the front door. She said she needed to speak with you. It was urgent. I told her you may be busy, but she insisted." She shrugged innocently, indicating the situation was out of her hands.

Samar's gaze trailed from Altaira to Ila, and his expression darkened considerably. Ila had to resist the urge to smirk. "You're dismissed, Altaira," he stated, his tone much less civil now. She nodded and hurried off. "Ila, tell us why you have shown up unannounced."

Clasping her hands behind her back as she met Samar's gaze, Ila told him, "It has come to my attention that corruption amongst this Council must be dealt with."

Murmurs of surprise passed through the Council. "You can't just come waltzing into our home and accuse us out of nowhere like this," one man challenged. She didn't recognize him, but judging by the scowl on his face, it was clear he allied with Samar in his opinion of Ila.

"As the acting chairman of the Auraes in Mariea's absence, I can. And this is no small matter," she pressed before giving them a succinct description of the events Altaira had informed her of.

As she finished, one man turned to Samar and stated, "She can't prove it. I didn't do any of what she just said." Realizing this must be Ezequiel, she studied him quietly. He had a bulkier, sturdy build, with curly golden hair and sharp facial features. Ila guessed he would have been quite attractive in his younger years. Under his stubborn anger, she noticed a hint of fear in his green eyes. *He's guilty,* she mused, allowing a slight smirk.

"As a matter of fact, I can prove it," she stated, and then pulled the journal papers from the inside pocket of her coat.

Samar gestured her forward, so she handed the papers over to him. He read them in silence for a long moment, his scowl deepening as he did. "Where did you get these?"

"An anonymous tip," she said with a shrug.

"They're just journal pages. This doesn't prove anything," Samar dismissed.

"But this might," Ila stated, raising the tape. "It details the conversation had during the transaction. I'll play it for you if you wish. Or will you hand Ezequiel over without making a scene about this? You know the laws. What he did was illegal. I have the right to prosecute him, and I intend to. I will not see corruption go unpunished."

Samar's jaw tightened as he stared at Ila, clear hatred written all over his expression. Eventually, he let out a heavy sigh and stated, "Fine, do what you will."

"What?!" Ezequiel exclaimed, staring at Samar in disbelief as he gripped the table before him. Ignoring his protest, Ila turned and signaled for the sentinels to enter.

"Ezequiel, we must abide by the law," Samar stated, sounding as if it pained him to say it. "You will receive a fair trial by the sentinels, but this blemish requires you to resign from the Council."

Ezequiel looked ready to kill Samar or Ila, or maybe both, but he glanced at the sentinels, and all sense of resistance vanished from his expression. Stiffly, he stood, straightened his uniform jacket, and stepped down from the Council bar. One of the sentinels approached and shackled his hands with a simple spell.

"Take him back to the entrance—I'll meet you there soon," Ila commanded. The pair nodded and led Ezequiel away.

Ila turned her gaze back to Samar. "I thank you for your cooperation," she told him with a cold smile. "See to it his replacement is chosen legally this time."

Samar gave a curt nod. "If there is nothing else, please be on your way so we can get back to our business," he snapped.

"Of course," Ila agreed. She reclaimed the journal pages and tape, and then left.

It took her much longer than she would have preferred to find her way back to the entrance. Altaira was waiting, as promised, with the two sentinels and Ezequiel. "Ready to head back to the city?" she asked.

"And back to civilization," Ila griped, glancing warily over her shoulder.

Altaira rolled her eyes, but thankfully spared Ila any snarky remarks. They started out, leaving the Brotherhood behind, Ila feeling the oddest mix of relief and triumph.

Mefune

Soon after Ila left, the Council erupted with angry comments and questions, so much so that it quickly became hard to keep track of everything going on around Mefune. It amazed him to see just how much of the Council was upset by Ila's actions. He had hoped more would be willing to accept justice, showing that they were potentially still loyal to the Brotherhood's true purpose, and not Samar, but it seemed that wasn't the case.

"Were those journal pages really enough to just let her take Ezequiel?" Darius asked Samar after a moment. Mefune barely heard his question over the others. Focusing on the two, he waited to hear Samar's response, hoping to make sure there wasn't any reason to suspect him for their appearance.

"Yes. She had clear evidence of what happened, and I'm sure the tape would have been even more incriminating," Samar grumbled just loud enough for Darius to hear. He met the other man's gaze. "Besides, they were from *Alec's* journal."

Darius' gaze widened slightly, clearly understanding the journal's significance. "I thought you destroyed his things after he died."

"Apparently, some evidence survived," Samar stated with a frustrated shake of his head. "I had to let Ezequiel take the fall. We don't want them looking further." *So, Samar and Darius are aware of Alec's murder*, Mefune mused, finding this little piece of information very useful.

"Wonder who brought them to Ila," Darius muttered.

"That's what I would like to know," Samar grumbled with a slight sneer, his gaze passing over the other members. "We must have a leak somewhere." Then he called for everyone's attention. They quieted and turned to him reluctantly. "As much as I hate to leave Ezequiel in the hands of the Auraes, there's nothing we can do now. We'll have to gather the entire Council so they can vote to replace him."

"That'll take some time, and we'll need the Auraes' permission to do it. Who will run his region while he's gone?" Daya wondered.

Samar considered it for a moment, and then his gaze found Mefune. "With only one base to run, I think you can handle both assignments."

Mefune nodded, as did the others. *Now we wait,* he thought.

As the Council dispersed, Samar approached Mefune. "Do you have a moment to talk?" he requested.

"Sure," Mefune confirmed, figuring he wanted to discuss details of the adjusted assignments.

Samar gestured for him to follow and headed for his office just down the hall. When the door closed, he asked, "Do you know anything about where these journal pages came from?"

"No more than you do," Mefune replied, frowning slightly in confusion. "Why?"

"You seemed the only one that wasn't upset over what happened," Samar pointed out.

Mefune shrugged slightly. "Why waste my breath? If Ezequiel was stupid enough to get caught, he deserved what he got. We move on without him. Do you feel otherwise?"

"Just had to double-check," Samar stated lightly, as if his accusation seconds ago meant nothing.

Mefune raised an eyebrow. "You think I'm the anonymous tip?" he questioned.

Samar shook his head. "It was simply a question," he corrected.

"Seemed oddly timed. Forgive me for finding it accusatory," Mefune stated, folding his arms against his chest.

"Everyone's a suspect until we find out who gave the Aurae this information," Samar said with a shrug. "If they keep snooping around in our business, our plans become complicated."

Mefune had to resist the urge to express his frustration over the irony of how Samar was handling the situation. It was as if he viewed whoever had helped Ila as the criminal, not Ezequiel. Instead, he stated, "I am committed to helping you, Samar. You shouldn't take that commitment lightly. I don't back out when I give my word."

Samar nodded, looking thoughtful. "I'll remember that." Despite his pleasant tone, Mefune caught on to the implied warning. If he didn't follow through, Samar wouldn't be quick to forgive.

Mefune nodded and dismissed himself. His thoughts raced as he walked away, wondering what he had done to make Samar suspicious. *How could he think I was involved? I was so careful not to leave a hint. What more could I have done?*

He trailed deeper into the base, wandering aimlessly as he reconsidered the day he had found the pages. No matter how many times he analyzed the situation, he couldn't find anything that would have directly incriminated him. Sure, Samar would know someone had been snooping in his office simply because the pages had turned up, but he wasn't sure how he would have figured out Mefune was the one who had found them—and so soon. And yet, he knew Samar wouldn't have singled him out if he actually believed everyone was a suspect. Something had tipped him off.

Deciding he needed to talk this over with someone, he paused in his wandering and started for the apartments on the second floor. He sought out Garrett first, but found he wasn't around. That left Daya and Altaira who were aware of the whole scheme, leaving him conflicted. He didn't know Daya well, and though Altaira had agreed to put their little conflict behind them to help him, she still seemed to only barely stand his presence. But he had to speak to someone.

Settling on Altaira, simply because it was a chance to show he trusted her, he started for her apartment. When he knocked, she seemed surprised to see him. "Have a minute to talk?" he asked.

She seemed at a loss for words for a brief moment, but then nodded. "Sure. Uh, come in," she told him, her attempt to sound inviting undermined a bit by her uncertainty.

Mefune followed her inside, his mind too occupied to pay attention to the situation entirely. "Samar thinks I had something to do with the journal pages," he stated after the door closed. He didn't bother to sit down, instead choosing to hover near the entryway.

"That could be a problem. What tipped him off?" Altaira wondered. She busied herself with straightening things around the room, though a quick glance over everything told him there wasn't much out of place.

"I'm not sure. But he asked to speak with me after the Council meeting was over, and something about it seemed off," Mefune started before he quickly filled her in on the details of the conversation.

"Hmm. It does seem odd he singled you out." She paused a moment. "But how would he know you had anything to do with the pages?"

"I took them from his office. He'd know that's where they came from, but I have no idea how he connected it back to me. The only person who knew I was looking there was..." his voice suddenly faded as he connected the dots, his gaze widening slightly, "...Garrett."

Altaira's brow furrowed in confusion. "You don't think he betrayed us, do you?"

"It would seem that way, but he's literally the person who pointed me towards this whole scheme in the first place," he stated with an exasperated wave of his hand. He shook his head in confusion. "It doesn't make sense for him to turn against us after leading us to the issue."

They fell silent, caught in the contradiction for a moment. Altaira settled on the couch, and eventually, Mefune moved to sit across from her in an armchair.

"I don't know, but there's something off about Garrett," Altaira started with a light shrug. "He's always been careful, but lately, he's seemed…paranoid. And he knows more about Creta's death than he's letting on."

Mefune nodded. "I picked up on that too." As he reflected on Garrett's involvement from the beginning, his gaze narrowed slightly in suspicion. "At first, I believed him when he said he was worried about setting off Samar. The man's clearly dangerous, but Garrett's acting as if he's already done something to anger him, and now he's just waiting for Samar to punish him for it or something." He paused a moment, thinking. "I wonder if he's not trying to set us up to take the fall for whatever he did."

"Do you really think Garrett would do something like that?" Altaira wondered, sounding a bit surprised.

Mefune nodded slightly. "He's usually a pretty decent person, but he can be incredibly selfish. If he saw it as the only way to save himself from Samar, I think he'd do it. Question is, what made Samar angry at him in the first place?"

"Maybe it's about time we find out before it leads us to more trouble than we know how to handle," Altaira mused. "That, and all he knows about Creta's death."

Mefune nodded in agreement. "Hopefully, he'll be willing to talk."

"You think he'll just lie to us?" Altaira wondered.

"Not if he seriously believes it's in his best interest to tell us the truth."

"How do we go about convincing him of that?" Altaira wondered. "Anything too forward, and he might just run to Samar."

With no definitive answer, Mefune stayed silent for a moment. Then an idea came to him. "We capture some Tarapor for Samar. Garrett agreed to go with us. We'd be away from base, meaning he'd have no allies, and the desperation might be enough to squeeze the truth from him."

Altaira nodded slowly, a small smile curving the corner of her lips. "And we could even bring back some Tarapor, which could help turn away Samar's suspicion."

Mefune nodded, realizing it wouldn't hurt to do so. "It may seem like too obvious an attempt to smooth things over, but...considering how I responded to Samar's challenge, it might be a good idea. When are you on patrol next?"

"I have the next few days off," she replied.

"It'll take us time to get to an area where there are enough Tarapor that we'll have a chance to catch one."

"How much time?" she asked, sounding a bit wary.

"Two days, if I'm remembering right," he mused, his gaze flicking away as he considered it. "The closest area is probably the western shore, unless we go to the northern half of the lake, but there's a lot of Tarapor up there. We could get swarmed."

"Let's avoid that," Altaira quickly agreed. "Two days it is, then. So much for a few days off."

He gave her a small, sympathetic smile. "Sorry."

She waved her hand dismissively. "This is more important than catching up on my lack of sleep, anyway."

He nodded. "Should we include Daya?"

Altaira considered it for a second and then shook her head. "She has patrol tomorrow—one of the random new ones. Plus, as far as Samar knows, she's not aware of his scheming, and I'd like to keep it that way, so it's probably best she doesn't come with us."

"Alright. I'll tell Garrett. We should leave early tomorrow morning," Mefune decided as he stood.

Altaira let out an apprehensive sigh. "This should be interesting. I guess I'll see you bright and early, then."

Chapter Twelve
Hunting Tarapor

Altaira

Altaira dragged herself from bed and showered quickly in an early morning haze. Caring little for how she looked, she threw on a gray t-shirt, a pair of jeans, and sturdy boots, braided her hair into its usual style, and then pulled on a sturdy jacket. The night before, she had packed a bag with the supplies she would need for the two-day excursion to the western shore. Grabbing it, she swung it over her shoulder and then added her sword around her waist and a pair of knives, just in case. Then she started out.

Garrett and Mefune were already waiting just outside the base entrance, speaking softly in the early morning light. Considering everything, it surprised her that Mefune could speak with Garrett so cordially. She worried she wouldn't be able to meet his gaze without him picking up on her change of opinion towards him.

As she approached, the dew on the grass darkened her boots, and she took a deep breath of the crisp morning air. At least it seemed it would be a nice day. It would make the trip much more endurable. Dealing with Tarapor, Garrett, *and* bad weather at once would have been an absurd streak of lousy timing.

Mefune glanced up at the sound of the door sliding closed behind her and gave a small wave in greeting. "Ready?" he asked.

Altaira nodded. "How far do you think we'll make it today?"

"Let's try to make it to the cliffs along the shoreline tonight. That'll give us a good staging point to search for Tarapor tomorrow morning," Mefune decided.

Garrett's eyes widened a bit in surprise. "The cliffs are pretty far. I don't know if we can make it in a day."

Mefune smirked slightly. "Guess you'll have to pick up the pace. I've made the entire round trip in a day. I think we can make it to the cliffs in half the time."

With that, he started into the forest, setting a quick, persistent pace. Garrett stared after him in amazement for a moment and then shook his head before following. Altaira couldn't prevent a little chuckle as she joined them.

As they crossed under the trees, the limited lighting dimmed a bit. The morning was still chilly, the last of winter lingering before the sun rose, and Altaira found herself grateful for the warm jacket she had chosen to wear. The familiar smell of pine and growth permeated the air, and silence surrounded them except for the occasional wildlife noise.

Altaira glanced at Mefune, wondering when he intended to speak to Garrett. They hadn't discussed that little detail, and it left her a bit antsy without knowing when to expect it. She was reluctant to bring it up first, feeling it would be best coming from him. But that left her with nothing to do but wait.

Her mind strayed to the second quarry of their little venture into the forest. She wasn't looking forward to fighting the Tarapor. Despite spending almost every day of her life on patrols scouting for the beasts, it was rare they actually encountered them anymore. Five years ago, a cure had been invented for the disease that created the Tarapor. With this to protect them from falling ill, the Brotherhood was finally able to drive the creatures away from civilization throughout the world, especially on Raidenya, where their numbers had always been highest. Though they had succeeded in their task, many members had died, and none of them reflected on their time in those fights fondly. They had come to call those couple of years the Purges.

Luckily, the fighting had brought some good—they had discovered some things about the Tarapor that gave them a few advantages. The creatures were naturally skittish, and they lacked the coordination to work together, meaning they could be overwhelmed with numbers and strategy even when they were in groups. And, with the Brotherhood's specially crafted weapons, it was incredibly easy to kill them—only a small wound was required. The metal destroyed their aura, and without it, they quickly died. Since then, the Brotherhood's job had become a bit easier. Their job was relatively safe as long as they stayed away from the more infested areas.

But now, they were purposefully seeking the Tarapor out, and it seemed counterintuitive. To say the creatures were dangerous was an understatement. Nobody really understood the magic-turned-disease that sustained their enemies, but it was highly contagious. If one were to survive a Tarapor bite, the chances of joining their ranks were surprisingly high unless the cure was immediately administered. And in the last decade, it had mutated to affect not just humans but also animals. The creatures that remained after the disease had its way with them were more relatable to a walking corpse than anything living. They were often so mutated in both behavior and appearance that it was hard to guess what they had been before they were turned.

In contrast to their appearance, they were nearly impervious to injury caused by magic or otherwise—except for the weapons Altaira and the rest of the Brotherhood carried. They seemed to have limitless lifespans, able to survive in the harshest climates as long as they had one thing—access to blood. They hunted after it in a feral frenzy, the drive for it making them unaware of pain or fatigue. A protein found in blood allowed the magic to maintain itself, which the disease stole from its victim while they still lived. Once the victim died, the condition modified the new host to allow it to steal blood from others, which would sustain the disease, and the corpse, after death.

Memories of her last encounter with the beasts flittered through Altaira's mind, increasing her nervousness. Glancing at her companions, she wondered if they felt the same. Garrett looked a bit nervous, but Mefune strode forward confidently as if unaware of the danger. It was more likely that he *was* aware of it and was perfectly fine with its presence. Altaira couldn't help but admire that confidence, knowing full well when they did find the Tarapor, he would give them a good challenge. That reassured her a bit.

Then she had to pause and contemplate that he, of all people, was comforting her by being near. Shaking her head slightly at the odd change of events, she pressed on, determined to think of something else.

The day passed uneventfully. After they had traveled for a good few hours and the Brotherhood headquarters was well behind them, Mefune stated, "Garrett, before we reach the Tarapor, we need to talk."

Right, Altaira thought. She had nearly forgotten they intended to confront Garrett. The man in question paused, his nervousness increasing, making Altaira wonder if he hadn't suspected something like this.

"What about?" Garrett asked, his tone forcefully light.

"After Ila left, Samar confronted me about the journal pages showing up. Somehow, he knew to be suspicious of me, even though I was careful to make sure I left no evidence behind of ever being in his office. The only other person that knew I intended to look there was you."

Garrett shifted uncomfortably, unable to meet Mefune's gaze. "Samar noticed something was off when he returned to his office after you had searched it. He thought I was the one who had stolen them, and he was furious. I had to give him something, or I probably wouldn't still be here."

"So, you did tell him it was Mefune who took the pages?" Altaira asked, surprised he had so willingly admitted it.

"Not directly," he quickly corrected, looking to Mefune. "I only told him that maybe he should consider that others on the Council didn't like his plans but wouldn't speak up. Then when he asked where I had been that morning—he confronted me the day you told us about the pages—I reminded him I was on patrol like the rest of the Council. I didn't think it would be enough for him to figure out that you found the pages, but I guess since you missed the patrol, he realized it was you."

Mefune shook his head, clearly annoyed. "Why didn't you point him towards someone else on the Council?"

"I don't know—I panicked! I'm sorry," Garrett defended, shrinking slightly as he took a step back. "You weren't the only one who missed the patrol. Honestly, I don't know how he guessed it was you."

"Samar won't trust me now. Even if he doesn't find evidence I was there, he's just paranoid enough that he'll write me off anyway," Mefune grumbled, shaking his head.

"I guess you'll have to leave the snooping to the rest of us," Altaira sighed.

"It's not that simple. If he catches on to the fact that you have a connection to me, he won't trust you either," Mefune continued. "He'll be watching us now, making it nearly impossible to find the information we need for our plan."

"I'm sorry. I really wasn't trying to sabotage you," Garrett stated with a shake of his head.

"Then why does it seem you're trying so hard to convince us to leave this alone?" Altaira asked.

"I...." Garrett hesitated, looking conflicted. "Because...I've known about Samar's plans for a long time now, and this isn't the first time I've been dragged into an effort to stop him."

Altaira's brow furrowed in confusion. "What do you mean?"

"The reason Creta died was because the two of us were trying to take down Samar." He ran a weary hand through his hair. "Samar approached me about his plans to attack the Auraes when he first started actively recruiting a few years ago. I played it off as if I wasn't interested in helping but wouldn't hinder him either. Then I told Creta, hoping someone with more seniority would be able to handle it and I could back out, but he dragged me along. When Samar realized what we were trying to stop him, he made me help him remove Creta. I thought he intended to just force him to resign. I didn't think it would end up with him dead. I tried to warn Creta, but he wouldn't listen."

He glanced at Mefune. "The minute you got elected, I realized you would follow right in Creta's footsteps, so I tried to warn you." He shook his head, letting out a small, bitter huff.

"Look where it got me. Right back to square one, watching someone run themselves into the ground trying to fight Samar."

Mefune seemed to contemplate this information for a moment. "So you had a hand in Creta's death," he stated softly, his voice colder now as he studied Garrett. Altaira shifted nervously. The look in his eyes sent a shiver down her spine, and she hadn't missed how he had tensed slightly, his grip tightening on the sheathed sword he carried in one hand. Would Mefune kill Garrett if the fool admitted to helping Samar kill Creta? Watching him now, Altaira didn't doubt he was capable of it. She bit her lip as she debated what she was supposed to do if it did come to blows.

"No! Not directly," Garrett quickly corrected as he paled slightly, clearly not missing Mefune's anger. "I just misled him, so he didn't realize Samar was on to him. But when I realized what Samar had planned for him, I tried to stop it, but I was too late. Creta knew why he was sick, but neither of us could figure out what Samar was using or how he was poisoning Creta. He even left headquarters for a time, but didn't get any better." He shook his head again in frustration, as if reflecting on the problem still upset him. He seemed to genuinely mean he hadn't meant Creta any harm.

Mefune didn't seem satisfied. "Who's to say you won't turn on us as well the minute things get difficult?" he wondered softly.

"I won't!" Garrett protested. "I already saw Samar kill one person. I'm not about to let him get away with it again."

"You sort of already did with the journal pages, though," Altaira pointed out.

"I know, I..." Garrett faltered, then let out a heavy sigh. "This is another reason I don't want to be involved. Samar already knows not to trust me. He knows I'll cave to him, meaning I'll always be a weak link in your plans."

"Then give us what we need to take him down quickly. Help us prove he killed Creta," Altaira pressed.

Garrett shook his head. "I would if I could."

"No, you're just willing to let Creta's murder go unpunished to save your own skin," Mefune griped.

Garrett shook his head again, more vigorously this time. "No! I would speak up if I had any evidence that would hold up! I only know bits and pieces, nothing substantial. Samar's a creative liar—he'd easily find ways to dismiss what I do have, or worse, turn it against us. I promise, Mefune, I would do anything to fix what happened to Creta. I regret every bit of it. That's why I'm trying so hard to keep you out of this. I know Creta wouldn't want you to die trying to fix this."

"He also wouldn't want us to stand by and watch the Brotherhood and Auraes turn against each other because doing something about it is a little risky to ourselves," Mefune countered forcefully. Then he shook his head, pressing his lips into a thin line. After a pause, he continued in a slightly calmer tone, "I realize I'll get nowhere debating this with you. Let's just get this trip over with." Then he met Garrett's gaze and added, "Don't make me regret forgiving you for telling Samar I found the journal pages." With that, he started into the forest, setting a surprisingly brisk pace.

Garrett sighed again, staring after Mefune, his expression conflicted. "Why do I get the feeling I just made a big mistake telling him the truth?"

"It's no surprise you feel that way, considering how upset Mefune is now," Altaira reluctantly agreed.

Garrett glanced at her. "I can't figure out if he was angry with me or Samar," he stated, his worry written all over his face. "Samar's bad enough. I don't need Mefune as an enemy as well."

Unsure of what to say to reassure him, she didn't bother replying. Part of her couldn't help but agree—she didn't want to see what would happen if Mefune ever had a chance for revenge against Samar. She also wasn't entirely convinced Garrett was safe from his anger, either.

Shaking his head with his shoulders slumped in defeat, Garrett numbly started after Mefune. After a moment more, Altaira followed, wondering just how the rest of their trip would turn out.

— ✑ —

Mefune

Mefune pressed into the forest, caring little if Altaira and Garrett followed. He wanted nothing more than to be alone because he wasn't sure how much longer he could control his anger.

Part of him wondered why Garrett's confession made him so upset. He had known for a while now that Creta had been murdered, and it hadn't upset him this much before. Maybe it was because a part of him had always doubted Garrett's claim. Creta had been clever. It seemed hard to believe Samar had fooled him and he had died because of it. Or maybe it was because part of him was still in denial the old medic was actually gone. It was easy to pretend he had just wandered into the forest again, as he often did.

But something about Garrett's confession, about realizing he could very well be meeting the gaze of Creta's murderer, had set him over the edge. And honestly, he wasn't entirely angry with Garrett. He was angry with Samar for manipulating him into helping him kill Creta. He wasn't sure how valid Garrett's account was, but it sounded like he had tried to make the right decision in the end. Unfortunately for Garrett, he had been present there in the forest, not Samar, so he bore the weight of Mefune's anger. And he would never fully trust Garrett again.

It made him nervous thinking of how angry the whole situation had made him. It had been a long time since he had felt that angry, and he knew all too well rage like that only drove him to do things he would regret. Like killing Samar. The thought had crossed his mind—it would be justified, he told himself. Murder for murder. But he was trying to be the better man. He didn't need Samar's blood on his hands, and it would serve no real purpose other than to add another regret to a list he already wished was much shorter.

But there was more than one way to make a man suffer for his crimes. He would see Samar's undoing, one way or another. That he was sure of.

The trio pressed on, Altaira and Garrett giving Mefune his space, which was probably for the best. When they reached the western shore, it was growing dark. They made their way down to the caves carved into the cliff side, staying far away from the sharp drop-off to their left. By the time they reached the cave, Mefune felt a bit more level-headed, but still way too restless to sleep, so he volunteered to take first watch. They hastily built a fire near the cave entrance, and then Garrett and Altaira settled down to rest farther into the cave.

Mefune sat on the edge of the cliff, staring out at the sea. His sigh billowed before him in a cloud of white as the temperature dropped low enough to make it chilly, but he didn't mind. The fire behind him warmed the cliff edge enough that it wasn't unbearably cold. It was too dark to make out much more than the white caps of the waves as they curled towards the cliffs far below, but he stared at the endless blackness of the ocean anyway, allowing the rhythmical pattern to calm him. Farther north, a waterfall poured over the edge of the cliffs, but its roar was only a gentle hum from this distance. He could still make out the white foam rising from where the falls met the ocean far below. The whole scene was surprisingly soothing, and he let his thoughts wander, wanting to put the events of the day behind him.

Altaira appeared a few hours later, her arms hugging her body in an attempt to preserve the warmth of the sleeping bag she had left behind. "You want to switch now?" she asked softly.

Finding himself still reluctant to sleep, he shook his head slightly. "I'm fine for a bit longer."

"Well, I can't sleep either, so mind if I join you?"

Deciding he wouldn't mind the company, he nodded slightly. Altaira sunk to the ground near the fire, tucking her knees against her chest and resting her arms atop them. "It's a beautiful night," she commented, her gaze on the stars above. "No moon, though. The Tarapor are probably in a frenzy tonight."

"Probably," Mefune agreed, his gaze on the sky as well.

They fell silent for a long moment. "I...I'm sorry about Creta," Altaira suddenly stated.

Mefune glanced at her, not sure how to respond. "It's in the past. There's no reason to dwell on it now," he muttered eventually, but it was hard to miss the insincerity in his voice. It wasn't an easy issue to dismiss.

"Yeah, that's what we tell ourselves, but it still hurts," she stated, the bitterness weighing down her words. Mefune turned away, staring down at the ocean again, worried the conversation would make his anger return.

"I remember when my mom told me about what happened to my dad," Altaira continued softly. "Revenge was my only thought for days. Nobody deserves to die the way he and Creta did."

This brought Mefune's gaze back to Altaira. The dim light offered little details of her expression, but he didn't need to see it to know the look in her eyes. It was reflected in his own. She understood on a much deeper level than anyone else just how badly he needed to see Samar's plans undone. Sure, saving Verndale and the Brotherhood from a potential war was plenty of motivation, but it became personal when the Council's corruption had targeted people close to them.

Samar is a fool for making an enemy out of us, he thought. "I guess Creta deserves to be avenged as much as your father does."

"He does," Altaira agreed readily.

"And I intend to," Mefune added.

She nodded slightly. Meeting his gaze, she smiled softly and told him, "I have to at least admit, Garrett is right; this could get ugly. But I'll help, wherever it takes you."

He nodded, grateful for the support. They fell silent, and for once, he found he was comfortable in her presence, enjoying the night in companionable silence. Now that they had finally realized just how entirely their goals aligned, it seemed they could put the last of their old animosity aside.

Altaira

The following morning, the trio climbed back up to the top of the cliffs and started into the forest again. "We shouldn't have to go much farther to find Tarapor," Mefune informed Altaira and Garrett. "The last patrol covers up to the river just north of here, but they only pass through here once every two weeks."

Altaira nodded. "How many are we going to take back?" she wondered.

"One or two?" Mefune guessed.

"That's it?" Garrett stated, sounding surprised.

"We have to drag them all the way back. Keeping them contained, and us safe isn't going to be easy. I don't want to take too many at once," Mefune replied.

"Maybe we should have gone to the lake. It would have been closer," Altaira muttered, sharing Garrett's disappointment a bit. It seemed they had traveled a long way to accomplish very little.

"It's too late for that now," Garrett dismissed with a wave of his hand. "Let's just get this over with."

They fell silent as they traveled. Altaira scanned the forest for the Tarapor, wondering if they would bother being out in the day. They usually hunted at night, but sometimes their desperation would draw them out even during the day. Their numbers would be fewer if they were out, meaning catching them would be easier.

Eventually, they neared the river that fed into the waterfall they had seen the night before. Here, it moved at a lazy pace, not yet caught in the frenzy of the waterfall, so it would be easy to cross.

But before they had reached the banks, Mefune paused. "Did you see that?" he muttered, his gaze glued to a part of the forest to their right, his hand straying for his sword.

"Tarapor?" Garrett asked.

"I think so," Mefune confirmed.

"How many?" Garrett wondered as he reached for his sword.

Mefune shrugged slightly. "Couldn't tell, but they rarely travel alone."

As if his words had summoned them, Altaira noticed movement through the trees to her right. *Here we go,* she thought, frowning slightly as she, too, reached for her weapon. Just as her hand closed around the grip of her sword, she heard a screech behind her and whirled, raising the weapon as she did. The Tarapor that had launched itself at her met with her blade, dying quickly. Garrett and Mefune drew their weapons as more Tarapor joined the fight. Luckily, it didn't seem like a large group, but even one or two were deadly. No mistakes could be made.

Just as she finished off one Tarapor and turned to search for more, a large Tarapor slammed into her from behind with impressive force. The impact sent her flying forward, her sword falling from her grasp as she fell in a heap. Her head smacked painfully into the ground, and she lost awareness of her surroundings for a brief second.

Immediately, a Tarapor tried to take advantage of her fall by launching itself at her. She barely caught a glimpse of it as she rolled onto her side, and she only stopped it from burying its fangs into her neck by raising an arm. Though the action saved her from a potentially lethal wound, the beast simply latched onto her wrist instead. Pain shot through her arm, but it was quickly replaced by a numbing sensation that spread through her body as the Tarapor's poison leaked into the bite.

She knew she had precious little time before she would lose too much blood to recover, but thinking around the drug quickly proved difficult. She punched the Tarapor weakly with her free arm as she tried to escape its grasp, but the creature stayed firmly latched on, its claws digging deeply into her arm and hand to hold her in place. Realizing punching it was doing her no good, she kneed it hard in the side, but it simply shifted away.

Then she remembered the pair of knives she had brought. Pulling one free, she lunged upwards with what little strength she had left and buried the blade in its neck. It died with a screech, finally freeing her.

She rolled to her knees, crouching as she watched the forest around her, trying to shake herself free from the mind-numbing grip of the poison. Her heart raced too fast, her breath echoing in her ears, and her eyes wouldn't focus. Swallowing hard, she pushed herself to her feet sluggishly.

Drawing her second knife, she held the two blades tightly, wishing her hands would steady. She wasn't as proficient with the smaller weapons as she was with her sword—and she definitely preferred keeping the Tarapor a sword's length away—but she couldn't see the ground well enough to find her sword, so she would survive with the knives. She shook her head slightly to try to dislodge the fog. It was fading, but not fast enough.

Mefune appeared at her side, glancing at her with a concerned gaze. "Are you alright?" he asked.

"Still breathing," she managed, noticing how slurred the words sounded. Mefune shifted to stand back-to-back with her, and some of her fear faded, reassured with him to cover her. But he couldn't fight them all alone, so she forced herself to function, despite just wanting to curl up and sleep.

She managed to raise her knives in time to kill the next Tarapor before it could get a grip on her. She dodged the next one, whirling to stab it in the back as it passed by. The more she fought, the better she felt as instinct kicked in to keep her moving.

As the fog slowly cleared, she became more aware of her surroundings and began working in sync with Mefune. She was surprised how easy it was; all those years she had spent becoming familiar with his fighting style to defeat him made it surprisingly easy to know how he would act. They managed to push the Tarapor back enough that Altaira no longer felt they were in danger of losing.

"Remember to keep some of them alive," Garrett stated as he rejoined them.

"Right," Altaira muttered. Things had become so crazy that she had forgotten there was a purpose to the fight.

The rest of the Tarapor began to scatter as they realized this wasn't a fight they could win. As the last one disappeared into the trees, silence followed it, and Altaira stumbled to a halt, panting. She glanced at Mefune. Besides a shallow scrape on his cheek, she never would have guessed he had been in a fight.

Glancing at Garrett, he seemed mostly in-tact as well. *We survived,* she thought, feeling immensely relieved.

"Are any of them alive enough we can drag them back?" Garrett muttered between breaths. She noticed he didn't sheath his sword, as if waiting for the creatures to attack again.

Mefune kneeled at the side of one beast. "If they were dead, they would have decayed," he stated.

That was another weird fact about the Tarapor; once they died, the magic sustaining their bodies disappeared, and it immediately returned to whatever stage of decay it would have been in if it weren't for the magic preserving it. The trio was surrounded by many skeletons as if a battle had taken place there long ago, but amongst them were Tarapor still in-tact.

"Yeah, I know, but I'd hate to take injured ones, and they die on our way back," Garrett muttered.

"Let's take this one and that one," Mefune decided, gesturing to another near Altaira. "They seem less injured."

She nodded and then sheathed her knives. As she moved her wrist, she couldn't prevent a small hiss, grimacing slightly as the wound pulsed with a fresh wave of pain.

"You're injured," Garrett noticed.

"Yeah, but it's nothing bad."

"Did you get bitten?" Mefune asked.

Altaira nodded. Garrett let out a quiet, fearful curse, surprising Altaira until her poison-addled brain remembered why that was a problem. "Oh," she breathed, fear making her heart skip a beat.

Mefune straightened. "I have an antidote. Garrett, finish tying this one up," he stated, gesturing to the creature he had been fussing with. "Make sure it's secure." He and Garrett swapped places as Mefune approached her, pulling his bag off his shoulder as he did. Gesturing to a nearby fallen tree, he told her to sit as he began sifting through his bag.

She followed his instructions as she set her bag down and pulled her jacket off, allowing access to the wound. Working with it was surprisingly painful, causing her to grit her teeth as she pulled the fabric free to reveal the jagged scrapes and puncture wounds along her forearm and hand and the nasty bite on her wrist. The skin around the bite was black, with thin white and red circles surrounding it, and the blood that still seeped from it was a good few shades too dark.

"That doesn't look good," she muttered.

"It'll heal fine as long as I get this applied quickly enough," Mefune reassured her. He pulled a small vial with a silver liquid from his pack and broke the seal with a knife. Taking her arm, he carefully held it steady without irritating the many wounds, and then warned her, "This is going to hurt."

He poured the medicine into the bite, and it was like pumping fire into her veins. She resisted the urge to pull away from him, but couldn't prevent a gasp as she squeezed her eyes shut, her hands clenching into fists involuntarily. As the searing finally ebbed, she let out a shuddering breath. At least it had cleared the last of the fog from her mind.

"Man, that hurt worse than the original bite," she complained.

Mefune allowed a small smile. "Hey, at least you know it worked. The burning sensation was it purifying your bloodstream. You should be fine."

He disinfected the rest of the wounds, which stung but weren't nearly as bad as the cure had been. Then he carefully wrapped bandages around most of her arm and hand as the pain finally began to fade to a manageable level. "Keep it dry and clean, and make sure the bruising fades within a few days," he instructed as he finished. "If the bite doesn't seem to improve, you should probably see a medic."

"Thanks. How did you get so good at this?"

Mefune's smile turned to a smirk as he began gathering his things. "Before Creta was elected to the Council, he had a habit of disappearing into the forest for weeks, and he always dragged me with him. Back then, the Tarapor swarmed the entire forest. I had to learn pretty quickly how to survive in those conditions."

Altaira let out an amused huff. "Sounds exciting," she joked.

"Very," Garrett deadpanned from his spot next to the Tarapor, reminding Altaira he was present. "I think this thing is effectively tied up. We should go before the rest come back."

Mefune stood, turning back to the Tarapor, which was now somewhat conscious and weakly struggling against its bonds. "This should be interesting," he mused apprehensively, before hauling the creature to its feet. Garrett and Altaira moved to help, and they started back into the trees the way they had come.

CHAPTER THIRTEEN
LEVERAGE

Altaira

Thankfully, they managed to make it back to base without incident. Garrett found Samar, and they handed the Tarapor over to him before heading their separate ways. Altaira made her way to her room, desperate for a shower and some painkillers. Her arm ached, and she was exhausted.

Just as she finished dressing and re-bandaging her arm after her shower, she heard a knock at her door. Grumbling to herself about her interrupted nap, she wrapped her still-dripping hair in a towel and went to the door. Opening it, she realized it was Daya, which lightened her disappointment slightly. Given she was dressed in her uniform, Altaira guessed she had either just left a Council meeting or was heading to one.

As Altaira invited her in, Daya asked, "Where have you been the past few days?" Then her gaze found Altaira's bandaged wrist, and her eyes widened slightly. "What happened?"

"I'm fine, just a small scratch," Altaira dismissed quickly, deciding she didn't need to let her know just how close she had come to dying.

Daya eyed her with one eyebrow raised, clearly knowing it was more than just a scratch simply by the length of the bandaging. Thankfully, instead of pressing the matter, she asked, "What were you doing?"

The pair moved to her couch as Altaira filled her in on their little adventure, including all she and Mefune had learned about Garrett.

"Wow," Daya muttered as she finished. "I wouldn't have guessed all that—about how Creta died or about Garrett."

"I know. It's pretty shocking," Altaira agreed as she stood and made her way to the kitchen to grab a glass of milk and some pain pills. "Mefune was pretty upset, but I think he's elected to let Garret slide. He's even more determined to stop Samar now."

"I don't blame him. The sooner we're rid of that worm, the better," Daya grumbled.

Altaira couldn't help but agree. After downing the medicine and most of the glass of milk, she asked, "Anything new happen while I was gone?"

"The Brotherhood has been talking nonstop about Ezequiel's arrest. Samar has been trying to cover up why he was arrested—and make the Auraes into the bad guys—but he's not having much luck convincing anyone. So I guess Mefune's plan is sort of working," Daya told her. "It's just not moving very fast."

"We didn't think it would," Altair admitted as she rejoined her on the couch.

"Yeah, I just hope we make enough of a dent in Samar's following before it's too late," Daya muttered. Then she shook her head and let out a small sigh. "Anyway, the last of the Council arrived just a few hours ago. They're getting ready to start the voting process, so I should probably get going. I just wanted to stop by and see if you were back from wherever you had disappeared to," Daya informed her.

Altaira nodded. "Come tell me how it went when it's over, alright? I'm going to take a nap," she decided as she finished her milk and wandered back towards her bedroom.

"Sleep well," Daya told her as she headed out.

After sleeping for roughly an hour, Altaira woke and decided to get some dinner in the dining hall. She made her way down and then claimed her food and a table, content to enjoy her meal alone.

Soon after, a large group began pouring in; she noticed it mainly consisted of Council members. She spotted Daya, Mefune, and Garrett in the crowd and waved them over. "How did it go?" she wondered.

Daya smirked as she set her plate down and dug into her dinner. "Believe it or not, the vote actually fell in your favor."

Altaira simply stared at her friend for a solid moment, unsure she had heard her correctly. "Wait, they voted me in? Seriously?" she wondered once she found her voice.

Garrett chuckled. "Can't say that I'm surprised. You are one of our best," he pointed out, amused by her surprise.

"Huh," Altaira muttered. A spot on the Council. It seemed too good to be true. She shook her head in disbelief. "Well. That's a pleasant surprise."

"The first one in weeks," Daya agreed.

"They'll make it official in the next couple of days after Samar makes sure you want the position," Mefune told her.

"The best part is, you'll be reassigned to our patrol, so we'll all get to work more closely together, and regular gatherings like these will seem less suspicious," Daya added.

"That'll be good," Altaira managed, but she was still focused on the announcement. Then she chuckled slightly. "I guess I get to join in on the drama now."

Mefune smirked slightly. "Welcome aboard," he stated as he raised his glass in a toast.

Daya laughed and joined in, and Altaira did too, smirking. Garrett reluctantly joined, but she didn't miss his small smile. Even he had to admit that things were going better than anyone had expected.

_— ✍ —_

A couple of days after Altaira's election, she sat in her new office, still trying to grow accustomed to the space. She and Daya had spent most of the days before cleaning out Ezequiel's belongings. Now the room felt bare, but decorating wasn't high on her list of priorities. In all her time around Daya, she had never once grasped just how much she had to do as a Council member. Now, a tiny part of her regretted being so ambitious— she was struggling to catch up.

Her job would be overseeing region five, which included the Mexico City, Houston, and Miami areas. Those Council members would report to her so she could keep the Council appraised of their situation. They also relied on her to relay information from the Council leader, approve recruitment campaigns, and handle any reassignments between areas.

After a very brief training from Garrett—which mainly was him repeating, "This is what I do, but you can manage your region however you would like" over and over—she was left alone. Over the next few days, she found herself trying to catch up on what notes Ezequiel had left and contact the Council members who were supposed to report to her. That was easier said than done, considering how she had to communicate with them. She spent a painful amount of time piecing together information over long strings of written messages. It left her wishing she had an aura so she could talk to them or didn't have to rely on magic to communicate. She also had to account for time differences—between her and the three areas, she was working with three different time zones. Now, she understood why many Council members found the Auraes' strict ban on tech so annoying.

She was working her way through another stack of papers when Mefune stopped by. He knocked on the doorframe, and when she glanced up, he walked to her desk and handed her a paper. "A message from Jocelyn for you."

"Jocelyn?" she repeated, wondering why the sentinel would want to speak to her. Briefly, she wondered why Mefune had the message before she remembered, as Raidenya's Council member, he was the official contact between Verndale and headquarters.

She turned her attention to the note, which read: *Ezequiel has requested to speak with you. The case against him is moving forward well, so it won't impact anything if you choose not to. However, he's claiming to have information about something that may be important to you and the Brotherhood Council, but he won't speak to anyone but you. Please come to my office in the capitol building if you choose to.*

Altaira studied the note in surprise, amazed Ezequiel had reached out to her. *What if this has something to do with my father?* "Did you read what it said?"

He nodded. "I had to, to write it down."

She nodded. "Think it's worth looking into?"

"What do you think?"

"I would like to think he might know what happened to my father. But this could just be a desperate move on his part to try to get out of trouble," Altaira responded.

Mefune shrugged slightly. "I'd go. Jocelyn said it wouldn't hurt anything if you talked to him, didn't she?"

She nodded. "Yeah. I think I will go. Cover for me if the Council asks where I'm at, alright?" He nodded, so she gathered her things and started out.

When she reached Verndale, she immediately headed for the capitol building to find Jocelyn in her office. She glanced up when Altaira neared and said, "Can I help you?"

Realizing Jocelyn must not recognize her, Altaira told her, "I'm Altaira Conover. I received your message about Ezequiel and decided it was best I speak to him."

Jocelyn's confusion faded, replaced by recognition as she nodded. "Ah, right. Follow me, please." She stepped from the office, gesturing for Altaira to follow.

The two made their way to the prison, which was only a few blocks away from the capitol building. There, Jocelyn led her down a small side hallway away from the cell blocks and administration area. She paused and gestured to a locked door.

"He's in there." Then she glanced at the sword at Altaira's side. "But first, I'll be needing that. I can't allow weapons in the prison."

Altaira resisted the urge to roll her eyes as she detached the sword from her belt and handed it to Jocelyn. The sentinel took the weapon with a nod and said, "I'll be close if you need anything."

Altaira nodded, so Jocelyn unlocked the door and allowed her in. Inside, Ezequiel sat at a small table, his gaze locked on the wooden surface, his expression tense. "So, you said you had something to tell me?" Altaira stated.

Ezequiel's gaze flicked up to her, and the amount of hatred she saw there surprised her. Then he glanced at Jocelyn over Altaira's shoulder. "Yeah, but she has to leave."

Jocelyn looked to Altaira for confirmation, who nodded, so she left, shutting the door behind her. Turning back to Ezequiel, Altaira moved to sit across the table from him. Letting out a sigh, she folded her arms and settled in. She had the feeling this wouldn't be a quick conversation. "Well then, get on with it," she urged.

"I know you brought those journal pages to Ila," he started. He shifted slightly, clearly restless.

"What makes you think that?" she wondered, one eyebrow raised in surprise. She couldn't help but be a bit worried he had guessed so easily, and if he had been given a chance to tell anyone else on the Council of his suspicion.

As if sensing her worry, he shook his head slightly. "Don't worry, the rest of the Council doesn't know, and they probably won't figure it out."

"Then how did you guess?" Altaira wondered.

Ezequiel shrugged slightly. "I know something they don't. Alec was your father. Somehow, they haven't connected the dots, probably because you look nothing like him."

"Ah," Altaira muttered. She hadn't realized it wasn't common knowledge her parents had been members of the Brotherhood. It wasn't like she had made any effort to keep it to herself, and she would have guessed at least somebody would have recognized her last name. It hadn't been that long ago that her father had died and her mother had left, and she was sure many of the older generations had served around them. But now that she knew the Council wasn't aware of her relation to Alec, she found herself grateful.

"And I know why you brought the pages forward," Ezequiel continued. "You think I had something to do with your father's murder."

"Did you?" Altaira asked. It was the first time someone on the Council had confirmed her father hadn't died of natural causes. She found herself conflicted by this—though it meant all her efforts hadn't been waisted, it only added to the sad truth that the Council had deviated from its intended purpose much farther than most would even guess.

"No," Ezequiel denied with a shake of his head. "But I know who killed him and why."

Altaira sat up straighter. This was something she desperately wanted to know, but she did her best not to allow Ezequiel to realize this. She didn't know what he wanted yet, and she didn't want to back herself into a corner. "So, tell me who did it," she pressed, trying her best to keep her voice neutral.

Ezequiel shook his head. "Not yet. First, you have to swear to help me."

Altaira only barely prevented the snort of contempt. "Why in the world would I help you?"

This clearly didn't sit well with him, but he contained his annoyance, and in a somewhat civil tone he told her, "Because I'm the only one who can stop Samar from murdering everyone."

This time, she couldn't prevent a small bemused chuckle as she shook her head slightly. "Even if Samar could somehow murder *everyone*, what are you going to do to stop it? Stop trying so hard to sell yourself for better than what you are. You're no hero; you're just a crooked guy who wants to get out of jail free."

"Listen to me!" Ezequiel snapped, slapping his hand on the table. Altaira startled slightly, sobering at the intensity of his stare and the sudden change in demeanor. "I know it sounds ridiculous, but Samar is—" he suddenly stopped, as if he realized he was starting to explain before he had what he wanted in exchange. He contained his frustration with concerted effort as he settled back into his chair, his hands pressed against the table before him. "Look, just promise you'll get me pardoned, and I'll tell you everything."

Altaira's gaze narrowed slightly as she processed all this. A pardon was a lot to ask for, and something only Mariea would be able to hand down, but it seemed Ezequiel didn't know that or didn't care. Altaira would prefer he rotted in a cell for the rest of his life for his part in her father's murder, but she doubted that would happen even if the case against him went well; he hadn't committed a serious enough crime for a long sentence, and so far, there was no link to Alec's death. She also had to admit she needed the information he had. It could very well lead to a solution for Samar's schemes *and* avenge her father.

"Fine, I'll talk to Jocelyn after we're finished. Tell me what you know."

Ezequiel let out a relieved sigh, sinking back into the chair as some semblance of calm settled over him. "Samar isn't working alone," he began.

"We know that," Altaira responded, immediately worried she had promised a pardon for nothing.

"You probably do know about the other Council members. But I'm not talking about them," Ezequiel corrected. "He has a contact, someone who isn't a member of the Brotherhood, who's directing his actions."

"Do you have a name?" Altaira asked, wondering why Ezequiel was being so vague.

"No. I've never seen him. But it's the reason your father died. He found out about this contact, so they ordered Samar to kill him."

Altaira's brow furrowed in confusion. She couldn't help but doubt knowing of one man's existence would be enough to urge someone to kill her father. "And how do you know all this?"

"I overheard Samar planned to do Alec in. I was pretty sure he had evidence about our deal, so if Alec ended up dead and the sentinels found that evidence, I knew I would be the first suspect on their list. So I went to his place, searching for the evidence. I didn't find it in time—it ended up with Samar—but what I did find was information about Samar's secret meetings with that contact of his. I've kept it to myself all this time because I knew Samar had dirt against me, and he could still frame me for Alec's murder. But now that has come forward, he has no bargaining chip, so I'm willing to tell you what I know."

He reached into his coat pocket and pulled out a piece of paper that had clearly been handled a lot through the years—it was folded several times, with faint crease marks that hinted at refolding, and the edges of the folds were soft and fraying. He carefully unfolded it and slid it to her.

"This is another page from Alec's journal. It shows the meeting schedule Samar followed. It was all speculative, but I've pieced together what he didn't know and confirmed what he did have. Samar doesn't know I know about this. If he did, there's no way he would have allowed the Auraes to take me alive. If you can find out who this contact is and get evidence that he's a threat to the Auraes, you'll have all you need to remove Samar from power."

Altaira stared at the page, trying to commit it all to memory. "So I can take this, then?"

"If you hold up your end of the bargain."

Altaira nodded. "I'll do what I can," she stated quickly.

He looked disappointed, his shoulders slumping slightly. "You never intended to help me." She paused, unable to deny it. He looked so dejected. Shrugging slightly, he sunk back into his chair. "Fine then. At least you know the truth. Whoever this man is, he's clearly dangerous. I don't want anyone else dying because of this."

She frowned slightly, suddenly feeling a bit sympathetic. It seemed, despite how desperate Ezequiel had been to save himself, at least part of him had wanted to share because it was the right thing to do.

Letting out a small sigh, she told him, "Like I said, I'll see what I can do. I don't have the power to pardon you, so I can't guarantee that. But Mariea does, and she's reasonable. If Jocelyn won't listen to me, I'll talk to Mariea when she gets back."

He nodded slightly. "I guess that's all I can ask at the end of the day." Then he frowned slightly, and his gaze flicked to the table. "I am sorry about what happened to Alec. He was a good man. I should have done something to stop Samar instead of worrying about my own skin. I was just young and stupid."

Altaira nodded, glancing away slightly as she resisted the urge to agree with him. By the look on his face, she guessed he had spent plenty of time torturing himself over the issue. She didn't need to add to his suffering. "Well, you did the right thing in the end. I promise we'll keep Samar from getting away with anything else like this."

Ezequiel nodded, so she left, taking the paper with her. She folded it and placed it into her pocket before meeting Jocelyn at the end of the hall. The sentinel glanced up as she noticed Altaira approaching and asked, "What did he want?"

"Nothing important," Altaira replied, deciding she would talk to Jocelyn about the pardon later. For now, she wanted to keep the information she had to herself. "He'll say whatever he can to get out of trouble."

Jocelyn shook her head slightly. "The desperation of the guilty always amazes me. I'm sorry you had to come all the way here for nothing."

"It's fine," Altaira said with a shrug. "The walk was nice. But I really should be getting back to work." Jocelyn nodded and handed back her sword before bidding her farewell.

When Altaira made it back to base, she immediately sought out Mefune. She found him alone in the basement gym, and he was just wrapping up a good workout, by the looks of it.

He noticed her approaching and asked, "How'd it go?"

When she was sure they were alone, she allowed a small smile and pulled the paper Ezequiel had given her from her pocket to hold it up between them.

"What's this?" he asked as he grabbed a water bottle from the cabinet and took a long drink from it.

"All the evidence we need to take down Samar. Ezequiel told me his whole scheme has some sort of outside connection. This paper has locations and times of their meetings." She handed it over to him.

After wiping his hands off on a towel, he carefully unfolded the paper and studied it. "This is surprisingly detailed," he mused, clearly amazed by what she had brought him. "Where did Ezequiel get this?"

"Long story short, from my father. This bit of information is apparently what caused Samar to order his murder."

Mefune sobered. "So, in other words, we should be very careful with this, and who knows that we have it."

Altaira nodded, catching on to his meaning. If Samar had already killed once to protect his crimes, there was little chance he'd hesitate to do so a second or third time.

"So, who exactly is it that Samar is meeting with?" Mefune wondered.

"Don't know. But if we were to show up at one of these meetings, we could find out," Altaira suggested.

Mefune considered it for a moment. "It's risky. We'd have to be careful not to get caught."

"Yes, but if we could get proof that Samar is working with an outside source to jeopardize the safety of the island, we could get him arrested without risking the safety of the Brotherhood. Ila would have no reason to believe the Brotherhood is involved, so we wouldn't have to worry about starting a war."

Mefune nodded slightly, and she could tell he was tempted to go through with her idea, but he was still concerned about the risk. "You think we can trust Ezequiel?" he asked.

"He seemed sincere."

"I'm sure he did. If I were trying to lie my way out of trouble, I'd do my best to seem sincere as well," Mefune stated, and suddenly she caught on to his meaning.

"I...don't know. It's hard to say for sure. He said Samar wasn't aware he had this information. He seemed like he really wanted to make sure Samar couldn't hurt anyone else."

"Why not bring it up before now?" Mefune wondered. "If he was so worried about Samar, why not say something before he killed Alec or Creta?"

"Because he didn't know about it until after my father died, and Samar knew about his deal with Alec. He said he was afraid Samar would frame him for Alec's murder. I could see why he'd be worried about that. With the deal he and Alec had, it made sense for him to want Alec dead," Altaira explained.

Mefune nodded slightly, and then he let out a small sigh. "It's at least worth looking into. Do you recognize any of these places?" he asked, tapping the sheet of paper.

"No. Most of the references are vague. That's probably on purpose. But all of them include coordinates, so if we can get hold of a map of the island, we could locate them."

Mefune nodded. "Let me shower quick, and then we can start working on figuring them out."

Altaira nodded in agreement. "There's bound to be an updated map in the library. I'll track one down. Meet me at my place when you're ready."

Mefune nodded, so they went their separate ways. After a bit of searching, Altaira found the needed map and returned to her apartment with it. Mefune joined her a few minutes afterward. They spread the map out on the kitchen table, and then Altaira set the piece of paper down next to it.

"Alright, how do we want to do this?" Altaira asked.

"Think the library will miss this map if we accidentally forget to take it back?" Mefune wondered.

Altaira shrugged. "They had several."

"Alright. I say we just mark all the locations and label the next date they're supposed to be there. Then we can decide which one would be the easiest for us to eavesdrop on without getting caught."

Altaira nodded, so she went to grab the needed tools as Mefune claimed a seat. "I'll read the coordinates, and you mark them?" she suggested as she rejoined him and handed him the pen.

He nodded as he took the pen and turned the map towards him. She grabbed the paper, and they began.

It wasn't long before they had ten or so marks on the map. "Okay, now for the times of the meetings," Mefune stated as he turned to her.

Altaira glanced over the paper again. "There are time intervals listed next to some of the coordinates. Three weeks. Two months. And a second set of coordinates." She set the paper down, pointing to the first on the list. "Look, this one is labeled two weeks, and then the second set of coordinates matches the one listed down there."

"So they meet at that first location, and then two weeks later they meet at the second location?" Mefune guessed.

Altaira nodded. "That would make sense. It seems the last meeting took place here," she said, pointing to the fourth listed set of coordinates.

"Let's figure out when they'll be meeting at each of these locations next," Mefune suggested.

This took more effort than initially marking the coordinates. After Mefune read her the final list of coordinates without a date, she considered the paper for a moment and then muttered, "I guess they're meeting there tomorrow night."

He glanced up at her, surprised. "Wow. The others are months out at the least," he muttered. He wrote the date next to the mark and then tapped the pen on the map as he thought about it. "It's not that bad of a location either."

"Where is it?" Altaira asked as she leaned closer.

He pointed to the map. "It's actually at the cove," he told her. On the southern shore, near the Brotherhood's headquarters, there was a small cove that allowed one or two small ships access to the island. It was well hidden and hadn't been used since Verndale's docks had been developed to allow easier access from large passenger ships. It was almost guaranteed to be abandoned.

"Could we eavesdrop without getting caught?" Altaira wondered.

"Possibly. I haven't ever been down there myself, but if I remember right, the cliffs above the cove are covered in vegetation. I just don't know if we'd be able to hear anyone down there or really see anything if it's late at night—it looks like the meeting time is pretty late."

"Hmm," Altaira muttered, studying the map. "Do you know anywhere in the actual cove we could hide and overhear?"

"I don't know—the amount of land available changes with the tide. We'd risk ending up in water if we stayed there too long. If we left any footprints on our way in, they'd know they aren't alone. At that point, we'd have nowhere to run to. We'd be forced to fight our way out if confronted, and without knowing who this mysterious contact is, I'd really like to avoid that."

Altaira nodded, understanding. "When's the next one?"

"Not until June." His brow furrowed slightly as he considered that. "I wonder what they discuss to feel the need to meet so regularly and at consistent locations and times."

"Unless they're not just meeting to discuss things. It could be some sort of handoff," Altaira guessed.

"That would make more sense than just exchanging information," Mefune agreed with a slight nod. "But handoff of what?"

Altaira shrugged. "Your guess is as good as mine. Maybe that's why the budget has been tight; Samar's been stealing funds and sending them to his benefactor."

"Could be," Mefune muttered, but he didn't seem convinced. "Though he'd have to be taking funds from other bases. I have control over headquarters' funds now, and everything is accounted for."

"So, what else could be of value to this person?" Altaira muttered.

"Without knowing who it is, your guess is as good as mine," Mefune stated with a shrug. They fell silent as they debated it.

Then Altaira shrugged. "I don't know, I say we go to the cliffs tomorrow, see what we find, and then if we don't hear anything, we can try again in June. But considering we don't know when Samar intends to act on his plans against the Auraes, I don't think we can afford to pass up trying tomorrow."

Mefune nodded. "I agree."

"Should we tell the others about this?"

Mefune shook his head. "I don't trust Garrett to keep this quiet, and I don't want to risk Daya. Having this information might as well be a death sentence." Altaira nodded, frowning slightly as she was reminded just how dangerous Samar could be.

"Well then, I guess we're paying a late-night visit to this cove."

Mefune nodded, sighing slightly. "I just hope Ezequiel got his numbers right."

CHAPTER FOURTEEN
ESPIONAGE

Mefune

Mefune paused in a thicker clump of underbrush a few feet away from the top rim of the cove. The cover ahead was thinner than he had hoped, making it difficult to get closer without being spotted. The darkness would offer some protection, but with the bright moon above and the clear night sky, he worried it would be easy for anyone below to spot them moving near the top of the cliffs. However, if they wanted the endeavor to be productive, they still needed to get closer. He scanned their surroundings, debating the best path.

Altaira came to stand next to him. "Have you seen Samar?" she whispered.

"No, but I think he's here."

"What makes you so sure?"

He shrugged. "Just a feeling." Then he pointed to a clump of bushes growing near a few larger rocks. "If we want to get any closer, that's probably our best bet. Just stay low."

Altaira nodded, so he moved forward in a crouch in an attempt to stay out of view from anyone in the cove. As he claimed a spot up against the rock, Altaira joined him. She tried to peer through the bushes to the cove below, but quickly discovered what he already had; it was too dark, and the bushes were too thick to see through.

They listened in silence for a moment. Then, from below, Mefune heard a voice. It was nearly too far away to make out what was being said, so he leaned closer, straining to make it out.

"Is it done?" the voice asked. Mefune didn't recognize it. It sounded as though it belonged to a middle-aged man, and it carried a surprising weight to it. Whether it was the clearly British accent that caused it or the deep tone, Mefune wasn't sure. His mind dreamed up an image to go along with it; a well-dressed businessman in a suit and long trench coat, carrying a cane, his graying hair carefully maintained.

"Yes," came the reply, and it was clear this was Samar.

Altaira glanced his way, a knowing look in her eye—it seemed Ezequiel was telling the truth, and the information on the paper was accurate. Samar was meeting in secret with some unknown benefactor.

"So then our plans are safe?" the man asked.

Samar hesitated before replying. "I don't know. When he tried to threaten me, he said he had overheard only one of our meetings. But I'm not sure if he left evidence of them anywhere. I sent people to search, but nothing has come up yet. If this knowledge spreads—"

"Then we will continue as we have and remove anyone who would challenge us," the man finished, as if it was the simplest of things.

"You think they're talking about Ezequiel?" Mefune whispered.

Altaira shrugged. "He said he had never seen Samar's informant, but maybe he had?"

It made sense now why Samar hadn't put up more of a defense for Ezequiel when he was arrested. He wanted him out of the way because of the information he knew. But Mefune had a sinking feeling there was a chance removing Ezequiel from power wouldn't be enough for Samar. He would want him silenced.

He turned to Altaira, about to voice his concerns, but before he could say anything, a bright, bronze orb of light appeared next to Mefune. He froze, staring at it in surprise before his mind registered it could give them away. He quickly threw his coat over it, pulling it towards him.

"What was that?" the man asked below while Altaira shot Mefune a look that seemed to ask much of the same question.

"I don't know. You better go, just to be safe," Samar urged. Mefune heard quick footsteps on the stone below, and it sounded as though one pair was approaching.

He straightened partly, backing away from the cliff as he gestured for Altaira to follow. They quickly made their way back into the trees. Once under their cover, Mefune straightened and continued at a slow jog away from any path Samar would take back to headquarters. Part of him wanted to sprint away, but he maintained his pace, favoring stealth over speed. Altaira kept glancing over her shoulder as they went, clearly worried they would be followed, but it seemed nobody had noticed them.

Just to be sure, he continued a while into the quiet of the forest, his attention on his surroundings to make sure he didn't stumble across any other surprises—such as Tarapor. There wasn't much chance they'd find any this close to headquarters, but seeing how his luck was going so far that night, he wouldn't be too surprised if they managed to find the only ones in the area.

Once they were far enough away that Mefune felt it was safe to stop, he found a sheltered grove and turned back to face Altaira. "What happened?" she hissed.

"Jocelyn sent me a message. A very *inconveniently* timed message," he grumbled as he opened his coat and the orb flittered free.

Altaira sighed slightly. "Of course, one had to come tonight. So what does it say?"

In response, Mefune tapped the orb's surface, and it expanded to reveal a short handwritten message. Altaira stepped closer so she could read it as well. *"There has been an attempt on Ezequiel's life. I need to speak with the Council right away."*

"Well, that was quicker than I expected," Mefune muttered.

"Wait, you knew this was going to happen?" Altaira wondered.

He shook his head. "I just guessed. It seems Samar somehow learned Ezequiel knew of his meetings. That's what he was discussing with his contact in the cove. After what he did to Alec for learning of those meetings, I guessed he wouldn't let Ezequiel live to possibly spill his secrets to the Auraes. It seems I was right, unfortunately."

Altaira shook her head, a mixture of amazement and disbelief in her expression. "You would think Ezequiel would be safe in the center of Verndale, surrounded by the Auraes. How did Samar get away with an assassination attempt there?"

"I don't know, but I'd like to find out. Let's head to the city," Mefune decided as he dismissed the message with a wave of his hand. He glanced up at the sky to get his bearings quickly and then turned northeast towards Verndale.

As she fell into step next to him, Altaira asked, "Shouldn't we tell the rest of the Council? Jocelyn did ask to speak to all of them."

He shook his head slightly. "If there's any sort of evidence of what happened, I want to see it before Samar has the chance to get rid of it. If we hurry, we can make it to Verndale before word spreads to headquarters. We'll just tell her we were nearby." Altaira nodded, so Mefune picked up the pace, moving at a jog; they had a bit of a walk ahead of them, and he wanted to guarantee they'd beat Samar or anyone he sent to the city.

As they traveled, he couldn't help but contemplate how stressful things had become in a matter of minutes. Samar had murdered someone for the information Mefune now carried in his pocket. Another man had nearly been killed for overhearing the same type of meeting he and Altaira had just eavesdropped on. If anything, this put into perspective just how dangerous Samar really was.

That quickly made him realize they would be Samar's next target if he found out they had been at the cove that night. Part of Mefune began to regret going. They hadn't learned anything useful except confirming Ezequiel's speculations that Samar had a partner in his planning. Now, it seemed he had taken an unnecessary risk with little to no reward. He was sure he could handle Samar. But it didn't sit well with him that he had also risked Altaira.

Finally, they reached the city, and Mefune quickly made his way to the jail, Altaira following closely. They were met by a team of sentinels outside the front entrance. One stopped them and said, "Nobody's allowed inside right now. There's an active investigation going on."

"We know what happened. Jocelyn sent us a message requesting to speak with the Council. Where is she?" Mefune responded.

"Right here," Jocelyn stated from behind, so Mefune turned to her. "I'm grateful you were able to come so quickly. Has the rest of the Council been informed?"

"Not yet. We were in the area, so I figured I'd save everyone a trip and just find out what happened myself, then report back," Mefune replied.

Jocelyn nodded. "Come on, I'll fill you in on what I know." She gestured them inside, so the sentinels stepped aside and allowed the three to pass.

"So, is Ezequiel alive?" Altaira asked as they made their way to the cell blocks.

"Barely. I just got back from escorting him to the hospital," Jocelyn replied. She shook her head slightly. "Poor bloke was in bad shape. We're still not sure he'll make it through the night, but we're hoping."

She paused outside an open cell and gestured for them to look inside. After one glance, it was clear to Altaira why Ezequiel wasn't so well off—there was an impressive amount of blood pooled in a corner of the room, and some had splattered on the walls. The bed had been overturned, and the blanket lay in shreds on the floor. A couple of sentinels moved around the cramped room carefully, documenting the scene and looking for evidence.

"This happened a couple of hours ago. Ezequiel should be dead, but by some miracle, the guard on duty happened to walk by and see him in time to get a medic down here. From what I saw, he had a major wound to the back of the head, and he had been stabbed at least twice. It was clear they intended to kill him, but his attacker did a messy job of it. I think they were interrupted by an approaching guard, or Ezequiel put up more of a fight than anticipated. Either way, his wounds aren't fatal, but he's lost a lot of blood, and we don't know what damage the trauma to his head did to his brain."

Mefune let out a sigh. "So, if he did see who attacked him, there's a chance he won't even be able to tell us," he muttered.

"Right," Jocelyn agreed with a grim frown. "There were signs of a struggle, so I would bet he saw their face, unless the attacker was disguised. I'm just amazed whoever did this managed to slip past the sentinels on duty. It's not easy to get past our magics."

Mefune wasn't particularly familiar with sentinel magic, but he at least knew it allowed them a hyper-awareness of their surroundings that was particularly hard to fool. "So it's probably safe to assume whoever did this either didn't have an aura, so they couldn't be sensed, or is trained to mask himself from the sentinels."

"Which, of the two, I think it's most likely someone trained to mask himself," Jocelyn guessed.

"What makes you think that?" Altaira wondered.

Jocelyn glanced at her, clearly debating whether to answer, before she shrugged and said, "It's just a theory. We might not be able to sense someone without an aura, but that means they wouldn't be able to sense us either. They would have made mistakes. This person didn't."

"Interesting," Mefune muttered.

Jocelyn nodded. Then she turned to Altaira. "You were the last person to speak to him other than my staff. Did anything he said lead you to believe he might be attacked? Or did he mention anyone he might have been afraid of?"

Altaira glanced at Mefune, clearly wondering if she should mention Samar, but he wasn't sure how to respond without Jocelyn seeing. Already, the sentinel's gaze had passed from Altaira to him briefly, and he guessed she hadn't missed the silent exchange. "No," Altaira eventually sighed. "He was throwing around random accusations against multiple members of the Council. None of it seemed even marginally believable. But..."

she glanced to Mefune again, "We've been keeping an eye on those he mentioned, just in case."

"So, only the two of you are aware of what Ezequiel said?" Jocelyn asked.

Mefune nearly missed her carefully hidden suspicion. He realized it did seem odd only they knew of Ezequiel's accusations. As members of the Council, there was a chance they were threatened by them. It seemed Jocelyn had come to the same conclusion. He guessed she was wondering if they had tried to silence him.

"Do you mind if we speak with you privately for a moment?" he asked. Altaira glanced at him, looking a bit surprised.

Jocelyn nodded and gestured them farther down the hallway, where they were alone. After making sure nobody had followed them, Mefune told her, "In reality, we are looking into some of his accusations. Altaira came to me and Daya—who is also on the Council—because we were the only ones Ezequiel didn't mention. He seemed most suspicious of Samar, but nothing he said holds up so far. We're not dismissing it, but after this, I'd say it's worth saying someone somewhere wanted him silenced."

"Hmm. That's good to know, though it's concerning members of your Council—and especially Samar—might not be trustworthy. Do you think he had anything to do with it?"

"It's hard to say for sure at this point," Mefune responded.

Jocelyn nodded. "Will you keep me informed about what you learn?"

"We will as best as we can," Mefune agreed. "Right now, it's tough to know who to trust or what is accurate. But if we find solid proof of any of Ezequiel's accusations, we'll tell you so we can work through proper legal channels to deal with it."

This seemed to satisfy Jocelyn. She nodded. "Just out of curiosity, what were you doing out so late?"

"We just got back from running supplies to one of the more eastern patrol camps," Mefune responded, coming up with the first believable story off the top of his head. It was something on his to-do list; just yesterday, the patrol who had passed through there said the supplies were getting low. Unfortunately, as an alibi, he realized it was a bit weak—there was nobody else who could validate their story. Hopefully, the fact that he so quickly had an answer and seemed confident in it would be good enough.

"Is there anything else you would like us to see here?" Altaira wondered.

"No, that was pretty much it," Jocelyn said with a slight shrug. "I'll keep you updated on Ezequiel's condition."

Feeling he needed to warn Jocelyn somehow, Mefune carefully added, "Hopefully, the killer doesn't return to finish the job."

She shook her head slightly, her expression darkening. "If he does, we'll be ready this time." Mefune didn't doubt it.

With that, Altaira and Mefune started back towards base. It was impressively late now, and Mefune was growing weary. Altaira seemed tired too. But there was still a lot on both of their minds. The situation had left so many loose ends, and Mefune didn't care for it. He could only hope Samar hadn't spotted him or Altaira that night.

"We should probably lie low for a little while," he muttered to Altaira once they were back in the forest. She glanced at him and then nodded, her gaze falling to the ground. He wondered if she was as worried as he was. "It's just a precaution," he added. "Just until we're sure Samar didn't see either of us. I don't think he did, but..."

"Yeah, I get it," she stated softly as if she didn't want to follow that thought to conclusion.

"Good thing is, we know Samar is willing to act. We have a heads up and can be careful."

"I just wished we knew who Samar got to go after Ezequiel. He's a fighter, like us. He wasn't a small man, either. Whoever it was would have had to be strong and skilled."

"Not necessarily. If they caught Ezequiel by surprise, they had the advantage; he was weaponless and confined."

"True, I guess. I just wonder how they even got to him. Could it have been one of the sentinels?" Altaira wondered.

"Why would the Auraes help Samar?" Mefune wondered. Though, the question left him wondering if it was possible Samar had allies amongst the Auraes. People who were displeased with the current government might be easy enough to sway—though it didn't seem there were many, from what little he knew of Aurae politics.

Altaira simply shrugged, so the conversation faded. After a while, she stated, "I'm surprised you told Jocelyn we're suspicious of Samar."

"I had to give her something. I think she found it a bit suspicious that we were the only ones who knew about Ezequiel's accusations, and then he was attacked. The last thing I wanted was for her not to trust us. If we learn something about Samar, we're going to need to be able to prove it without a shadow of a doubt, or he could play it against us."

Altaira nodded. "We should probably fill Daya in on this then, just in case Jocelyn asks her about what we told her." Mefune nodded. After a moment, she asked, "So what do we do about Samar's secret contact?"

Mefune let out a small sigh, shaking his head. "I don't know. I feel like tonight ended up being an entire waste of time. We still don't know who he is or have solid proof he has any ill intentions towards the Brotherhood or the Auraes, despite how obvious it is that he does. And we can't wait until their next meeting in June to learn more. Plus, if Samar believes his meeting locations are compromised, he'll probably change things up."

Altaira nodded. "Do you think you'd get anywhere if you asked Samar about it?" she asked. Clearly, she didn't believe he would, but it seemed she had to ask, anyway.

"I doubt Samar will trust me with that level of information. He's been more tight-lipped after the thing with Garrett and the journal pages. The chances of him immediately lumping me with Ezequiel and Alec are high."

"So definitely not a good idea," Altaira grumbled with a shake of her head. "I guess we try to find evidence against other Council members and move forward with that plan."

Mefune nodded, but he had the feeling they were running out of time. Samar clearly wasn't as much of a fool as he would like to believe—he had caught Alec, Creta and Garrett, and

Ezequiel in their attempts to uncover his secrets. It was only a matter of time before he decided Mefune and possibly everyone connected to him was too much of a threat to keep around.

Which led him to wonder why Samar hadn't already confronted or attempted to silence him. If he was suspicious, it seemed reasonable to assume he would act. *Maybe he isn't as suspicious of me as I initially thought,* he mused. *Or could there be another reason he's leaving me alone?*

He shook his head slightly, quickly realizing the rabbit hole of anxiety that thought would take him down. He couldn't lose his nerve now, not when it was so blatantly obvious Samar had no intentions of showing mercy to anyone who may be an enemy. It seemed his life had now become a race against Samar. Whoever found out the truth first would win and most likely be the only party left. Or, they could both fail, and a war would start in the middle of it all.

CHAPTER FIFTEEN
FEAR OF THE DARK

Ila

Ila sat at her office, mentally going over the list of things she wanted to talk about during the Council meeting she had later that night. On the top of her list was updating the Council on Mariea's progress. The only unfortunate thing about that was she hadn't heard from Mariea since she had left Raidenya. It left her with depressingly little to report. And made her more than a little worried for her friend.

She let out a heavy sigh, swiveling in her chair to face the large window behind her. The sun was setting in the distance, reflecting brightly against the ocean far away and the city's buildings below. Life went on, as usual, but she had begun to sense a tension in the streets she hadn't ever felt on Raidenya. Despite how Ila and Gavin tried to keep the news under wrap, the public was getting restless over the mysterious attacks. It was hard to find it in her to keep reassuring them when she was starting to get just as impatient as they were. She wanted answers. She just didn't know where to turn for them.

She had tried to call Mariea several times since she left, with no luck. With the meeting quickly approaching, she decided to try once again. She figured she had waited long enough for

Mariea to be awake, so she brought her aura to light and crafted the necessary spell.

After a painfully long time, the golden orb before her expanded, and Mariea appeared before her. Ila let out a relieved sigh. "I was starting to think something had happened to you," she told her.

"No, nothing too major. Sorry I haven't called sooner," Mariea told her with a sheepish half-smile.

"Wait, nothing *too major*? That means something happened," Ila quickly questioned.

Mariea winced slightly. Clearly, she hadn't intended for Ila to read into her words too much. "There…was a bit of an incident at the airport. Mae and Bracken were arrested because their IDs weren't set up properly. Luckily, we got it cleared up."

Instantly, Ila's festering anger and frustration turned towards Samar, knowing he had been in charge of supplying Mariea and her companions with the needed documents to travel to New York safely. "The Brotherhood probably sabotaged you."

"I don't think they did. Cato, who runs the base in New York, was the one who helped us get everything fixed. If the Brotherhood sabotaged me, why would they help us fix it?"

"Still seems suspicious," Ila grumbled. She knew she'd never convince Mariea that the Brotherhood wasn't trustworthy, so she decided to change the subject. "Well, are things going well other than that? Have you learned anything useful?"

"Nothing yet, unfortunately, but I at least know where to look now. We're working on getting the funds we need to buy a boat from the Brotherhood."

"A boat?"

Mariea smiled slightly as she nodded. "I'm following a bread-crumb trail of sorts. My next destination is an island somewhere in the Caribbean. Considering it's uninhabited and not listed on any maps I've found, we decided sailing there ourselves was best."

Ila nodded, trying not to seem disappointed. "Any idea when you'll be back?"

Mariea shook her head. "No idea at this point. I'll do better keeping you updated, though."

Ila nodded. "I better let you go, then. I have a meeting to get to."

Mariea nodded, and the image faded. Sighing, Ila stood and made her way upstairs, where the other members of the Council were already starting to gather. Once again, Samar chose to show, which was both a relief and annoying. Ila would rather never have to interact with the man, but if she wanted to confront him about his latest crime, that unfortunately required him to be present.

She started the meeting as soon as the last member, Misha, joined them, and impatiently waited while everyone reported on their respective duties. She was disappointed but not surprised to hear of the growing number of attacks and that more were fatal. This only added to her anger. If Samar were trying to sabotage Mariea, that would only confirm her suspicion that the Brotherhood was somehow behind everything happening to the Auraes. She knew she wasn't alone in her beliefs—since his visit to the Brotherhood a few months ago, Gavin had struggled to trust them. Now, if she could only convince the rest of the Council.

When it was finally her turn, Ila told the group, "Mariea has made it to New York, though she ran into trouble upon arrival. For some reason, some of their IDs didn't work." She turned her gaze to Samar. "Do you know why this happened?"

"The New York base reported as such. I'm looking into it," Samar replied, but his tone suggested he couldn't care less what had happened.

"I'll wait anxiously for that report," Ila told him, making it clear she didn't intend to allow him to brush the matter aside. "I would hate for anything to happen to Mariea. It seems a bit suspicious that she'd be interrupted by something like this on such an important trip."

Samar's fist tightened on the table, his lazy posture and disinterest evaporating quickly as his gaze snapped to her. "Are you implying I purposefully sabotaged her?"

"No, of course not. But maybe someone who works for you did," Ila stated with a shrug.

"Making IDs for people who don't exist is far more complicated than you think. If you would just allow us to maintain false records for you, it wouldn't be so suspicious to the world's governments for people to just appear in their systems. Their computers and technology advance faster than your magic, and we're stuck using ancient technology in an attempt to keep up. We did our part as best as we could, considering the circumstances."

"Hmm," Ila muttered. It was clear she wasn't going to get anywhere with this argument, considering the Aureas were somewhat guilty of what he was saying. Ila hated technology. She much preferred using magic to solve their problems. "Well, like I said, I eagerly await that report." Samar seemed to debate arguing further, but then he nodded curtly and turned away.

The meeting went on, and by the time they wrapped everything up on the agenda, it was dark. This time of year, the sun set well before what Ila considered properly night. It didn't help that the meeting ran long. Since the attacks had started, she hated being out after dark, but she had made a point not to change her habits. She didn't want the people to see her fear. So, she had no choice but to walk home as planned.

Before heading home, she had a few things to grab from her office, so she headed there first. As she picked up her bag and reached to turn the desk lamp off, she heard a soft knock at the door and turned to notice Jocelyn standing in the doorway.

"Have a moment?" she asked.

"I was just on my way out. Can this wait until the morning?" Ila wondered, trying not to sound annoyed.

"No, but I'll be brief," Jocelyn stated, her voice stern, warranting no room for disagreement. That was one thing Ila admired about Jocelyn—she stood by her convictions and could be just as stubborn as Ila herself, something Mariea never seemed to manage. She'd give Jocelyn her time.

"What is it then?" she asked, abandoning the lamp and straightening to face Jocelyn.

"I'm worried your hatred towards the Brotherhood will stir up contention we do not need," Jocelyn stated bluntly.

Ila scoffed. "Please. I'm not doing anything but pursuing the truth."

"I'm almost certain the Brotherhood has nothing to do with the threat we're currently facing. You chastising Samar over every little thing will drive a wedge between us and them, one we cannot afford. If we have to fight off whatever is attacking us, we will most likely need their manpower," Jocelyn pressed.

Ila sighed, leaning against her desk as she folded her arms. "I'll admit, I can be a little biased. Old grudges are hard to let go of," she muttered, before looking up to meet Jocelyn's gaze. "You're sure you can trust them?"

"In this regard, positive."

Ila nodded. "Alright, I'll lay off of it for a while, I guess. But if I learn they are involved, I expect you to back me in removing them from the playing field."

Jocelyn nodded. "And I will if it comes to that. I just don't want a war on our hands." With that, she turned and left.

Ila watched her leave, then shook her head as she finished gathering her stuff. Jocelyn was a good fighter, even a good leader, but sometimes she missed the smaller nuances of the political side of their jobs. Ila wouldn't back down from protecting her people, even if nobody around her seemed to understand what she was doing. The Brotherhood wouldn't get away with crimes just because the Auraes needed them.

With that, she started outside, into the streets of Verndale. The city at night had always been a peaceful place. Despite Ila's mistrust of the darkness, she had always felt comfortable wandering the streets. As the nights grew warmer, more and more people were out, enjoying a night on the town, and such was true that night. A decent crowd bustled around the shops near campus, brightening the darkened city. For a while, Ila passed through them without thinking much of her surroundings, instead dwelling on the frustrating afternoon.

But as she moved farther from the busy throngs of downtown, she found herself more wary, her aura barely kept invisible. Despite her casual stance, she scanned the streets around her, feeling tense with anticipation for something she could not see. Something wasn't right—she swore she could sense it.

It's just these mysterious attacks that's got me all antsy, she thought, remembering Mariea telling her of her own close call. *But I don't need to worry. They've never been so close to the city center, so out in the open,* she told herself. *There are too many witnesses, too many sentinels.* Her reasoning did little to calm her nerves. Deciding stressing over it wasn't worth it, she picked up her pace, wanting to get home as soon as possible.

A scream from behind snapped her from her pretend calm as Ila whirled around, her golden aura flashing to view around her. Dark figures slunk through the night, lit by murky, ill-colored auras. They attacked a group of Auraes who had wandered from the main crowds like Ila.

As she rushed to assist them, she studied her enemy in the time it took her to reach them; they seemed human, nothing like the Tarapor, making her wonder if these beings weren't something different. And they knew how to use their auras. They met any resistance easily, and, as Ila watched, the Auraes began dying, too suddenly to make sense. One minute, they were fighting off their attacker; the next, they fell to the ground in agony.

She reached the group and quickly joined the fight, dragging one of the mysterious enemy away from his intended victim by the collar of his shirt. Before she could pull him far, he twisted from her grasp and quickly turned his attention to her. Her aura reacted naturally to block the acidic green energy he threw her way, but she was surprised by the strength of the attack.

Deciding she would need every advantage she could get, Ila called on an old favorite of hers—Fire Magic. Flames leaped to life to surround her fists just as she threw a punch at her attacker, managing to clip him on the chin before he could stumble out of her grasp. The flames caught on the scruff on his chin and quickly spread, burning unnaturally fast. It winked out almost as soon as the fire started, leaving nothing behind except for a pile of ash. Ila blinked in surprise but had little time to contemplate it; there were more enemies.

Noticing one approaching her from behind, she sent flames her way, but the woman dodged easily, moving with a grace Ila quickly envied. *What are these people? And why are they attacking us?* she wondered for the umpteenth time that night alone. Her attacker quickly closed the distance, despite Ila's best efforts to fend her off.

When she was a few feet away, Ila was suddenly engulfed in an unholy pain. Her aura shuddered, and she lost control of the flames as they winked from existence, and she collapsed. The intensity of her pain made her muscles seize up, paralyzing her. She couldn't even scream, despite how badly she wanted to.

Just before she blacked out, the pain left her. Gasping for air, she rolled onto her side and pushed herself up on one elbow. She looked around for her attacker with bleary eyes, but found instead a familiar figure standing over her. Arlen, her younger brother, contended with the woman who had attacked her. As she watched, still dazed, he quickly ended the fight, leaving behind another pile of ash.

Turning to her, he hurried to her side. "Arlen? What are you doing here?" she asked as he approached.

"Saving you, it seems," he replied, offering her a hand to help her up. Concern had replaced his usual bravado, despite how Ila knew he would try not to let it show.

She smiled slightly as she reached up to take his hand. "Well, thanks." Unsteadily, she rose to her feet, leaning heavily on him for support. Pain exploded through her head, briefly making it hard to focus on her surroundings, but it faded to a bearable level. *Man, what did she do to me?* Wanting to hide her apparent weakness, she attempted to stand straighter as she asked, "How did you know I needed help?"

"I'm a sentinel. It's my job to know when there's trouble, and it's even easier to know when my family is involved."

Another Aurae approached, bearing the markings of a medic. "Are you alright?" he asked Ila.

Annoyed that she had seemed weak, Ila quickly replied, "Besides the pounding headache and nausea, I'm fine." The medic nodded, heading off. By the looks of the crowd around her, she wasn't the only one who had been injured, and the medic had many to tend to.

Glancing at Arlen, she asked, "What were those things?"

"They're responsible for all the recent deaths. We don't know where they come from, what they are, or how to stop them. They're killing even the sentinels faster than we can keep up with, and they grow bolder with each attack. We can't catch them or find where they disappear to. And we can't fight them, either; somehow, they disable our auras," he admitted, looking grim.

"Is that what she did to my aura?" Ila wondered, attempting to bring it to light. It did, though its glow was weak and sporadic, and it made her headache worse—a clear-cut sign it had been stressed close to its limits by whatever the woman had done to her.

"Yeah. We haven't been able to figure it out. It's like they exhaust our auras instantly," Arlen agreed. "Did you hear your attacker use a spell before your aura freaked out or anything that might explain what happened?"

She sighed. "No. All I can tell you is it hurt like none other."

He nodded, looking a bit disappointed. "That's pretty much what everyone is saying," he grumbled.

Ila nodded, too tired to think of anything else to help at the moment. Glancing around, she took stock of the situation. The attackers had disappeared, and medics poured in to help those who had been involved in the fight. "Mind walking me home? I don't think we're needed here anymore."

He glanced around, obviously reluctant to leave, but then he relented with a nod. He helped her through the streets and the quickly growing crowd, his uniform and authoritative commands clearing a path. Finally, they reached her apartment. She let them in and then promptly sank into an armchair in the front room, letting out a heavy sigh.

"Will you be fine if I head back out?" Arlen inquired.

"Do you really need to leave so soon?" Ila asked in surprise.

He nodded. "That attack was a lot bigger than the others. And in a more populated area, too. They're getting bolder. Jocelyn will probably be calling in more sentinels. I'm sorry, I wish I could stay longer. I can find a medic if you don't feel well enough to be alone."

"I should be fine," she managed, her words heavy with exhaustion.

Obviously uncertain of that fact, he hesitated. "Here, let me get you something to drink before I leave. Water will help." He moved to the kitchen, which was adjacent to the seating area. He quickly found a cup and filled it with water from the dispenser on the fridge. Returning with it, he pressed it into her hands.

She took a sip, if only to make him feel better. She felt nauseous enough that she worried she wouldn't handle it well. But the cool liquid did seem to refresh her a bit, calming the ache in her head and settling her stomach.

Leaning back against the chair, she asked, "What are we going to do about this?"

"I don't know," Arlen admitted. He hesitated a moment and then sunk into the chair across the coffee table from her, despite his earlier comment about needing to leave. "What we really need is more people to defend the city. Ways to protect ourselves."

Suddenly, an idea came to her as her mind strayed to her conversation with Jocelyn earlier that evening. She *had* suggested the Brotherhood should help them fight off their attackers. "I know someone who has a ton of fighters ready to go."

"Who?"

"The Brotherhood," she stated, sitting up as the idea grew on her. The Brotherhood easily outnumbered the Auraes, and they were all trained to fight without auras, giving them an immediate advantage over this new enemy; their odd power to disable auras was useless. And, if Jocelyn's pleas earlier hadn't convinced Ila the Brotherhood wasn't involved in the attacks, her experiences that night had. Clearly, these beings wielded powers the auraless Brotherhood wouldn't be able to manage. But that didn't mean they couldn't do their part to help fight the new threat.

"You think they'll help?" Arlen wondered. He was well aware of the tension between the Brotherhood and the Auraes at the moment, and Ila's opinion of the matter.

"I'll make them," she decided, feeling determined. "I'm done playing their games. It's time they prove they're actually loyal to us. Now's their chance." She nodded, set on the idea now. "I'll speak to them tomorrow."

Arlen looked uncertain, but he simply nodded. He knew better than to argue with her. "I'll inform Jocelyn. She'll be grateful to know there may be backup coming."

Ila nodded. Jocelyn would be happy to know Ila had taken her advice to heart and even gone a step beyond. Then she let out a sigh, deciding she had done enough about it for tonight. "Now, I think I'm going to sleep," she announced before she unceremoniously finished off her glass of water and shuffled to her room.

$$- \wp -$$

Mefune

Their plans ground to a halt after Altaira's election and the fiasco with Ezequiel. Mefune still felt it wasn't safe to pry into the Council's business, at least for a little while. Ezequiel remained in a coma, and though there was a chance he'd wake up, Mefune wasn't optimistic.

Altaira didn't like waiting. It was quickly apparent she wasn't a patient person, and now that she knew Samar had been the one to order her father's murder, she was even more set on seeing an end to his power. Even Mefune had to admit he was growing frustrated with the current game of cat and mouse. But he knew he had to keep her from doing anything irrational in her eagerness.

So, on impulse, and to pass the time and give them a chance to talk when nobody would be suspicious, he decided to see if he could get her to train with him in the mornings. After dressing in light exercise clothes, he went in search of her. He found her in the library, perusing books in a way that made him guess she wasn't finding anything interesting.

As he approached, she glanced his way and asked, "Need something?"

"I was heading to the practice circles to get a little sparring in and wondered if you wanted to come with me," he told her.

She paused, looking slightly surprised. "Like...to spar with you?"

He raised an eyebrow slightly, confused why she was so surprised. "Of course. What, did you think I wanted you to watch?"

She scoffed, shaking her head in annoyance and a hint of embarrassment. "No thanks, I'm busy. Looking for something."

He shook his head, slightly annoyed she was being so difficult. It was like this every time he asked her to do something other than hunt Tarapor and scheme against Samar, as if she couldn't understand why he bothered. Part of him wondered as well, but for some reason, the more she resisted, the more he felt the need to try.

So, he decided to make the offer a little more tempting. "Come on, don't you want to know how I beat you?" he asked her.

She stilled, pausing with a book halfway off the shelf, and glanced sidelong at him. Then she let out an annoyed huff as she shoved the book back on the shelf. "Fine, just this once. Let me change into something else. I'll meet you down there."

He resisted the urge to smirk in triumph as he nodded and told her, "See you there."

Leaving the library behind, he started down to the same arena where he and Altaira had dueled a few weeks ago. When not being used for large competitions such as their duel—which didn't happen often—the space was split into several smaller rings for sparring. It sat at the base of the cliff headquarters was built into, on a strip of sand surrounded by large boulders on all but one side. It had once been a cove, but with some help from the Auraes, the Brotherhood had dried it up decades ago to give them a secure outdoor sparring area. Bleachers had been carved into most of the rocks, allowing for spectators, but now they were empty. Save for a few others sparring in different sections, Mefune was alone.

He took up a pair of wooden practice blades from shelves near the door and staked out a corner of the arena to wait. Luckily, it wasn't long before Altaira joined him. She hurried towards him, still looking a bit miffed.

Handing her one of the two practice swords hilt first, he told her, "You didn't have to come."

"I wanted to," she replied as she took it. "I do want to know how you beat me."

He smiled slightly and nodded. "It was simple, really. Your grip is loose when you deflect an attack on your left side."

She sighed slightly. "I never did fix that," she muttered. "It's from an old injury from the Purges. I learned to compensate for it, but it weakened my form."

"So we fix it," Mefune stated with a slight nod. "Don't be too surprised I beat you so quickly. Most of the Brotherhood is actually a little weak when actually fighting someone armed."

"Fighting with swords is literally what we do. How could that be true?" she wondered, confused and almost annoyed he would suggest such a thing.

"Most of us only maintain the basics of proper use of a sword. With the Tarapor, the only thing that really matters is speed. We don't need to be horribly accurate in our strikes, as long as it lands, since it only takes a small wound for the magic in our swords to do their job. On the other hand, I make sure to maintain proper technique, which gives me an advantage."

"Huh," she muttered with a nod, considering his words for a moment. "Well, now that I know it's still a problem, let's spar, and I'll work on it."

He nodded, so they stepped apart, facing each other. She gave the practice blade a couple of experimental swings and then lunged. He met her attack easily, and the sparring began.

At first, he was entirely in teaching mode—doing what he could to help her correct the mistakes he had noticed. She always scowled at him every time he pointed something out, but she took his suggestions to heart, and he even saw improvement in the little time they were there.

After a while, he forgot he was supposed to be helping her and simply found himself absorbed in the fighting, enjoying himself. Once she let go of her initial annoyance, she relaxed and seemed to actually enjoy herself too, something he had thought impossible while in his presence.

He won another match, and she stepped back, panting slightly. "One more round," she urged after only a few moments.

"You sure?" he asked. He didn't want to admit he was tiring any more than she did.

Altaira nodded, her eyes bright with determination. "I'm going to win one of these times."

He chuckled. "We'll see," he agreed before attacking again. He caught her off guard, and she backed up, stuck on the defensive against his onslaught. They were already close to the bleacher walls, so it wasn't hard to force her back against them with a hard shove against her blade. He pressed close, pinning her in place with the weight of his sword against hers.

"Give up?" he teased.

She didn't answer, just smirked slightly as she debated her options. For someone who was cornered, she seemed way too optimistic. Elated, even. He decided she was actually quite beautiful when she wasn't scowling. This close, it was much easier to notice the little details, like how her eyes weren't black like he had originally thought, but more a deep indigo.

Suddenly, she slipped sideways and escaped his grasp, making him realize he had backed off slightly while lost in thought. She swiped at his unprotected back, and he barely managed to get his blade up in time to defend himself.

"What was that?" she called. "Why did you let me go?"

"I...don't know," he admitted, bewildered. He couldn't remember the last time he had lost a match because he was distracted. Dismissing it as a brief lapse in judgment caused by his growing exhaustion, he pressed his attack again and eventually won the duel.

She sighed, allowing her sword to fall to her side as she ran the back of her hand over her forehead in a futile attempt to wipe away the sweat that had gathered there. "Well, I'll just have to beat you next time."

"Next time?" he repeated with a raised eyebrow. "I thought this was a one time thing."

"Don't get too excited. I'm only allowing another round because I want to win," she corrected quickly.

He smiled softly. "Alright. Just once more." He mentally noted not to let her win, just to see how long he could drag this out. He found himself surprisingly excited for round two.

It became a routine of theirs quickly after. When they didn't have a patrol or weren't hunting Tarapor for Samar, they spent their mornings together. Altaira continued to claim it was just because she wanted a real chance to beat him, but he knew she enjoyed it as much as he did. The mornings had always been his favorite part of the day, and now they were even better.

As they wrapped up another morning, Altaira let out a small huff. "I'll beat you one day," she decided.

He smirked slightly. "Maybe. If I allow you to," he teased. She rolled her eyes, but her smile didn't fade. In truth, she was improving fast, and he was hard-pressed to keep up with the rapid pace. He was sure she'd manage her goal sooner rather than later.

"Mefune?" a voice called from behind. Turning, he discovered Garrett standing behind him. "Sorry to interrupt. Samar needs the Council to gather immediately," he informed the pair.

"Again? We just met yesterday," Altaira complained, her shoulders slumping slightly. "Do these emergency meetings happen a lot?"

"Just recently, they have," Mefune replied as he started after Garrett. "Think we have time to clean up a bit?"

"If you hurry," Garrett agreed with a nod, so they went their separate ways. Returning to his apartment, Mefune showered quickly and then dressed in his uniform, despite guessing most of the Council wouldn't have time to honor the formality. He made a point of doing so, knowing Samar approved of the tradition and was insistent on following it himself. It seemed like just the not-so-subtle pandering Samar would expect from him.

As Mefune reached the Council room, he was surprised to find Ila sitting in the front row near the Council, watching the members trail in with a hint of impatience. *This can't be good*, he thought.

It took a good while to gather the Council—many of the international members were still present from Altaira's election—and the longer Ila had to wait, the more irritated she became. When the last member joined them, Samar turned his angry gaze to her and nearly spat, "Alright, Ila, what do you want this time?"

She stood slowly, strolling to the center of the space before them with her hands resting against her back. "Two nights ago, I was attacked by these strange creatures that have been assaulting the city for a month now."

Before she could say more, Samar interrupted. "We've told you, we know nothing about them. We're doing everything we can to protect the city. We can't offer anything more!"

Ila raised a hand to stop him. "I'm not blaming you for the attacks," she stated. "But there is something more you can offer."

"And what would that be?" Garrett asked.

"Fighters. We need many more of them in the city to help combat this threat, and you have them."

Silence fell as her statement hung in the air. Whether it was an order or a request, Mefune couldn't tell. Finally, Samar started from his stupor. "We're already fighting the Tarapor," he spluttered.

With an acknowledging nod, Ila stated, "Yes, but you have more than enough men for that. I'm only asking you to do your part to defend the city."

Quickly realizing the situation was spiraling out of hand—and that Ila was only feeding into the anger that fueled Samar's plans—Mefune felt he had to say something to smooth things over. "As much as we would like to help protect the city, our priority has to be with the Tarapor. We don't have the manpower to sacrifice from there. Not unless you would like to deal with both the Tarapor *and* whatever these new beings are."

"You have members scattered across the globe. Pull some from there," Ila insisted.

"Then those cities would be left vulnerable," one of the international members protested.

Ila's gaze passed over the Council as she frowned slightly. When it rested on Samar, she stated, "Maybe I'm not making myself clear. If it weren't for the Auraes, this island and your entire organization wouldn't exist. Therefore, we are the ones with the power here. You will support us in this effort, as you rightfully owe us, or I will be forced to repay you with the same favor—no supplies, no money, no weapons."

"Here's another fun fact for you," Altaira spat, clearly irritated by Ila's patronizing demeanor. "If it weren't for the Auraes, the Tarapor wouldn't exist either! Don't forget, we're the only ones standing between you and them. You'll quickly learn what happens if we aren't there to defend you."

"She's right, Ila. I will not bend to your threats. See what happens when you turn your back on us," Samar stated coldly.

Ila stared at him for a solid minute, as if she couldn't quite comprehend that he was telling her no. Then she sighed. "Very well. I hate to see the end of such an old alliance over something so petty."

"You have only yourself to blame for that," Samar dismissed, his tone heavy. "Leave before I have you removed from the premises."

Ila seemed to debate saying more before she turned on her heels and left. The door echoed loudly through the vast room as it closed behind her, emphasizing the tense, anger-filled silence.

"That Aurae will pay," Darius growled after a moment. "Nobody threatens us like that."

"They all will," Samar spat. "I'm done dealing with people like her. Our plan moves forward now."

This sent ripples of surprise through the crowd—clearly, nobody had expected him to move forward so quickly. What surprised Mefune more was how few seemed confused by this statement. Clearly, everyone knew what he was referring to, or at least was feigning understanding. *His influence goes farther than we thought,* Mefune worried silently.

"When will we attack?" another Council member asked, sounding all too eager. Mefune glanced at him, realizing it was one of the international members. He searched for a name, or at least a location, but found he had never been introduced. As he glanced around the room, he realized he didn't recognize any of the international members, despite having met a few over the years. Either all of the ones he knew were conveniently off the island, or Samar had been replacing Council members with ones loyal to him.

Mefune forced his thoughts to the side, focusing on the conversation at hand. Samar debated the man's question for a moment in silence, clearly weighing his need for vengeance against their chances of success. "A week. Sooner, if we can manage it. We only need to finalize the last details of how we want things to play out, and then we're ready."

It took a lot to keep Mefune's despair contained. All their efforts unraveled before him as he watched helplessly. One week. With how bent on revenge Samar was, Mefune wasn't expecting to get an entire seven days. He glanced at Altaira. Seeming to understand the problematic turn things had taken, she gave a subtle nod, and he remembered her promise from earlier. *Wherever it takes you.*

Well, we're about to find out where that will be.

Altaira

Altaira, Garrett, Daya, and Mefune gathered soon after the Council meeting, tucked in a quiet corner of the base far from prying ears. The minute they were sure they were alone, Daya stated, "Now what do we do?"

"We have to prevent this attack somehow," Altaira stated, hearing the desperation in her own voice.

"But how? We have no support. Just the four of us—three, since he won't actually help," Daya reminded them, shooting a frustrated glance at Garrett, who shrugged helplessly.

"He can't attack the city if he doesn't have Tarapor," Mefune stated.

They paused, turning to him in surprise. "What are you thinking?" Garrett wondered.

"If we destroy the Tarapor he's collected, we prevent him from attacking the city, at least for a little while," Mefune clarified.

"There's only one problem with that," Altaira pointed out. "We don't know where he keeps the Tarapor. Only Samar does."

"Yeah, every time we've brought some back, he's insisted on handling them himself instead of letting us come with him," Daya added.

Mefune nodded. "And the only reason I went along with it was so I didn't blow our cover. But I think the time for doing this carefully has passed. If we bring back more for him, then one of us could follow him to the stash. Later, we go back and destroy them before he plans to attack the city."

"That could work," Altaira muttered. "We don't have a lot of time to pull it off, though."

"But he'll know someone's working against him afterward," Daya pointed out. "There's no way they won't notice something like that, and if any of us get hurt, or they see us out when it happens, it'll be hard to convince him we weren't involved."

Mefune nodded in reluctant agreement. "He'll know someone betrayed him, but if we're careful and make sure we all have good stories, we may be able to avoid his attention for a little while." He let out a small sigh. "I knew it would come to this, eventually. We wouldn't be able to fight Samar quietly forever. I'll do what is necessary to protect us all from whatever he does in retaliation, but I'm not about to stop just because the risk to myself is greater."

"Same," Altaira stated softly. Daya glanced at her, looking worried. Meeting her friend's gaze, Altaira added, "Too many people will die if we give up now, between Samar's recklessness and the war he would undoubtedly start. I can't stand by and let that happen."

Daya sighed. "Alright. If you're sure, then...I'll help." All eyes turned to Garrett next, who quickly glanced between the three, then shifted nervously, frowning.

"When I said I'd do what was necessary to protect us from Samar, that meant you too," Mefune told him. "We could really use your help."

Garrett let out a heavy sigh. "Fine. What do you need me to do?"

Altaira couldn't resist a triumphant smile. Finally, it seemed they had won him over. Mefune, however, was all business as he began delving out orders. "I need to know who's actually loyal to Samar and who isn't. I get the feeling some of the Council may be pretending to keep out of trouble, like we are, but it's hard to tell. If this comes to some sort of fight, I want to be ready."

Garrett nodded. "I can handle that."

"And I'll bring back some Tarapor for Samar," Mefune decided. "Daya and Altaira, you follow Samar to where he's keeping them when I get back."

"Wait, you want to go after the Tarapor alone?" Garrett wondered, one eyebrow raised in surprise.

"You're good, but not that good," Altaira added. "We barely all made it back in one piece last time."

"You doubt me?" Mefune wondered with a hint of a smile, clearly not taking it as seriously as the others.

"Only your sanity right now," she grumbled. When Mefune didn't seem ready to let it go, she added, "At least let me come with you; we have a better chance of surviving together."

He considered it for a moment. "I guess Daya can follow him alone. I wanted the two of you together just in case you got caught; that way there's less of a chance the fight could go bad."

"I think you have more to worry about fighting the Tarapor," Daya stated. "I'll be fine on my own. Let Altaira go with you."

Mefune glanced at Daya, clearly not satisfied with the idea, but then he gave a short nod and turned back to Altaira. "Fine. Can you be ready to leave in an hour?"

"You want to leave today? It's almost four," Garrett pointed out.

"We don't have time to wait for better circumstances," Mefune confirmed with a nod.

"I'll pack my things," Altaira agreed.

"Let me know when you get back," Daya stated.

— ℰ —

An hour later, Altaira headed for the exit to the forest, carrying her freshly packed bag and dressed in a long-sleeved t-shirt, cargo pants, and her usual sturdy pair of boots. She hadn't had a chance to purchase another good jacket since the last one had been ruined by the Tarapor that had bitten her, so she had been forced to resort to a dark-colored rain poncho instead. It wasn't nearly as warm, but it acted as a good wind blocker, and combined with the warmer shirt and better weather, she figured it would be good enough.

She met up with Mefune just as she reached the exit. "Ready?" he asked. She nodded, so he pressed the button to open the door, and they started into the forest.

"So, where do you plan to find the Tarapor this time? Same place as usual?" Altaira wondered as they reached the bottom of the hill and started into the trees.

Mefune shook his head. "Let's go to the northern lakeshore this time."

Altaira paused. "Wait, that's where you said it was pretty heavily infested. We specifically chose not to go there last time."

"Yeah, but we don't have the time for a two-day hike to the western shore like usual. I doubt Samar will actually wait a full week. He could attack tomorrow, for all we know. Even if he does wait, we don't know what it will take to destroy the Tarapor he's collected. I want as much time as possible to deal with that," Mefune pointed out.

"True," Altaira muttered. "But it's not going to do anyone any good if we get ourselves killed out here."

"I'm hoping to find some stragglers far enough south we can stay away from the worst of it. I've been in that area before; it isn't too bad if you're on your guard. Besides, if we're quick, we might even make it back tonight."

Altaira let out a heavy sigh. "I hope this goes well. And you wanted to do this alone."

Mefune allowed a small smirk. "I guess Creta wore off on me a bit."

Their conversation lulled to a halt as they traveled deeper into the forest. Breaking from the familiar paths the patrols usually took, they started north. The trees were dense in that area, blocking almost all the sky from view. They traveled in silence, as if unwilling to shatter the fragile peace around them. It was almost unnerving to Altaira just how quiet it was. Usually, there were birds or other wildlife, but she couldn't see or hear any. She couldn't help but wonder why.

When the trees parted slightly, and a somewhat familiar river came into sight, Altaira realized how far they had come. *Maybe we will manage to find a Tarapor and make it back before dark,* she mused, but part of her still seriously doubted it. They would most likely have to find shelter for the night somewhere in the forest, hunt down a Tarapor in the early morning hours tomorrow, and then make it back before noon. Still, it would be faster than traveling all the way out to the western shore.

Reaching the riverbank, they carefully crossed over a makeshift bridge, which was nothing more than a few fallen logs. The river below them was shallow and clear, passing quickly through broader, deep banks. Altaira had seen this form of erosion before and knew the banks had formed when the river swelled from spring runoff and heavy storms.

Time passed slowly. They continued on a mostly northern trajectory, passing through familiar and unfamiliar areas of the forest. Eventually, Altaira found herself in a part of the forest she had never traversed before. In the distance, she caught glimpses of the mountains' snowy peaks above the tree line, and the sun sometimes caught the lake's surface and shone through the trees to her right. Eventually, it too fell away, leaving her with no familiar landmarks other than the distant mountains. The sun continued to sink towards the horizon, and under the trees, it seemed to grow darker much faster.

As the trees thinned again, Altaira noticed the sky was now overcast and a constant breeze had picked up, gusting at times enough to worry Altaira. "I don't like the change in weather," she commented, knowing how dangerous it could be to be caught out in the forest when the weather grew nasty. The patrols planned for it and had plenty of magic-sheltered camps along their routes, but out here, things were much less organized. It would be easy to get lost in an unfamiliar location.

"Hmm," Mefune muttered, his gaze narrowing as he glanced up between the swaying pines. "I don't like it either. But we have to keep moving forward at this point; with how fast it's rolling in, there's no way we'll make it back to base before it breaks, and I don't want to have to deal with the river."

"Where do we go then?" Altaira wondered.

Mefune glanced around the forest, taking in his surroundings in silence for a moment, making Altaira a bit worried. "There...should be places up ahead we can take shelter in."

"Are you sure?" Altaira asked.

"Not entirely," he admitted. "It's been a while since I've been in this part of the forest. But if I remember right, there are a series of caves behind a waterfall near the lake that should be just northeast of us."

Altaira bit her lip. "Are you sure we shouldn't just head back? I'd hate to be stumbling around in the storm looking for a cave that's not there."

As Mefune considered it, Altaira heard the last rumblings of distant thunder. He glanced in the direction of the sound and then stated, "If we're going to try, we go now." Altaira didn't like the urgent tone of his voice. She simply nodded, and they started back the way they had come simultaneously.

It began to rain before they had made it far, and the thunder seemed closer now. Altaira pulled up her hood, tucking her braid inside her poncho. As she glanced up at the trees, she felt both grateful and fearful of their presence; they protected them from the rain, but she also knew with thunder came lightning, and being near trees was not an ideal place to be.

They scaled down a gentle slope as another clap of thunder resonated through the forest. The wind howled through the branches above, and the rain grew increasingly more intense. *Spring storms like these can get real nasty,* Altaira remembered. Despite its claims of being waterproof, her poncho was soaked through, and the growing darkness made it difficult to see; night was coming, and the thick tree cover and dark clouds made it seem like midnight. She couldn't help but silently marvel at how quickly the storm had blown in and hoped it wouldn't get any worse, despite knowing it had the potential to.

With the thunder now so loud it seemed to shake the ground around Altaira, sending shivers of fear down her spine every time, they finally neared where she remembered the river had been. Mefune suddenly stopped in front of her, causing Altaira to stumble to a halt behind him just in time to prevent herself from running into him.

"What?" she began as she stepped up next to him. Before he could answer, lightning eerily lit up her surroundings, and for the first time, she noticed the shallow water rushing past her boots. She stared at it in shock. The original riverbanks weren't for another few feet. The storm had already forced the water well beyond it, and she guessed it would only worsen the longer it rained.

"We can't cross. Who knows how fast the current is at the center, or how deep?" Mefune stated grimly.

Altaira cursed their lousy luck under her breath, her hands on her hips. "Now what?" she asked.

Mefune simply turned around. If he had said anything, it was lost to Altaira in another deafening clap of thunder. As she followed him back through the trees, she distracted herself from her quickly growing fear by counting the seconds between the lightning flashes and the thunderclaps. But that did little to calm her nerves; she quickly realized the storm was steadily moving closer.

The wind intensified as they continued, and the rain was forced sideways in its path, pelting Altaira in the face. It became impossible to see anything other than Mefune's form before her, like a living shadow in the darkness. She figured in normal circumstances, her eyes would have somewhat adjusted to the lack of light, but the lightning flashed frequently enough to disorient her, like someone occasionally flicking on a flashlight in a dark room. She stumbled along behind Mefune, focusing on keeping her feet moving forward and stopping herself from panicking. She was quickly discovering another issue with the encroaching night—the dropping temperatures were made unbearable by how wet she was. *I'll take Tarapor over this any day,* she grumbled inwardly. *Give me a whole hoard of them right now. At least that I can fight.*

Mefune made his way around an ancient, obviously dead pine just as another gust ripped past. Altaira heard the snapping of wood and paused in her tracks, fear making her heart skip a beat. She had no idea how close she was to the tree without the lightning to illuminate her surroundings, but she remembered how precarious it looked when she first glimpsed it.

Another gust ripped past, followed by more snapping. The next couple of seconds passed almost as if she was watching it happen to someone else, everything moving painfully slow. Lightning flashed again, allowing Altaira a brief glimpse of the falling tree moving towards her. Eyes widening, she burst into action, hoping to get out of its path before the tree landed, but she only had a general idea of what direction it was falling.

When the branch hit her, she was launched sideways, her shoulder smashing painfully into the ground. A crash loud enough to compete with the thunder echoed behind her, and excruciating pain shot through her leg. She cried out, but it took her ears a moment to register she was making any sound. All she could hear was the pounding of her own heart.

She heard Mefune call her name as he kneeled beside her. Lightning flashed again, and she caught a blurred glimpse of his concerned gaze. In the new lighting, his gaze snapped to a dark form near Altaira, fear in his eyes. Then he disappeared into the blackness again, and Altaira almost gave in to the pain, fighting to stay conscious. She could hear him struggling with something heavy, and then he cursed quietly. She could feel the weight on her now and realized part of the tree must have pinned her. Then she saw a silver flash before the pain suddenly lessened and the weight lifted away.

He appeared at her side again. "I'm going to have to..." he started, but part of his words were lost to her—whether from thunder or her blacking out, she wasn't sure. "Altaira?"

"Just get us out of here," she managed through gritted teeth.

He nodded, and she only briefly caught it in the haunting glow of more lightning. The ground fell away moments later as he pulled her into his arms and lifted her up. She clung to him, quickly growing disoriented. The movement jarred her injuries, and she let out another yelp, tensing as she rode through the pain.

He started into the forest, moving as quickly and carefully as possible. Altaira slipped in and out of awareness as the pain threatened to overwhelm her over the next moments—she had no idea how long it was, but it felt like an eternity.

When the rain stopped, she glanced up but could see only darkness, and the echoing thunder told her she was definitely still in the storm. "We made it," Mefune sighed in relief. He carefully set her down.

As if knowing she was safe was finally enough to allow her to give in to the blackness, she found it impossible to fight it anymore. Deciding its emptiness was better than the painful world she existed in now, Altaira welcomed it as she passed out.

$$- \wp -$$

Mefune

When Altaira lost consciousness, Mefune couldn't help but wish he could sleep as well, but knew there was still a lot that needed to be done before he could allow himself to rest. First, he checked to make sure she could breathe easily and that her heart rate seemed steady. When he noticed she was very cold to the touch, he quickly lit a small fire with some dried leaves and twigs he found on the cave floor.

In the craziness of the storm, it had been hard to see the extent of the injuries she had suffered. Now, it was a bit easier under the light of the fire. The shoulder she had landed on had a deep gash that soaked her poncho and sleeve in blood, and there were several other minor scrapes and bruises covering her arm and one side of her face. By far, the worst of her injuries was definitely her leg. The bone in her shin had snapped in two places, the top break protruding through her skin a few inches above the rim of her boot. The wound was bleeding horribly, making him worry she had passed out due to blood loss. He quickly realized how dangerous it was to have moved her. At this point, he could only hope he hadn't made it worse. Considering the storm, he hadn't had much choice. Leaving her in the rain would have been a death sentence.

His lips pressed into a thin line as he considered his options. Setting his sword aside, he pulled his bag off his shoulder and rummaged through it for a moment, assessing his supplies. It was a nasty break, and it had been a while since he had first learned how to treat it. His mind raced as he tried to remember what he needed to do, and in what order. Stopping the bleeding and setting the leg right was crucial for her survival and her future use of the limb. Even if he did it right, she wouldn't be able to walk on it for a long while, and they were far from civilization.

Part of him reluctantly admitted there was another option. There were dangers to what he was considering, and he had promised himself he would never venture down that path again. Not since the accident with Creta. But he was desperate. His eyes squeezed shut, his hands clenching into fists, torn between helping Altaira and staying away from his troubled past.

In the darkness, he could almost imagine Creta hovering behind him as he often had, the subject of his pestering before Mefune—usually an injured animal, something the old medic had stumbled across and had determined to use as a teaching moment.

"Your doubt is the only thing holding you back, Mefune. You can do this," Creta told him, his hands resting behind his back, a calm expression on his face.

"I can't," Mefune denied. *The memory of his mistake was way too fresh on his mind.*

Creta kneeled next to him, resting a hand on the boy's shoulder. He reluctantly looked up at the older man, his gaze full of the torment he felt inside. "I know you're scared. But I don't hold what happened against you. I knew the risks of taking you as my apprentice. I want you to realize your past doesn't have to control you."

The memory haunted him as Mefune opened his eyes again, his gaze resting on Altaira. He hadn't succeeded then, refusing to act on what Creta told him. From that moment on, he had always seemed lightly disappointed with Mefune.

But that was a long time ago. Though he was still scared, he had learned to work around that fear. There was something stronger now urging him on as he thought of Altaira.

Just this once, he told himself as thin wisps of silver light appeared around his hands, and he got to work.

Altaira

Altaira stirred, disoriented, as she took in her unfamiliar surroundings; she seemed to be in some sort of cave, a blanket thrown over her, and the remnants of a campfire smoldered nearby. The air smelled of damp earth and wood smoke, irritating her nose enough to make her sneeze—which she quickly wished hadn't happened. Her whole body ached, and the sneeze made it spike to an almost unbearable throb. Her left shoulder and right leg were the worst.

When it settled to a more bearable level, she searched for Mefune, remembering he had been with her the last time she had been conscious. "What happened?" she managed, swallowing around her parched throat.

"You passed out," Mefune supplied as her gaze finally found him.

"Passed out...why?" she asked, bewildered. Then memories from her last conscious moments came crashing back, and she blinked and pushed the blanket away, wanting to know how bad her injuries were. She glanced at her leg first, remembering the pain, and immediately noticed the bandaging that covered most of her shin from just below her knee to about where her boot would start if it were still on her. Glancing around, she found it sitting next to her, thankfully. Her poncho was gone, revealing the sleeve of her shirt had been cut free, and her shoulder and upper arm were wrapped similarly.

"That's why," Mefune muttered, sounding almost sarcastic. Turning back to him, she decided exhausted was more the word for it. He looked surprisingly ruffled, his complexion pale.

"I remember now," she muttered. "How bad are they?"

Mefune hesitated a brief moment and then shrugged. "Not as bad as they look. Mostly just surface wounds and bad bruising. I thought your leg might have been broken, but it was just a pretty deep cut. You'll have to be careful with it, but it shouldn't take long to heal. Your shoulder's in similar condition, but not quite as bad."

She nodded, taking in the information. It surprised her; she would have guessed her injuries were worse, judging by the amount of pain she had been in the night before. Glancing at the opening of the small cave behind Mefune, she noticed there was hardly any trace of the storm except for the large puddles in random places. "How long was I asleep?"

Mefune reached for his bag and began searching for something inside as he replied, "A day. Hungry?" He produced a small wrapped package and offered it to her.

"Yeah," she muttered as she accepted it, recognizing one of the pre-bundled ration packs all the members of the Brotherhood carried with them on patrols. They were simple, palm-sized, slightly lumpy brown squares with an almost doughy texture and a shelf life of about a thousand years. Packed with nutrients, one could survive on them alone for a long time. Despite how unpleasant they looked, they tasted decent, and Altaira was so famished she felt she could eat a hundred of them.

After swallowing the square, she brushed her hands clean and carefully leaned back against the cave wall. Glancing up, she studied the little space; it was made from an ancient tree leaning against an enormous boulder, thick moss and tangled roots creating a roof of sorts. It wasn't waterproof, leaving a good portion of the interior still slightly damp from the rain, but the area around Altaira and the fire's remains were kept dry by the thick tree trunk. She noticed her shawl hanging from a tree branch, still damp, one side bearing a new stain, probably from her shoulder. *Man, another one ruined,* she thought, remembering the jacket destroyed by the Tarapor that had bitten her.

Mefune held out a closed fist and her canteen. "Here, these will help with the pain a bit. I don't have much, so only take what you need."

Trying not to act too obviously relieved, Altaira accepted the canteen and allowed Mefune to drop a couple of pills into her open palm. After swallowing them, she commented, "You literally have everything in that bag, don't you?"

Mefune managed a half-smile, bringing some light back to his tired expression. "It pays to be prepared."

"Yeah, and I keep benefiting from it," she pointed out. "Thanks for last night." He dismissed it with a slight shrug, glancing down at his hands. She smiled slightly, bemused by his reaction. "No, seriously. You saved my life. Thank you."

"It was the right thing to do. I couldn't leave you there." Then, after a brief pause, he attempted to change the subject by asking, "How are you feeling? Are you cold? I could start another fire."

She smiled slightly, allowing him to move on. It was almost charming that he didn't know how to take her gratitude. "No, I think I'm okay right now."

"Alright. Keep me updated, okay?"

She nodded, shifting slightly to pull the blanket back over her—which she realized was actually Mefune's jacket. They hadn't come prepared for more than a night's stay in the woods, and as she glanced around, she realized her pack was missing, meaning half their supplies were as well. She frowned slightly, realizing that could be problematic.

"So, if the bridge is washed out, will we be able to cross the river?" she wondered.

Mefune frowned slightly. "Probably not. I haven't seen the river yet, but it's likely still too deep and moving too fast for us to cross any time soon."

Altaira sighed. She had been expecting this but still didn't like hearing it. "So, how do we get back?"

"We can wrap around the lake, which will take a couple of weeks. We don't necessarily have the supplies for that, but we can survive off the land," Mefune told her, sounding as if he didn't like that idea but was reluctant to suggest the other.

"We can't afford a couple of weeks. We only have a few days before Samar moves against the Auraes," she reminded him. "There has to be another option."

"We could try to wait out the river. But there's no telling how long it'll stay flooded," he suggested next.

"Still leaves us with the same problem, though. We don't have the time to wait," she replied.

Mefune sighed. "Just a bit to the north, the river is smaller just before it merges with a few streams. There's a chance it would be shallow enough there that we could cross. That'll take about a day, but it's most likely our fastest option." He paused and then added, "But that would take us directly through the thick of the Tarapor hives."

Altaira slumped, shaking her head slightly. "And I'm in no condition to fight on that level," she muttered, realizing their predicament.

"You...might be surprised," Mefune mused, eyeing her carefully. "The leg will hold your weight as long as you're careful, and if I'm not mistaken, your injured shoulder isn't your dominant hand, so you could still hold your sword without too much trouble."

Altaira raised an eyebrow, considering him for a moment. "You want to take the third option."

"*Want* is a bit strong," he sighed. "Like you said, we don't have time for the first or second options. I don't like the odds any better than you, but I'm not sure we have any other choice."

Altaira's lips pressed into a thin line as she debated how to answer. It seemed ridiculous to even consider stepping into such a place, even with her at full health, and yet, he seemed set on the idea. She couldn't help but feel a bit miffed her health seemed of little concern.

"Give me a day, then, to rest and get used to my injuries," she requested after a moment, her tone a little sharper than she meant it.

He nodded. After a long moment, he glanced up and met her gaze, looking as if he wanted to say something, and then hesitated. "What?" she wondered.

He seemed to debate what he wanted to say for a moment more before finally telling her, "I don't want you to think I made the decision lightly."

"I don't," Altaira said in an attempt to reassure him, but she was amazed by how well he had read her.

"You do," he insisted. "Why?" his voice was still soft, but she squirmed under his piercing gaze. She couldn't help but remember how he had reacted similarly to Garrett admitting his involvement with Creta's death, making her nervous.

She sighed. "I guess...I just..." she stammered, "I just worry I won't be able to keep up with you, and this will be dangerous. I hope you haven't misplaced your trust."

"I haven't," he stated confidently. "You're a better fighter than you give yourself credit for."

She shook her head slightly. "That's just it—I know I can fight. But I'm injured. Badly. And we're debating walking into the most Tarapor-infested place in probably the entire world. I don't think I'm up for that right now."

"Then what do you suggest we do?" he questioned, his frustration making his careful control slip slightly. "I've been debating this constantly while you've been resting. I know you're in no condition to fight, but people will die if we don't make it back in time. Garrett hardly wants to help, and I doubt Daya will act alone. What is she supposed to do? At best, she could warn the Auraes, but that won't stop the war. I can't just sit here and let that happen."

"I know," Altaira huffed, crossing her arms against her chest, before immediately regretting the motion as it irritated her shoulder. She hated admitting he was right, but it still didn't seem like the brightest idea. Then she paused, another possible solution coming to mind. "You could go back alone. You'd make it."

He raised one eyebrow in question. "What, and leave you alone with hardly any supplies and surrounded by Tarapor? This area's crawling with them. They've been trying to swarm the cave since we got here. Our odds of survival are much higher if we stick together."

"I'll just slow you down and make you feel like you have to protect me. It would be easy for you to make it back in time to stop Samar if you went alone," Altaira pressed.

Looking a bit surprised, he inquired, "Do you really think my only interest in your well-being is because of this whole scheme we're caught in?"

This surprised Altaira, making her realize that was exactly what her words implied. It hadn't been her intention, but she knew she had thought similar things of him in the past, giving her words more validation than she had meant them to have.

But why do I think that? she asked herself. *He's only ever done things to show me he's not that type of person.* Her whole reasoning was based on the reputation he had and the few moments where she had glimpsed a surprising coldness to him when they were younger. But she realized she couldn't think of a single incident that validated the rumors that circled about him. Her mind trailed to the time she spent with him in the mornings, his interest in helping her improve, and the companionship she felt with him during those sparing sessions. She thought of his determination to make things right for the Brotherhood, and how he took her and Daya's opinions seriously and seemed to genuinely value their input and support. And, she had to admit, dragging her out of that storm could have put himself at risk. Twice now, he had come to her rescue.

Realizing she had never replied, she blinked and quickly stated, "No, of course not."

"You do," he pressed, and she realized she had hesitated way too long.

She met his gaze, wondering if she had offended him, but his expression remained an unreadable mask. "That's not what I meant," she said with a sigh. She shook her head, feeling heat rise to her cheeks with embarrassment. Now that she had confronted her own thought process, she realized how ridiculous it was to think he'd be willing to abandon her. And she found herself desperately wanting him to know she didn't believe he was a horrible person. Not anymore, at least.

She paused a moment to gather her thoughts and then began by saying, "Honestly, sometimes I've wondered. There's just...something about you—maybe in your demeanor or the way you carry yourself, I'm not sure, but it's intimidating. It makes it easy to believe the rumors about you. I guess I just fell into the trap of expecting the worst of you, just like everyone else did. But you've proven you're better than we—*I* give you credit for. I'm wrong to judge, and I'm sorry."

He held her gaze for a long moment, silently appraising her words. She squirmed slightly, hoping he realized she meant what she said. She didn't want to make an enemy of him for multiple reasons, but what seemed most important at that moment was making sure he didn't hate her for her cruel judgment. What an odd turn of events it was.

Then he smiled slightly, his gaze flicking down. "It's funny how often I get that. I've always wondered what I did to start the rumors. I promise I don't mean to act that way."

"I realize that now," she stated. "If you were like that, you wouldn't still be here. You wouldn't have pulled me out of that storm. You wouldn't have cared if the Auraes died in Samar's schemes. So...yeah. Clearly, you're a lot better person than I thought."

She bit her lip as her voice fell away, suddenly unsure of where she was going with her comment. It amazed her how quickly she had gone from accusing him to defending him, but it felt right. Still, she hadn't expected the amount of emotion behind her words; she was genuinely grateful for his help, touched by it more than she had first realized.

He seemed just as surprised by her comment as she was, but then he slowly smiled. She realized then it was probably the first time she had seen him smile openly, enough to allow it to reach his eyes. She found herself smiling too, warmed by how pleased he seemed. There was just a hint of uncertainty, as if her gratitude was unexpected and something he experienced infrequently, but it was a welcome surprise. *Maybe people need to tell him* that *more often,* she thought. Suddenly she found herself considering the possibility of playing that role, just to let him know she thought of him as a good person.

Suddenly, Mefune turned to the cave entrance, his gaze locked on to something Altaira couldn't see. "What?" she asked, surprised by the sudden switch in his demeanor.

"More Tarapor." He reached for his weapon resting against his leg as he stood. The sword split into two with a quick twist, and then he waited, watching the forest in silence.

Altaira shifted, debating trying to help, but the minute she tried to put any weight on her arm to push herself to her feet, the immediate pain made it clear trying wouldn't go over well. As she watched, a figure materialized out of the underbrush. Just as it crossed the threshold of the cave entrance, Mefune ended its life. The second tried to catch him off guard while he finished the first Tarapor, but he was more than ready for the creature; it died just as quickly as the first. He watched the forest for a moment more, but then seemed to sense the danger was gone.

As he turned back to her and sheathed his sword, Altaira sighed in relief, allowing herself to relax against the cave wall again. "How did you know they were there? I couldn't even see them," she wondered.

He smirked slightly. "Guess I'm just that good," he joked, avoiding her question as he reclaimed his spot near the remnants of the fire between them.

She laughed at his sarcasm, surprised by it again. "Well, I hope whatever ability grants you this foresight sticks around. It'll make being stuck out here a lot easier."

His smirk only grew. "See, it is good having me around."

"I guess," she readily agreed, realizing how much she was glad he was there. As much as she dreaded the coming days, suddenly, part of her was grateful that of all the people she could have been stranded with, she was lucky it was him.

Mefune

They passed the afternoon with small talk, interrupted only by the occasional Tarapor that wandered their way. As night approached, Altaira eventually dozed again. But Mefune found himself too restless to sleep, just as he had been the night before. Between the mad dash through the storm, trying to keep Altaira alive, the constant threat of the Tarapor, and worrying over a solution to Samar, he couldn't get himself to stop thinking long enough to do much more than doze. It was good he had bothered to learn a simple spell that would allow him to go without sleep for a while. He had a feeling it would be needed over the next couple of days. Altaira was too exhausted to take a turn on watch duty, and the forest was too busy with Tarapor for them both to sleep.

He wasn't sure they would survive the next few days, not with Altaira in this condition. That was the biggest reason he couldn't rest; he found himself stuck in the same debate he'd had the night of the storm. He could do more for her, but she would notice if he healed the wounds any further than he had. There was no way he'd be able to explain away them magically healing.

His original plan was to let them finish healing on their own. But the more he thought about it, the more he realized Altaira wouldn't have the strength to fight the number of Tarapor they were about to face. He had noticed her struggling to get to her feet on several occasions throughout the day, and it made him realize just how vulnerable she was. He couldn't condemn her like that just to keep his secret safe.

The problem was, he wasn't sure he trusted her on that level. It wasn't anything she had done, he was just incredibly slow to trust. And there were reasons, more than he would ever like to explain, why he hardly ever used his aura, especially around others. *But if we're going to make it back, I just might have to trust her with this*, he thought, not for the first time.

Debating it endlessly would get him nowhere. Finally, he let out a sigh, throwing caution to the wind as he moved to her side. He brought his aura to light around him again and got to work.

Though his training was rudimentary and her injuries seemed extreme, they were luckily pretty easy to heal. To effectively use most medical magic, a person had to know how to treat the injuries *without* magic—so in this situation, he had to know how to set the broken bone properly and how to clean and bind the wounds. The spells were useful because they were exact. If he told it to set the bone by reducing the fracture, it would align it precisely and avoid damage to the surrounding tissue. Then, he could use other spells to encourage the body to heal as it normally would, but at a much faster rate. Those spells only worked if the body could naturally handle the wound on its own —so regrowing a limb or organ wasn't an option—but Altaira's injuries were perfect candidates.

However, he couldn't bring her entirely back to health. His aura had its limits, and medical magic was extremely exhausting, especially since he hardly used his aura. Plus, if he encouraged her leg to heal too fast, he'd risk the integrity of the bone, making it likely to break again under normal strain. Luckily, between his work the night before and then, he was able to bring it to a point where he was confident she'd be able to walk on it without pain or risk of further damage. If anyone were to look at the bone, it would seem like she had broken it weeks ago. He focused on that and healing her shoulder enough that she'd be able to fight without problems. The other wounds would have to heal on their own.

By the time he finished, he was so exhausted he probably would have passed out if it weren't for the sustaining spell keeping him going. He could feel the weight of his lack of proper rest hovering in the back of his mind, but until he reached the limit of the sustaining spell or dismissed it, he would be able to remain alert. He retrieved his sword and settled against the cave wall with a sigh, preparing for another long night on watch.

Chapter Eighteen

Hunted

Altaira

Soon after Altaira woke the next morning, Mefune slipped off to look at the river and decide if it was crossable. As she forced down another ration bar for breakfast, she noticed her injuries weren't nearly as sore as they had been last night. In fact, without even noticing it, she had picked up the ration bar with her left hand, and the motion hadn't hurt. If it weren't for the obvious bandages, she would have forgotten she was injured. It seemed like quite an improvement.

After finishing her breakfast, she decided to try standing. Shifting slightly, she tried moving her leg first and was relieved to find the motion didn't make the pain increase. The swelling had gone down considerably, making her hope she'd be able to get her boot back on without trouble. Rotating her shoulder, she found it in a similar condition.

Unable to entirely believe her luck, she cautiously climbed to her feet. She stretched and worked the kinks out as she shuffled to the cave entrance, amazed. *This shouldn't be possible,* she thought.

Mefune stepped from the forest into the small clearing near the cave. Noticing her standing at the entrance of their little shelter, he called, "I'm surprised you're up."

As he reached her, she gave him a flabbergasted shrug. "They hardly hurt. I have no idea what happened overnight, but it's like they've had a whole week to heal."

His eyes widened slightly in surprise. "That's amazing," he congratulated.

Something about his tone of voice made her wonder if her announcement surprised him. Fixing him with a pointed look, she asked, "You didn't have something to do with this, did you?"

He let out an amused huff. "Me? I'm no miracle worker. All I did was bandage them and keep you alive."

"Yeah, but they're suddenly healed. You're the only person around," she pressed. "What did you do?"

"I mean, I just..." he started, but then let out a sigh and shoved his hands in the pockets of his jacket as he glanced down at the ground. For a long moment, he didn't continue, and when he did, his voice was soft. "There's a reason Creta wanted me to be his apprentice."

It took her a minute to figure out his meaning, but finally, she realized the one connection between Creta and the current conversation. Creta had been a medic. medics could heal wounds quickly, like hers had. She could only see him specifically requesting to train someone because he wanted to pass down those skills. And by the condition of her injuries, she was beginning to think he had.

"But..." she muttered, her brow furrowing in confusion. "...I didn't know you had an aura."

"Nobody but Creta knew," he admitted, confirming Altaira's suspicions despite how his expression made her feel he would have rather left her guessing.

"Why don't you ever use it?"

He shifted slightly, and by the way he wouldn't meet her gaze and seemed almost tense, she could tell this was a topic he didn't like to visit often. "I do for little things, sometimes." He paused, searching for words. "There was an accident a long time ago. I haven't entirely forgiven myself for it."

"Oh," she stated, still bewildered. What could have happened that would warrant never using his aura again, to the point nobody knew he even had one? From what she knew about Auraes, using their aura was instinctual as breathing. It would take a lot to change that.

As if sensing her need for more information, he added, "Creta nearly died. It took a week for him to recover, and he was never the same after. The whole thing was my fault. He never blamed me, but he never really forgot, either, and neither could I."

"Ah," Altaira managed. She wasn't sure what else to say. *I guess if something like that had happened to me and my mentor, I would be reluctant too,* she admitted to herself. "Well, I'm glad he taught you. This will make things a lot easier."

"That's why I used it now, even though I honestly would have preferred to avoid it," he told her.

"I'm guessing that means you would rather me not tell anyone about it," she assumed.

He nodded. "I know it's foolish to hold what happened against myself for so long, but I need to allow myself to deal with it my way. If everyone knew I have an aura, they would expect me to use it."

That she could agree with. Their need for medics willing to assist the Brotherhood was always high, considering the danger they regularly faced. But she would respect his wishes—she owed him that. "Hey, I get it. Don't worry, your secret's safe with me."

"Thank you," he stated, soft enough that Altaira almost didn't hear him.

"You're welcome," she told him with a smile. "Now, considering how much better I'm feeling, I don't think we need to wait any longer. We should start back. How does the river look?"

He sighed, glancing over his shoulder. "It's slowed down a bit but is still pretty flooded. It's definitely not safe to cross there."

She nodded, disappointed but not surprised. "Well, here's to hoping we'll find a place to cross before we reach the worst of the Tarapor."

"Yeah," he agreed as he began to gather his things. Altaira followed suit, though, without her backpack, there wasn't much for her to take. Part of her was a bit grateful she didn't have the extra weight to carry. As much as she trusted Mefune had healed her wounds well enough, she didn't want to push her luck.

Instead, she turned to getting her boot back on her injured leg without aggravating the wound. It took loosening the laces and tucking the edge of the bandages inside the rim to get it on comfortably, but she felt a bit sturdier with it on again. Then she pulled on her poncho, deciding to ignore the stain. The bit of warmth it offered was worth it.

Soon, they were heading out into the forest again. They stayed near the river as best they could, searching for a way across, but at times it dropped below them in steep ravines, or the landscape forced them away from it for a while. After walking for a few hours, Altaira started to think they wouldn't find a crossing any time soon. The river was still just as swollen and didn't seem to be getting any better the farther they traveled.

They walked in silence, Altaira glancing over the forest, wondering how long it would take before they started encountering Tarapor. She couldn't help but wonder how many they would have to deal with before the misadventure was over. The more she thought of it, the darker her imagination became until she had nearly freaked herself out with haunting images of her and Mefune falling to massive swarms of Tarapor.

Deciding she needed to focus on something else before she lost her courage, Altaira searched for something to talk about. Her mind strayed back to their conversation from that morning as her gaze found Mefune a few steps ahead of her. She couldn't help but reflect on her memories of him, wondering if anything would be different now that she knew he had an aura.

Quickly, one thought came to mind that sparked her curiosity. If he had a fully functional aura, why choose to join the Brotherhood? Having an aura and carrying the weapons they did was dangerous—it was why the auraless were tasked to protect Verndale from the Tarapor in the first place. Why risk his life daily like that when he didn't have to? Creta was the only other person she had heard of who had made that decision. And, just about everyone had agreed that despite how wise and kindhearted he was, he was also completely crazy.

She debated asking for a while, biting her lip as she did. She knew he was an extremely private person—more so than she had ever guessed—and he didn't like talking about his aura. Would he be annoyed if she asked?

It's probably a bad idea, she thought, trying to push away her curiosity. But with nothing to distract her, her mind dwelt on it incessantly. Eventually, she settled on bringing up a relatively safe, somewhat related topic in hopes she could gauge how willing he was to talk about his past.

Catching up to him, she matched his pace. After a minute, she asked, "Sometimes I wonder what my life would have been like if I hadn't joined the Brotherhood."

Mefune glanced her way, looking a bit surprised by the sudden start to the conversation. But if he found it odd, he didn't say anything. Instead, he replied, "It would be very different, that's for sure. We at least wouldn't be stuck in this situation."

Altaira chuckled. "I guess not." Her gaze turned far away as she reflected on that train of thought and what her life would actually be like. "But you know what? I wouldn't trade it. Our job gets hard sometimes—I mean, look where we are now—but I'm doing something good with my time. I'm protecting people. It gives me purpose."

Mefune nodded. "Couldn't have put it better myself. It's why I'm trying so hard to save the Brotherhood from Samar's schemes. Most of its members are good people like you, who are just trying to do their part to make life a little better for everyone. They don't deserve to fall to his greed."

"Exactly," Altaira agreed. Then her head tilted to one side as she reflected on the past month and came to an interesting realization. "You know, if you hadn't won that duel forever ago, I don't think we'd be here either."

"What do you mean?" he wondered, glancing at her.

"Well, if you hadn't joined the Council, Garrett wouldn't have approached you. Samar's schemes would have gone unnoticed until he attacked Verndale, and we would have had a war on our hands."

He considered her words for a moment. "I guess you're right. But if I had for some reason lost, you would be the one with the Council seat, and I'm sure you would have figured Samar's plans out."

"I don't know that I could have, not before it was too late."

"You were already looking for evidence to take down your father's murderers. It makes sense that would lead you to find out about Samar's schemes, especially since there's actually a connection between the two," he insisted. Then he shrugged slightly. "You know, now that I think about it, if I had known why you wanted the Council seat, I probably would have given it to you."

She paused, caught off guard by this. "You would have just handed it over?" she questioned, audible disbelief in her voice.

He stopped and turned to face her when he noticed she wasn't keeping pace. "I only wanted it because Creta had promised it to me. Something of an inheritance of sorts, I guess. And I didn't mind the idea of something new, of a challenge. But you wanted it for a legitimate reason—to prevent the wrongs your family suffered from happening again. If I had known, I wouldn't have stood in your way."

"Wow," she muttered, not sure what else to say. She hadn't ever heard of anyone amongst the Brotherhood so willingly giving up their power for someone else. It was something so selfless, so opposite of the person everyone saw him as that it warmed her heart. "Thanks. For being willing to help, I mean," she managed, struggling to express her gratitude properly. *How in the world did I manage to misjudge him so completely?*

He shrugged, looking slightly uncomfortable, making her think he hadn't expected it to mean so much to her and now didn't know how to proceed. Then, as if he had caught on to an idea, a hint of humor entered his expression. "Though I don't know if my pride would have allowed me to throw that duel. So, it might have been a moot point anyway," he joked.

Altaira laughed, surprised by his sudden sarcasm. "Oh, I see how it is."

"Yeah, still have to give you a reason to hate me," he stated, as if it was something he truly considered crucial.

"I don't hate you!"

He raised an eyebrow. "You sure about that?" he wondered, meeting her gaze.

"I don't!" she pressed. "After all this, I couldn't hate you even if I tried."

His smirk faded to a genuine smile, and he glanced away, shoving his hands in his pockets. "Good," he muttered, sounding surprisingly pleased.

Altaira brightened at the sight of his smile, all thoughts of their conversation gone. There was just something about that smile that made it impossible to think of anything else. It still wasn't lost to her how rarely she saw it. She loved the way it chased away the shadows and made him seem so happy, just for a brief moment. Watching him, she found herself wanting to make him smile like that every day. She couldn't exactly pinpoint the moment when she had started caring so much, but he had gone from one of the people she hated the most to someone she genuinely cared for.

He started into the forest again while she was lost in thought, reminding her where she was and what they were doing. She shook her head, trying to process her little realization while keeping her mind in the game—now wasn't the time to forget how dangerous her surroundings were.

But first, before she could move on, there was one more thing she had to do. Catching up to him again, she told him, "I'm glad things went the way they did, though. If it hadn't, we would probably still be rivals. This whole thing gave us a chance to put our differences aside and work together. And I'm happy it did," she told him.

He considered it for a moment, and then nodded. "You and me both."

— ℰ —

By dusk, the pair had covered a lot of ground but still hadn't found a place they could safely cross the river. It rushed past them to their left, a constant flurry of water.

Mefune paused, sighing as he glanced around. "What is it?" Altaira asked.

"I'm a bit worried I might have been mistaken about how the river is structured. I don't know how much farther we'll have to go before finding a place to cross," he replied. "I say we stop, find somewhere safe to spend the night. I'm just not sure where that would be in this part of the woods."

"Is there anywhere along here you think we'll be able to cross?" she wondered, glancing at the river again.

He shrugged. "Judging by how far north we've traveled, we might be pretty close to the mouth of the river at this point. There are caves there we could take shelter in, and we might even be able to cross there. Though, getting there before the Tarapor show up will be tricky. I've already started to notice them stir."

"Wait, you've seen them?" Altaira glanced around quickly, surprised and worried she hadn't noticed them.

"No, I can sense their auras. They're moving this way," he explained.

She blinked, realizing she hadn't once considered his aura would give him that advantage. He smiled slightly, clearly amused. "How else do you think I always know when they're approaching?"

"I guess that makes sense," she mused. "Honestly, I'm still getting used to knowing you have an aura."

"Understandable," he muttered.

They fell silent as they continued. Soon dusk turned to night, leaving Altaira on edge. Every little stir pulled at her attention, her eyes wide as she tried to keep track of her surroundings in the darkness. She was beginning to tire after a whole day's trek through the forest, and she knew it was partly because she was still healing. But she wasn't about to rest, not while they were so exposed.

After a moment more, Mefune paused. "They're close," he whispered.

Altaira immediately went for her sword. "Where are they coming from?"

"East," Mefune replied. He turned towards the river that still ran to their left. "We need to get across, or we'll get swarmed."

Altaira bit her lip and turned to the river as well. "It still looks pretty deep here."

He nodded and started towards the water. Getting as close as he dared, he continued along the river, searching for a spot they could cross. Knowing the Tarapor seemed to have an aversion to water, Altaira hoped their nearness to the river would keep them away. It at least created a natural wall to one side so the beasts couldn't surround them from all directions.

Altaira heard a distant howl, making them both quickly turn back towards the forest. "We need to hurry. I think they know we're here," Mefune warned. He broke into a light jog, and Altaira followed suit, despite how her weary body protested.

They hadn't made it far when Altaira heard a noise approaching from behind. She turned, drawing her sword, just in time to see a darker shadow separate itself from the underbrush and launch at her. She quickly sidestepped around the Tarapor and ended its life as it careened past. More Tarapor poured from the trees as Mefune returned to her side and joined in the fight. It was quickly apparent to Altaira that her injuries would affect her abilities, but she ignored them. She couldn't afford to favor them now.

Luckily, as it became clear the pair had the upper hand, the remaining Tarapor scattered into the forest. "They'll be back, most likely in greater numbers," Mefune muttered. "Let's keep moving."

He started back along the river, still searching for a way to cross, Altaira following. She could hear beings following them through the darkness at times, but couldn't see them. Tense with the anticipation of another attack, she watched the forest, knowing Mefune was right—now that the Tarapor knew they were present, they wouldn't give up on their prey.

Just as they had predicted, the Tarapor did come in random spurts as they continued up the river. The noise of the fights attracted more, and the larger the group became, the longer the struggles lasted before the pair managed to drive them off. Exhaustion was quickly setting in, leaving Altaira to wonder how much longer she could keep fighting.

As they drove off the horde for the fourth time, Mefune paused to catch his breath, turning north again. "I think we're getting close to the caves," he told her, pointing to a darker patch up ahead. "If we can make it there, we'll survive." With that, he started north again at the same grueling pace.

She nodded, saving her breath for running. They sprinted through the forest between attacks, trying to get as far from their enemy as possible.

But they kept coming, keeping pace with the pair easily, their enhanced agility hard to beat. The only thing that kept them away was the toxic metal of Mefune and Altaira's swords, and even that fear wasn't enough to drown out their desperate hunger for long. Eventually, as good as they were, there would be too many for them to fight at once. That growing fear kept Altaira going despite her exhaustion, knowing she would basically be accepting death if she stopped.

They approached from the north and east when they came again, swarming the pair on both sides. Altaira and Mefune pressed close, keeping the river behind them. She found herself killing two or three Tarapor with every stroke, immensely grateful it didn't take much damage to end their lives. Sometimes she'd barely nick one, killing it seconds before it could bite her. The fact that they were managing to get so close left her heart racing, her fear only increasing as the fighting continued.

Finally, the Tarapor began to scatter as their dead piled up and their fear of joining the growing pile of corpses won over. Altaira shifted towards Mefune, making sure those he faced were also retreating. He stabbed one and pushed the rotting corpse away, but didn't quite manage to turn fast enough to stop the next one from grabbing onto his arm. Before it could bite him, Altaira lunged forward, burying her sword in the creature's back.

"Thanks," Mefune breathed, straightening as he quickly inspected the gouges on his arm from the Tarapor's claws.

Thankfully, they were minor; his jacket had taken the brunt of them.

Altaira nodded, unable to find the strength to reply. She stepped back and glanced around as she struggled to catch her breath. She closed her eyes for a moment, trying to block out the pain of her throbbing injuries. Her sword drooped at her side, and the very thought of lifting it again seemed too much. She had reached her limit.

Obviously noticing, Mefune asked, "You alright?"

"Just taking a break," she managed. She lifted a hand to steady herself against the tree next to her, but winced as she moved her bad shoulder. She glanced at it, noticing a thin, dark line running down her arm from underneath her poncho. She wiped at it, confused, until it dawned on her it was blood.

"Not good," she muttered under her breath, frowning.

"What?"

"My shoulder's bleeding again," she told him softly, meeting his gaze. They both knew what an open wound meant.

"So that's why they're so persistent," Mefune sighed, sounding weary and actually a bit afraid. He glanced over the forest behind him, searching for their enemy. "Come on, we have to get to the caves."

"I need to catch my breath." She wasn't sure how she was even standing at this point, much less running through the forest.

"We're close. We need to go now while we have the chance," he urged, and she could hear the desperation in his voice. Knowing he wouldn't force her onward unless he seriously thought there was a chance they wouldn't make it if he didn't, she gathered what little strength she had left and pushed away from the tree.

Suddenly, she caught a glimpse of movement out of the corner of her eye and called out a warning. Mefune was already ready, and he met with the first Tarapor as it leaped from the trees.

As the Tarapor attacked and Altaira found herself again fighting for her life, she felt a pang of fear as she realized her exhaustion was causing her to make mistakes that could very well lead to her death. Thankfully, Mefune seemed to pick up the slack, which she figured was the only reason she survived with every passing moment.

Mefune shifted, moving to stand on her right, so he was directly between her and the largest group of Tarapor. "Keep going, I'll cover you."

"They'll just follow," Altaira pointed out as she turned to deal with the couple Tarapor that immediately moved into the space Mefune had been occupying on her left.

"There's too many," he managed, and she knew what he meant—they were about to be overwhelmed. They needed to get out of there quickly. She turned to the cliffs and pressed forward, cutting down the Tarapor that stood in her way.

Mefune followed closely, and somehow they managed to keep the horde at bay just enough to continue to make progress. They hurried through the forest, Altaira simply focusing on one thing; moving forward. It took all her willpower to continue to put weight on her bad leg.

The Tarapor fell back again, allowing Mefune to catch up to her. They continued to follow, not ready to give up yet, but reluctant to attack. Luckily, it seemed there was a chance they would make it; Altaira noticed the rush of water was growing louder, and the cliffs had morphed from a dark patch on the horizon to a dominating structure taking up most of her view ahead.

"Will the Tarapor try to follow?" Altaira managed between breaths. Usually, they wouldn't, but she was worried the frenzy her wound had encouraged would be enough to drive them beyond their usual limits.

"They hate the water. It should be enough."

Soon enough, he veered away from the river to a path that started up the cliffside at a surprisingly steep angle. It had obviously been cleared by man, but was hidden well enough that Altaira wouldn't have found it if it weren't for Mefune pointing it out.

The path wrapped around the cliffs, away from the waterfall, and grew steeper until they were forced to climb. Altaira's muscles burned, and her limbs felt weak and rubbery as she pulled herself upward. She refused to look down, her heart racing with the fear of falling. When the cliff became sheerer, ropes were embedded in the rock wall, giving her leverage. Relieved, she clung to them, feeling a bit more secure in her assent.

Finally, they reached a plateau about halfway up the cliffs. The waterfall rushed past them ahead, spraying the small space with a gentle mist. Mefune pulled himself up onto the ledge and then turned to help her up. She stumbled away from the edge and collapsed in a heap, trying to catch her breath. Her eyes squeezed shut, trying to fight the quickly growing headache. She was slightly dizzy, too, making her wonder just how much blood she had lost.

When the world steadied again and the pounding in her head faded, she managed to look around. Mefune stood near the cliff's edge, his sword still in his hand, his gaze on the ground below.

"They aren't following," he muttered, his shoulders slumping in exhaustion as he sheathed his sword and stepped away from the edge. Then he turned to her, and his gaze immediately went to her wounded shoulder. "We need to take a look at that," he muttered, kneeling next to her as he set his sword aside and pulled his bag off.

She nodded, too tired to reply. She rested her sword next to her and then carefully pulled her poncho over her head. The bandages encasing her shoulder were a deep scarlet now, but thankfully, it hadn't soaked through. Mefune handed her a roll of gauze and bandaging strips to hold. She watched as he began removing the soaked bandages, working quickly as he frowned slightly. Now that the wound was exposed, she could see just how bad it was. The cut started just above the point of her shoulder, running down her arm a good few inches, the skin around it raw and bruised. He sanitized the wound, clearing away the blood, and then his frown deepened when he could see it clearly.

"The stitches broke in a couple of places. I'll have to redo them," he told her. She nodded, now frowning as well. She hated stitches.

Oddly enough, he hesitated. Then he shook his head, letting out a small sigh. A silver light surrounded his hands, brightening the ledge. As he muttered a few short phrases in

Shidokian, the stitches faded, replaced by new sutures that closed the wound without a bit of pain. She watched, fascinated. It was one thing for him to tell her he had an aura. It was entirely another thing to see him use it. When the stitches were finished, his aura disappeared, and she found herself missing the gentle silver glow.

He carefully covered the wound with gauze soaked in a fragrant cream, and the last of the ache faded as it absorbed into her skin. She let out a relieved sigh, some of the tension leaving her. She watched as he carefully wrapped bandages around the wound, the rhythmic pattern oddly soothing. He worked carefully, his hands steady despite the rush of the night, his touch light against her skin. She found herself unable to look away, amazed that the same man who had just spent all night fighting for his life could turn around and care for her so easily.

As he finished, he pressed the last piece down, taped it in place, and then gently rested his hand on her shoulder. "There," he muttered. "It should be fine, I think." He looked up at her, his expression a mix of indecipherable emotions.

"Thank you," she whispered, acknowledging he had once again saved her life. It seemed he was making a habit of it.

"Don't thank me. I nearly got you killed," he dismissed, shaking his head as his expression changed slightly.

Suddenly she understood he was angry, but at who, she wasn't sure. "You saved my life. Again," she corrected gently. Shifting towards him, she reached up and rested her hand on his, giving him a small, weary smile. "I don't think I would have survived these last few days without you."

His anger faded, his expression softening slightly. "I had to keep you safe," he admitted. As he spoke, he lifted his hand from her shoulder and took hers in his, running a thumb over her knuckles as if in an attempt to wipe away the dirt. It was such a simple gesture, but it sent shivers down her spine and made her heart skip a beat. She shifted closer, unsure what was urging her on, but willing to embrace it.

But as she moved, she put pressure on her bad leg, sending a flair of pain up the limb. She gasped as she flinched back, but then immediately regretted it, sensing how quickly it shattered the moment.

"I should probably check that too," Mefune muttered after a pause, his gaze on the ground. His tone was forcefully light, but it couldn't entirely hide the emotion from his words, making it impossible to simply accept his attempt to move on.

She sighed and muttered, "Yeah," but her heart was still racing as she attempted to process what had just happened.

It didn't take him long to check the second injury. The stitches had held, and it was in much better condition than her shoulder, just sore. Mefune bandaged it again, adding more disinfecting cream, just to be safe.

When he finished, Altaira muttered, "I'm going to try to sleep. Is the cave any drier?"

"Should be," Mefune replied as he cleaned up his supplies.

She nodded and then attempted to stand, but found it nearly impossible without causing more pain than she had strength left to deal with. Her legs were weak and shaky, and she still felt a bit lightheaded. But asking for help seemed just as difficult, for some odd reason.

Finally, she asked quietly, "Mefune?"

His gaze didn't stray from his work, but he muttered a quick, "Hmm?"

"I hate to ask, but...I don't think I can walk on my own right now," she started, sounding sheepish even to herself.

He stood before she could even get to the question and moved to help her. "There's no reason to be ashamed," he muttered as he crouched next to her. "You've been through a lot. Most would have given up a long time ago."

With his help, she made it to her feet, and then the pair limped into the cave. The entrance was damp like the ledge, but farther in, it was drier. Mefune lowered them to the ground near the cave wall, settling next to her. They both let out a weary sigh of exhaustion, and then Altaira chuckled. "I'm so tired I could sleep for ten years," she grumbled.

"You and me both," Mefune agreed as he relaxed against the cave wall. Surprisingly, he didn't move away. Blaming her exhaustion, Altaira didn't bother to either. She dozed quickly, finding it surprisingly comfortable leaning against his shoulder.

CHAPTER NINETEEN
THE COLONISTS

Mariea

After a week of waiting for the needed funds from the Brotherhood for their random boat purchase, finding and purchasing said boat, gathering supplies for an undetermined length of time, and then four days sailing, Mariea had never been happier to see a strip of land in her entire life. The small island from her vision appeared on the horizon not long after dinner, and they arrived at their destination just as the sun was setting over the island.

When they arrived, it took everything in Mariea to stay and help anchor the ship before exploring the island. Once finally on the beach, she took in her surroundings, hoping something would give her a clue about what to do next. There was a thick stretch of soft white sand for many miles to her left and right, and before her, it gave way to a dense tropical jungle. Distant hills rose above the tree line, but for the most part, the island was low and flat, nothing like their mountainous island home, which was much larger than this island.

But despite how beautiful the island was, she found it all a bit disappointing. She had been quietly hoping the solution to their problem would be finding a thriving Aurae community who happened to have all the answers, but it was clear nobody had been to the island in a long time.

"There are still remnant spells here," Bracken mused as he came to stand next to her. "They hide the island, but they haven't been maintained in a long time. They won't last much longer."

That Mariea could sense, and it was a bit of a relief. Solid proof that these colonists actually existed at some point made her feel a bit better. Maybe they had left behind something useful. Pushing forward, she began searching, unsure of what she was looking for but desperate for answers. As she glanced around, she realized some of the planks of wood lining the shore were the remnants of old docks, and she started towards them, hoping that from there she could locate where the settlement had been. She stood at the head of one and then turned to look inland, scanning the tree line.

When the vision came to her again, the dock reformed behind her, followed quickly by an image of Elinore. She hurried down the pier to meet a group from the ship that was now anchored there, gripping her skirts in her hands to prevent herself from tripping. Mariea recognized Rupert from her previous dream, and Elinore greeted him warmly, along with another man Mariea didn't recognize. He was younger, and judging by how Elinore treated him, Mariea guessed he was most likely a romantic interest. Then they moved towards the town, and Mariea followed.

— ℘ —

Elinore

Elinore embraced her father as they met on the dock and then turned to Densin, who quickly pulled her into a kiss, smothering her more public-appropriate greeting. She stood between the two most important men in her life, relieved they had returned home without incident. "How was your trip?" she asked them.

"Surprisingly, the first half was rather enjoyable," Rupert replied. "We didn't have any incidents when we made it to port. I think the magic there is finally working to make them stop questioning who we are and where we're coming from."

"That's good to hear," Elinore mused, knowing getting supplies would be so much easier if they could do it discreetly. The more people pried, the more questions they were forced to answer, and the more that exposed the Auraes to persecution.

"The journey home was stressful, however," Densin added. Elinore glanced at him, surprised by how weary he looked. He glanced at her, and then his gaze trailed to the town. "Having to leave port early without all the supplies we need is always hard. But we heard about the sickness. We had to know if our families were alright. Messages can only do so much."

Elinore frowned, sharing in his quiet worry for a moment. Living in such raw conditions, disease wasn't unexpected. Despite this, the medics kept everyone healthy, and their little town was growing more sophisticated by the day.

But the disease that had caused the supply ship to return early was particularly difficult to beat. It was like nothing the medics had seen before; it destroyed a person's aura, chipping away at it one piece at a time until they finally died after weeks of suffering. The medic's best efforts to contain and solve the problem proved insufficient. At first, they had tried to keep the situation quiet, but as it grew more urgent, the colonists noticed their preventative measures and the growing number of sick. Elinore hoped they would give them more details soon. Since she and Densin had a six-month-old son and a three-year-old daughter at home, she hardly ventured out, afraid of bringing it home to them.

Deciding she wanted to change the subject to something more positive, Elinore informed them, "There's a meeting in the town square. The governor said he had some important announcements to make. You made it back just in time to hear what he has to say if you want to head for the square."

"Very well then," Rupert agreed, and he started towards town. Densin offered Elinore his arm, and the couple fell into step behind her father. They passed into town, winding through the streets, the crowd around them slowly growing. The town center was surrounded by administration buildings and shops, which were temporarily closing as their workers started for the city center. The dirt roads kicked up dust as the crowd pressed forward, and the bright sun beat down on them from above the buildings. It was always hot on the island—something Elinore was sure she would never come to like, but at least she was growing accustomed to it.

Just before they reached the square, Elinore noticed one of her oldest friends, Clare, and her younger sister, Shareece. Elinore waved and called to them.

Clare turned and smiled, moving to walk with Elinore. "I'm surprised to see you here this morning. Where's the baby?" she wondered.

"With my mother. I needed to leave the house," Elinore admitted, earning a sympathetic chuckle from Clare. She had a young baby only a few months older than Elinore's son, so she understood the difficulties of being a new mother quite well.

"What do you think this meeting is about?" Shareece added as she joined them.

"No idea," Elinore said with a shake of her head.

Shareece shrugged and then switched the subject to her new job with the town seamstress. She seemed excited, her pale eyes bright as she smiled, but as Elinore listened, she couldn't help but notice the dark circles under her eyes and the pale tint to her skin. Usually, Shareece had more energy than this—normal conversation with the girl was like trying to keep up with a racehorse—but this one lacked her usual vigor.

Elinore found that her worry for Shareece was only made worse with everything going on, and she had to ask about her well-being. But she feared frightening everyone simultaneously, so she tried something less direct. "They're not working you to death there, are they?"

Shareece paused and then shook her head, managing a small laugh. "Oh, no. I'm just tired. I don't sleep well in the summer; it's just too hot," she admitted. Then something to her right caught her attention. She brightened, gave a rushed explanation that Elinore couldn't understand, and then disappeared into the crowd.

Densin chuckled. "I've never understood where she gets all that energy."

"Trust me, I've known her all her life, and I'm still trying to figure it out," Elinore agreed as she glanced at Clare, sharing a knowing look with her old friend.

Surprisingly, Clare's smile seemed less genuine. She glanced after her sister, her expression sobering a bit. "I'm worried about her," she admitted. "She hasn't looked well for a bit now. And, well, she looks even worse today."

"You don't think..." Elinore ventured carefully, but she found herself unable to finish her sentence.

Clare quickly caught on to her meaning, her gaze snapping to Elinore, a hint of fear there. She shook her head in denial. "It... it couldn't be." But then she bit her lip, her brow knitting in worry. "Could it? It's so hard to know what's going on."

Elinore couldn't find the words to reassure her; she knew as little as her friend did. Instead, she patted her shoulder gently, the best she could do in the crowded street. *If Shareece does have this new sickness, we'll know soon enough*, she thought with a frown. Quickly, she realized if Shareece had caught the mysterious disease, it would put Clare and her family at risk, as well as Elinore and Densin. So far, she hadn't witnessed the sickness in anyone she was close to, but a part of her began to wonder if she would be able to avoid it forever, considering how quickly it was spreading.

Soon they reached the town center, where everyone was gathering. It was packed, and as the remaining colonists filled the square, Elinore felt proud to realize just how much their numbers had swelled in the past few years. So many Auraes were pouring to the island, drawn by the promise of safety it offered.

The town's mayor, Woodrow Carson, stepped forward and raised a hand, asking for silence. It took a long while for the crowd to quiet. When it finally did, he began, "I gather you here today to discuss the recent problem we have been facing; this new disease. It's claiming lives faster than we can catch up. We need to find a cure quickly. Several are ill now and need our help."

Elinore let out a small sigh. She had hoped the announcement would be something positive, but it was good to finally get more information on the situation. Gesturing to the man at his side, the mayor told them, "This is Joseph Redro, our senior medic. He will explain further what we need of you."

Joseph stepped forward to take over the conversation. "My friends, we are very close to finding a cure, but we need some of you to assist us. We are looking for young people with fresh, lesser developed auras, particularly people between twelve and twenty-five. These auras are still moldable and will work best for our experiments. It's a bit hard to explain exactly what we're looking for, and I won't attempt to for the sake of time. If you want to help, we can tell you if your aura will work. We also need volunteers to help us make the cure. You don't need any medical training to help us with either task. If you are willing to assist, please gather here on the stage. The rest of the public can be dismissed. We will give you more details when we have them."

As Joseph finished and the crowd began to disperse—more so towards the town than the stage—Elinore glanced at Densin, wondering what he was thinking. One look at his expression, and she realized he wanted to help.

"I want to volunteer," he told her softly.

Elinore nodded. "I'd help too, but the children," she muttered.

"You go," Rupert interrupted, surprising Elinore. "If this is what you want to do, your mother and I will take care of the grandchildren as long as you need." He glanced at the stage. "It doesn't seem like they're getting very many volunteers as it is. I would, but I'm obviously too old. So we'll support you in your efforts to help."

Elinore smiled gratefully. She hugged her father, muttering a quick thank you, before retaking Densin's hand. The couple made their way to the stage. As they joined the small group gathering with the mayor and Joseph, he turned towards them. "Ah, more volunteers? What are your names?"

"I'm Densin Remar, and this is my wife, Elinore," Densin introduced.

Joseph nodded, scribbled their names onto a notepad, and then told them, "Thank you for your assistance." Turning back towards the town square, he let out a small sigh, realizing almost everyone had left, and the remaining few had little interest in joining them on the stage.

Elinore couldn't help but feel a bit disappointed. But then again, most of the age group he had requested were still children.

With so few details about what was happening, she was sure she'd be reluctant to allow her children to participate. Luckily, after a quick headcount, she realized they had still collected roughly forty volunteers.

"We'll go to our lab, and my team and I will explain what we need of you in more detail." Joseph continued. "Please, follow me."

With that, he started into town, and Elinore and the others followed. They made their way to the edge of the settlement, where the jungle rose to meet the buildings; thick foliage and tall, ancient trees reached for them, the sounds of wildlife echoing from within. Joseph started down a narrow path. The jungle was still an eerie place to Elinore, even after living among it for over a decade, making her a little hesitant to follow. But Densin plowed on, oblivious to her concerns, and since he was still holding her hand, he pulled her along as well. Elinore took a deep breath to steady her nerves and tried not to think about what might be hiding just beyond the foliage.

The journey was mostly silent. They hadn't traveled long when a large, square structure appeared from among the trees. It was surrounded by deep gorges, leaving only a narrow ledge to the structure's opening. It lacked windows, leaving Elinore to wonder how they kept the building lit. A thousand candles would never be enough. The walls were entirely made of the surrounding soil, which she guessed would explain the deep holes. Despite how impressive it was to have formed the building from the earth, it gave it a primitive appearance that was far from inviting.

"Is that really the lab?" Elinore wondered quietly as she leaned towards Densin. She couldn't imagine staying a day in the drab structure.

"That's what I was thinking," Densin muttered in agreement, eyeing it warily.

As they neared the rugged building, Joseph informed them, "It looks less than pleasant. We just needed a simple structure quickly, so we used elemental magics to form the surrounding earth into this. It's crude, but it gets the job done." With that, he gestured them inside.

The walk across the narrow strip of land to the door was a bit nerve-racking. The gaping holes on either side were deep enough that one would probably suffer some severe wounds if one were to fall. At least there were plenty of medics nearby to help if that were to happen.

One by one, the group filed into the building and then gathered on the other side of the entrance. As Elinore stepped through, she first noticed it was impressively light, and the air was comfortably cool, allowing her to escape the jungle's oppressive heat for the first time in a long while. She couldn't resist a small sigh, smiling slightly.

Then she noticed Densin and most of the others with her were staring upwards with expressions of surprise and wonder. Elinore looked up, wondering what had drawn their attention. Instead of the rocky ceiling she had expected, she discovered a solid wall of what looked like a contained aura, thousands of colors swirling across its surface. It lit the room but didn't hurt to look at, as if it only gave off the gentle light of a typical aura.

"Ah, I see you've discovered our little *dan*," Joseph commented as he entered the room behind them. Elinore recognized the Shidokian word for sun. "It maintains the temperature in the room and supplies us with hassle-free, consistent lighting. We figured that was easier than constantly sweating while working in poor lighting." He paused, allowing them some time to admire their work, and then waved them on, saying, "Come now, there's much to be done and little time to do it."

The group reluctantly moved on, Elinore and Densin among them. Joseph led them through the lab, which was full of multiple workstations set up in a haphazard way that suggested they had been placed there quickly with little thought for organization. medics buzzed about, working on a thousand different things at once, their auras and expressions reflecting the strain Elinore was sure they felt. They glanced up at the group, and some seemed relieved to see the volunteers. Elinore only hoped they'd be able to assist them as much as the medics needed.

Joseph led them to a more open area near the center of the large structure, where a couple of other medics waited for them. There were low wooden benches placed in rows before the medics, and the volunteers were invited to take a seat.

Joseph joined his comrades at the front of the group before addressing them again. "I would like to introduce you to the medics leading the research on this project." Gesturing to the middle-aged woman with brown hair and hazel eyes and a stern expression, he continued, "This is Sariah Ashcroft, the mind behind the idea for the cure and its creation."

He then indicated the man standing next to Sariah, who had blond hair and light brown eyes, and seemed much younger than the other two medics. "This is Andrew Griesenbeck. He oversees a very specialized part of the experiment known as grafting, which we will explain in a moment." Turning back to Sariah, he asked, "Please, could you explain the basic functions of the cure and how it was created?"

"Of course," she replied with a nod. "The cure is what you might call an artificial aura. It can temporarily collect someone's aura within it without harming the person, and then essentially purge it of the disease while encouraging it to regenerate faster than normal. We refer to this process as *purifying*.

"Although our early tests were promising, we quickly realized there was one flaw in the cure's design. Ridding an aura of the disease doesn't work if we try to purify it a bit at a time. The disease spreads very rapidly, and when confronted by the cure, it only spreads faster, meaning it will most likely kill the person before the treatment can do its job. This leaves us with only one option—an entire aura must be purified at once, which would require a whole aura's worth of the cure. Unfortunately, it becomes nearly impossible to contain and control the cure once there is that much of it in one place. This left us with a solution, but no way to use it.

"Eventually, we came up with a solution. If we graft the cure to a healthy aura, it would adopt the abilities of the cure and essentially allow that Aurae to become the cure. They could then purify as many auras as needed, allowing the cure to be more efficient. That is why we need young, fresh auras." She paused briefly and then asked, "Any questions?"

A woman raised her hand, and when Sariah glanced her way, she asked, "How is the grafting even possible? I didn't think we could modify auras."

"I believe Andrew will have more useful insight into the matter." Sariah gestured to her colleague, who stepped forward to take her place.

"The grafting has proven to be the most troublesome part of this experiment," Andrew began. "As you said, we've never been able to alter the nature of our auras, but I've long since believed it to be possible—we just haven't tried it because of the danger it poses. The aura is so intertwined with an Aurae's life that tampering with it could have serious consequences. Unfortunately, we did run into these consequences in our early experiments. We have only attempted a small handful of grafts, and almost all were rejected. The one that did take almost instantly killed the Aurae."

Gasps and nervous whispers passed through the crowd, to which Andrew raised a hand in a reassuring gesture. "That incident was regrettable, but it was a one time ordeal that we have guaranteed will not happen again. This is the reason we need younger, less developed auras. They're far more capable of adapting and, therefore, capable of receiving the graft without immediate risk to their life. We aren't sure what side effects could present afterward, but we believe it is possible to retract the graft with some work."

This seemed to reassure the crowd. Elinore at least felt better about it.

"With this, we know there may be some of you unwilling to take such a great risk, and we understand that," Andrew added. "Please, if you feel you cannot participate in these experiments, at least consider staying to help create the cure. But if you would rather not participate at all, feel free to leave at any time during this meeting. Just remember, this is our only hope of stopping the spread of this disease. I must be frank; at the rate it is spreading, it poses a serious threat to our community. We must get ahead of it quickly if we want to survive."

Elinore was surprised by how few chose to leave. Most were parents with younger children close to the cut-off age who had decided they didn't want them to take the risk. It warmed her heart to know so many were willing to help.

Obviously pleased as well, Joseph smiled as he told the group, "Thank you again for your willingness. From here, we need to determine where you can best help us. For those of you who are willing to accept the grafts, we must test your aura to make sure it will be compatible. Andrew will help with this, so please remain here if you would like to be tested. For those of you who do not qualify or would rather just help with the cure, please meet up with Sariah. She will help find a place for you within the process of creating the cure. After this, you will be immediately shown to your workspace. Good luck!"

As the crowd began breaking into two groups around Sariah and Andrew, Elinore glanced at Densin. "What would you like to do?" she wondered.

His gaze trailed towards Andrew. "I would at least like to check if my aura is compatible." Elinore nodded. He glanced at her and asked, "What about you?"

She hesitated, glancing towards the group Densin would be joining in a moment. "I...don't know. I'm a little worried about the danger it poses. I have to think of the kids."

Densin nodded. "Would you rather me not, then?"

Once again, Elinore wasn't sure how to respond at first. The group around Andrew was considerably smaller than the group around Sariah. And the volunteers hadn't numbered that many to begin with. As much as she wanted to tell Densin no for the sake of their family, she also couldn't forget Andrew's warning towards the end of his explanation. They needed this cure, which meant they needed people willing to risk themselves and accept the graft. Her family was still at risk if they didn't have a treatment.

She let out another sigh and then told him, "No, they need you. Just get tested, I guess. We can worry about the details later."

Densin nodded. "See you in a moment, then?" he told her.

She nodded, so he started for Andrew's group. As Elinore joined the back of Sariah's group, the older woman began making her way through the crowd, asking them questions briefly before writing a few things down and then handing them a small piece of paper.

As she reached Elinore, she asked, "Your name please?" Elinore supplied it, causing Sariah to glance over her ledger before finding Elinore's name. "We're mostly looking for people with skills in elemental magics and crafting spells. Which would you feel you'd be better at?"

Elinore debated it briefly. She hadn't spent too much time with either, but she knew she was more experienced with the elements. "I'd say I lean more towards the elemental magics."

Sariah nodded. "Take this, and when we split into smaller groups, stick with the others with similar dot colors." She handed Elinore a palm-sized piece of paper with a small, orange dab of paint in the center. Elinore nodded, and Sariah moved on.

After she finished, they broke off into smaller groups based on their dot color and were led to workstations. Elinore and about ten others were directed to an area with several long rows of tables. A group of Auraes were scattered among them, keeping fires lit underneath small pots, their auras swirling around them as they worked.

The Aurae leading Elinore's group paused, his gaze on the tables as he explained, "During a point in the creation of the cure, it must cook at an exact temperature for a certain amount of time. We found it easiest to use Fire Magic in this case because it's the only way to guarantee the correct temperature. You will each be assigned a table to manage, but don't worry if you can't keep the fire going for long or manage many at once; we will work with whatever you can." With that, he began assigning them to tables.

Soon, Elinore found herself working. It wasn't hard for her to maintain the small fires on her table, and she quickly realized the task would become very monotonous. Somehow, she kept herself focused well enough, and time flew by. Towards the end of the day, they were given more details about the schedule for the foreseeable future and when the medics would like them to return the next day before they were sent home. Elinore couldn't help but feel relieved the busy day was over. She found she desperately wanted to find Densin and learn how his day had been, and return to their children.

As she neared the entrance, she recognized his black hair and tall form among the crowd and hurried to him. "How did it go?" she asked.

Densin smiled as he greeted her. "My aura's perfect for the graft," he informed her, his words borderline a brag. Elinore nodded, a rush of concern and excitement immediately competing for her attention. When she didn't immediately respond, he asked, "You're still alright with me going through with this, correct?"

"Yes, yes. I just...I worry. But it's my job to worry about you, is it not?" she told him with a reassuring smile. "Just be careful."

"Of course. If I ever feel things are getting too risky, I'll back out. I promise I won't leave you to raise our children alone, no matter what," he told her before placing a gentle kiss on her temple. Then he took her hand and put it on his arm. "Come. I'm in desperate need of a good meal and a bed. We should get home."

CHAPTER TWENTY

GRAFTS

Mariea

The vision retreated, but Mariea did not return to her world yet. She watched as several days passed quickly. Elinore continued to work on her part of the cure. Luckily, more volunteers joined them as time went on, swelling their numbers to one hundred. With the extra hands, things went much faster. Despite this, the heavy sense of worry did not leave them, emphasized by several more colonists falling ill even as others lost the battle with the disease. They were racing against time to get the cure for their comrades and loved ones before the sickness managed to wipe out the whole colony. No amount of quarantining or precautions seemed to prevent its spread.

Then, three weeks later, they had finally created enough of the cure to attempt the first graft...

— ❧ —

Elinore

Elinore pushed her way through the throng of busy people, clutching a small vial close to her chest. In the vial swirled a murky green gas, the result of hours of grueling work by the team of medics and volunteers gathered in their makeshift lab. After seeing just how much of the chemicals had been poured into the final pot to cook, Elinore had hoped they would have enough cure to attempt several grafts. However, when the final vial emerged, hardly anything was left of what had been poured in. Now, it wasn't hard to see why they needed so many Auraes working on the process—it would take years to finish with the small group of medics available.

When she reached a closed-off area near the far end of the laboratory, Elinore slowed her pace as she stepped through the curtains. About a dozen medics were gathered there. She searched the group for the now-familiar splash of blond hair and finally found Andrew.

He noticed her approaching and then brightened when he saw the vial in her hands. "Finally," he muttered before asking one of his team to go retrieve one of the graft volunteers. He turned back to Elinore and took the vial from her hands. His brow furrowed slightly as he studied it. "This is all of it?"

"Yes. Did you need more?" Elinore wondered, worried he would say yes and the graft would be delayed again.

"No, this will do for one graft. But I was hoping with the number of volunteers we brought in, the process would have been sped up. It seems we're moving slower now," he muttered.

Another medic entered before Elinore could reply, followed closely by Densin, which made her frown slightly. She had said she was okay with him helping, but volunteering first seemed rash. When Densin noticed her, he gave a small wave. He smiled at her, but it couldn't entirely hide the nervousness in his expression.

"Would you excuse me?" Elinore asked Andrew. Before he could reply, she was already moving toward her husband. When she reached Densin, she stepped close and quietly asked, "You volunteered first?"

"Yes," Densin confirmed with a shrug.

"Why? It's dangerous, remember?" she reminded him.

Densin glanced at the medics, who were all waiting for him, but were simultaneously trying not to eavesdrop. He gently pulled her out of the room before continuing. "I didn't want to wait any longer. They weren't allowing me to do anything with my aura. I was just sitting around, waiting while you and the team worked, when all I wanted to do was help. I couldn't take it anymore. When I heard the graft was ready, I had to volunteer first. I thought you said you were okay with this," he replied.

"Well, yes, I am, but I was hoping you would at least let them work out the kinks before jumping in headlong," Elinore pressed.

He shrugged slightly. "It's risky, but I'm sure they can handle it. Only one person has died so far out of the several they've tried. I'll be fine."

Elinore didn't respond. She knew much more was playing into his decision than just him wanting to help find a cure. Though that was the majority of it, she knew he also saw this as an opportunity to prove himself. He would never admit it, but she knew his father's disappointment over Densin's weak aura still lingered in the back of his mind. He had told her repeatedly he didn't let it bother him, but his actions often spoke differently.

He seemed to realize she still wasn't happy with the situation. "I can back out if you want me to," he told her, though he didn't sound very enthusiastic about the idea.

Elinore let out a sigh and shook her head. "No, if this is what you want, then go ahead."

He smiled softly. "I'll be fine," he promised before giving her a gentle kiss and heading back inside.

Elinore hesitated a moment and then followed him in. Typically, only the medics were present for graft attempts, but she hoped Andrew would make an exception for her, considering her relation to Densin.

Finding the medic again, she asked, "Would it be possible for me to stay?"

"Sorry, my dear, no spectators allowed, I'm afraid," he responded quickly. His team was already busy giving Densin instructions and situating him on the bed near the center of the room. Andrew's gaze trailed towards them, clearly eager to return to his work.

"Please," Elinore insisted. "I'm his wife. I just want to make sure he'll be okay."

Andrew glanced back at her, his gaze softening slightly. After a brief hesitation, he let out a small sigh and relented, "Alright. But just this once. Don't let word of this spread, or I'll have the whole island peering down my neck for a glimpse at my work."

Elinore brightened and nodded. "I promise, not a word."

Andrew smiled. "Alright then, let's get to it," he stated as he turned towards Densin. "Are you ready?"

"I believe so," Densin agreed. His gaze trailed to the small vial Andrew still held. "So that's it, then? Looks harmless enough, I guess."

"Looks can be deceiving," Andrew stated with a bittersweet smile, his words carrying the weight of experience. "Let me remind you, this process is not risk-free. Are you willing to accept those risks?"

Densin nodded. "People need this. I'm not backing out now."

Seeming a bit reassured, Andrew nodded. "Alright then, we'll proceed—one more thing. Throughout the grafting, you must listen carefully to my every instruction. Even if things get a bit worrisome, don't panic. You're in good hands here." Densin nodded, managing a half-smile.

The medics gathered around him, and then Andrew waved Elinore over. She cautiously approached, taking up a spot on Andrew's left. "As long as you don't involve yourself in the magic and maintain your distance from Densin while the graft occurs, feel free to stay here," he told her softly.

Elinore nodded. She felt quite out-of-place standing with the group of medics, but she stayed put, trying not to seem nervous for Densin's sake.

"Let your aura be free," Andrew instructed Densin, so Densin's pale gray aura surrounded him. The medics followed suit, first with Andrew's bright yellow aura. They shared a glance, and then Andrew nodded. He began a spell, and the others quickly joined in, layering their magic with his as the room filled with the sound of many Shidokian phrases blending together. Elinore couldn't help but be fascinated. She knew building intertwining spells simultaneously was incredibly complicated. Whatever they were doing was magic far beyond anything she had ever tried.

After a bit, Andrew opened the vial, and the ugly green vapor slowly leaked from it. Before it could get too far, he spoke a couple of muttered words, and it was suddenly caught in his aura, pulling towards him. Static electricity danced between the two substances where they touched. Elinore could sense the tension the interaction caused and couldn't help but worry about it. If this was supposed to merge with Densin's aura, should it be reacting that way to Andrew's aura?

As the medics continued to craft the spells, the green mist left Andrew's aura to surround Densin's. He watched it curiously, as did Elinore. The words of the spells changed as the medics continued, and Elinore sensed a shift in the magic; it was hard to keep track of what they were saying with everyone talking at once, but there was something strangely wrong about the spells. She shivered slightly, hating the ominous undertone that settled over the room. Never had she been uncomfortable around Aurae magic, but the spells they were using left a dark feeling in the pit of her stomach.

As the spells continued to progress, the line between Densin's aura and the cure began to blur. He frowned, seeming a little uncomfortable, and then he gasped, his eyes widening for a second before squeezing shut as his whole body tensed with pain. Elinore's breath caught, surprised by the sudden shift. She stepped closer, but then remembered Andrew's warning. There had to be a reason he had explicitly told her to keep her distance.

Her worry only grew as Densin's pain seemed to grow worse. Without realizing it, her fear brought her aura to light, causing it to surround her faintly. The spells continued, and Densin seemed to be growing weaker. Elinore glanced at Andrew, wondering if this was normal and if he was as worried for Densin as she was. He seemed a little nervous as he took in Densin's condition, but he wasn't panicking. She forced herself to calm a little at this. If he wasn't overly concerned, she had to believe things were going the way they should. She just hoped his lack of reaction wasn't simply because the pattern was following the failed experiments, and it no longer concerned him to see such a reaction.

Finally, it became impossible to tell the difference between the graft and Densin's aura as the murky green replaced his usual gray. The medics began sealing their spells, which she knew was the last step in any spell. Elinore could tell Densin's strength was fading fast, and she desperately hoped they would finish soon. He was no longer conscious, and she would have questioned if he was still breathing if it weren't for the obvious reactions to the pain he still felt and his aura surrounding him.

When the medics finally stopped chanting, Densin's aura disappeared quickly. The pain was finally gone, but it left him looking so lifeless. Elinore couldn't stand it anymore. She stepped into the center of the circle to take his hand in hers. His skin was clammy, but now that she was closer, she could tell he was still breathing softly, which reassured her.

"Did we lose him?" one of the medics asked softly.

"No," Andrew reassured them with a slight shake of his head. "If we were going to lose him, he would have died already. He'll make it." He glanced up, and his gaze passed over the group as he managed a smile, albeit a weary one. "Congratulations, my friends. We've accomplished something truly extraordinary."

"But at what cost?" the medic to Elinore's left whispered, so quietly Elinore was sure she was the only one who had heard it. The woman stared at Densin, and her expression sent chills down Elinore's spine.

Before she could ask her what she meant, another medic stated, "I wished there was something we could do to help him. His aura is so weak."

"It will recover, as will he. We should let him rest. I can monitor him from a distance," Andrew told them.

The medics slipped away, but Elinore stayed. She sunk onto the bed next to Densin, suddenly overcome with a wave of intense exhaustion that she wasn't sure she had the strength to remain standing. She steadied herself, her brow furrowing in confusion at the sudden lack of energy. She hadn't been doing anything to warrant it.

One of the medics returned after a while with a blanket, which she helped Elinore place over Densin so he could sleep more comfortably. She stayed by his side, gently stroking the back of his hand. Slowly, the color returned to his face, and he seemed to be resting soundly. Elinore's hope that he would pull through increased with each slight improvement.

Elinore hadn't even realized she had dozed until she was shocked awake by a gasp as Densin sat up partly. He glanced around, disoriented, until he found her.

Relief chased her worry away, and her shoulders slumped as she managed a smile. "Hey," she greeted softly.

He tried to push himself into a proper sitting position with a quiet grunt, and she quickly moved to help. "What happened?" he managed.

"From what I can tell, the graft worked, but you passed out," she informed him. Immediately, he brought his aura to light around his hand and raised it slightly, studying the change to it in silence. Elinore noticed the murky green of the cure had faded, allowing his aura to return to its natural pale gray. However, it still felt odd, like the cure had, and she frowned slightly, not sure she cared for the change. It left a wrong impression on her, like something wasn't right about his aura.

Then his aura faded as his focus shifted to her. "Thank you for staying. It was good to have you near. I...really think you being here gave me the strength to survive."

"I wasn't about to leave you," she reassured him. "But you did this on your own. You were so strong and brave."

To her surprise, he shook his head slightly. "I didn't mean it like that. I meant it literally. Somehow, I was able to draw on the strength of your aura. It was endless, and when my strength failed, you easily supported us both, maybe without even noticing it."

"Oh," Elinore muttered, surprised. *Maybe that's why I felt so tired earlier*, she mused.

Just then, Andrew poked his head in and then brightened when he saw Densin was awake. "Ah! Densin! I thought I sensed you were awake. How are you feeling?" he asked as he stepped into the small room.

"Better now that I've had time to rest," Densin replied.

"Good, good. We were worried there for a moment," he commented. "But I knew you would be fine." Elinore couldn't help but note he now spoke with a confidence that had definitely not been there earlier. "Now. How about your aura? Does it seem any different?"

"Mmm..." Densin muttered, his aura appearing around him again. "It seems stronger. Much stronger."

"Hmm," Andrew contemplated, studying the aura curiously. Elinore wondered if he sensed the change she could and if it bothered him as much as it did her.

"And I noticed I can hear better and see much clearer now. Suddenly, life seems so detailed and clear, like I've been living underneath a sheet," Densin added.

"An unexpected but welcome bonus, it seems," Andrew mused. "It does make some sense; the graft was designed to enhance the aura's natural regeneration processes. It seems it does the same thing for other functions as well."

"Now we just have to see if the cure works," Densin stated.

"Oh, it will. But I think it would be better if we wait a few days and allow you to rest," Andrew suggested.

Densin sighed, clearly reluctant to wait, but Elinore could see the exhaustion in his expression. "I should be ready by tomorrow," he decided.

Andrew smiled, a hint of admiration in his gaze. "Tomorrow then. We'll talk about the details then. You rest."

"Yes, doctor," Densin agreed with a mock salute and a weary half-smile, and then settled back into the bed with a sigh.

"We should leave him be," Andrew suggested to Elinore.

She glanced at Densin, reluctant to leave him alone, but he was already dozing. "You're probably right," Elinore agreed, and followed the medic out.

As they stepped from the room, Andrew paused and said, "He'll have to remain here overnight for observation. I can arrange for a place for both of you to stay if you would like."

"I should probably go home," Elinore reluctantly decided. "We have two kids I need to care for. You'll tell me if anything changes?"

"Of course. But before you go, could I speak to you in private for a moment, please?"

"I have time," she agreed, so he gestured for her to follow.

He led her to his makeshift office along one of the lab walls; it was one of few rooms with actual walls and a door within the entire building, though it lacked a roof, allowing the makeshift *dan* above to supply light still. Inside, he sunk into the chair behind his desk with a heavy sigh.

"Is everything alright?" Elinore wondered.

He nodded. "Quite alright, actually. It's just...something about this whole thing unsettles me." He waved his hand as if to brush away the worries and said, "Never mind. That's not what I wanted to discuss with you."

Leaning forward, he rested his arms against the desk and looked up to meet her gaze. "By my account, Densin should not have survived."

Elinore's brow furrowed in confusion. "What do you mean? He's obviously fine."

"Yes, but something happened during the graft to make that possible. Something none of us had planned for," Andrew explained.

"What?" Elinore pressed.

Andrew shook his head slightly, his gaze falling away slightly as he contemplated the question himself. "I'm not entirely sure, but I think it had something to do with you."

Elinore blinked in surprise, staring at him. When she finally found her voice, she managed a breathy, "Me?"

"Yes," Andrew confirmed. "I'm not sure how, but he drew from your strength. We will have to learn to compensate for that in future grafts."

"Oh," Elinore muttered, reflecting on the brief conversation she had shared with Densin before Andrew had joined them. *I guess he was right*, she mused.

"I wanted to ask if you knew anything about it," Andrew added.

Elinore thought about it for a moment. "Not really. I was pretty tired afterward, and Densin mentioned he believes something similar, so I think you might be right, but...well, I don't know."

"Hmm," Andrew muttered. "Well, think about it. If you come up with anything, let me know, alright?"

"Of course," Elinore agreed with a nod.

Chapter Twenty-One
Healing

Elinore

About a week after the graft was completed, Densin was finally allowed to begin using his new aura. He and Andrew traveled to a nearby quarantine camp, leaving everyone else waiting in anticipation. At the lab, little work was accomplished that day—Elinore found herself too anxious to focus on much for long, and she wasn't the only one.

When Densin and Andrew returned near nightfall, a crowd gathered around the entrance to the lab. Once Elinore realized why, she hurried to join them, eager to see Densin again and hear how his new aura had worked. As she reached the door, she quickly realized she had arrived too late to get close to him right away. Andrew was speaking to the crowd with Densin at his side, who watched them all with a sheepish half-smile. She couldn't hear what Andrew was saying, but she figured it was good news when the crowd began clapping, bringing a smile to her face.

After a bit, Andrew escorted Densin through the crowd. Elinore quickly moved to intercept. Everyone wanted to talk to him and Andrew, making it difficult for her to reach them, but Densin noticed her and redirected Andrew to meet up with her.

They finally managed to escape the crowd with Andrew's help, and Elinore embraced Densin as she told him, "Congratulations!"

"Thanks," he sighed as he pulled her closer. He lingered, and suddenly she sensed a weight to him that didn't make sense. When he finally stepped back, she met his gaze, giving him a questioning look.

Densin glanced over his shoulder at Andrew and asked, "Do you need me anymore?"

Andrew shook his head. Densin nodded and took Elinore's hand. He slipped through the lab, moving quickly without explaining where he was heading. He led her out of the lab and into the dark jungle. Despite her original apprehension of venturing into the trees at night, she only hesitated a moment before following him, knowing he wouldn't take her there without good reason. Once the lab was no longer in sight, he finally stopped and leaned against a tree with a heavy sigh.

"Are you alright?" she asked, unsure of how to interpret his behavior. He seemed very melancholy for someone who had just spent the day helping people and moving the entire island one step closer to beating the disease. She hoped it was just exhaustion after a long day's work, but something told her this was more.

"Mostly," he muttered, sounding very uncertain. "I think."

"What's wrong?" she asked, stepping closer to take his hand.

Instead of responding, he brought his aura to light around his hand and muttered a quick spell to create a small orb of light that hovered to his left, illuminating their small grove. Doing so allowed her to realize his aura had changed colors again to the murky green of the graft.

Before she could consider what that meant, he told her, "Sorry, I didn't choose the best place to talk."

Knowing he was probably worried she would be fearful of the jungle, she forced what apprehension she did feel away and told him, "I don't mind. Tell me what's bothering you."

"Something happened today, and I need to tell someone," he started, shifting slightly. He wouldn't look at her, which only made her worry more. He stayed silent for a moment, gathering his thoughts. "Healing those people was one of the most amazing things I've ever experienced, but...not for the reasons I had expected. It was nice knowing I was helping them, but there was...something else. Something with my aura. I don't know how to explain it." He shook his head slightly, clearly annoyed words were failing him so entirely.

After a pause, he continued. "When I had total control over their aura, there was this...I felt...powerful. Limitless. I've never known what it's like to have a strong aura, but for a minute there, I did, and it was an amazing feeling. It was almost irrational just how happy it made me—how *good* it felt. I wanted it to stay. At first, I thought it was because I was helping. But the feeling only grew stronger the more I used my aura, and when I gave their aura back, it would fade."

He looked up at her warily. "The worst part is, I know if I were to keep their aura, that feeling would stay for much longer. And...I think I could. I could take their aura and make it part of mine."

"But that would kill them," Elinore pointed out, shocked they were even discussing it.

He nodded, his gaze on the ground. "I know. But the longer I worked, the harder it was to ignore the urge to see if it was possible. It seems so obviously wrong now, but in the moment, I had a hard time ignoring that urge. I almost lost it with that last aura. It was so powerful." He shook his head, a hint of shame in his expression. "The problem is, the desire to steal those auras never went away. There's still a tiny part of me that wants to run back right now and see what would happen if I tried it, as revolting as that is. I worry it will never go away. There's been something different about my aura since the graft. I'm far more aware of the auras around me. Now, it's nearly impossible to ignore them."

For a moment, Elinore didn't know what to say. She stepped closer, tightening her grip on his hand slightly in an attempt to comfort him. After a moment, she quietly asked him, "What do we do about this?"

Densin shrugged, his frustration returning slightly. "I have to keep healing them. This is the only answer we have right now."

"Should we tell the medics? They might be able to help."

He seemed to consider it for a moment, and then his lips pressed into a thin line as he shook his head. "I wanted to. But after seeing the joy and excitement among them, and seeing the sick get better, I couldn't take that away from them. If the medics know what I experienced, I'm sure they'll make me stop. I'll wait until I've healed everyone I can, and then I'll tell them."

"But...what if you..." Elinore started, but found she couldn't finish. She didn't want to imagine what would happen if he did slip and gave in to the temptation to keep an aura.

"I won't let that happen," Densin insisted with surprising force. He swallowed hard, a haunted look in his eyes. "I can't."

Elinore let out a small sigh and told him, "If you think you can handle it, I trust you."

He smiled slightly, meeting her gaze again. "Thank you. I don't know what I would do without you," he told her, before placing a gentle kiss on her temple.

She didn't respond, part of her wondering if they had made the wrong decision. It seemed like a significant problem, and leaving it alone didn't seem reasonable. And the medics were about to attempt another graft in a couple of days. Would they all suffer from the same temptation?

"I wonder what caused this. I'm sure the medics didn't want this to happen," she muttered.

Densin shrugged as he shook his head slightly. "Who knows? All of this is so experimental. I didn't realize just how impossible the graft should be until I saw how baffled some of the medics working in the quarantine camp were. Even they couldn't understand what my aura could do. I guess we're in uncharted waters now."

"I guess," Elinore agreed quietly. "I just hope, after you tell the medics about all of this, they'll be able to find a solution."

He nodded slightly. "Hopefully." Then he pushed away from the tree and took a deep breath as he glanced up at the sky. "But I could use a good night's rest for now, and it's late. We should get home. I don't want our kids to start forgetting us."

Elinore let out a small, amused huff and nodded. They made their way back to the path leading away from the lab and started for home.

— 𝑒 —

The following day, work began more vigorously on making more of the cure, newfound energy amongst the team brought on by Densin's success. He continued healing over the next few days, but he was more careful not to overwhelm himself. He found spending his free time alone and keeping away from large crowds of Auraes soothed the need to steal auras slightly. But Elinore hated to see him so isolated, so when he would allow it, she accompanied him. More often than not, she was with him. She figured he didn't want to be alone either but didn't have much choice in the matter.

Despite the graft's major disadvantage, there were also some advantages. His increased awareness of the world around him remained, and his aura seemed more potent, more capable. When he used it for magic, Elinore couldn't help but be amazed by how quickly he caught on to new techniques and how easily he completed previously difficult tasks.

It wasn't long after their first day spent healing that Elinore heard another graft was attempted and succeeded. She eventually learned from Andrew how they managed to compensate for the strength she had accidentally lent Densin— energy drawn from spells such as was used to create the artificial lighting in the lab. It wasn't as clean a solution as her aura had been, but it somehow worked, satisfying the medics. Elinore didn't pretend to understand, but she was grateful they had found a solution, and the whole situation had benefited from her accidental contribution.

Over the next few weeks, several more grafts were completed. Each graft was more straightforward than the last as the medics explored the possibilities the spells offered and altered them to make things easier.

Beyond the lab, word spread quickly of their success, and, somehow, the few benefits of the graft leaked as well. It made Elinore a bit uncomfortable to see how it excited the general populous, especially since they didn't know anything about the adverse effects of the graft. She asked Densin a couple more times if he wanted to speak to somebody about his struggles, but he seemed set on keeping it quiet. Eventually, she stopped asking.

Then, one day, the medics gathered the whole settlement together at the town square and announced they could now offer the graft to anyone willing to take it, regardless of their aura, and with none of the previous risks. Many stepped forward. Though most of the new volunteers seemed to want to help Densin and the other healers, Elinore wondered if at least a few of them were interested in gaining the extra power the graft offered.

As the crowd dispersed and a much larger group began heading back to the lab, Densin let out a small sigh. "It'll be nice to have more hands to help."

"It will," Elinore agreed. Despite her apprehensions, she realized more grafts would speed up the healing process, meaning Densin would be able to find a solution to his struggles sooner.

"Now that you can, will you take the graft?" he asked.

Elinore didn't answer for a moment. "I don't know."

"If you don't want to, nobody will judge you for it," he reassured her, obviously picking up on her hesitation.

She sighed. "I'm just worried. There's still so much we don't understand."

"That's understandable. I wouldn't wish this burden on anyone," he admitted. "Plus, you're already doing plenty by helping the medics make the cure. We're going to need a lot more of it now."

Elinore nodded. "I'll stick to that, then, I guess." Glancing at him cautiously, she added, "Do you think we should warn them about the side effects before they start spreading the graft to so many people?"

He frowned slightly, and part of her wondered if she had annoyed him by asking again. "No. The other healers and I are learning to deal with it, so it's not nearly as much of a problem."

Elinore nodded again. She couldn't help but be worried they weren't making the right decision, but she figured he knew best. He was the one dealing with all the change, not her. It wasn't her call to make. Plus, she trusted him.

— ✑ —

Mariea

The vision faded slightly, but Mariea could still see Elinore for a moment more. Over the next few months, the colony finally managed to cure the last of the diseased, and life seemed to return to normal. Time passed as if she was watching the next couple of years in fast forward. After a time, Densin and Elinore's family were able to move to the farm they had bought on the outskirts of town. Their children grew, and they were happy.

But it seemed their peace would not last forever. Just as the vision began to fade, Mariea heard rumors of unrest beginning to circulate through the town, and it seemed not even Elinore's young family would be able to escape.

Snapping back to reality, Mariea found herself laying on the sand, Bracken at her side, looking incredibly worried. "I'm alright," she grunted, and immediately his shoulders slumped in relief.

Pushing herself up into a sitting position, she leaned her elbow against her leg, pinching the bridge of her nose between her fingers. It was hard to get her mind back to the present; the vision had seemed so real that she felt she had been yanked from one reality to another. She had been there, feeling and living everything Elinore had to the point the images seemed more like memories.

"You sure you're alright?" Mae asked, reminding Mariea she wasn't alone. She was kneeling on Mariea's left, opposite Bracken, and seemed just as worried.

"Yes, I'm fine," Mariea reassured them, lifting her head slightly as she finally managed to gather her thoughts. Her gaze trailed to the remnants of the dock just a few feet away, and she realized that was the second time she had stood in the same place as Elinore and a vision had been triggered. "It seems when I come to places Elinore has been, I see more of what it was she wanted to show me. I see her life. It's almost as if I'm living it."

Bracken gently brushed the sand from her hair and back. "You had us worried there. We couldn't wake you up to save our lives."

"Not even magic would do it," Mae muttered, sounding a little miffed.

Mariea managed a weak smile. "I get the feeling this will become a regular thing until I know all of Elinore's message," she warned them.

"I guess that means you don't have any clues about what's happening back home then, huh?" Bracken asked, sounding disappointed.

Shaking her head, Mariea replied, "Not yet, but I think I will soon." She paused a minute, trying to process all that she had learned. "There was a settlement here a long time ago." Shifting to face the jungle, she was surprised to find no sign of the town. Saddened, Mariea stood, wondering what had happened to it. Obviously, several years had passed, but she would have thought at least some of the structures would have remained.

Her companions followed, obviously eager for details, so she told them, "I...don't know what happened to it. There was a disease, and Elinore helped to cure it. It felt almost similar to what we're dealing with back home." She rubbed at her temple, fighting a slight headache. "They used magic that was way beyond us—creating artificial suns, building whole buildings out of the earth, modifying auras on a basic level." She paused, shaking her head slightly as she marveled over it all.

"Wait, you mean they changed the basic composition of an aura?" Bracken repeated, staring at her with amazement and disbelief. "That shouldn't be possible."

"I know, but they did it. The magic seemed odd," she muttered, remembering how it seemed everyone was disturbed by it, but nobody seemed to want to talk about it. She wondered if that was simply because it was so unique or if there wasn't a deeper reason behind the feeling. Considering the struggle Densin had been left with at the end, Mariea worried it was more they were ignoring a bigger problem in their desperation.

The three fell silent for a moment, and then Bracken asked, "So, now what? Where do we need to go for the next dream?"

Mariea's gaze returned to the jungle warily. "I think it's going to be somewhere in there." She pointed in the general direction of where the settlement had been.

Glancing warily at the uninviting jungle, Bracken muttered, "I'm not sure how I feel about going in there."

"What, are you afraid of a few trees?" Mae mocked, smirking.

"We don't know what's in there," Bracken argued.

"I don't think there's any wildlife on this island," Mariea commented, cutting Mae off before she could pester Bracken anymore. Though she had no way to know for sure, Mariea had noticed how silent it was once they had reached the island, and she hadn't seen a single bit of life anywhere.

Her companions looked at her in surprise. She simply shrugged and told them, "Listen."

After a pause, Bracken nodded in agreement. "I think you're right. It's too quiet—no animal calls, no birds, not even insects."

"If it's empty, then what are you afraid of?" Mae wondered, glancing between the pair with an incredulous look.

"Just because the jungle is empty doesn't make it any less creepy. In fact, it makes it *more* creepy," Bracken decided.

"Yeah," Mariea agreed. "What caused it to be so void of life?" Mae's confusion faded slightly, and she frowned, glancing back at the trees in question with more reservation.

Mariea sighed. "But I'm sure that's where the rest of the message will be, so...I guess it's into the creepy jungle whether we like it or not," she muttered.

They all hesitated for a painfully long moment, none of them feeling very confident in that statement. Then Bracken glanced up at the sky. "It's late. Maybe we should just camp here. I think I'll be a lot less reluctant if it wasn't getting dark."

"Yeah, I like that idea," Mae quickly agreed.

"I'll grab our stuff from the boat," Mariea decided just as quickly.

They set up camp facing the water, and after a while, Mariea was able to push away her worries. But she couldn't help but wonder if there was more to the feeling of apprehension they all shared.

Mefune

Mefune woke early the next morning. He was usually up near dawn, and today he was too restless to sleep late. Carefully, he slipped away from Altaira, who was still deep asleep. Worried she would get cold if he left, he shrugged out of his jacket, draped it over her, and then slipped outside.

The forest was peaceful that morning, covered in a light fog that disappeared slowly as the day warmed. Memories of when he had first laid eyes on such a view played in his mind, reminding him of how beautiful he had thought the forest was. At the time, he had been unaware of the dangers that hid underneath its canopy—dangers they had to face again that day. He let out a sigh, glancing back towards the cave where Altaira still slept. He had done all he could for her wounds last night, but he worried it wasn't enough. She had been surprisingly weak last night. There wasn't anything he could do for exhaustion or blood loss, and they were still so far from home.

This left him reflecting on the chaos of the night before. When they had reached the cave, and he had seen just how badly she was suffering, he was suddenly angry. Angry at the Tarapor for putting her at risk, angry at himself for forcing the idea of their reckless trek through the forest, and angry at nature itself for the storm that had caused the injuries in the first place. He knew it was irrational anger, but he couldn't dismiss it easily. Suddenly, keeping her safe was all that mattered.

But as he had patched up her wounds and relief replaced his fear, he was left to consider what had caused such a need. He wasn't one for attachments, but from the moment the tree had fallen, something had changed. He wasn't sure what, but it had already pushed him to do things he had told himself he never would—like use his aura to heal her. Or tell her about it. Or stay there, with her sleeping against his shoulder, without a second thought. At the time, he had dismissed it as exhaustion, but part of him knew there was more to it than that, whether he wanted to admit it or not.

He shook his head, trying to focus on the issue at hand, but his thoughts wandered. He, too, was exhausted—he was reaching the limit of the sustaining spell much faster than expected—but he couldn't afford to be. He had to get them both home safety and still deal with Samar. There had to be a way he could manage both.

She joined him after a few hours, still wrapped in his jacket. She settled next to him, just close enough that their shoulders touched, and then handed him a ration bar.

He smirked slightly as he took it. "Can't say I'm looking forward to another one of these," he muttered.

She chuckled as she ripped hers open. "What, you're not enjoying this exotic cuisine?"

"Not entirely," he replied with a shake of his head before taking a reluctant bite of his bar.

They ate in silence for a moment. "Thanks for this," she stated after a moment, indicating his jacket.

"You're welcome. Didn't want you to get cold."

She smiled softly, shaking her head slightly. "You think of everything."

He let out an amused huff. "Apparently, lately I do," he muttered, more to himself than anything.

She gave him a curious look, but he decided to change the subject. No need to explain where *that* little thought came from. "How are you feeling?"

"Better. Achy though. And entirely not looking forward to another day fighting Tarapor," she admitted.

"Honestly, I don't think you should keep fighting. As tired as I am, there's not much more I can do to heal those wounds any faster, and they didn't fare as well as I had hoped they would last night. You need to rest."

"But we still have a way to go before we make it back," she pointed out.

"Luckily, I think we're past the worst of the Tarapor. We'll be heading away from the more heavily infested areas from here on out, and I'm hoping we'll cross back into patrolled territory before nightfall," he told her.

"So we can cross the river here?"

Nodding, he pointed to the cave behind them with a thumb. "There's a path behind the waterfall that leads to the other side."

"That's good," she breathed, clearly relieved.

"Yeah, if we had to go any farther north, I don't think we'd survive," he muttered grimly.

She nodded, her expression making it clear she had no interest in testing his theory. After a pause, she pointed out, "We still need to catch at least one Tarapor."

"Maybe I'll just find the stash without one," Mefune suggested.

"I thought the whole reason we were doing this is that we couldn't find it. We don't have time to look for it, especially not now," she pointed out.

"I know," Mefune agreed with a weary sigh.

"Don't worry about me," she told him.

"It's hard not to," he told her before he could stop himself. "You scared me last night. I don't want to lose you to those creatures."

Giving him a weary smile, she told him, "I've got you to keep me alive."

He shook his head slightly. "You put way too much trust in my skills."

"I think you underestimate yourself," she countered. Then she sighed. "You're probably right, though. I don't know how much more fighting I've got in me, not for the next couple of days. I just don't like the idea of giving up. Of letting Samar win."

"Neither do I," Mefune readily agreed. He paused, thinking for a minute. "I'll just catch one on my own. We'll keep going, make it as close to base as we can by daylight, and then, when night falls, I'll find a nest."

"So, it's back to you facing the Tarapor on your own then," she said with a frown.

He nodded slightly. "I think that would be our best plan."

She shook her head. "The whole reason I came with you was to keep you from doing something so reckless."

"I'll be careful," he reassured her.

"It's still stupidly dangerous! I can't lose you either," she pressed.

They paused for a moment, Mefune surprised by her statement, and both of them stuck on the problem it presented. Eventually, he sighed. "I don't know what else to do."

She debated it for a moment, her lips pressed together in a thin line, clearly not pleased. Eventually, she stated, "I guess if there are no other options, we'll do what we have to."

"If we find a group before dark, we might be able to catch them by surprise," Mefune guessed. "Their fear will make them scatter, so we shouldn't have to fight too many."

"That might work, but how are we supposed to find them? I don't know where they hide during the day."

He thought about it for a moment. "It's possible I could sense their auras, and use that to track down a group," he guessed. It wasn't exactly easy—he had to be relatively close to sense them—but it wouldn't be the first time he had used that trick. It wasn't one he relied upon heavily because he didn't want others to start thinking he had some uncanny knack for finding them. But now that Altaira knew about his aura, there was no reason not to.

"Right, I nearly forgot about that. You think you could find them?" she wondered.

He thought it through, nodding. "It's not easy. Their auras aren't strong, meaning I can't sense them from too far away, and I have to be careful not to use my aura too much while carrying my sword. But we know they like to sleep away from the sunlight, so we'll know where to look."

She sighed slightly. "Alright, if you're sure about this," she muttered.

He nodded, standing. "I'm sure, trust me." Then he offered a hand to help her up. "We better get going. We have a lot of ground to cover if we want to make it back tonight."

She nodded and accepted his help. He led her into the cave and gathered his things as she did hers, and then he led her to the back of the cave.

As it grew darker, Altaira paused. "Geez, it's dark back here."

"Yeah. Hold this, will you?" he asked, handing his sword back to her.

"Why?"

"Can't have it in hand while I use my aura," he replied, before bringing it to light around his hand. He blinked a bit to adjust to the bright silver light after the darkness of the cave, before gathering a ball of it in the palm of his hand and letting the rest fade. The remaining orb floated just above his hand, lighting the path ahead.

"Right, right. I'll get used to this eventually," she said with a shake of her head. He smiled slightly, finding it amusing how quickly she kept forgetting. She glanced at his sword as they started into the tunnel. "Guess that would explain why you always carry this in your hand."

"Exactly. It's a habit I picked up from Creta. He had to be extremely careful, since his aura was a lot stronger than mine."

"I honestly thought it was impossible for someone with an aura to even handle these. The Auraes always made such a big stink about it," Altaira mused.

"It is pretty dangerous," Mefune admitted with a shrug. "It's like walking around with an explosive in your hand. One wisp of your aura touches that metal, and you're dead, and since Auraes' auras react so easily to their emotions, it's easy for an accident to happen. It comes alight when they're afraid or angry, and it's over. Creta was just crazy enough to risk it, anyway. For me, though, it's not as bad since I hardly use my aura."

"Huh," Altaira muttered. "Guess that makes sense." She paused a moment, glancing sidelong at him, and then carefully asked, "So, why risk it? If it's really that dangerous, why did you and Creta choose to join the Brotherhood?"

"Creta wanted to research the Tarapor. He was bent on finding a cure, but the Brotherhood was reluctant to send patrols into the more dangerous parts of the forest just to protect him. So he decided to learn to protect himself and make it work," Mefune replied.

Altaria nodded. After a pause, she softly added, "And what about you?"

He paused, realizing she had initially asked about both of them, and, like usual, he had directed the attention away from himself. She seemed oddly curious, and he couldn't blame her. His situation was an odd one.

He debated how to answer, wondering how much he wanted to tell her. For the first time in a long time, he found he didn't mind someone being interested in his past, so eventually, he gathered his thoughts and told her, "When I came to the island, I found I didn't fit in with the Auraes' way of life much. I came from a rough place. It's not something I like to think about often. Someone suggested I might be happier here. So," he shrugged, "here I am."

"Makes sense," she mused, nodding slightly as she did. Thankfully, she didn't pry further, seeming to sense he had shared as much as he felt comfortable doing so.

They approached the other end of the cave tunnel as the roaring of the waterfall became increasingly louder. "We're right behind it now," he yelled over the noise. "It'll be pretty wet once we get outside. Be careful not to slip."

They crossed out of the tunnel into the early morning light and found themselves behind the waterfall. It roared over the rock above them to their left, surrounded by sheer cliffs down to a small pond below. On the other side of the waterfall was another small plateau, and near their way down; they just had to pass behind the waterfall to get to it. The rock surrounding them was dark with water, and the cold mist engulfed them, making Altaira shiver a bit. It wouldn't take long for them to be soaked, so Mefune began carefully picking his way across the gap, wanting to get to the other side as soon as possible.

But Altaira didn't follow. She stood staring down at the sheer drop before them, looking a little uncertain. When he noticed she wasn't following, he turned back. She glanced sidelong at him, but then her gaze quickly returned to the gaping hole before her. "This might be an interesting moment to mention that I'm terrified of heights."

"Never would have guessed that, considering how you climbed that cliff last night."

She chuckled bitterly. "Well, you'd be surprised how much of a motivator a mad horde of Tarapor can be."

He laughed. "True. Don't worry, though, it's not as slippery as it looks. If we're careful, we'll make it across fine." He gestured for her to follow, waiting for her to catch up. She steadied herself with a breath and then started after him. Once she was right behind him, he continued forward.

They reached the other side. "Now we just have to climb down," he told her.

"Right," she muttered, taking a deep breath as she stepped towards the edge. She stared down at the steep drop, paling slightly as her lips pressed into a thin line. Then she turned and handed his sword back. He set his bag down, rested the blade against his back, then picked the bag up again.

"You first," she told him. It wasn't much of a suggestion, making it clear there was no way she'd be going down first. *She wasn't kidding about the fear of heights,* he silently noted.

He nodded and moved to the cliff edge. There were ropes embedded into the edge of the ledge and down the cliffside, just as there had been on the other side of the waterfall. He reached down and gave the top one a heavy tug, grateful to see it still held. Grabbing ahold of it with both hands, he carefully lowered himself down the cliff.

"So, who put these here?" Altaira wondered. Her voice shook slightly, and he guessed she was trying to distract herself from the drop as she maneuvered herself over the edge after him.

"Not sure. I stumbled upon them a long time ago. They're clearly not regularly maintained, but the ropes never wear out. Must be some sort of magic involved," he told her as they continued down.

"I wonder if it's an old campsite we just don't use anymore," Altaira mused.

During the Purges, the Brotherhood had set up several locations throughout the forest to give the fighters safe places to rest during the night when the Tarapor were most active. After the Purges, they had adjusted their patrols to cover the area they felt they needed to continue monitoring regularly. Several camp sites had been abandoned in the process.

"Could be," Mefune agreed.

They fell silent as they climbed. Once at the bottom, Altaira took a second to catch her breath—and most likely relish being on solid ground again—while Mefune glanced around.

"Alright, so the Tarapor aren't going to be close to the river, so I say we start by heading more south. Just watch for clumps of undergrowth or any sort of overhang they could hide in."

"Lead the way," she urged, and once again, the pair started into the forest.

They walked well into the day, staying silent as they searched, their path meandering a bit, but with home always in the general direction they kept going in. With his sword now back in its usual location—carried lightly in one hand—Mefune could use his aura just enough to allow him to sense any others in the area. It wasn't enough to make it appear around him; it took hardly any effort to discern the auras around him.

Just as the sun reached its apex in the sky, he paused. Off to their left, he could just sense the half-dead aura of a Tarapor. It had such an odd feeling, making it distinctly different from any others.

"There's a group over there," he told her, gesturing with his sword.

She paused and glanced in that direction. "You sure?"

He nodded, and she looked a bit relieved. It seemed they had some luck left. They changed course, now moving more cautiously. Sure enough, just ahead, he noticed a large clump of trees growing closely together. Mixed with the thick underbrush, they made a natural shelter of sorts. He could sense a handful of Tarapor inside, but he assumed they were asleep by how quiet it was.

They approached carefully. "Sure you still want to face them alone?" Altaira asked, sounding worried.

He nodded. "This group doesn't seem very big, so it shouldn't be a problem. Just stick close. You'll know if you need to help."

They reached the edge of the clump of trees and peered through to study the small group of Tarapor. It seemed they had been caught in the morning light and had made dens of whatever was around them, leaving many vulnerable. He unsheathed his sword as quietly as he could. Setting the sheath down, he straightened and began to make his way through the underbrush.

Before he could get far, Altaira stopped him by laying a hand on his arm, turning him back towards her. "Be careful," she requested quietly.

"Of course," he promised, giving her a reassuring smile.

She nodded. Then a hint of humor entered her gaze, chasing away the worry for a brief moment. "And remember to keep at least one alive."

Mefune smirked slightly. "I'll try to remember," he promised before turning back to his quarry.

Passing through the underbrush, he appeared behind the nearest Tarapor, melting from the shadows to incapacitate it before it could even wake. The Tarapor nearest him jumped, sensing the movement, and let out a warning hiss that woke the others. Before it could launch at him, he lunged at it and killed it quickly.

Just as he had expected, the Tarapor scattered, but not before a good few attempted to attack him and quickly perished. Silence fell as the den emptied. He straightened from his stance and glanced back as Altaira joined him.

"The first one I attacked should still be breathing," Mefune guessed as he gestured to the only in-tact Tarapor amongst the already rotting remains.

Altaira nodded and moved towards its unconscious form, Mefune joining her quickly. After making sure it wasn't at risk of dying from injury, they quickly tied the Tarapor up, including a tight bandana around its mouth to prevent it from being able to bite them. Then they began the long walk home.

Darkness approached much sooner than Mefune would have liked. It seemed they wouldn't make it back that night as he had hoped. Luckily, they were farther from Tarapor territory, meaning they had a lot less risk of getting swarmed.

"We've crossed back into the area we patrol," Altaira pointed out.

"Right," Mefune agreed, realizing he recognized this part of the forest.

"Shouldn't there be a camp spot around here somewhere?" she wondered.

"Should be," he agreed. After some searching, they found one—a small ravine covered with many layers of concealing magic. They tied their unwilling third party member to a nearby tree and slept in peace.

In the morning, after yet another ration bar breakfast, they continued. Finally, as the day grew old, the familiar hill where the Brotherhood headquarters was located appeared through the trees.

"Can't say I've ever been happier to see this place," Altaira said with a relieved sigh.

"Yeah," Mefune agreed, feeling equally relieved. Then, his thoughts shifted to his plan, and he told Altaira, "You should go find Daya, send her out first to hide somewhere around here. Then find Samar. I'll wait here with this thing until he comes for it. We'll have Daya meet us at the overlook afterward and tell us what she learns."

She nodded. "And if we're too late?" she asked cautiously.

"Then...come back, and we'll figure something else out," he muttered, not willing to consider the whole trip might have been for nothing.

She nodded. "See you in a while then," she stated, before starting up the hill.

It wasn't long before Daya passed by, giving him a nod in greeting, and then disappeared into the surrounding trees. Considering she didn't seem worried, and Altaira hadn't returned with her, Mefune guessed it was safe to assume they had made it back in time.

A while later, Altaira and Samar approached. The Council leader grinned as he neared. "You're timing is perfect; we attack the day after tomorrow."

"So soon?" Mefune wondered, trying to hide his surprise.

"Things are going better than we thought," Altaira mused, meeting his gaze. Clearly, she understood as well as he did just how close they had come to failing and how little time they had to release the Tarapor.

"Well, with the injustices we've suffered by the Auraes' hands to motivate the Council, it hasn't been hard," Samar stated.

"I would assume not," Mefune guessed. "Want help taking this thing wherever you're keeping them?" He had to ask, even though he already knew what the answer would be.

Samar shook his head. "I can handle one Tarapor on my own. I'll fill you both in on the details of the plan tomorrow morning. Meet me at my office at eight."

"Sounds good," Mefune agreed, and then passed their prisoner off to the Council leader.

He joined Altaira, and the pair started back into the base to the overlook, where they planned to wait for Daya. Once there, Altaira sunk wearily onto a boulder that rested up against the base, turning her gaze to the ocean. Mefune settled next to her.

"I'll be happy when this is all over," she told him.

"Yeah. Maybe then things will settle down," he mused. "We can go back to quarreling over nothing whatsoever."

She let out an amused snort, shaking her head in disbelief. "I think we both know that's one aspect of our lives that will never go back to what it was," she assured him. As if to prove her point, she shifted closer ever so slightly, earning a small smile from Mefune.

Time wore on, and he grew impatient, worried Daya had run into trouble. Finally, she joined them, but her expression did little to calm Mefune's nerves.

"What's wrong?" Altaira asked as she stood to meet her friend.

"There's a ton more than we expected," Daya replied. "There's no way the three of us can kill them all."

Mefune sighed. "I was worried about that. He's been collecting Tarapor for a long time," he muttered as he stood.

Altaira's shoulders slumped with exhaustion. "So, what do we do?" she wondered.

They stood in silence as they thought for a moment. "How many would you estimate they have?" Mefune asked Daya.

She shrugged, looking overwhelmed just thinking about it. "Hundreds. It's like they intend to wipe out the Auraes instead of just scare them into submission."

"I wouldn't be too surprised if that were actually his goal," Altaira grumbled.

"Probably," Mefune agreed with a disbelieving shake of his head. "How is he keeping them contained?"

"A metal cage of some sort. It looked like it was made of the same material as our weapons," Daya supplied. "It's just southeast of here, but I think it's concealed by magic."

"What makes you think that?" Mefune wondered.

"I couldn't see it until I was right on top of it, like the base entrance. I backtracked a couple of times to make sure I could find it again," Daya explained.

Mefune nodded. *Who would have put up a concealment spell over it for him?* he wondered. He was well aware he was currently the only one amongst the Brotherhood with a functional aura. There was a small handful with weak, unusable auras, like Samar, but definitely none strong enough to create a spell like that. There were the medics that worked in the infirmary, but because they rotated out regularly, Mefune guessed none of them were around long enough to be swayed to Samar's cause. Mefune couldn't see any of them willingly helping him, anyway. *Could it be Samar's mysterious contact?* If Samar was using him for magical support, it would explain the need for regular meetings. But when he and Altaira had listened in on their conversation at the cove, Mefune hadn't sensed an aura from the stranger. He might have been hiding it, though, like Mefune usually did.

Deciding that was a mystery he would have to sort out later, he focused on how to get rid of Samar's collection of Tarapor. "Maybe...instead of killing them, we just release them," he suggested, a plan slowly forming.

"They're close to Verndale. A lot of them might head for the city," Daya speculated.

Mefune gave an allowing nod. "They'll most likely scatter once they're released, but some might end up at the city. Maybe it would be enough for the four of us to handle."

"I don't know, it sounds like it'll take a whole patrol to protect the city, and since Samar and Ila broke up our alliance, I doubt we could get away with sending a whole group," Altaira muttered.

"Oh, you guys don't know about that," Daya muttered. "Sometime after you left, Jocelyn contacted us. She managed to undo what Ila had done. On the surface, our alliance is officially broken to satisfy Ila, but the patrols are still operating, and we're still receiving support. It's a temporary fix until Jocelyn can get the legal backing she needs to overrule Ila's decision."

"Seems not all the Auraes approve of how she's handling things," Altaira mused.

"So that means there will still be a patrol guarding the city until right before Samar's attack," Mefune realized. "If we give them a heads up, say we saw a bunch moving through the area, they should be able to handle it. Maybe we'll even send others to reinforce them."

"We'd have to. They're going to need all the fighters they can get," Daya stated.

"I'll join them. You could, too, Daya. And maybe we could convince Garrett, just this once. He might be willing to help if we bring others," Mefune guessed.

"Garrett also told me we can trust Desiree. She knows of Samar's plans but has kept quiet about them because she didn't know how to handle them. Now that she knows we're working to stop him, she wants to help. We could bring her," Daya suggested.

Mefune nodded. "I'll come too," Altaira interjected.

"You sure you're feeling up to it?" Mefune asked.

Altaira nodded. "There's no way I'm letting you face that many without me," she pressed.

Daya raised an eyebrow, glancing between the two as if noticing the change between them for the first time. While it would have been easy to assume Altaira's comment was directed at both of them, something about how her gaze lingered on him made Mefune think she had meant it for him, and it seemed Daya felt the same.

She glanced at Altaira. "What happened?"

"Long story. I'll fill you in if we survive tomorrow," she reassured her.

Daya nodded and then asked, "So, how do we go about releasing them?"

Once again, they fell silent as they debated this. "Samar must have had a plan to do that without getting anyone killed," Altaira guessed.

"Yeah, but we don't have time to figure out what he had in mind. I doubt he'd just tell us," Daya pointed out.

"Could we destroy the cage somehow?" Altaira wondered. "Maybe from a distance, so we wouldn't have to interact with the Tarapor?"

"That might work," Mefune agreed as an idea dawned on him. "The Auraes have a spell for breaking down any extra metal leftover from creating our weapons. If we could get ahold of one of those, we could collapse the cage and let the Tarapor run free. We could even have it created to break down at a slower rate, so then someone could start it and be long gone by the time the spell took full effect."

"How do we get one of those spells?" Daya wondered.

"I'll take care of it," Mefune dismissed quickly, earning a knowing glance from Altaira.

"Okay, when do we do this?" Daya wondered.

"Samar said he'll fill us in on his plan tomorrow morning. It might be a good idea to wait until at least after then to make sure there aren't any details we're overlooking. That'll also allow us to gather some reinforcements for the patrol. So, tomorrow night."

Daya nodded. "I'll tell Garrett and Desiree so they'll be ready."

Altaira nodded. Then she let out a heavy sigh. "If that's everything, I'm going to go take a shower and sleep in a real bed," she decided.

Mefune chuckled. "Yeah, you've earned that."

"So, that means I actually have to wait until morning to hear the details of this little adventure you two went on?" Daya asked, pouting a little.

"Yes," Altaira stated bluntly, earning a disappointed huff from her friend. "But it'll be a better retelling if we wait until I'm coherent, anyway."

Daya gave an allowing nod of her head and then stated, "Fine, fine. I'll be patient." Then she grabbed Altaira's arm and began pulling her inside. "Come. The sooner you go to bed, the sooner you're awake, and you can tell me."

Altaira protested weakly, but then let out a defeated sigh as she shook her head, smiling at her friend's antics. Mefune watched them go with a smile of his own, amused by the two.

CHAPTER TWENTY-THREE

GUARDIAN

Mariea

Walking through the jungle, Mariea wiped the sweat from her forehead again, quickly hating how muggy it was under the trees. It made her wish for her island home, where the weather was cooler. Usually, she would use her aura to keep her comfortable, but for some reason, she was reluctant to call it to light; the feeling of apprehension from last night hadn't left since crossing under the trees. For some reason, it made her oddly defensive of her aura.

They took a break after another half hour or so of hiking. Grateful for the rest, Mariea took the opportunity to pull her hair up into a bun. The humidity and heat made it wild and frizzy, but finally, she managed to get it away from her face. Sadly, the resulting effect was not as dramatic as she had hoped—she was still way too hot. As she drank from her canteen, she found it as disappointingly warm as everything else. *Okay, this is ridiculous. How did Elinore survive in all the layers they wore back in her day? And it's only April.*

Bracken let out a heavy sigh as he lowered his canteen, running a hand along his forehead in a futile effort to remove the sweat. Then his brow furrowed in confusion as he tilted his head to one side. "What's this?" he mused, taking a few steps into the jungle.

It took Mariea only a moment to realize what he was talking about. Before them was a barely noticeable cobblestone path and wooden structures that looked like the remnants of buildings. There wasn't much other than foundations and the occasional pole or part of a wall randomly protruding from the jungle, but Mariea could still tell they were on a street. "I think this is the edge of the settlement. Maybe it was further into the trees than I thought?" she wondered.

"Hmm. Well, there was obviously something here once. I guess this is as good as anywhere to start looking," Bracken decided.

The three moved forward cautiously, Mariea leading them down the former street. Once they were farther into the remains of the settlement, the ground sloped upward to the right slightly, and Mariea felt a wave of nostalgia. "The houses were mostly built on that hill. The city center is that way," she explained, pointing to sections of the jungle. More recognizable structures surrounded them now, but they were still hardly buildings. Mariea realized the dark black color of the wood wasn't from exposure but a fire. *That would explain why there's so little left of the town. What happened?*

When they reached the town center, she looked around at the vaguely familiar square. The fountain that had once been there still held water, its basin thickly covered with moss, but the statue adorning it was gone, and so were most of the surrounding buildings. The cobblestone was now easier to see as it poked through the thick underbrush. Though a few trees had grown in the square, it seemed it wouldn't be long before the jungle reclaimed it entirely. Mariea could imagine the courtyard in its prime—even see it if she just closed her eyes—bustling with activity. Now it sat in hallowed silence, the lingering taste of sorrow and pain almost palpable.

"A lot of people died here," Mae muttered, her arms wrapped tightly around her, pain in her gaze as she scanned the dilapidated square. Tears built in her eyes, and she glanced away.

Mariea blinked in surprise, amazed by how much the place affected Mae. "Are you okay?" she asked, taking a step closer.

When Mae seemed too upset to answer, Bracken supplied one for her. "medics are especially sensitive to the passing of fellow Auraes. They can sense it like you and I can sense auras. It can be upsetting if they aren't prepared for it."

"Oh," Mariea muttered, a bit surprised. She hadn't known that little detail about medics.

"But this is so potent even I can feel it," Bracken added, frowning.

Mariea nodded slightly, realizing it must be what was responsible for the dreadful feeling that had haunted her since entering the jungle. It was far more potent in the square, making her shiver slightly.

The three fell silent, as if they were all reluctant to break the eerie quiet after such a realization. They took a moment to respect the people who had passed, if only to appease whatever caused their pain to linger.

Mariea sighed. "I need to know what caused this," she stated, a hint of desperation in her voice. Somewhere in the back of her mind, she couldn't help but worry she was looking at a possible future for her own home.

"So, we have to keep going?" Mae asked, clearly reluctant.

Mariea glanced at her, wondering just how much she could handle if they continued to linger in such a place. "Only if you'll be okay," she told her.

Mae stayed silent for a moment, her gaze on the ground. "I'll be fine. I know how to block it out. I just wasn't ready for this."

Mariea nodded, turning her gaze to the remnants of the settlement. "Then we'll keep going. We have to figure out what's going on," she decided.

They started forward again, picking their way around the fountain and farther into the square. Beyond, it seemed some buildings had been spared from the fire that had claimed most of the settlement, and many of them still stood. The impression of being on a street strengthened as they started into the more intact area, even if it was an eerily empty street.

They hadn't traveled far when suddenly she sensed something that made her stop abruptly—there was an aura nearby, and a powerful one too. A shiver ran down her spine as she considered it, amazed by its presence and that she was just now noticing it. She glanced around nervously, trying to identify whatever she was sensing.

Bracken bumped into her, glancing at her in surprise. "Something wrong?" he wondered when he noticed her expression.

"We're not alone," Mariea muttered, her aura appearing in thin wisps as she prepared to defend herself. She instinctively feared the source of the aura, knowing it wouldn't be friendly.

"Wait, what happened to there not being anything living on the island?" Mae quickly protested.

"I think we're about to find out why there isn't," Bracken replied warily, making Mariea realize he could now sense the aura as well.

"Well," a voice stated just before a lone figure stepped from the shadows of a nearby ancient structure. His silvery hair and youthful face were an interesting contrast, but his bright green eyes drew the most attention. There was something distinctly off about him, and despite not being able to decide precisely what bothered her, it left Mariea uncomfortable in his presence.

"It's been a long time since I've encountered Auraes here," he continued. "Especially after what happened." His voice carried an odd accent Mariea couldn't quite place but was vaguely familiar. His metallic purple aura surrounded him, and as Mariea watched him, it was quickly evident he was the source of the power she had felt moments earlier.

"What do you want?" Bracken demanded, his gaze narrowed in suspicion, his deep umber aura surrounding him.

"Nothing, actually. It intrigues me to know why you bothered returning here after so many years, but I, unfortunately, have other orders. Besides," slowly, his grin turned wicked, and his aura came to full light around him, "I haven't had a good fight in so long, and you two have quite strong auras. This should be fun."

Mariea's gaze narrowed, her aura coming to full view around her as it reacted to her sense of danger. Most of what he said left her confused, but his purpose was clear enough. "Mae, get out of here," she ordered, knowing the medic wasn't trained to defend herself.

"Right, just don't get yourself killed. I'll be nearby," she informed them as she backtracked slightly, her gaze on the newcomer.

"Leaving so soon? Bummer," he stated. "Don't worry, I'll find you after I'm finished with these two." His aura briefly flared brighter as a wave of energy burst away from it and shot towards them.

Luckily, Bracken was already reacting; a shielding spell hardened between them long before the attack reached them, deflecting it easily.

Mae hurried away, but Mariea was too occupied with keeping ahead of her enemy's attacks to worry about her anymore. As Bracken deflected another stream of energy, Mariea darted around him and attacked from the side, her power rippling through the air in a bright flash. To her surprise, the stranger deflected it almost casually, looking bored. *Who is this guy?* she wondered, amazed by his power. Suddenly, she wished she had brought at least one sentinel with her. They would probably know how to handle the situation much better than she and Bracken.

They exchanged shots for a while before the man paused, letting out a small annoyed huff. "This is boring," he complained and then blinked from existence.

Mariea stumbled to a halt, her aura sparking with energy around her as she stared at the spot he had once been in bewilderment. Seconds passed in silence, and then a dark shadow grew where he had stood, surrounded by the same deep purple of his aura.

As Mariea watched in stunned silence, a beast reared up before them, something like she had never seen before. It grew in height, towering over them, its giant mouth sliding open to reveal brilliant white teeth, the canines long and deadly. Great leathery wings appeared against the creature's arched back, but they were so torn and full of holes Mariea doubted it was capable of flight if it ever had been. A long tail slapped the ground, sending shudders through its surroundings. The obsidian scales reflected the sunlight dimly, as did the claws that dug deep grooves in the road. Eerie green eyes stared down at them with slit pupils, and Mariea was sure the beast was grinning at them.

"Is that...a dragon?" Bracken whispered, staring up at the beast in fear and wonder.

The creature opened its mouth wider, and flames poured from its jaws. Mariea reacted in the split second before the fire reached them, gesturing upwards with a hand as her aura glowed brighter. A wall of ice appeared between them and the flames. The ice instantly transformed to steam against the fire with a hiss, briefly surrounding them in a blinding cloud of white.

As the steam cleared, Mariea realized the beast had closed the distance between them and raised a giant paw to smoosh them, moving incredibly fast and quiet for its size. She and Bracken broke apart, lunging in opposite directions to avoid the attack. Mariea was knocked off her feet as the dragon smashed its foot against the ground with a heavy thud.

Taking advantage of their vulnerability, the dragon tried to torch Bracken, but he managed to defend himself with a shielding spell. Mariea pushed to her feet and sent an angry wave of earthen spikes into the creature's side. They shattered harmlessly against its scales, but it drew its attention back to her long enough for Bracken to recover.

The beast seemed to contemplate them for a moment, then it charged at Bracken, moving so fast it was hard for Mariea to follow. Simultaneously, it sent a blast of power her way, strong enough she knew her aura wouldn't be able to deflect it. She dove into the remnants of the building behind her as the magic passed over, stinging her skin as it went. It shattered the top half of the wall she hid behind, raining her with debris and dust, making her cover her head and flinch away, coughing on the dust it kicked up.

When everything settled, she pushed the wreckage aside, grateful nothing heavy had fallen on her. Still, she felt several minor cuts and bruises across her arms and back. She turned back to the dragon quickly, not wanting to give it a chance to attack her while she was down. It seemed focused on finding Bracken, but it had already proven it could multitask quite well. As she raised her hands, a boulder formed from the rubble, and then blue flames leaped to life across its surface before it slammed into the dragon. It stumbled a bit but didn't notice, as if she had just bumped it. Clearly, the flames did no harm.

The dark creature's tail swung towards her, but she saw it coming just in time to dodge out of the way. Before the beast could try the same move again, an umber-colored shell formed around it, pinning it to the ground. Mariea spared a glance to her left, finding Bracken poking out from behind a wall, his aura surrounding him as he muttered spells under his breath. A cut on his forehead was bleeding, but other than that, she was relieved to find he seemed alright. She hurried to him, stepping over the dragon's pinned tail as she reached his side. They carefully backed away from their enemy as it yanked its tail free, shattering the spell.

Bracken frowned. "That wasn't supposed to be breakable," he grumbled as they crouched in the shadows of a building.

"Yeah, well, you saw how well my magic is working against it," Mariea griped. "What do we do?"

"Run?" Bracken suggested.

"We can't leave the island yet. There are still answers here," Mariea reminded him. She paused a second to redirect more flames, and they scrambled to a new hiding spot, feeling much like the dragon was hunting them. "And I get the feeling, now that he knows we're here, he isn't going to just let us leave," she finished.

Bracken sighed. "I knew you would say that. How do you intend to fight it, then?"

"It has to have a weakness," she muttered, her mind racing for solutions.

The dragon spotted them again and sent fire their way, but Mariea pressed her hands together before her, and the fire parted at her fingertips to pass on either side of them. Then she harnessed the last of it as it trailed past her, bending it back behind them to shoot toward the dragon. It smacked against its scales and disappeared as if she had thrown feathers at it. Luckily, it at least blocked them from view for a few moments, and the pair took advantage of the distraction and bolted down a side street.

"This is going great," Mariea joked sarcastically as they ran.

"Just wonderfully," Bracken agreed, carrying on her sarcasm. "Have you tried piercing the scales?"

"Yeah. No luck," she replied.

The dragon suddenly appeared on their left, sending more fire at them. They scrambled back, nearly tripping over each other as they careened around a corner, barely escaping the flames.

Bracken suddenly grabbed her arm and yanked her into the trees, hiding in the shadows of a large palm. Peering back into the town, he watched for the dragon. "I think its scales are enhanced by magic. That would explain why you can't break them and why my spells keep collapsing against them. We'll have to try something stronger," he suggested.

"Like what?" Mariea wondered. "I don't exactly have a wealth of strong, sharp objects lying around."

In response, he opened his palm and muttered a quick few Shidokian phrases. A sword made of his aura formed in his hand and then hardened. "Maybe something like this?" he stated as he offered it to her. "Here. I'll distract it, you try stabbing it. Go for a vulnerable spot."

Mariea glanced down at the sword, the very idea of approaching the beast sending shivers down her spine. Then her mind registered the other half of his suggestion, and her gaze snapped up to him. "No, you're not going to act as bait," she said, rejecting the idea quickly.

"What else are we supposed to do? You need it to focus on something other than yourself. I'll be fine, I promise," Bracken reassured her.

"You can't promise that," she corrected.

He rolled his eyes slightly. "Well, yeah, but still. I'll be careful, at least."

Mariea bit her lip, her hand closing around the sword's hilt. "You better be," she told him forcefully.

"I will. That I can promise." Then he straightened and charged out of their cover.

Mariea heard the dragon growl as Bracken called out to it, and saw it pass by her hiding spot as it pursued him. She took in a shaky breath, hoping Bracken was okay, and then started after them, trying to approach from behind.

She rounded a dilapidated building and discovered the dragon standing in the street beyond, its tail pinned under some rubble, a spell wrapped around its mouth, and its wingtips pinned to its hind legs with more magic. It growled in annoyance as it struggled to free itself, but Bracken kept adding more spells as she watched.

Deciding not to let it get a chance to free itself, Mariea rushed to its side, raising the blade and slashing it across the beast's stomach.

To her dismay, the sword shattered in her hand as it ground across the scales with a sickening screech. The dragon let out another growl as the magic surrounding its jaw broke free, smoke billowing from its jaws as it exhaled. Mariea backpedaled, hoping Bracken would do the same. Ducking behind a wall, she barely avoided the stream of flames that followed, the heat making her raise an arm and squint to protect her face.

When the flames dissipated, she glanced around the wall, noticing Bracken had once again drawn its attention; it snapped at him as he deflected it with more barrier spells, creating artificial walls to dodge behind. Turning her gaze to where she had passed the blade along the beast's side, she frowned when she noticed she hadn't even broken the scales. But there was a long, thin scratch, barely noticeable.

Her gaze passed over the dragon, searching for a weakness. The scales were too hard to pierce, but she was sure if she could find a softer spot, the dragon would be vulnerable to her magic. As her gaze trailed to the back of the beast's head, she suddenly saw what she needed; tucked underneath the long fins behind its eyes, there was a small fleshy spot, usually hidden by the fins but left exposed to Mariea's angle. But now, she just had to get herself to it. Considering how tall the dragon was, that wouldn't be easy.

Glancing around, she looked for something to climb on, then turned her gaze to the building she hid behind. The low shed next to it was just short enough that she figured she could use it to reach the roof. Scrambling onto the small structure, she quickly hoisted herself onto the top of the larger building. With little thought for whether it could still hold her weight, she hurried across it to the opposite ledge and the dragon.

Just as the fight came into view again, the beast managed to yank its tail free of the rubble across the street. It thrashed to her side fast enough that when it smacked into the building she stood on, it easily plowed through the weakened walls. The building fell from underneath her seconds before she jumped from the roof. She flew through the air, falling short of her goal of landing on the creature's back. Slamming into its side, she felt it flinch away from her as she slid down its scales, but before it could dislodge her, her fingers found purchase in an old gash that left a tiny ledge. She jolted to a stop that sent pain flaring through her hands and shoulders. Quickly, she realized she wouldn't be able to hold on to the tiny indent for long.

The dragon let out a growl as it glanced over its shoulder at her, its acidic gaze glowing with annoyance. Bending its neck back, it snapped at her, its lips brushing her side as its jaws closed a fraction of an inch from her. Mariea shuddered, closing her eyes briefly as she let out a gasp of fear. But as she realized she had escaped unscathed, she also acknowledged the beast had given her a footstool. Acting quickly, she pushed off its mouth with a foot, gaining momentum. Then, with a blast of air, she jolted herself upward, grabbing onto the base of the creature's wing above her. With all of her strength, she pulled herself up into the small crook between its body and the wing, even as it gave a violent shake to try to dislodge her. She clung to the base of the wing, barely staying put.

Umber-colored magic flashed past her, and the dragon turned away from her just long enough to send more fire Bracken's way. Mariea pulled herself farther onto its back, grabbing onto the ridge of spikes along its spine. Quickly realizing she had no way to hold on once she was up there, she found herself precariously crouched on its back, uncertain of how to proceed.

Bracken glanced upwards, noticing her crouched on the dragon's back, and looked relieved. But in that brief moment of distraction, the dragon sent more fire toward him. Without time to completely finish a spell to protect himself, the fire broke through the magic, and he disappeared behind the blaze. Mariea stared in horror, waiting for the flames to dissipate, but she couldn't see him through the smoke.

Tears built in her eyes as her hands shook with shock. Her nightmares were coming true, despite all she had tried to do. But before she could lose herself to the despair, she shook her head, wiping the tears away furiously. She had to believe Bracken was still alive, or she wouldn't be able to finish what she had come to do—and if he were alive, he would need a distraction to escape.

The dragon shook again, reminding Mariea of her own predicament. She slipped and nearly fell off, but she miraculously continued to cling to the dragon's spikes until the shaking stopped, ignoring how they painfully dug into her hands. She dragged herself onto the dragon's back again, breathing heavily as she kept her gaze on its head, ready for it to try to shake her off again.

When it did, she used carefully timed bursts of air magic to keep balanced and stay aloft on the shaking beast. It turned and snapped at her in response, but it couldn't bend its neck back enough to reach her.

Remembering the phrase Bracken had spoken moments before, she mimicked his magic and created a long dagger, the metal tinted a metallic blue. She launched forward, running the short distance along the dragon's spine. She barely managed to keep her footing as the beast continued to try to shake her loose, but despite her growing fear, she pressed on.

Luckily, she didn't have far to travel; she reached the base of the neck after only a few steps. At this point, she knew she had precious seconds before the dragon figured out what she was doing and how to get rid of her. She crouched, waiting for a good angle on her target. As she did, the scales below her began to buzz with power, stinging her fingertips, and she couldn't begin to guess what was about to happen. Deciding she didn't want to stick around long enough to find out, she launched herself forward and smashed the knife down into the vulnerable gap in its scales, burying it to the hilt. With nowhere to land, she was jerked free when its head jolted upward, and she fell, landing hard on her ankle.

The beast let out a pained roar, and its legs gave out. Mariea crawled out of the way just in time as it collapsed to the ground inches away from its shoulder. Her ankle throbbed, and she figured she had broken it. But she had won. She lay with her eyes closed for a few seconds, desperately trying to catch her breath.

Then she remembered Bracken and forced herself upwards despite her body's protests. Mae appeared at her side, helping her to her feet. "Bracken," she gasped, wanting to tell Mae to help him instead, but she didn't have the energy to form the words correctly.

"He's alright. I moved him out of the way," Mae told her. The pair hobbled to the edge of the road, where Bracken leaned against a tree. Fresh bandages covered one arm, but Mariea was simply relieved to see he was alive. She pushed away from Mae, half falling to reach him.

When she collapsed at his side, he caught her in a one-armed, tight hug. "I thought you were crushed when the building collapsed," he muttered.

She let out a relieved half chuckle, half sob. "I thought I told you to be careful," she teased as she turned to look up at him.

"I tried," he said, shrugging apologetically and then wincing as he moved his bandaged arm.

Mae collapsed next to them, looking tired. She, too, bore a few bandages, making Mariea wonder what had happened. Bracken glanced at the medic. "If it weren't for her, I wouldn't be alive. She jumped in the way and managed to deflect enough flames that we both survived, and then dragged me out of the way while the dragon was distracted."

The medic gave a small, weary smile. "What else am I here for?" she mused. "Mariea, I think you broke your ankle."

"Figures," Mariea grumbled, turning towards her. But she couldn't get herself to move away from Bracken, and he seemed reluctant to let her, so instead, Mae moved to them and quickly examined the ankle before splinting it with a bit of magic.

"It'll heal alright, but you should stay off it the rest of today," Mae urged.

"The rest of today? We don't have time for that," Mariea protested.

"Honestly, you shouldn't be walking on it for the next couple of days, but I'll do what I can for it," Mae clarified. "My aura's exhausted, so there's no way I can heal it today. I'll try again tomorrow."

Mariea sighed and nodded, disappointed, but she had to admit they were fortunate. Somehow, they had all survived, and she guessed it was only because their enemy had been too cocky to kill them quickly.

"Hey, we might want to move," Bracken interjected.

Mariea glanced at him and then followed his gaze to the body of the creature they had fought. Oddly enough, it was beginning to bloat, a dark orange light emanating from underneath its scales, like molten lava about to spill through the cracks.

"That might be a good idea," Mariea mused as she struggled to climb to her feet. She didn't know what the change meant, but she didn't want to stick around long enough to find out.

Mae managed to stand and then pulled Mariea up. Bracken climbed to his feet and started away, searching for somewhere they could take shelter. Mae followed, urging Mariea to do so as well. Her injured ankle wouldn't hold her weight, forcing her to hobble on one foot while leaning heavily on Mae.

The three had only traveled a few feet when a loud boom echoed behind them. Mariea glanced back to see a ball of orange flames shoot upward from the dragon's corpse, quickly engulfing everything around it. Mae cursed under her breath and picked up the pace, dragging Mariea with her.

"Over here," Bracken suggested, gesturing to an ancient brick wall that looked sturdy enough to survive the blast. He hurried back to them, and between him and Mae, they practically carried Mariea behind the wall. The blast rushed past, collapsing several weak structures around them before silence fell over them again.

Carefully, Mariea glanced around the wall to where the dragon had been. Fires had started on some of the underbrush, but nothing too major. With how wet the plant life was, she was sure they wouldn't burn for long. Then she turned back to her comrades, glancing over them quickly to ensure they were all still okay.

When she was sure they would all survive, she let out a relieved sigh, her shoulder slumping in exhaustion. "Well. That was interesting."

"We all survived at least," Bracken mused.

Glancing upward, Mariea considered what time it was; the sun was beginning to set. Then she turned towards the smoldering town. "Let's make our way to the outskirts and then take a break for the rest of the day."

Everyone seemed more than willing to agree to this. They started for the edge of what was left of the settlement, moving at a painfully slow pace. Glancing over her shoulder, Mariea couldn't help but wonder, *What was that thing, and where did it come from?*

When they found a spot to rest, they quickly set up camp and ate a small meal from their supplies. Bracken glanced at her and then back to the city. "It almost sounded like whatever that was didn't want us to be here. Like it was some sort of guardian or something," he mused, his brow furrowed in thought. "It makes me wonder if it didn't have something to do with what's going on back at home."

"Guess it doesn't matter; it's dead," Mae pointed out.

"I don't know about that," Bracken disagreed with a shake of his head. "It said it 'had orders.' Someone powerful enough to order that thing around..."

His voice faded away, but he didn't need to finish that sentence. A tense silence fell over the three as they all contemplated what that could possibly mean. Mariea glanced back at the city once more, for the first time wondering if she wasn't in way over her head.

Chapter Twenty-Four

Response

Mefune

Mefune waited in the darkness before the city, the patrol spread out around him. They had just settled on the north-western edge of Verndale, where they had a temporary camp set up to give them a place to rest for the night. The day before, Mefune had spent time reorganizing the patrols to make sure there would be plenty of people guarding the city. It seemed excessive, and most of the patrol seemed confused why so many people had ended up there, but they weren't about to question him. At first, he had attempted to get the reassignment orders out discretely, but as he considered the number of Tarapor Daya had reported, he had eventually decided he would have to move too many people to keep the whole thing under the table. It would be easy for anyone aware of Samar's plot to see that people had been moved to guard the city the same night the Tarapor had been released. Mefune hoped he'd be able to play it off as a rookie mistake—he had simply confused the patrol schedules, trying to deal with so many extra ones to keep the Auraes appeased—but he didn't expect Samar to buy it. It made him a bit nervous, wondering what Samar would do in response, but he took comfort in the fact that since the orders had come from only him, there was no reason for Samar to suspect anyone else had been involved.

Most of the patrol seemed relaxed, comfortable in the idea the Tarapor wouldn't venture so close to Verndale, but among them were those who knew what was actually happening—Mefune, Garrett, Altaira, and Desiree. Though they tried to blend with the crowd and give no indication of uneasiness, Mefune could see the tension in how they couldn't quite sit still, and their hands never strayed far from their weapons.

Verndale was quiet behind them. It was well after midnight, and the early morning hours approached steadily. Darkness still surrounded them, but the sky along the eastern horizon had turned a deep blue instead of the black of night, hinting at the coming dawn. Daya had volunteered to set the spell to release the Tarapor and then planned to head to them and raise the alarm of the coming enemies. All they had to do was wait for her arrival.

Altaira sat next to Mefune, her gaze searching the forest for her friend. After a moment, she let out a heavy sigh as she leaned forward to rest her elbows against her knees.

Taking in her expression, Mefune noted how nervous she looked. "Hey," he muttered, nudging her arm gently to draw her attention. She blinked and looked up at him. "You okay?"

She forced a smile as she straightened, more for those around them than anything. "Yeah, just...thinking."

"Tonight should go well," he told her, getting as close as possible to directly reassuring her without revealing his foreknowledge of the coming events.

She nodded slightly. "I figure it will," she agreed lightly, but her expression said otherwise.

Because of the circumstances, Mefune knew there wasn't much more he could say to reassure her, so he took her hand instead and gave it a gentle, reassuring squeeze. "Whatever happens, we'll survive it, just like we have the rest of this week," he muttered softly.

She smiled slightly, nodding. "And then we should do something entirely boring."

Amused, he asked, "Like what?"

"I don't know. Literally anything that doesn't involve Tarapor. And ration bars."

He chuckled. "Sounds good to me."

"Well, I have to say I like this better than you two fighting," a new voice stated behind them.

Altaira straightened quickly, turning to see who had approached as Mefune glanced over his shoulder. Daya stood behind them, her arms crossed against her chest, looking pleasantly surprised.

"Later," Altaira commanded. The darkness made it hard to tell, but Mefune could have sworn she was blushing slightly. "Have you told the patrol leader yet?"

Daya shook her head. "I was on my way there when I got distracted by something I thought I'd never see," she teased.

"Daya," Altaira griped, glaring at her. Daya chuckled and hurried off before Altaira could scold her more. Altaira glanced at Mefune nervously, then stood, muttering, "Let's get this over with."

Deciding to let the whole incident slide to keep himself on task, Mefune didn't say anything. It wasn't long before the silence of the night was shattered by the patrol scrambling to prepare as the alarm was raised. Campfires were put out, and those that were sleeping were roused. Weapons drawn, they gathered along the city's edge while scouts moved into the forest to search out the coming Tarapor.

"You're sure they're headed this way?" the patrol leader asked Daya as the pair moved towards the head of the group. Mefune recognized Amara, one of the older Brotherhood members still actively participating in patrols.

Daya nodded. "They weren't far behind me. I barely made it here in-tact," she replied, managing to sound sufficiently affected by her apparent mad dash through the forest. Mefune couldn't help but smirk a bit at that.

Amara nodded. Then, noticing Mefune just ahead, her gaze widened slightly. "Mefune," she greeted. "I didn't expect you to be here tonight. Are you who brought the extra people?"

He realized she was probably wondering how the command structure was supposed to work; it was expected for patrol leaders to defer to Council members who joined their patrols, but Mefune had never liked this since he didn't know her men as she did. To reassure her, he stated, "It wasn't planned, but it looks like it's turning out to be a good thing. Where would my patrol be most helpful?"

Amara shook her head, letting out a heavy sigh. "Daya said there's a ton coming. Just keep the Tarapor out of the city, I guess. This unprepared, that's the best we can do."

Mefune nodded and began helping her redirect forces to reinforce the line, pushing them more towards where Daya said the Tarapor were coming from. Within minutes of the adjustments, a cry of warning echoed from the western edge of the patrol, and the rest of the group quickly shifted that way. Sure enough, frenzied Tarapor poured from the forest, caring little for the weapons held by their intended victims. They flew mindlessly at the patrol, dying as quickly as they came, but their numbers steadily increased.

Altaira and Mefune joined the fight as the rest of the patrol did. The stream of Tarapor seemed just as endless as Daya promised, and their desperation made them a formidable foe. Maybe even more so than usual. Mefune kept close to Altaira, knowing she was still healing, but she proved to him once again she was more than capable of handling herself.

As he killed what had to be the thousandth Tarapor in just that week, he turned as someone rushed past him. The man quickly approached Amara, who still fought nearby, and announced, "A handful got past us; they're headed into the city."

Knowing it was best to allow the members of the regular patrol to stick together where their strategy was strongest, Mefune immediately offered, "I'll take care of them." Amara turned to him and nodded. Glancing at Daya and Altaira, he motioned for them to follow and gathered the other reinforcements. He directed some to help reinforce the line where the Tarapor had broken free, and then he and the rest spread out through the city in search of the Tarapor that had gotten through.

Mefune stuck with Altaira and Daya, moving silently through the darkened streets. They found the first Tarapor almost immediately after crossing into the city and dispatched them quickly.

"Do we know if any got farther than this?" Altaira wondered, glancing through the darkened streets.

Mefune glanced back at the fighting, assessing the situation. It seemed the patrol had the problem under control, at least for now. "We better check. The last thing we need is for the Auraes to wake to a few stragglers." Altaira and Daya nodded, so the three continued.

"The problem is, we can't search the whole city tonight. How are we supposed to find them?" Daya wondered. The area was primarily residential, and the houses were all dark, leaving only the occasional streetlight to dispel the shadows.

Altaira glanced at Mefune, clearly wondering if he would be able to sense them—which he usually would be able to, but with so many auras around, it was nearly impossible to discern the weaker Tarapor auras.

"We'll just have to keep looking until we're sure they're all gone," Mefune replied.

Suddenly, a Tarapor launched at them from the darkened alley to their right. Altaira dove out of the way as Mefune raised his blades to meet it, killing it quickly.

A strangled cry from behind alerted him to more Tarapor, and he turned just as the beast Daya had killed flopped to the ground. Noticing a few others attempting to flee back down the alley they had come from, Mefune hurried after them, and his companions fell into step quickly.

Feeling a strange sense of déjà vu, they pursued the Tarapor through the darkness. It felt almost like the nights he had spent running from them with Altaira, but this time they were the hunters. They struggled to keep up with the Tarapor—now that they knew they were being pursued, they kept far away from the three, using their superior speed against them. They'd be hard-pressed to catch them all before morning.

Luckily, the Tarapor's unfamiliarity with the city worked to their benefit. After a suggestion from Daya, they managed to corral them towards a dead-end street, where they perished in a heap as the three fell on them.

Altaira let out a huff as the last one died, glancing at the buildings whose doorstep the corpses now laid on. "That'll be a sight to wake up to tomorrow," she muttered.

"We'll have to warn the Aurae leaders," Mefune replied, realizing this would put another damper on their already tense relationship, but there wasn't much he could do about it now.

They spent a good few hours trailing through the streets but encountered few Tarapor. Eventually, as dawn began to break over the horizon, they made their way back to the rest of the patrol. Despite the odds against them, the damage done was more minor than he had expected; there were a few with severe injuries, but most had escaped with minor wounds. Those that were injured were quickly transported to the hospital nearby.

"Well, this probably did little for the Auraes' opinion of how well we're handling the Tarapor," Amara huffed as Mefune and Altaira found her in the chaos.

"The Council will handle the mess," Mefune reassured her. "I'm just glad we mostly survived the night."

"Where did all these Tarapor come from, anyway?" Garrett wondered as he joined them, glancing at Daya.

She shrugged, feigning innocence. "I just noticed them as I was on my way to the city."

"Someone should head back to base, let everyone there know what happened here. And thank you for sending reinforcements. I know it wasn't planned, but you chose a good night to end up in the wrong place," Amara told Mefune.

"I'm glad we were here, too. We'll head back, tell the rest of the Council," Mefune decided. Gathering his reinforcements that were still healthy, he started back towards base. He allowed the patrol to travel on ahead, he and his allies dropping back so they could talk without eavesdropping.

"Well, that went a lot better than expected," Garrett mused once they were far enough away they were out of earshot.

"It's about time we had some good luck," Altaira muttered. They all nodded in agreement.

"Think we got away with it?" Garrett wondered.

"There was one slight complication," Daya quietly interjected. "There were guards at the cage; I had to draw them away before I could open it. I couldn't bring myself to leave them there to be slaughtered."

Mefune frowned at the gruesome idea. "Except now those guards know you were there," he pointed out reluctantly.

"It was dark. I...tried my best not to let them see my face," Daya stated in a weak attempt to reassure them all. It didn't go over well.

Mefune let out a heavy sigh. "Honestly, at this point, I don't think Samar will be fooled by our attempts to seem loyal to him. There wasn't much I could do to hide that I redirected so many people here tonight. But I'm hoping he'll just blame me, and, well, maybe Daya, since the guards saw you. He can't attack us in broad daylight, though, or while we're around the other Council members—I don't think many of them are loyal to him enough to put up with the murder of one of our own. We'll just have to stick together and be on guard."

"And somehow be ready to respond to whatever his next attempt to be rid of the Auraes will be. I doubt he will give up on that just because we freed the Tarapor," Altaira added.

"Probably not," Mefune reluctantly agreed. "And since he doesn't trust us, we won't have a heads up on what he's planning next."

"He...might tell me," Garrett reluctantly inserted.

Mefune glanced at him in surprise. Garrett looked up to him, uncertain, and then shook his head. "It's just a thought. I hinted that you stole the journal pages, but maybe now I should be a little more straightforward. Tell him a 'I told you so' sort of thing. Let him believe he's beaten me into helping him willingly."

Mefune considered it and then shook his head. "It's an option, but he won't trust you easily, even if he does think you're too scared to continue protesting. I don't know that we could rely on any intel you managed to gather."

"So, do we tell the Auraes at this point?" Daya wondered.

"I still think Samar will just use that to his advantage. Play the martyr," Altaira pointed out.

"I agree," Mefune said with a nod.

"But maybe, since you gave Jocelyn a heads up, she'd be willing to help us work on it without causing a civil war," Daya added.

"But it's not Jocelyn I'm worried about," Mefune countered. "She doesn't technically have the authority to act without Ila's permission, and I'm sure if Ila learned she was working with us behind the scenes, she'd be furious—she might even go as far as to say Jocelyn had betrayed her for us, or something. It's hard to know for sure with that woman. Considering she was willing to dismantle our entire alliance just because we didn't have the forces to spare for her fight proves she's prone to irrational behavior."

Altaira let out a heavy sigh. "Wish we could get rid of her like we did Ezequiel," she grumbled.

They fell silent, clearly stuck on the issue. Then Mefune let out a small sigh and told them, "It's late. Let's give ourselves some time to think about this. I don't want to do anything too overt for the next few days to give Samar time to cool off, anyway. Just...try to stick with each other, be careful, and keep our eyes open for any signs he's trying to move against the Auraes in some other way."

The group nodded, seeming equally tired and willing to let the matter rest for tonight. When they finally made it back to base, Garrett offered to report what had happened to Samar, so Mefune bid the rest of them a good night and gratefully headed for his apartment.

$-\wp-$

Altaira

As Altaira was preparing for the day the next morning, she heard a knock at her door. Opening it, she discovered Daya.

"Got any plans for this morning?" her friend wondered.

"After this week? No, I'm hoping today will be insane-plan-free."

"Well, how about breakfast with your best friend? Too crazy?" Daya wondered.

"Sounds nice, actually," Altaira agreed with a smile.

Daya smiled, nodding slightly. "Good. Come. You owe me a story, and you're not getting away this time."

Altaira let out a chuckle, shaking her head slightly, but allowed Daya to take her by the arm and lead her to Daya's apartment. As they walked, she debated what to tell her. She was reluctant to share, but also curious to find out what Daya would think of everything that had happened.

When they reached the apartment, Daya let her in and showed her to the table, where she had eggs, pancakes, and bacon prepared with milk and orange juice.

"This looks great," Altaira commented, surprised by how much effort Daya had put into it.

"Well, you haven't eaten much of substance for a bit, living in the woods and all, so I figured I'd fix you a good breakfast," Daya told her as the two sat.

"Thanks, Daya," Altaira told her with a smile.

Daya nodded, returning the smile. As soon as Altaira was settled, she pressed, "Come on then, spill! What happened? You guys weren't supposed to be gone for more than a day."

Altaira smirked slightly as she shook her head at Daya's persistence. "Fine, fine," she muttered. Pausing a moment, she began scooping eggs on her plate as she gathered her thoughts. Her smile slowly faded as she began. "Things went pretty bad." She proceeded to explain what had happened in as much detail as she could remember. It was all a bit of a crazy blur, punctuated with a few bright moments that she knew she would never forget.

When she came to the retelling of the night they reached the cave behind the waterfall, she hesitated, reflecting on it for the first time. She couldn't help but dwell on the brief moment she and Mefune had shared or how she had fallen asleep essentially in his arms. Since then, there was a closeness between them she appreciated, but still wasn't sure she understood.

"So you made it to the cliff, then what?" Daya pressed. She was sitting on the edge of her seat, her breakfast all but forgotten, despite the forkful of egg she held in one hand.

"Then we slept, found a Tarapor the next morning, and made it back," Altaria finished quickly before taking a bite of her pancakes.

Daya eyed her suspiciously, smirking slightly. "That's clearly not all."

"What do you mean? There's nothing else to say," Altaira denied, sounding defensive even to herself.

Daya's smirk grew. "Not true. You're blushing."

"And you're ridiculous," Altaira countered, her attention suddenly entirely glued to furiously cutting her pancakes into tiny pieces. She knew Daya was right—she could feel the heat in her face—but she hated admitting that.

Daya laughed, clearly watching her reaction and reading way too much into it.

"It was nothing!" Altaira stated firmly.

"I saw you holding hands the other night. You're realizing he might *actually* be your type, aren't you?" Daya teased.

"No."

"Liar. You're my best friend. We've known each other for way too long for you to be able to hide this from me," Daya chastised, eyeing her with a smirk.

Altaira let out a sigh and abandoned her cutting with the clang of silverware against her plate. "I don't have time for all that," she protested with a small wave of her hand. She tried to sound genuine, but she knew at this point she was grasping at fringe excuses that wouldn't hold up under Daya's scrutiny.

"Says who? You can make time if this is important to you," Daya countered.

Altaira didn't bother arguing. She knew she couldn't defend her point for long. She searched for another excuse, another reason to deny herself, but she struggled to come up with anything substantial. *Why am I trying so hard to scramble my way out of this?*

Daya sobered slightly as she watched her and then let out a small sigh. "I know you've been reluctant to date lately. Believe me, after everyone you've lost, I think I'd feel the same way. But I don't think you should let that stop you from going after something if it'll make you happy."

Altaira glanced up at her, meeting her gaze. She realized Daya had hit her real concern dead on, the one Altaira had been skirting the entire conversation. She was trying to escape because she was afraid. This wasn't the first time she'd been drawn into a potential romance, but she'd always called things off before they became too serious. She had no interest in growing attached, only to see life take them from her.

She shifted in her seat and went back to pushing her food around her plate for a moment. "I know," she finally muttered. The weak response didn't convince even her.

Daya considered her silently for a moment and then shrugged. "I don't know. I don't want to push you into something you don't want. But you two could be good for each other. You've suffered a ton of loss in your life. I think it's only fair you have the chance to gain someone this time around."

Altaira nodded, though she wasn't entirely sure she agreed. After her parents, her mentor, several friends throughout the Purges, and, in a sense, her brother, since they were far from close, she had a hard time trusting she'd have any better luck this time around. Life didn't seem interested in being fair or giving her extra chances.

"But please, don't leave me out of this if things change between you two. I need some good gossip in my life," Daya added in an attempt to lighten her mood slightly.

Altaira scoffed. "I'm glad you find my confusion amusing."

Daya chuckled, knowing she meant it sarcastically. "Hey, you know my love life is spectacularly lacking, but if it weren't, you'd be in the same spot as me, wanting all the details."

Altaira shook her head, though she couldn't entirely argue. "Whatever," she grumbled, though she was smiling.

After finishing breakfast, Altaira found she wasn't sure what to do with herself. For a while now, she and Mefune had met for a bit of sparring in the morning, but they hadn't discussed meeting this morning with how crazy last night had been. Now, she had long since missed their usual rendezvous. She was both equally disappointed and relieved—part of her wasn't sure she'd be able to handle a conversation with him after the one she had just finished with Daya.

She did have work to attend to, and was sure she had missed some things while lost in the forest, so she eventually made her way to her office. But after only a few hours of attempting to read through a few reports, she found herself too antsy to sit still. She had been on the move almost constantly for the past week, and now being at a desk wasn't working for her. She had already stopped at the infirmary yesterday, before the whole ordeal with releasing the Tarapor, and they had finished healing her wounds beyond what Mefune could, so there was nothing preventing her from doing something more active. Deciding a good workout might be just what she needed to get the restlessness out of her system, she put her work away and made her way towards the outside practice ring. She figured she could just find a sparring partner there, or, if nobody was available, the gym downstairs was an option.

Once there, she stood near the entrance, realizing there was only one group present, and they were cleaning up. Just as she was about to turn to head downstairs, a familiar voice stated behind her, "Why am I not surprised to see you here?"

Altaira smiled and turned to Mefune, her heart skipping a beat as so many thoughts crossed her mind at once. Apparently, it still hadn't been long enough since her conversation with Daya for her heart to behave properly at the sight of him.

"Hey," she greeted, hoping she sounded and looked more composed than she felt.

He glanced across the open space. "Looks like we have the place to ourselves again. Did you have a plan for your time here?"

"Nothing really. Just, after the past few days, I couldn't stand sitting still," she replied.

He let out a small, amused huff. "Yeah, me neither. Even when I wanted to be lazy, I still found it boring. Well, I've been meaning to work on a little hand-to-hand sparring. Care to join me?"

"Sure," she agreed. "Though I'm not nearly as practiced in this."

He shrugged. "I'm probably a bit rusty myself. We can work on it together."

They quickly fell into their usual rhythm, and the familiarity was comforting. The last of her stress melted away, and Altaira found herself relaxing, teasing him easily as they sparred. For most of their rounds, he had her on the defensive as usual, but she didn't mind for once. She was just happy to be safe and enjoy some time with him.

When she found herself pinned in a corner against the bleachers, he smirked slightly and said, "Well, this is familiar."

She chuckled. "You going to let me escape this time?"

His smirk took on a mischievous edge. "Mmm, I think not. I'm not distracted this time."

"Darn. Guess the novelty of me smiling instead of scowling has finally worn off," she lamented.

"Oh no, it hasn't. I've just learned to ignore it. I know your tricks now."

She struggled for a while to escape, but he was stronger, and she was growing tired. Finally, she announced, "Alright, I give."

He let out a relieved sigh and shifted to lean against the wall next to her, no longer blocking her path. She collapsed against the wall next to him, equally as tired.

"We should really learn to stop before we've beaten ourselves to death," he mused.

She managed a small chuckle. "Where's the fun in that?"

"Well, I'm not complaining, but I do think we both have jobs to attend to, and we've spent most of the day here. If we did this every day, we might get ourselves fired," he mused.

"It hasn't been that long," she denied, unable to believe it.

"It's three."

She blinked, glanced up at the sky, and then back to him. He slowly smiled, and then she started laughing as he did.

As their laughing subsided, his gaze found her again. "Nope, definitely hasn't worn off," he muttered absentmindedly.

She paused, confused. "What?"

"Sorry, just thinking out loud," he muttered as he quickly turned away, and she realized he hadn't meant to voice the thought. He almost seemed embarrassed, something she hadn't seen from him before. She couldn't help but feel surprised. What in the world could leave him—of all people—flustered? And it was something about *her*? There was no way she wasn't going to press for details.

"What do you mean?"

He stayed silent for a moment, clearly debating whether to explain. Finally, he told her, "It was just..." he paused, looking so uncertain, which was so uncharacteristic of him, it nearly made her laugh. "The first time we sparred, I let you get away because I was distracted."

"By?" she urged, even more confused.

He shrugged slightly, as if desperately trying to make it seem like no big deal. "I just happened to notice your eyes are such a fascinating color. I just thought they were dark blue, but I realized they're actually almost purple. Random, I know, but... they're pretty."

She blinked, surprised by the sudden compliment, and sure she was blushing. "Well, my brother used to tease me as a kid, said they made me look strange. I've never thought of them as fascinating."

"They're beautiful," he corrected.

She looked at him, realizing just how sincerely he meant it. She decided not to take the compliment lightly, considering who was saying it. He wasn't one to throw around meaningless words.

She opened her mouth to thank him, but then she met his gaze, and the words were lost to her. He watched her intently, clearly gauging her reaction, a vulnerability to his expression she hadn't seen before. It drew her to him, and she took a half-step towards him.

He shifted closer, tensing slightly with the hyper-awareness often felt during a fight, but there was something softer about this. Reaching up, he brushed a loose strand of hair away from her face, leaning forward slightly as he did. She could almost imagine the space between them disappearing with every breath she took as she waited in silent anticipation.

He moved close enough that their foreheads nearly touched, his fingers tracing her jawline until his hand rested against the back of her neck. When his lips found hers, something inside of her exploded with joy, and she realized she had been waiting, ever since that brief moment on the cliff a few nights ago, to see where it could have led them. It was such a tentative kiss, but it was all the reassurance she needed. There was something there, building between them, and she hadn't been wrong in assuming he had sensed it as well.

She wrapped her arms around his neck and kissed him back. In response, he pulled her closer, all sense of uncertainty gone. She let out a small sigh, content to forget the world and stay in his embrace forever.

But all good things had to come to an end. Across the space, the door to the base opened with a clang, and voices from a rather large group forced their way into the silence of their moment. Altaira gasped and took a step back, looking at the group. When she realized they weren't paying them any attention, she relaxed again, relieved. She smiled slightly, glancing sidelong at him. "Guess that's reality once again trying to remind us it exists. We should probably get back to it."

"Yeah," he muttered, but he sounded reluctant to leave. He glanced over his shoulder at the group, looking almost annoyed.

Altaira laughed. "Oh, don't worry, my job won't keep me busy forever, and neither will yours," she reassured him.

He turned back to her and gave an allowing nod. "Fine, fine, back to life it is, then. See you at dinner?"

"I'll be there."

He nodded, and then after another pause, he started across the room.

Once he was out of hearing range, she let out a sigh and melted against the wall, sure her jello legs wouldn't hold her for a moment more. *Well,* she thought as her hand trailed to her lips. *I think I need to update Daya.*

Chapter Twenty-Five
Betrayal

Altaira

By mid-afternoon the next day, everyone had heard of what had happened at Verndale and the strange surge in Tarapor activity in the area. The Brotherhood was alive with the news, wondering how the Auraes would react and where such a large group of Tarapor had come from. It was interesting to Altaira to note who knew of Samar's plans; their surprise over the phenomenon always seemed less than genuine.

Samar's reaction, however, surprised Altaira. He wasn't anywhere near as angry as she had expected him to be—in fact, he hardly reacted at all, except to inform Mefune he would have to reorganize the patrols to compensate for the increased number of Tarapor near the city. It worried Altaira that he didn't seem to care his plan had been thwarted.

But there was a lot to worry about. Altaira was still adjusting to her new duties as part of the Council on top of all of her regular duties as part of the Brotherhood, and there was the constant threat that Samar knew who was acting against him and would retaliate hanging over her head. Mefune continued to keep a close eye on him, and he often told her it seemed Samar wasn't suspicious, but they were all slow to believe it wasn't more than just a ruse to get them to drop their guard. Samar wasn't the type of person to forget or dismiss when he was betrayed.

Two days after they released the Tarapor, Samar ordered the entire Council still on the island to gather for an extra patrol. After the release of Samar's gathered stash, the amount of Tarapor near the city and headquarters had swelled to a dangerous number, so the patrol was specifically looking to thin the Tarapor's numbers, not just to make sure they were keeping to their territory.

As Altaira made her way outside to join the gathering patrol, she noticed Mefune just starting down the hill ahead of her and smiled. Hurrying to catch up with him, she fell into step next to him and took his hand as she greeted, "Good morning."

He smiled. "Welcome to another day of Tarapor hunting," he joked, earning a chuckle from Altaira.

That was something else that was on Altaira's mind—Mefune. She spent every spare moment with him for no reason other than she could. And wanted to. It was good to have something to look forward to and enjoy in the chaos that her life had become.

And despite her original trepidation, she quickly realized she wanted to see where their budding relationship would go. He seemed to understand almost subconsciously just how nervous she was about it all because he didn't push to move things too fast. Either that, or he partially shared in her concerns. She wasn't sure. But they both seemed content to allow it to develop how it would. She wasn't even sure what to call their relationship, but she was satisfied with what it was at the moment.

As they reached the bottom of the hill, they discovered they had beaten the rest of the patrol. "Hopefully, they won't take too long," Altaira muttered.

"Yeah. The sooner we get this adventure over, the better," Mefune agreed. Then he let out an amused huff as he shook his head slightly.

"What?" Altaira wondered.

He glanced back towards the base, ensuring they were still alone, and then told her, "I just realized we're basically helping to clean up a mess we created."

Realizing what he meant, Altaira smiled slightly. "I guess that's only fitting." Then her smile faded. "Can't say I'm looking forward to fighting the Tarapor again." Her thoughts immediately turned to how badly things had gone last time she had ventured into the forest.

Though good came of those days spent in the forest, she reminded herself, knowing that if it weren't for that little adventure, she and Mefune wouldn't be nearly as close as they were. Maybe something good would come of this little venture.

"At least this time, they'll be a whole patrol, not just the two of us," Mefune pointed out.

"Yeah. That'll make things easier." She allowed his words to reassure her slightly.

After a time, the rest of the patrol slowly trickled in. Altaira was surprised to see how many international members were still present; she thought they had left days ago, after her election. But counting them, she found eight of the fifteen Council members from beyond the island had joined the patrol. She didn't know any of them well, and she only knew a few of their names. Of those she did know, she quickly realized they all favored Samar. If she had to guess why they were still around, she figured it was so they could reconsider how badly their plan had failed and develop a new one. Maybe they already had, and that was why Samar didn't seem so upset about losing his stash of Tarapor. That thought made her frown slightly as her worry returned.

At least there were familiar faces amongst the patrol she knew she could trust. Daya joined her and Mefune, and she noticed Garrett and Desiree nearby. It was nice to know she wasn't entirely surrounded by potential enemies.

Finally, when Samar joined them and directed them onward, the patrol started into the forest. Altaira stuck close to Mefune, and Daya never strayed far. The forest was surprisingly warm that day, and the sun was bright in a cloudless sky above. After a while, she found her worries melting away as she moved with the patrol, relishing in the sense of familiarity. It was amazing how everyday events were so enjoyable after a week like the one she had just survived. She found herself smiling, enjoying herself despite everything.

Sadly, it didn't last long. They hadn't gone far into the forest before they found the first pocket of Tarapor, and the fighting began. They spent the better part of the day trailing after them, resting only when necessary, working at a grueling pace. Samar seemed determined to mop up the entire mess in one go. On more than one occasion, Altaira wondered if he was silently punishing them for releasing the Tarapor.

They took a break around four, and Altaira found a fallen log to take a seat and find her canteen in her pack. Daya settled next to her, and Mefune sat facing the other direction behind her.

"How much longer do you think we'll go today?" Daya wondered.

Altaira shrugged as she finally paused in her water chugging long enough to breathe. "Much farther, and we'll have to stay the night in the forest."

"That's probably what Samar has in mind," Mefune guessed.

"But we weren't planning for an overnight trip," Daya protested.

"Yeah, he definitely didn't give us much of a heads up, that's for sure," Altaira grumbled in agreement.

"We'll survive," Mefune dismissed.

"Most likely because you somehow came supplied for all three of us," Altaira added. He allowed a small smile, shaking his head slightly with a hint of exasperation.

"There's another group up ahead," Darius announced, appearing from the trees. "Let's get moving."

Altaira wasn't the only one to grumble about her exhaustion as they gathered their things and regrouped. Samar waited only long enough for the last member to stand and then gestured them into the forest. With a sigh, Altaira followed, Mefune and Daya close behind.

They approached the pocket of Tarapor silently, their weapons ready. They outnumbered the group easily, so Altaira figured it would be a quick fight. As they attacked, the Tarapor began to flee almost immediately, as she had expected they would, but the patrol pursued.

Suddenly, as they crossed into a small clearing, they realized the Tarapor had been leading them to another nearby group, and their numbers swelled as the new enemies reacted to the threat. Altaira frowned, feeling a little uncomfortable with fighting such a large group. She tried to close the distance between her and Mefune, knowing it was suddenly crucial not to be fighting alone, but the patrol was already scattered among the Tarapor, and it made maneuvering difficult.

Then Daya joined her. "It's been a while since we've fought together," she mentioned as she cut down a Tarapor and stepped up to stand back-to-back with Altaira.

"It's good to have you back," Altaira greeted. For the longest time, the two had served on the same patrol before Daya's appointment to the Council. Sometimes Altaira still missed it. Together, they managed to stay ahead of their enemy much better than if they were fighting alone. *But if I'm here, is Mefune alone?* Altaira wondered with a hint of worry, scanning the chaos for him as best she could between fights.

Suddenly Samar stumbled into her, almost knocking her off her feet, as a much larger Tarapor stalked after him. Altaira turned on the opponent, realizing it was one of the beasts that had once been animal instead of man. After a moment of avoiding its huge, clawed paws, she recognized the deformed, mangy creature as a bear.

Daya joined the fight as well, and despite the beast's size, they had the upper hand working together. When Samar saw an opportunity, he killed the beast with a decisive final blow, stumbling back as it tumbled towards him. Stepping away from the quickly rotting carcass, he turned back to the fight, as did Daya and Altaira.

Despite the odds against them, the patrol managed to pull through. The clearing fell silent as the last Tarapor died, the familiar halt after a battle settling over them. Altaira glanced around the clearing, taking in the others with her. As she took in the group, it was clear there were more injured than healthy, some with pretty severe wounds. She shook her head, annoyed. Samar had pushed them too hard, leaving them vulnerable. At least now, he'd be forced to turn back. There was no way they'd be able to keep fighting with injured members.

"Think that's the last of the Tarapor?" Darius asked from nearby, his gaze on Samar.

For a moment, Samar didn't answer, glancing around the patrol from his spot between her and Daya. Then he shook his head. "It is," he confirmed, his words oddly heavy. Altaira glanced at him, a bit bewildered. How could he know they had killed every last one? Had he been counting or something?

While she was busy puzzling over his comment, she didn't notice he never returned his sword to its sheath, nor did any of the others hovering around the clearing. As soon as Daya turned away from Samar to scan the forest, he lunged toward her, his blade raised to attack. She let out a cry of surprise and pain as Samar thrust his sword into her upper back.

Altaira froze, unable to comprehend what she was seeing, as her eyes widened in shock and horror. Samar pushed Daya away unceremoniously, and Altaira watched her fall as if in slow motion. She started towards her, unable to process what was happening, her body growing numb with shock.

Before she made it far, she was yanked back by the collar, strong arms pinning her in place. Her sword fell from her grasp as she was pulled back, leaving her weaponless. She struggled weakly, too dazed to entirely comprehend what was happening, until a cold blade pressed against her neck.

Altaira stopped fighting, but she strained against her captor's grip despite the deadly weapon at her throat. She couldn't just stand there and let Daya die. "Let me go!" She demanded.

"That's for betraying me and ruining my plans," Samar seethed, his voice close to her ear. "Now cooperate, and I might let you live."

Altaira didn't respond, her gaze glued to Daya. She heard struggling across the clearing and noticed Mefune trying to reach her, but other Council members stepped in his path, refusing to allow him to help. As she watched, helpless to do anything about it, the last of Daya's life faded. The fight left Altaira, and she stared unseeing, her body limp, unable to care. Daya was gone, and she couldn't even begin to understand why.

It took a long moment for Altaira to realize someone was speaking—first, a voice close. It was her captor again. Then a familiar voice, one that grounded her. Mefune.

"You know the minute Altaira's free, you're dead," Mefune promised, his voice surprisingly steady, filled with cold anger that would have sent most men cowering.

"I guess I'll just have to keep Altaira close for a while, won't I?" Samar replied, his words deceptively sweet. He tightened his grip slightly, as if to emphasize his words.

Realizing he must be trying to use her as leverage against Mefune, Altaira scowled, anger rising to clear away the fog of grief for a moment. She wouldn't let him use her to hurt more people, not if she could help it.

She found Mefune and met his gaze, hoping he could understand she didn't want him to bend to whatever Samar was demanding. She had missed that part in her confusion, but she was confident it wouldn't be good. Then she took in her surroundings, searching for options. As she did, she realized most of the Council watched the debate with impassive acceptance, maybe even anticipation, making her realize just how many they were up against. It seemed they had been wrong to assume they wouldn't stand by if Samar turned against other members. The odds weren't in their favor.

"So, what will it be, Mefune? The only way we all leave this scene alive is if you agree to help me." He paused, and Altaira felt him shake his head slightly. "Honestly, I'm surprised this is even a debate. Does she really mean so little to you?" Altaira could imagine him smirking at Mefune as he continued. "Or is she just another one of your games to pass the time?"

Mefune's expression hardened, and he looked ready to slaughter Samar right then and there, but instead, he turned his sword point downward and jabbed it into the ground. He raised his hands in surrender, and Altaira slumped slightly in defeat, unable to believe he was actually giving in to Samar's demands. The patrol shifted, seeming surprised he had given up so easily, but now, none dared to approach him. Even unarmed, the anger in his gaze was a clear-cut message. He was still very much a threat.

"You know, Samar, you said you didn't want to make an enemy of me," he stated softly, his words devoid of emotion. Something about how he said it sent a chill down Altaira's spine. He took a couple of small steps closer, his gaze still locked with Samar. "There was a reason for that fear. You should have listened to me when I warned you."

Then, to Altaira's surprise, his aura surrounded him. Before she had time to contemplate what he intended to do, a similar glow surrounded Samar's hands before her. The minute it touched his sword, it sparked, blinking from existence as quickly as it had appeared.

Samar let out a pained grunt, and his grip loosened as he collapsed behind her. Altaira stumbled away from him. Mefune's aura disappeared, and he reclaimed his sword. Splitting the sword into the two separate blades with a twist, he tossed one blade to her as she slid behind him, and then the patrol swarmed them.

The next few moments became a blur of fighting. Altaira hated killing those she had just spent the day fighting alongside, but the bitter taste of betrayal and pure anger over Daya's death drowned out any sense of conscience she felt. She considered every death an attempt to avenge Daya as she fought, but nothing satisfied her. Nothing could ease the pain.

Mefune stuck close, fighting without mercy. He seemed to have lost any sense of respect for the lives he was ending. After what they had tried to do, Altaira could hardly blame him.

To her surprise, she discovered they didn't fight alone; Garrett and Desiree both defended them. After how long they had spent trying to convince Garrett to truly help, it amazed her he was willing to now, and Desiree had hardly been involved in their struggle. But she wasn't about to question it. The numbers were not in their favor—nine against four. Luckily, the injured among their enemies made for easy targets, and few could match Altaira and Mefune's skill or anger.

It ended almost as quickly as it began. Altaira stumbled to a halt as her last enemy fell, and she took in the carnage around her. These deaths wouldn't fade from her memory as easily as the Tarapor did.

Garrett let out a grunt of pain as he kneeled at a woman's side, and Altaira realized it was Desiree. He sighed and shook his head, straightening. "She's dead," he muttered, then grimaced as whatever wounds he bore were aggravated by his movement.

Altaira turned to Mefune. There was a superficial wound on his arm and a few other scrapes and bruises, but he seemed okay. As he sheathed his sword and his anger calmed, his shoulders slumped, and he suddenly looked a thousand years older as the weight of everything that had happened settled on him like a stone. She glanced at Samar a few feet away, wondering what Mefune had done to force his aura to appear. She hadn't even known he had one before he had died, but she was grateful it had given Mefune an easy solution to the situation.

Then, not far from Samar, Altaira found Daya's body. Without the anger, there was only her grief, and as the rush from the fighting faded, she was left to process all she felt. Numb again, she approached Daya's cold form. She collapsed to her knees next to her, her borrowed sword forgotten at her side. *I'm sorry*, she thought as she raised a trembling hand to close Daya's eyes, unable to handle how lifeless they were.

Daya was gone. In seconds, Altaira's whole world had collapsed around her. Tears clouded her vision, and she found it suddenly hard to breathe, her heart seeming to seize in her chest. Her tears fell silently, the physical pain almost more than she could bear. She had lost too many, and all her grief seemed suddenly compounded in this one last straw. Everything she had tried so hard to accomplish had been towards one goal—to protect those she still had from being taken from her. But here she was, once again trying to process why she had to lose someone else.

Then a hand rested on her shoulder, and she jumped slightly, glancing up to see Mefune. His gaze met hers; once bright, it was now dull with a pain she knew they both shared. She shifted closer when he crouched next to her, searching for comfort. He pulled her close, and she buried her face in the crook of his neck, trying to hide from everything she had lost.

"I'm so sorry," he whispered as he hugged her close. "It wasn't supposed to end this way. If I could fix this, I would." His words were heavy with grief, his voice shaking slightly with unshed tears.

Suddenly, she realized she wasn't left alone in her grief for the first time. Mefune was there for her. Even if everything seemed lost, and she didn't want to keep fighting, he was there. She would cling to that as long as she could.

After a long moment of silence, Garrett asked softly, "What do we do now?"

"Tend to our wounds, bury the dead," Mefune replied wearily.

Realizing she had to function, Altaira forced herself to straighten and stand as she wiped away her tears, but Mefune stayed close. He carefully tended to their few injuries, and then the three got to work burying the fallen.

As they began to take stock of the situation and figure out how best to handle what they had to do, Garrett pulled away, searching through the bodies for any survivors. After a moment, he called, "Darius is alive!"

Mefune hurried to him, and Altaira reluctantly followed. Garrett had stepped around a tree near the edge of the clearing. When they joined him, Altaira noticed Darius at the base of the tree. His breathing was heavy and raddled, and his hands pressed to a large wound in his side. Despite his obvious disadvantage, he glared up at the three with pure loathing.

"Well, this makes our lives a little easier," Mefune stated before stepping around Garrett to crouch in front of Darius.

He immediately tried to scramble away from Mefune, a hint of fear replacing his anger, but Mefune raised his hands in a placating gesture. "I'm not going to kill you—you're too valuable alive. But looking at that wound, I doubt you'll live long unless I help you." He paused just long enough to let this sink in and then continued, his voice soft. "Now, tell me what you know about Samar's schemes, and I might find it in me to patch you up."

Darius seemed to struggle with the idea. "Why should I tell you?" he managed through clenched teeth.

"Well, I could let you bleed out here if you don't cooperate," Mefune stated with a light shrug.

Darius swallowed hard. "I don't know anything."

"Liar. I saw how much you hung around Samar, how you seemed to know before anyone else did that he intended to turn against us today. He obviously trusted you with details he wouldn't tell anyone else. What was he planning?"

Darius shook his head. "I don't know; all he told us was what he told you."

Seeing he wasn't getting anywhere with that question, Mefune asked next, "Who else is loyal to him? What was my part in all of this?"

"I don't know what he had planned for you," Darius managed as he tried to sit up straighter, but succeeded only in aggravating his wound. He seemed to be getting weaker.

"What about the rest of the Council? Are they loyal to Samar?" Garrett asked.

Darius shook his head slightly. "Samar...couldn't convince them. That's why he sent them away before today."

"Is anyone else aware of Samar's plans? Anyone who might try to act on them?" Mefune pressed.

Darius shook his head. His breathing was growing shallower.

"Mefune, he's going to die," Garrett pointed out.

Mefune let out a heavy sigh, obviously realizing the same thing. "Swear to me you will confess all you know to the Brotherhood, and I'll let you live."

Darius let out a weak, bitter chuckle. "Why bother? They'll kill me for my crimes. Might as well die here."

"Suit yourself," Mefune muttered, straightening.

"Wait," Darius clamored. "Please. I don't want to die."

"You'll swear it?" Mefune pressed.

Darius hesitated and then gave a curt nod. Mefune kneeled at his side again, meeting his gaze. "You back out on that promise or do anything harmful to any one of us, and you'll wish I let you bleed out here," he promised. "Got it?"

Darius nodded, this time with more vigor, clearly believing Mefune could carry out his threat. Satisfied, Mefune reached for his bag and got to work tending to Darius' injuries. As he worked, Darius lost consciousness, urging Mefune to move faster.

This would be much easier if he could use his aura, Altaira realized. Glancing at Garrett, she stated, "He can handle this. We need to get everyone else buried before all this attracts more Tarapor."

Garrett nodded and followed Altaira back to the clearing where so much death had occurred.

Without the proper tools, it took much longer than necessary, but each fallen soul was finally laid in a shallow grave. After dealing with Darius's wounds and tying him securely to the tree he had rested against, Mefune joined Altaira and Garrett. They worked well into the night, and Altaira was ready to collapse, but she couldn't bring herself to leave Daya behind. She stood forlornly over the grave, staring at it without really seeing. Her tears had stopped, but she felt it was simply because there weren't any more left to cry. Her heart still ached plenty enough for the tears to fall.

Mefune stepped up next to her silently, taking her hand in his. Altaira glanced at him briefly and then back to the makeshift grave, complete with the crooked pile of rocks to mark its location. "She deserved better than this," she muttered. "Buried among traitors."

"We'll honor her properly when we get back," he promised.

She nodded, understanding there wasn't much they could do now. It still hurt to have to leave Daya behind, but that was always what happened when someone died on patrol—they couldn't risk trying to carry the body back, knowing it would attract more Tarapor. It wasn't the first time she had been forced to bury someone in the forest, and part of her worried it wouldn't be the last.

Glancing at Garrett, Mefune stated, "We should rest, figure out what to do next in the morning."

"I second that," Garrett agreed, sounding just as weary as Altaira felt. He was nursing some pretty severe wounds. As he limped into the forest, Mefune followed, gently guiding Altaira away from Daya's grave.

They went just far enough that the scene of so much bloodshed was no longer in sight, and then set up camp quickly. Mefune volunteered to take first watch, and Altaira didn't have it in her to protest. With him watching, she knew she'd rest easily, and desperately wanted the escape sleep would bring. Hopefully, she'd somehow figure out how to function again without Daya by morning.

Mariea

The day after facing the dragon proved to be uneventful. Mae's aura was still too tired to care for Bracken's wounds and fully heal Mariea's ankle, and Mariea quickly found it was way too painful to walk on, much less go hiking through the jungle. So, she reluctantly agreed to wait another day to allow herself and Bracken time to heal. Towards the end of the day, Mae worked on healing Mariea's ankle enough she could walk, and then they called it a night.

The next morning, Mariea woke long before her companions. As she straightened, she let out a pained grunt, as she discovered she was surprisingly sore. Between the fight with the dragon and sleeping on the ground with nothing but a sleeping bag to shield her from the rocks, her body wasn't too happy with her situation.

Carefully, she extracted herself from Bracken, who was sound asleep next to her, and glanced around their camp. Mae slept on the other side of the small clearing they had made, curled up in a ball inside her sleeping bag. It was still a relief to see both of her companions alive and well, considering what they had been through. Part of her still marveled at how the whole ordeal was even possible. It felt like a bizarre dream. But the minute she took a few steps, her ankle reminded her it had, in fact, been real.

It was cooler that morning, the sky overcast, which was a big relief. While she waited for Mae and Bracken to wake up, she carefully took stock of their supplies. To her dismay, she discovered they were dwindling fast. They only had enough for another three days on the island. They had more supplies on the boat, but they had to be saved for the return trip. If they didn't find their answers fast, they would be forced to leave to restock and then return.

She hadn't heard from home since she had left New York. Though she told herself it was because of the problems a glowing aura message showing up on a crowded New York street could cause, part of her worried it was actually because something had happened to them. *Maybe I should send them a message,* she mused, remembering her promise to Ila to keep her updated. Maybe they were waiting for her to reach out. But then she frowned when she realized she had nothing positive or even remotely helpful to tell them. She would wait.

Glancing back at her sleeping companions, Mariea debated waking them. She knew they were both exhausted, so she found herself reluctant to bother them. She sighed and began pacing, deciding she wanted to move around and stretch out the kinks so she'd be ready to go once everyone was awake. It took all her willpower to keep herself nearby. She didn't want to leave them behind, but she had already wasted a day, and her nagging worry for home wore down her patience.

Her circles slowly widened as she paced and eventually wandered back into the settlement. Suddenly, she realized she recognized where she was; they had set up camp near where the path had been that had led to the medics' lab. Curious, she began searching the tree line for any indication of the trail. She hadn't gone far into the trees when she began to feel dizzy. She blinked, trying to steady herself.

Suddenly, she was standing in the settlement, near the busy downtown area. Time had passed, and the colony had grown. The streets were now paved with cobblestone, more of the buildings seemed better furnished, and the businesses surrounding Mariea seemed to be thriving.

Her gaze rested on the nearby church, realizing it was packed. At first, she thought it was for a happy occasion, but as the scene moved her into the building, she felt the sorrow hanging over the room.

Near the front of the chapel, the governor spoke to the gathering in a soft, heavy tone. Mariea's gaze found Elinore and Densin near the front of the room. Elinore was crying silently, clinging to Densin, who stared at the front of the room, his face a blank mask. Mariea could feel their pain, and it took her breath away when it hit her, immediately bringing tears to her eyes. It took her a moment to understand what had caused them to suffer so much, but then her gaze followed Densin's, and she saw the casket at the front of the room. Mariea quickly realized it was way too small for an adult, and a feeling of dread grew as her mind turned to the two young children of Elinore and Densin.

As the governor finished, the crowd passed by the casket to pay their last respects to whoever had passed. Mariea followed with Elinore and Densin, against her will, to the casket's side. She peered inside apprehensively and laid eyes on the all too still form of their daughter.

$$-\,\wp\,-$$

Elinore

Finally, the funeral ended. The small casket was raised from its spot, Densin and his father among the pallbearers, as well as Elinore's father and older brother. Elinore trailed behind them with the rest of their family and friends as they carried it to the cemetery.

Once the burial was finished, the crowd slowly disappeared, but Densin lingered. Elinore wanted nothing more than to leave Amberlie's grave behind, but he seemed to want to stay. He stared at the headstone, his face a cold mask, his hands clenched into fists at his side.

When an hour passed, Elinore finally stepped up next to him, gently placing a hand on his arm. "Let's go home," she whispered.

He glanced at her and then turned back to the grave, his jaw clenching as tears built in his eyes. It was the first tears he had shed since he had found her body, the first emotion he had shown. He had hardly even spoken a word since telling her what had happened. Leaning her head against his shoulder, she felt fresh tears gather in her eyes at the sight of his pain, his evident confusion and frustration.

He cried silently for a few minutes and then dried his tears with a shaky sigh. "What happened to her wasn't an accident," he muttered, so softly she almost didn't hear him.

"What do you mean?" Elinore wondered.

"She was murdered," he continued, his voice surprisingly devoid of emotion despite the weight of his announcement.

Surprised, Elinore stayed silent for a moment and then asked, "What makes you think that?"

"She hadn't passed yet when I found her." He paused, swallowing as he fought away another bout of tears. Elinore's sorrow deepened as she realized he had been forced to witness Amberlie's death. "She had wandered to the back field. Her aura was collapsing. I tried to repair it like I had others, but it was impossible. It had been destroyed by an Aurac spell," Densin explained quietly.

"Who would do something like this?" Elinore managed, her voice shaking with emotion as she stared at him in horror.

"That's what I would like to know," Densin sneered, his sorrow quickly warping into anger.

Suddenly, Elinore feared that anger. "Please don't get wrapped up in this," she requested. "Let the sentinels know so they can handle it."

"I can't tell them what I know," Densin told her, sounding reluctant to continue.

"Why not?"

"Because..." he paused, clearly searching for words. "After I tried to repair her aura, I knew there was no way she would survive, but she was dying so slowly. She was in so much pain. She didn't understand and kept trying to get me to help her, but there was nothing I could do. I...I couldn't sit there and let her suffer, so...I took her aura to end it."

"What?!" Elinore gasped. She couldn't believe he had done such a thing, even if she somewhat understood his reasoning. It was something he had promised to never do, and she couldn't help but wonder what the ramifications of such a decision would be. And to think, he had broken that promise to take his daughter's aura, of all people. She simply couldn't believe what he was saying was true.

"What was I supposed to do?" he protested with a helpless shrug. "Even if I had gone for help, she still would have died before I made it back to the house, and she was already so scared and confused. She wasn't going to make it. I had to, Elinore." He ran a hand through his dark hair, fighting tears again. "All this power, and I couldn't save her," he muttered bitterly. "I saved thousands, but when it came to one of the people I love most, I couldn't stop this from happening."

Elinore bit her lip, tormented by the way he blamed himself and the realization of how Amberlie had died. "There was nothing you could do. This wasn't your fault," she told him.

He stayed silent, giving no indication whether he believed her. Eventually, he let out another sigh and muttered, "Let's go. We still have Ansem."

"Yeah, he's probably going crazy waiting for us," she said, managing a half-smile as she thought of her baby boy. Her smile quickly faded when she thought of him growing up without his sister. The two had already been close, even at such a young age. She wondered if Ansem was old enough to realize she was missing.

In silence, they made their way back through town to Clare's house. Elinore's friend gave them a bittersweet smile and invited them in. Ansem was sitting on the floor playing with Clare's daughter, Marie.

"He was very well behaved, considering how upset he was when you left him," Clare commented.

"That's good," Elinore managed.

When the little boy heard her voice, his blue gaze snapped to her, and he grinned. Climbing to his feet, he tottered over to her. "Mama," he greeted, wrapping himself around her leg. She laughed softly, bending to gather him into her arms. He giggled and squirmed, but then wrapped his little arms around her neck and snuggled closer.

For a moment, she held him tighter, sure he had no idea how much that hug meant to her. Then she forced herself to focus, turning to Clare. "Thanks for watching him."

"No problem. He's a sweet boy," Claire replied. "If you need anything else, let me know."

"Thank you," Elinore sighed. "It's good the funeral is over, but...it'll take some time." Time to heal, time to feel like she could function without breaking into tears, time to forget the anger and pain. Time couldn't pass fast enough, in her opinion.

Clare nodded, obviously understanding. Elinore turned to Densin, realizing he was watching her and Ansem. She forced a smile and told him, "Let's go home."

He nodded and stepped out the door. Elinore followed, waving goodbye to Clare. They made their way out of town and to their farm. Once inside their modest house, Elinore paused, the feeling of something missing so overwhelming she had to bite her lip to fight more tears. The home suddenly felt so empty and quiet without the patter of her little feet and constant chatter. Setting Ansem down, Elinore headed for the kitchen, deciding she needed to keep busy. Densin disappeared into the fields behind their house, obviously with the same plan in mind.

Weeks later, things hadn't improved much. Though Elinore was doing everything possible to move past her grief and let Amberlie rest in peace, Densin couldn't. He almost seemed to fall deeper into his sorrow as time passed, drowning in it. He tried to act as if nothing was wrong, but his smile never reached his eyes, and he seemed to spend most of his time deep in thought, shut off from her. Nightmares tormented him frequently, and sometimes he became so angry or upset Elinore didn't know what to do to calm him. He always showed an outpouring of love towards her and their son, but she knew he was still hurting. It frustrated her to no end there was nothing she could do about it. She could barely handle her grief, much less help him figure out his own.

One day, he left to go into town, looking to sell some of their crops. He promised to be back before nightfall, but, as dark came, he didn't return. She tried messaging him, but he didn't answer. After putting Ansem to bed, she decided to wait up for him, figuring he wouldn't be much longer. A few more hours passed as she dozed periodically in the rocking chair by the fire. Finally, she gave up her vigil when she became too exhausted, but she hardly slept, too worried for Densin to relax.

The next morning, soon after she had sat down to eat breakfast, he walked in, looking tired but well. She sighed in relief, hurrying to him. After a quick hug, she asked, "What happened? Where were you?"

"I'm alright," he reassured her. "I just got sidetracked, and it ended up very late before I realized how much time had passed. I figured it was better to just stay in town instead of trying to make my way back in the dark. I was going to send you a message but got caught up in things and forgot. I'm sorry."

She managed a smile, grateful to hear nothing had happened to him, but she still found the ordeal odd. "It's okay. It's just...not like you to disappear like that, so I was worried," she said before heading back to the table and her forgotten oatmeal. "Are you hungry? I made breakfast."

"Yeah," he admitted, joining her at the table.

She grabbed another bowl from the cabinet behind her and served him some of the oatmeal from the pot on the stove. "What were you doing that kept you out so long?" she wondered as she handed it to him.

"I ran into an old friend," Densin began as he started into his breakfast. "We were talking for a while. When I told him about Amberlie, he asked me to allow him to buy me dinner. He couldn't think of any other way to offer help, but wanted to do something, so I accepted. It took longer than I expected. He let me stay the night at his place."

"Ah," Elinore muttered, picking at her breakfast, her appetite mysteriously absent. Eventually, she gave up and started cleaning up. "Well, at least it was something good that kept you for so long." Though she felt slightly relieved, something still seemed off, but she had no idea what. It nagged at her as he moved on, making it hard for her to concentrate as he told her about his successful sale and his plans for next year's planting. Even as the day went on, the strangely uncomfortable feeling lingered, especially when he was near. It made no sense whatsoever, but she just couldn't shake it.

They settled into their usual routine for a week, and she pushed her worry from her mind for a time. But then he went to town and didn't return after nightfall again, and all of her fears returned. This time, he did warn her he might be late, but it didn't calm her nerves for some reason.

But as time went on and he spent more and more time away, she fell into a weary acceptance of the absences, deciding he might just need his space for a time. It seemed to be helping him a bit—after the absences, he seemed more like himself for a time. As much as she didn't like not knowing what was going on, she didn't pry, figuring he would talk when he was ready.

Later, she would wish she had asked. As time moved on, he slowly began to change. Though there were brief moments where he seemed more clear-minded, he gradually became fixated on finding the man who had killed Amberlie and was willing to do anything to see her death avenged. Elinore watched, helpless, as his grief slowly consumed him a bit at a time, leaving an angry, hollow shell. He refused to tell her what he was doing when he disappeared, and he never used his aura around her. She figured it was because he was ashamed of taking Amberlie's aura, but it almost seemed irrational just how much he kept it hidden. She couldn't even begin to consider any other possible explanation.

And her unease around him only grew. She couldn't explain it, but he made her nervous. She guessed it was his erratic behavior. She told herself he wasn't a danger to her or Ansem, but at this point, she couldn't even guarantee that.

At the same time, rumors from town slowly began to reach Elinore. Reports of mysterious attacks. Unexplainable deaths, some of which the medics were calling murders. A sense of uneasiness settled over the town, and Elinore withdrew, spending more and more time at home.

By the time six months had passed since Amberlie's death, she had become so accustomed to Densin not being around that she often lost track of how long it had been since she had last seen him. A part of her worried there would be a day he simply never returned, even though he promised he would come back each time he left.

So when he appeared in her doorway late one afternoon after being absent for nearly a month, she stopped dead in her tracks, at first unable to recognize him. He was filthy, and a deep cut ran along his cheek. There were what looked like burns on his sleeve, and she couldn't decide if the dark patch on the side of his shirt was grime or dried blood. Despite his horrid condition, there was a smug triumph in his eyes.

"Densin, what in the world happened to you?" she managed.

"I found him, Elinore," he stated softly, his gaze slightly unfocused. "I found the man that killed our daughter."

Elinore's breath caught in her throat, and she found she couldn't speak for a few moments, dreading the next question she would have to ask. "And what happened when you found him?"

"He's dead," he stated, his words entirely lacking any emotion. There was no remorse, but there was no pride either. It was simply a fact.

"Densin," Elinore breathed, wanting to reprimand him for what he had done, but she was too afraid of how he would react to finish her sentence. "Why did you do it?" she finally asked.

"Isn't it obvious?" Densin stated, his eyes flashing with deep hatred. "He was dangerous. She wasn't the only one he had killed. He had to pay for what he did. Nobody else would do anything about it, so I handled it myself. He deserved to die."

Elinore's hands clenched into fists at her side as her fear grew. Her husband was many things, but cruel had never been one of them. But that was the only word to describe what she saw in him now. "It wasn't your place," she told him.

His anger only increased as his gaze snapped to her. She couldn't ever remember a time he had been angry with her. Sure, they had disagreed occasionally, as all married couples did, but he had never raised his voice.

"I did it for you and Ansem, Elinore!" he snapped. "He could have come to finish off the rest of the family. I couldn't let that happen! I couldn't lose you too." He paused, taking a deep breath, forcing himself to calm down. "It's over now. You're safe. I've guaranteed that monster can never hurt anyone again."

She swallowed back her first response, wanting to point out how he wasn't any better than the murderer. Or that he had nearly lost them anyway by entirely withdrawing from their lives.

She sighed, searching for a better response when Ansem tottered up to her unexpectedly. "Momma, up," he pleaded, tugging on her skirt. As she bent to pick him up, she couldn't help but be amazed by the fear she saw in his wide, blue eyes. Around his little hands, thin wisps of his recently found indigo aura appeared, reacting to his anxiety. He tucked his head underneath her chin, curling up into a ball in her arms. To her amazement, she realized he was trembling.

"What's gotten into him?" Densin wondered, echoing her thoughts. Looking at him, she noticed something of the Densin she knew and loved shone from underneath the grime as concern for his son brought him back to reality.

"I don't know," she replied, giving the small child a reassuring pat on the back.

Densin took a few steps forward, his eyes on their child as if he meant to comfort him. The minute Ansem noticed Densin approaching, he buried his face against Elinore's chest, whimpering quietly, his trembling increasing.

Densin stopped in his tracks, horror written all over his expression. Then his shoulders slumped. "I guess I deserve this. I have been away a lot lately. He's probably forgotten who I am," he muttered.

"Or maybe he just doesn't recognize you under all that filth," Elinore pointed out.

Densin sighed. "Maybe," he muttered. "I'll go clean up." He disappeared into the washroom attached to their bedroom. Elinore heard water being poured into the washbasin as she moved to sit in the rocking chair. She cradled her son close, rocking gently, until he relaxed and dozed, his head resting on her shoulder. As she trailed a hand over his back soothingly, she couldn't help but wonder what about the child's father was more terrifying—how he looked, or what he was slowly becoming.

She placed Ansem in his crib after a moment more, allowing him to sleep. After a few more hours, she retired, not sure she wanted to spend more time than necessary in Densin's presence. But as he joined her, her apprehension faded, and she allowed herself to remember what life had been like and to relive that memory for just a little while.

She hadn't slept for long when she was suddenly jerked awake by Ansem's terrified screams. She shot up, startled and disoriented, before realizing it was just him. He had never suffered from nightmares before, sleeping soundly through the night despite his young age.

Densin awoke when she did, looking around in confusion, thin wisps of his aura appearing around his hands as it reacted to his surprise. That's when she noticed the change. His aura was a dark, ugly green-brown. She stared at it, knowing when his aura interacted with others, it would change colors because of the graft, but never had she seen it so dark. Usually, the color faded quickly.

Feeling his gaze on her, she glanced up at his face. He eyed her carefully, his expression guarded, but there was a hint of disappointment to it. Then Ansem let out another cry. Silently, he stood and went to the boy, lifting him from his crib.

This almost seemed to upset the child more, his screams no more frantic as he squirmed against his father's grasp. Elinore hurried to him, taking him from Densin. Suddenly, she wondered if she knew what it was about Densin that terrified Ansem so much.

In her arms, his cries slowly subsided. Elinore paced, giving her an excuse to turn away from Densin so he couldn't see the anger in her eyes, but she figured he would pick up on it nonetheless.

"What is it, Elinore? Why are you so upset?" he asked softly, as she had expected he would.

She could imagine his shoulders slumping, his gaze unfocused as he looked her way, searching for answers, but part of her refused to give them. But she had to know if her suspicions were correct. "Why is your aura different?" she demanded, her words harsher than she meant. Ansem squirmed in her arms, disturbed slightly by the sharp tone.

"I tried to keep it from you. I didn't want you to worry," he sighed, avoiding her question.

She turned back to the crib, placing Ansem down now that he was asleep again. Then, she grabbed Densin by the wrist and pulled him through the house and outside, where they wouldn't disturb their son.

"*Not worry?*" she snapped, turning on Densin as she folded her arms against her chest. "How did you expect me not to worry? You've basically disappeared, cutting me out of your life, and for what? So you could seek your revenge? I doubt that's what Amberlie would have wanted."

"She was four. She wouldn't have understood," Densin deadpanned as he stared at her with a mix of disdain and frustration.

"*I* don't understand!" she countered, throwing her hands in the air in frustration. Then she locked gazes with him, daring him to turn away, to lie to her. "You took that man's aura. The one who killed Amberlie. And others, too, if I'm not mistaken."

His hands tightened into fists at his side, but his expression didn't change. "I did," he stated flatly, with the same dismissive tone he had used when first announcing the murder he had committed.

"You promised me you wouldn't use your aura like that," she reminded him, her voice cold as her anger cooled to despair and disbelief.

He shrugged, as if it was that easy to dismiss. "Things changed. Amberlie's death makes everything different. He had to suffer as I had, and that was the easiest way. The others were... unforeseen consequences."

"You chose to allow her death to change things. It didn't have to be this way," she argued, but she realized her words fell on deaf ears.

He let out an annoyed huff. "Do you think I wanted this to happen? That I wanted Amberlie to die? I didn't choose this."

"That's not what I said," she corrected with a shake of her head. "Whatever you're feeling because of Amberlie's death is understandable, but you shouldn't have used it as an excuse to give in to the temptation to abuse the power of your aura. It was meant for good, Densin. Now you've corrupted it."

"What do you know about it?" he growled.

"*I helped make it*, remember? I watched you use it to heal hundreds. That's the man I fell in love with. Not this! What you have done has changed you, Densin, and I'm not sure I can stand it!"

He shook his head, running his hands through his hair as he turned away from her for a moment, clearly trying to calm down before he responded. "I'm *trying*, Elinore," he finally said, and his words were so heavy that she felt her anger fade a bit. "You don't have to carry this burden. I've been trying so hard. But I couldn't do it anymore. I lost everything when Amberlie died. My daughter was gone, and with her my happiness. My control. You want to know why I keep away? Because I didn't want to accidentally steal your aura when I was too deep in my anger or grief to realize what I was doing. And now Ansem's aura is visible. I figured, if...if the man who killed Amberlie died, maybe some of this pain would go away, and I could keep things under control again."

She watched him for a moment in silence, finally seeing the bone-deep exhaustion that weighed him down and clouded his judgment. "Did it help?" she wondered softly.

He shrugged slightly. "I honestly don't know if anything can help me now."

"Maybe letting Amberlie go would."

He stared at her, and she could see the conflict in his gaze. Even after all this time, he still desperately clung to her. He let out a shaky sigh, his gaze dropping to the ground. "I don't know how to."

"Let me help you," she offered, taking a step closer. "Densin, we were supposed to face this together. Like we promised each other. Remember? I still hold to our vows. I'm here for you. But you can't keep shutting me out."

He met her gaze, his eyes bright with unshed tears, and nodded heavily. "I'm sorry. I let everything get out of hand. I...I'll try again."

The last of her anger faded, and she closed the gap between them. He caught her in a hug, gripping her tightly with the desperation of someone terrified to let go, and she relished in it, intending never to let him get so far away again.

After a long moment, she sighed as she pulled away slightly and said, "We never did tell the medics about the side effects of the graft. Maybe we should have. Maybe we should now."

He nodded, his gaze on the ground. "I realize that now. For some reason, I just didn't want to. Neither did any of the others. In the morning, let's fix that. Will you come with me?"

She nodded, elated he already seemed willing to involve her more. "Of course. I'm here for you," she promised.

He smiled, and then gently pulled her towards the house. "Come on. It's late. Let's go back to bed."

Elinore

The next morning, Elinore woke to find Densin missing. The last bit of grogginess quickly left her, and she climbed from bed to search the house, wondering what had changed since last night. She searched the dwelling, but couldn't find him anywhere. Deciding she wasn't sure she trusted him to be alone after last night's conversation, she gathered Ansem and quickly took him to her parent's house, then started for the town to search for him.

She hadn't quite reached the town when she heard a scream and paused. Another echoed through the air, followed by others. Rushing forward the remaining distance into the town, Elinore searched for the source of the screams and was met by chaos.

People scattered through the streets, running in all different directions. There was so much going on at once that it was hard to follow what was happening or who or what they were running from. It took a moment for her to process others were chasing them. At first, she wondered who was causing such a scene until she sensed their auras—they felt just like Densin's. Her mouth fell open with surprise, and she shook her head, unable to contemplate what was happening, even as her aura rose around her instinctively to protect her.

A woman tripped in front of her, letting out a terrified squeal as she tried to scramble back to her feet, but she kept getting tangled in the fabric of her dress. Elinore stared down at her, too dazed to decide what she could do to help. Finally, her body responded to her brain's weak signals, and she moved to help the fallen woman. But she was too late; the rogue Aurae chasing her caught up to them, and the woman's aura was gone in an instant and a flash of color.

The murderer turned her gaze on Elinore, and she suddenly found herself running for her life. With no idea how to protect herself against their power, she knew her only chance was to stay far enough away they couldn't take her aura. She dashed through the streets, her skirts clutched in her hands to prevent her from tripping as she desperately tried to outrun her pursuer.

Suddenly, someone pulled her roughly from her path, steadied her against the wall of a building, and then stepped around her to deal a deadly blow to the woman who chased her. She disappeared in a flash and falling ashes.

Elinore stared at the spot where she had been, her eyes wide and unfocused, as she struggled to catch her breath. Then she finally tore her gaze to her benefactor, who approached her with a look of concern. Recognizing the uniform of a sentinel, some of her fear faded a bit, knowing she'd be safe in his company.

"What's happening?" she demanded.

"There's been an uprising," he replied, his gaze searching their surroundings warily. "Those that received the graft a few summers ago have been hunting other Auraes. At first, they tried to keep their activities hidden, and we were trying to contain it, but something changed last night and, well…this happened." He gestured at the chaos just beyond the alley they stood in. Then he turned to her, obviously noting her dazed expression. "You should head somewhere safe. I can escort you."

Elinore immediately thought of Densin and couldn't help but wonder if he was somehow a part of it all. Then she considered what she knew of his aura, and subsequently, all of them like him. Blinking away her confusion, she met his gaze.

"No, I don't want to hide. I know these people. Let me help," she requested.

The sentinel eyed her for a moment, clearly debating how wise it would be to allow her to act on her request. Then he sighed. "I'll take you to headquarters. Amon will want to hear what you have to say."

Recognizing the name of the head sentinel, Elinore nodded, feeling slightly relieved he had agreed.

He motioned for her to follow, and they made their way through the streets. The rogue Auraes left them alone long enough Elinore was beginning to think they would make it to their destination unhindered. But it seemed she had relaxed her guard too soon—just as they stepped onto the main road leading to downtown, one lunged from the shadows of a side street, attempting to tackle her companion. They wrestled for a moment before the sentinel kicked the other man away and then sent a blast of energy after him. The man danced away from it, moving faster than Elinore thought possible, but the sentinel quickly pursued. She watched, unsure how best to help or if she should get involved at all.

Then, another snuck up behind the sentinel, and with a greed-filled grin, he began stealing the other man's aura. Realizing the sentinel was powerless to stop it, Elinore called her aura to light in a split-second decision and sent a blast of energy towards their enemy. The explosion forced their attacker to let go of the sentinel's aura to deflect her power. The sentinel had passed out, so when the two assailants closed in, she stepped in to fight both of them. Despite her fear, she simply acted on instinct, managing to protect herself and her companion and even gain the upper hand against her enemies.

Finally, she ended the life of one of their assailants, and the other fled. She stumbled to a halt to lean against the nearest building, her breath coming in gasps and her stomach nauseated she had been forced to kill. Thankfully, the man's body had disappeared the minute he had died, turning into a pile of ash. It was a welcome surprise, leaving no reminders of what had happened, but Elinore couldn't help but wonder what caused it.

Turning back to the sentinel, she discovered he was coherent and carefully pushing himself to his feet. "Are you alright?" she asked as she moved to help him stand.

He nodded, grimacing. "I'll live." He leaned against the building next to him wearily, looking unsteady on his feet. "You fought well," he told her. "Thank you for your assistance."

She gave him a weak smile. "I did what I could."

He motioned for her to follow, and they made their way carefully through town, keeping to the backstreets to prevent drawing attention to themselves. Her companion's aura was too weak to fight now, and she wasn't sure what she would do if she had to kill again.

Finally, he stopped before a building near the town square; it bore the logo of the sentinels, making Elinore realize they had reached their headquarters. Two guards stood near the door, dressed in full battle armor—a sight worth seeing. They were both intimidating and regal, a haunting mix that made Elinore glad they were on her side. They watched the pair from underneath their helmets carefully.

The sentinel she was accompanying stepped inside. Beyond the doorway was an expansive, open room. People rushed past, but a few gazes turned to the pair. A woman rushed to meet them, dressed in the same uniform as the man. "Al, what happened?" she gasped.

"Just ran into...one of them. I'll live, I'm just exhausted." After a pause, he added, "What are we calling them now?"

"The *Doushidok*," the woman replied as she approached. "Are you sure you're alright?"

"Dou..." Elinore muttered, translating the Shidokian word to English. "Changed aura?"

The woman glanced at Elinore, noticing her for the first time. "Basically," she confirmed with a slight nod. Her gaze on Al again, she asked, "Who's she?"

"I never caught her name," Al admitted, surprised. Their gazes turned to her.

"Elinore Remar," she supplied.

"Elinore. Nice to meet you. I'm Charlotte, and this is Alphonse." Glancing back to Alphonse, she asked, "I can't help but wonder why you brought her here? It's not safe."

Plopping down into the nearest chair, Alphonse sighed and ran a tired hand over his face. "She said she had information about the Doushidok. Something we could use."

Charlotte turned to Elinore, looking slightly surprised. "How did you come by this information?" she wondered.

"My husband..." Elinore started but paused, unable to classify him in the same group as those attacking the colony, "... has an aura like theirs. He told me some things."

The woman nodded slowly, her gaze sympathetic. "I'm sorry," she commented softly.

"Sorry about what?" Elinore asked, confused.

"If he is one of the Doushidok, he's undoubtedly involved in all of this," she explained regretfully. "None of them seem to be listening to reason. Half the colony has turned against us, blindly killing friends and loved ones. We don't understand what happened."

Elinore's brow furrowed in annoyance. "He's not..." she began, but her voice faded as her mind trailed back to their conversation from the night before. His aura was so dark. What if he had been helping, somehow?

Charlotte seemed to follow her train of thought as she watched her reaction and gave her a sympathetic smile. "Either way, we're grateful you're willing to help us. You should speak to Amon right away. I could show you to him."

Elinore nodded, deciding she would just have to sort out Densin's place in the mess later. "Lead the way then."

The two women made their way deeper into the busy headquarters. Charlotte led her to a larger man in the center of the chaos. He had a carefully trimmed beard, and his hair was pulled back into a tight ponytail. Despite how he whirled around, responding to a thousand questions and barking orders in response, he didn't seem the least bit frayed—clearly, he was in his element.

He glanced over his shoulder as the two women approached. "I thought I sensed an unfamiliar aura. Elinore, isn't it?"

"How did you…" Elinore muttered, taken off guard, but he was distracted again, listening to a man reporting a fire that had started near the town square.

Charlotte leaned closer, as if letting her in on a well-guarded secret, and muttered, "He can basically sense everything that goes on in this building and with any of the sentinels. It's one of the many abilities of the head sentinel."

"Oh," Elinore muttered. Amon turned back to her, giving her an expectant look as if he had never turned away and was still waiting for her to answer his question. "Well, yes, that's my name," she confirmed awkwardly.

"Good, good. Tell me what you know about the Doushidok. Do you know why they're attacking us? And how are they so strong? Does it have to do with why their auras feel so foul? Are they using some sort of dark magic?" His questions came so fast that it took Elinore a moment to process them.

"They…their…how much do you know about the graft that modified their auras?" she asked.

"They were designed to allow them access to others' auras to repair and heal them of the plague," Amon answered.

"Right. And to do so, they were given the ability to hold someone's aura in theirs," Elinore added. "Since gaining this ability, they've all been haunted by this…temptation." She frowned slightly, her gaze unfocused as she remembered what Densin had shared with her.

"Temptation? What could you possibly mean by that?" Amon wondered, his curiosity only growing.

"They could absorb the aura they held, making their aura stronger," Elinore continued. "But to do so would kill the person they took the aura from. The urge to do so is always there, and nothing satisfies it. So they're attacking people for their auras."

It was difficult for Elinore to admit that was what was happening, which surprised her. Maybe it was because she had known it was a problem all along and hadn't done anything about it. Or perhaps it was because she had watched the darkness consume her husband. The idea of all of them warped by the same anger and pain she had seen in Densin made her sick.

"Which would explain the deaths we've noticed, of people whose auras have suddenly disappeared," Amon mused, breaking Elinore from her thoughts. "Why hasn't this problem been mentioned before?"

"I...I don't know," Elinore muttered, feeling heat rise to her face slightly at the wave of shame his question brought on. She realized then just how guilty she was for the mess they were in. Why hadn't she been more insistent that Densin sought out help? And why had he resisted so much?

"The longer this goes on, the stronger they get," Charlotte added, pulling her from her thoughts. "We have to stop them before they become too powerful. They may be faster, but other than the sentinels that turned against us, we're the better fighters. If we could just defend against their ability to steal our auras, we would stand a chance."

Amon nodded and then turned to Elinore. "Do you have any idea how to go about doing that?"

"I've never had to think about it before, but...I bet if we could learn more about the spells imbedded in the graft that allowed it to manipulate others' auras in the first place, we might be able to learn more about how to defend against it."

"Sounds like a good start," Amon agreed. Turning to the other sentinel, he instructed, "Charlotte, round up a team. I need you to find Joseph Redro, Sariah Ashcroft, and Andrew Griesenbeck, and get them here so we can question them. They're the only ones who could possibly give us the answers we need."

Charlotte nodded. "Find them, bring them back in one piece. Got it," she told Amon, giving a small salute as she hurried away.

Amon turned back to Elinore. "I overheard you talking about your husband being one of them. This must be hard for you. Thank you for being willing to help despite that fact," he complimented, the same look of sympathy in his gaze that she had seen in Charlotte's moments before.

Once again, Elinore opened her mouth to protest, but found she had no words to defend Densin. She simply nodded, her gaze falling to the ground. Amon gave her a comforting pat on the shoulder before stepping past her. Elinore watched him go and then sought a quiet spot in the building. Once she was alone, she tried to message Densin, but he didn't answer. A dark feeling settled in the pit of her stomach, making her feel sick. *Where are you, Densin?*

Twenty minutes later, Amon received a message from Charlotte. He invited Elinore to join him as he stepped up to it and tapped the smooth surface. The orb expanded, and an image of Charlotte dyed in the same purple tint appeared before them.

"How goes the mission?" Amon asked.

"Somewhat good," Charlotte replied cautiously and then flinched as what sounded distinctively like an explosion echoed behind her. "We found Sariah and Andrew, but Andrew is badly injured. Joseph's dead. Sariah's working on getting Andrew back on his feet, but it will take a while. We're surrounded inside a barn on the edge of town. I think the Doushidok know these medics have the information we need." Another explosion shook the building, and Elinore caught bits of yelled warnings. Looking desperate, Charlotte told them, "Reinforcements would be nice. Got to go!" With that, the image blinked from existence.

"Wait, Charlotte!" Amon protested, reaching a hand for her even as she disappeared. He scowled, resting his bearded chin in his hand. "Hmm. We'll have to assist her," he muttered after a moment. Then, glancing over his shoulder at Elinore, he added, "And I want you to come with me."

"Me?" Elinore gasped. "I'm no sentinel." The very thought of venturing out into the battle-torn streets made her stomach twist into sickening knots.

He nodded. "That may be true, but you know what these people can do, and you fought like a sentinel against them with Alphonse. We're way outnumbered as it is. We need people like you."

Elinore sighed. As much as she dreaded the fighting, she knew he was right and couldn't push away his call for help. "Fine. I'll come with you. But I can't promise I'll be of any help in this situation. I'm not used to fighting," she warned.

"We're all fighters now by circumstance. Whatever you can manage will be enough," Amon reassured her. He hurried away, calling over his shoulder for her to wait by the door.

She let out a sigh and made her way there, shaking her head as she tried to comprehend the bizarre and terrifying turn their lives had taken.

She didn't have to wait for long before Amon reappeared, followed by three other sentinels. They were all dressed in aura-crafted armor. Pointing to them, Amon introduced, "This is Gideon, Benedict, and Jessamine."

She nodded a brief greeting to them and then turned back to him. "This is all you're bringing?"

"It's all we can spare. We're taking them from the guard of headquarters, and if this place falls, we lose the magic that unites us. We will lose the battle if we allow that to happen." Elinore nodded, understanding his hesitation.

"Is she going with us?" Jessamine asked, looking doubtful. Amon nodded, seeming slightly confused she was questioning the idea. "If she goes out dressed like that, it'll paint a target on her back. She looks like a normal civilian," Jessamine pointed out.

"Hmm. I didn't think of that," Amon muttered, glancing towards Elinore, his eyes taking in her dirty dress and frizzy hair. She fidgeted slightly, self-conscious under his gaze. "Grab her a spare uniform. It'll have to do."

Jessamine nodded and hurried off, returning a moment later with a neatly folded sentinel uniform and a pair of boots. She handed them to Elinore while Amon told her, "We don't have time to teach you the spell to create armor, but this'll protect you better than a dress and deflect extra unwanted attention." She took the uniform in her hands, hoping she didn't look as surprised as she felt. Amon jerked a thumb over his shoulder as he added, "There's a closet over there. Change quickly."

Elinore nodded weakly as she made her way to the closet, deciding she didn't have the energy to protest. Changing quickly in the dark proved difficult, but she managed. She pulled the uniform on, which fit her surprisingly well. The pants were tight but flexible, far from what she was used to, and the top had a high collar and square shoulders. Both were made of thick, sturdy material, giving her a sense of protection, even if it was just basic. She could sense the magic in the uniform and knew it would absorb more power than it looked capable of taking. She pulled her feet into the boots and quickly tied her hair back into a bun to keep it out of her way. Without a mirror, she could only guess what effect the uniform had on her, but she hoped it made her look more powerful than she felt.

Stepping from the closet, she rejoined the group. "There, that's better," Jessamine commented with a small smile.

"Alright, we need to get to Charlotte's team quickly. The two medics with them are the top priority. We must get them back here in one piece," Amon explained quickly, and then with a wave of his hand, they started out.

The streets were as much of a mess as Elinore remembered, but now a thick fog had rolled in from the ocean, shrouding everything in shadows. They passed through the town unhindered for a while, and Elinore was given a moment to take in the carnage. Several buildings were on fire, the acrid scent of smoke hanging heavy in the air, and bodies littered the streets— more than Elinore was willing to or could ever count. A cold silence fell over them; the horror of their surroundings hushed any conversation that may have passed between them.

As they neared the barn, they met with resistance. The little group was almost overwhelmed, but the sentinels fought with such strength and determination that Elinore took courage and did what she could to help. Finally, they pushed their way into the barn. They found the remaining sentinels from Charlotte's team crowded in the back of the barn, surrounding Sariah.

Amon moved to speak with his team, so Elinore turned to Sariah. She seemed worn and full of sorrow, something that was becoming a common element in Elinore's life. Kneeling next to the other woman, she told her, "We're here to help."

"Elinore," Sariah greeted, leaving Elinore surprised she remembered her. "It's good to see a familiar face. I didn't know you joined the sentinels."

It took Elinore a second to follow her comment until she remembered the uniform she was wearing. "It's sort of unofficial," she replied sheepishly.

Sariah gave a weary half-smile. "Well, the uniform looks good on you."

Elinore returned her smile, grateful for her support. "How's Andrew?" she asked, turning back to the task at hand.

The medic's smile faded, and she glanced at the ground. "I couldn't save him. His injuries were too severe, even for me. He was practically already gone when we found him. I did what I could to ease his passing." She sighed heavily.

Resting a hand on Sariah's shoulder, Elinore muttered, "We'll fix this. His death won't be in vain."

"He died thinking he was responsible for all this. We both are. We made the Doushidok," she muttered, thick self-loathing in her words.

"No," Elinore argued. "Don't blame yourself. You did what you had to in order to save those you loved."

Sariah shrugged wearily, unable to be comforted. "But at what cost? Most of them died anyway."

Before Elinore could fully contemplate that statement, Jessamine interrupted. "We need to get out of here. The wounded have been identified. Sariah, can you help them?"

"I'll try," the medic promised, standing.

"We'll hold the enemy back until you finish," Jessamine promised. The medic got to work, even as the sentinels continued to battle the Doushidok. As she finished doing all she could for those that had been injured, the group prepared to head out.

They poured from the barn, the sentinels surrounding Sariah. The older woman flinched away from the carnage, and Elinore couldn't help but feel the same way; outside was crowded by many desperate people, and magic flashed everywhere as they clashed, the smell of fire and the screams of the injured filling the air. Unfazed, the sentinels jumped into the battle, pushing back the remaining Doushidok that clambered at the barn. As their enemies fell, they turned towards the town center, ready to start back.

They hadn't traveled more than a block when suddenly Amon halted, raising a hand for everyone to pause. Elinore followed his gaze, wondering what had caused him to stop. A lone figure approached through the fog, and though she couldn't yet see him entirely, she could sense his amazing power, wanting to shrink away from it. Then he stepped through the thickest of the fog, suddenly becoming clearer. Elinore's gaze widened as she met a pair of familiar gray eyes, feeling as though someone had slammed her to the ground, knocking the air out of her and leaving her dazed and in pain.

Densin.

The sentinels tensed, watching him approach carefully. He eyed them with a level of contempt and disgust Elinore had never seen in him. His aura swirled around him, but it was unrecognizable; it seemed formed of living shadows, and the light it gave off was weak.

"Running away so soon?" he called to the sentinels, the faintest smile curling the corner of his lips, sending shivers down Elinore's spine.

"That's their leader," one sentinel hissed, surprising Elinore. The group reacted immediately, their auras appearing around them, ready to defend themselves from Densin, but before they could attack, she quickly stepped forward, putting herself between them.

"Wait," she ordered, grateful her voice didn't give out on her despite how it felt her throat was being squeezed shut. "I know him. Let me handle this." She met Amon's gaze, and suddenly he seemed to understand.

With a half nod, he commanded, "Let her take this one."

Elinore turned back to Densin, approaching cautiously. He watched her, his gaze devoid of emotion. She paused, staring at him through the fog, the battle fading from her attention.

"You know, I could kill that entire group with a simple wave of my hand," Densin informed her casually.

"I don't doubt that you could," Elinore admitted. "Your aura has become quite powerful."

He flashed her a malicious grin. "I'm glad you noticed."

"Why are you doing this?" she asked.

His grin faded, and she saw a fleeting shadow of the man she had married under the surface of the monster before her. But it was gone as quickly as it came. "I did it because I had to. You would never understand; you were too blind to see what needed to happen."

"But what about last night? I really thought you meant it when you said you would try harder to be a better person," she stated, trying not to sound like she was pleading.

"That's just it—it made me realize this was necessary. You and Ansem would never be safe, and we'd never be able to move on until they were all gone."

"They? They who?" Elinore wondered, bewildered and unable to comprehend how he had reached this conclusion.

"The Auraes," he stated, as if it was obvious.

She stared at him, dumbfounded, and then stated, "Densin, *you're* an Aurae."

He shook his head. "Not anymore. Haven't you heard what they've been calling us? Doushidok—it's a surprisingly fitting name, don't you think? We are changed. And for the better."

She shook her head, wanting to argue that this was definitely not an improvement, but she realized she would get nowhere with that line of thought. He was too far gone to see reason and probably had been for some time now, she had just been too blind to see it.

Deciding she was done passively allowing things to happen around her, she steeled herself and told him, "I can't let you do this. I can't let you kill so many innocent people."

For the briefest second, he looked conflicted, but then his expression hardened into a cold mask, his eyes glinting dangerously. "I still love you, but if you stand in my way, I will do what I must."

She swallowed hard, fighting the tears that threatened to fall. If he had dealt her a physical blow, she guessed it would hurt less than the pain that erupted in her heart. Her whole body stiffened, her hands clenched into fists. "Then...so will I," she whispered, unable to find the strength to say it louder, but she somehow held her head high nonetheless.

He hesitated a brief moment, and she wondered if something she had said had reached him. Then he sneered and sent a wave of power towards them, more potent than she imagined possible, more than she could ever defend against. She felt the magic in her armor react to shield her, and her aura did as well, but to her surprise, the darkness bent to avoid her, rippling instead towards those behind her. She heard their screams as if they were far away, everything moving in slow motion. As the magic faded, she slowly turned, taking in their fallen forms, in how still they were. *Are they all dead?*

Realizing she had left herself vulnerable, Elinore quickly turned back to Densin, but she was surprised to find he was gone. She looked around for him for a moment but found no traces of him. She was about to follow after him when she heard a pained grunt from behind her.

Looking back, she realized one of the sentinels was still alive. Gideon sat up carefully, wincing as he aggravated obvious wounds. Amon stirred but didn't rise from the ground, letting out a pained moan. Relief flooded Elinore even as she took in the rest of the fallen. Then Sariah pushed herself free from underneath Jessamine's smoking form, standing carefully. Elinore quickly realized Jessamine had sacrificed herself to protect Sariah, giving them one last chance to win.

Elinore hurried to her. "Are you alright?" she asked. Sariah nodded numbly, her gaze on Jessamine's body, her eyes wide.

Gideon limped to the two women. "We need to move quickly."

"Amon's hurt badly," Sariah whispered, sensing what neither of them could see. "Let me help him first."

"There's no time," Gideon replied, though he sounded reluctant to leave behind his commander.

"Please. We need all the help we can get," Sariah pleaded.

"Tell us how we can stop these things first, then you can heal all the wounded that you can manage," Elinore promised.

Sariah glanced between the two, then to the ground. "When the idea for the graft first came to me, I knew there was something wrong about it. I could sense it. But I was so desperate for answers, I ignored the warning signs. Luckily, I at least had enough sense to design a failsafe over the years; it's a prison of sorts, tied to their auras and powerful enough to hold them for centuries. All that needs to be done is say the final spells to enclose them, and they'll be trapped for as long as the magic will last. But the only problem is these spells are so strong, no aura could survive creating them."

Feeling something of a sense of relief settling over her, Elinore immediately volunteered, "I'll do it. If I perish, so be it."

Sariah studied her carefully and then nodded. In as much detail as she could manage, she explained the magic needed. Elinore listened, accepting her fate with a surprising level of clarity. She realized it would be a painful end, but it hardly mattered. She deserved to pay the ultimate price for the part she had played in all of this.

As Sariah finished, Elinore turned to Gideon and told him, "Get her to safety."

"What about you? Will you be alright on your own?" he asked.

"Yes. I just need to do one thing before I finish the magic," she told him.

"You want to find him," Gideon stated. She nodded. "I can help," he told her, surprising her. He closed his eyes as his aura surrounded him brightly for a few moments, and then he stated, "He...went to a farm on the outskirts of town."

"He went home?" Elinore muttered under her breath, surprised. She considered that for a moment, wondering what he intended to do there, but then she realized she was wasting valuable time. To Gideon, she stated, "Thank you. Good luck, both of you."

"You as well," he told her with a nod, respect in his gaze. She stood quickly, feeling she did not deserve his admiration, and turned toward home.

Chapter Twenty-Eight
The Shadow

Elinore

It took some time for Elinore to make it back to her home. On more than one occasion, she was forced to contend with the Doushidok, but once she made it past the town line and started up the simple dirt path leading to the farm, she was left with only her thoughts as company.

Approaching her home was surprisingly hard. The burden of what she was about to do weighed on her shoulders so heavily it was almost too much to carry. She knew he was there waiting for her—she could sense his aura now. She wasn't sure what had possessed him to stay, but she was grateful for it. Part of her knew there was no reason she needed to be with him to complete Sariah's prison, but she wanted to see him one last time.

Stepping into the building, she scanned the living room, attempting not to see the home she loved. But there was no escaping the memories that flooded her mind. They filled her with nostalgia as she longed for the days when it had been a happy home, but they were gone, and she was resigned to that fact. Nothing could bring them back, no more than stop the aching in her heart.

Then her gaze found Densin in the kitchen, leaning against the counter as if he had been waiting for her, his gaze on the small window across from him. He didn't turn to her as he commented, "I knew you would come."

"I had to," she replied.

"Where's Ansem?" he asked.

"Safe," she responded vaguely, wondering if the boy was why he had returned. She could only hope he and her parents were alright.

There was a pause, and then Densin finally looked up to meet her gaze. "Did you come to kill me?" Even if she had a reply, Elinore found it impossible to speak, the cold realization of what she had come to do hitting her like a slap to the face.

He smiled softly as he straightened, his aura appearing around him, sending shivers down her spine. "Let's get on with it then," he stated softly.

"Densin, no, I didn't come to kill you. I came to help you," she exclaimed, suddenly finding her voice again. He froze, surprised. "I love you. I don't care about anything else. As long as we're safe and together, nothing else matters to me."

He blinked, and then his aura disappeared as he dropped his guard. He stepped closer, and she closed the gap between them, embracing him, her heart aching. Then he kissed her, and she allowed him to, responding to his touch with a bittersweet passion she couldn't control, as she knew it was the last time she would feel him close, the last time he would love her.

Then she pulled away slightly, just enough that she could whisper, "I love you."

"I..." he started, but then she began the spells as her aura flashed to life around her. The magic caught him so quickly he had no chance to react, his aura wrapped in her power. He stumbled away, collapsing to his knees and clutching his chest as if she had stabbed him.

It surprised her, but it was a welcome relief; there was no way she could have brought herself to fight him if he had resisted. The pain of betrayal filled his eyes as he watched her crafting the spells, using every last drop of her strength. Her aura strained to keep up with her demands, but she pushed onward, refusing to allow her own weakness to get in the way of her task.

As the spells continued, her aura expanded around her with a blast, rippling through the small room and causing slight damage. She could feel the spells reaching out, finding the Doushidok one at a time, slowly catching them as it had Densin.

"Elinore, stop!" Densin growled, infuriated.

But he couldn't harm her, she knew that. Meeting his gaze, she paused, knowing she had precious moments before her aura was exhausted, and she perished. "I'm sorry," she whispered, tears streaming down her face. She muttered the last few words, and the spells finished, clicking into place with such power and finality she almost heard it.

And then he was gone. She knew the rest of his kind went with him, locked in the prison she had created. Silence filled the house, interrupted only by her quiet sobs and the racing of her heart as it fought to keep up with the demands she had placed upon her body. Her aura sparked and fizzled around her, barely still in existence. As her legs gave out, she crashed to the ground, numbly aware of the pain in her knees. The world was darkening around the edges, and she knew she would pass out. Whether or not she awoke again, she wasn't sure, nor did she care.

But there was one last thing she had to do before allowing herself to collapse into the all too welcome darkness. Though the spells would hold Densin and his kind for many years to come, she wasn't sure if there were any survivors on the island. She had to guarantee someone would know of the prison and could be ready to rebuild it before the spells collapsed and allowed the evil it contained to enter the world again.

Bringing her fading aura to light once more, she added another spell. With it went the last of her strength, but she refused to let go until it was finished. She was too weak to create a proper message, but the images and the emotion she poured into it would suffice. She had to believe that. As the spell was finished, she thought of who to send it to and how to guarantee it would actually reach someone. She thought of Ansem and, deciding it was the only sure way she could ensure her message would make it safely, she linked it to her bloodline, hoping the boy had survived the nonsense of the day.

Finally, as her aura blinked from life and she was engulfed in the most unholy pain she had ever felt, she allowed herself to let go and sink into the darkness.

— ✒ —

Mariea

Mariea stood over the remains of the island settlement. She watched the few survivors bury their dead and then gather to leave the island behind, Elinore's son and parents among them. On a second, familiar island, they found refuge with another colony of Auraes. Then, deep in the forests of that island, Mariea saw a simple door frame appear, mist the color of Elinore's aura surrounding it for a brief moment before dissipating. Mariea could sense that beyond the doorway—which would be invisible to the naked eye—laid the prison Elinore had created.

Time continued forward. Years upon years, passing faster now, and Mariea watched the prison. It left the island for a time, appearing in random places throughout the world, and then settled in New York, where it remained for a long time, still invisible. It was so subtle at first, but suddenly she realized the spells were starting to deteriorate. When she saw the first of the Tarapor and, soon after that, the distinctively clad members of the Brotherhood, Mariea realized time was nearing the present. Things continued forward. After a while, the door returned to the island, and she saw glimpses of people she knew. It was on Raidenya.

Then she found herself approaching the door, an ominous feeling settling over her. She was drawn to it uncontrollably, her feet taking steps she wished they wouldn't. As she paused before it, she studied the rippling surface of the dark spells between the doorposts, sensing just beyond a growing power that was much stronger than it had been when the prison had first formed, terrifying Mariea with its presence.

Suddenly, a hand shot through the doorway, grasping at her with clawed fingers. She stumbled backward, surprise making her heart skip a beat. The hand disappeared, replaced seconds later by a being with the aura of a Doushidok. He dragged himself free of the spells' control, dark energy crackling over his pale skin as the spells tried one last time to hold him and his kind in place. Mariea stumbled away, fearing the man, but then she turned to her aura, ready to defend herself. To her dismay, it refused to come to light, leaving her helpless. She ran, instinct kicking in to keep her alive. She ran for her home, hunting for its safety, but as she neared the city's edge, she stopped dead in her tracks, her eyes widening in fear.

Before her, Raidenya crumbled as a giant cavity opened in the ground, swallowing buildings and people quickly. Dark creatures flooded from the forest, preying on the people as they tried to flee the destruction. She heard their screams and fear, and tried to go to them, but she couldn't move. A cold sweat broke out over her skin, and she thought she would cry, but instead, she felt herself go numb with shock, her mind unable to process what she saw, to accept it as reality.

Then a cold hand wrapped around her shoulder and turned her around. She looked up into the face of a man that wasn't much more than a shadow with a grin. She tried to struggle from his grasp, her heart racing in her chest, her eyes wide in horror. But it wouldn't let go, its grip on her like steel. She was engulfed in pain as the shadows pierced her, and she plunged into darkness.

Snapping upright, Mariea let out a shrill scream. She looked around, panting, realizing she was alone in the jungle outside the settlement, but her body refused to acknowledge the horrors were gone. She pulled her knees to her chest, resting her head in her hands, trying to steady her breathing and racing heart. Tears threatened to spill over, the residual emotions from the vision so potent it was as if she had watched her home burn.

"There you are," she heard from above her, but she didn't have the strength to lift her head, too afraid to face reality.

Bracken kneeled next to her, resting a hand on her shoulder. "Mariea, are you alright?"

She finally straightened and attempted to wipe away her tears. "I...I just...another vision—that one was...it shook me up a bit," she stumbled, attempting to explain, her voice shaking from fear and unshed tears.

He pulled her to him, and she allowed herself to attempt to hide from the nightmarish images, but she couldn't stop running them over and over again in her mind. Suddenly, it dawned on her that she had been the one to receive Elinore's warning. The prison must be ready to open.

With that thought, she quickly climbed to her feet, pulling from Bracken's embrace. He stood with her, looking concerned and at least a bit confused. "I need to get a message to Ila immediately," she told him. She felt guilty leaving him in the dark, but it was the only explanation she thought she had time to spare.

Her aura came to light as she quickly crafted a messenger spell, pouring all the knowledge she had learned into it, her haste and anxiety deepening the spell's color. Mariea knew Ila would sense her distress and may be bothered by it, but she decided it was a good thing. The quicker the other Aurae acted, the better.

As she finished, Bracken stepped up next to her. "So, you want to explain what's happening?" he requested gently.

She turned to him, her blue eyes wide with fear and her aura still surrounding her. Briefly, she explained the prison, what it contained, and how the spells were weakening. "When that thing opens, the Doushidok will be released on our home. They could kill everyone. I watched them do it."

His eyes widened, and he paled considerably as she explained, seeming to come to realize her worst fears.

Shaking her head, she swallowed hard and added, "Bracken, we're on the brink of a war we're far from prepared for. We have to get back now. It may already be too late."

Author Bio

Jessica Duckworth lives in Ogden, Utah. When not writing, she loves to play the piano, read, or create simple computer programs. For behind-the-scenes info about her published books and other projects, visit www.jaedbooks.com.